THE LION
AND THE
LEOPARD

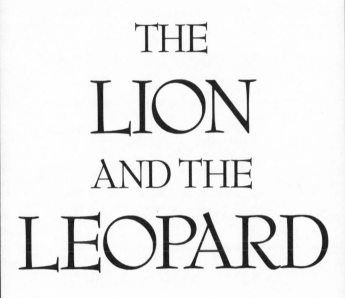

THE
LION
AND THE
LEOPARD

A NOVEL BY
MARY ELLEN JOHNSON

CROWN PUBLISHERS, INC. NEW YORK

Published by Crown Publishers, Inc., One
Park Avenue, New York, New York 10016 and
simultaneously in Canada by General
Publishing Company Limited.
CROWN is a trademark of Crown Publishers,
Inc.
Manufactured in the United States of America

Book design by Dana Sloan.

Library of Congress Cataloging in Publication
Data

Johnson, Mary Ellen, 1949–
The lion and the leopard.

I. Title.
PS3560.03816L5   1985   813'.54   85–11399

ISBN 0–517–55727–4
10 9 8 7 6 5 4 3 2 1
First Edition

To Mom and Dad, who instilled in my brothers and me a love for the printed word, as well as the belief that we could achieve anything we truly desired.

AUTHOR'S NOTE

Though I've tried to accurately portray life during Edward II's disastrous reign, some events have been altered for the purposes of my story. According to historical records Richard, Maria, and Phillip did not exist, but I believe they did—somewhere, sometime. Richard's discovery of what modern man calls "The Shroud of Turin" is indeed possible. There is written speculation that the disbanded Templars did hide the shroud in a remote English monastery during the early fourteenth century.

Out of the hundreds of books and articles I read about the Middle Ages, I would like to publicly mention Thomas Costain's *The Three Edwards*, for its always lively overview of the era; William Stearns Davis's *Life on a Medieval Barony*, for its charmingly detailed account of daily life; and Natalie Fryde's *The Tyranny and Fall of Edward II 1321–1326*.

Many people offered me advice and encouragement during the rewarding—and frustrating—years of writing *The Lion and the Leopard*. I would like to thank fellow authors Diane Hoover, Maggie Osborne, and Beth Harper for their support, as well as my parents, my brothers, John and Vic, and Vic's wife, Merri, who along with her husband suffered through several early drafts. A special hug to my children, Erich, Terrence, and Erin, who put up with many haphazard meals, much perfunctory housecleaning, and a mother who was sometimes more patient with rewrites than their various needs. My husband, Mark, complained—sometimes with good reason—about unmatched socks and reams of papers and books scattered from the living-room couch to our bed, but he never doubted my writing ability and worked long brutal hours so that I could travel to England. I am also extremely grateful to my agent, Diane Cleaver, who took a chance on an unpublished housewife. Without her I would still be on the outside looking in—and "someday" might never have arrived. I thank my editor at Crown, Pam Thomas, who believed in the book, despite its many flaws, and guided me skillfully through the laborious task of editing, which included weeding out hundreds of excess pages and scenes. Neither Pam nor Diane ever made me feel like an amateur, and I appreciate their kindness to me on a personal as well as a professional level.

When I began writing *The Lion and the Leopard* I realized the monumental odds against my novel ever reaching publication. Long ago I placed my manuscript in God's loving and capable hands. I humbly thank Him now for bringing my lifelong dream to fruition.

THE LION AND THE LEOPARD

ONE

aria d'Arderne stood in the bailey of Fordwich Castle, cradling her pet rabbit, Saladin.

"Hold him still," Maria's sister commanded. "or I cannot properly wrap his paw." As Eleanora fumbled with the dressing she chewed at her thin lower lip. Her long, bony nose and uncertain chin appeared even more pronounced because of her severely braided brown hair. Though the d'Arderne girls were twins, they neither looked nor acted alike. Physically, Maria favored their mother; Eleanora possessed the nature of their father. Or so people said.

"There now, Saladin," Maria crooned as the rabbit flinched. "Eleanora will not hurt you. She has the healing touch and will mend you better than new, that I promise."

Maria stroked her pet's soft flecked fur. She loved rabbits and had sheltered a multitude suffering from various afflictions. Currently, her rabbit hutch contained three. Besides Saladin, whom she'd rescued from a poacher's snare, there was Lionheart, blind in one eye, and Jerusalem the Runt. Maria had named each after her favorite time period, the hallowed—and long past—crusades. The last crusade had taken place in 1270, forty-four years ago.

When Eleanora released Saladin's bandaged forepaw, she lifted her brown woolen skirt and made ready to leave. "Do not forget, sister, that you must have your Latin verbs conjugated ere suppertime."

Maria's blue eyes momentarily darkened. As she stroked her rabbit, she sighed. "Have you ever thought, Eleanora, that the world might not cease if we knew not Latin, nor how to properly extinguish our bed candles and make a smokeless fire? Why cannot mother be like papa and relate interesting tales like those of Beowulf and the monster Grendel or our knights and the great crusades?"

"'Tis mother's duty to teach us about household affairs. Soon you, at least, will have your own manor to run, your own lord to please."

Maria tossed her head impatiently, trying to return a bothersome strand of auburn hair to its rightful place. Unlike Eleanora, she refused to wear a wimple or even braid her waist-length curls unless their mother, Henrietta, threatened her with more embroidery or the needle and shuttle. "I never intend to grow up, nor marry," Maria said. "I shall stay thirteen forever."

Her twin smiled tolerantly. "I believe you've said the very same thing from the time you were six."

Maria traced the curve of Saladin's spine with a slender finger. "Someday it will happen. I can think of nothing worse than growing up and marrying some old man who will boss me about worse than mother. I'll leave marriage to you."

Eleanora began picking her way from Fordwich's rabbit hutch to the keep, careful to avoid the chicken, pig, and horse droppings scattered amidst the bailey straw. "With my sight, I wager I'll be betrothed about the same time the Seven Trumpets announce Judgment Day."

Glancing up from her rabbit, which was sniffing at its bandaged paw, Maria called after her twin. "Have you dreamed of him again—the knight who shines like the sun?"

Eleanora shook her head. "Now do not forget to conjugate your verbs."

"Perhaps the golden knight was meant for you," Maria said,

but Eleanora had already disappeared inside the great hall. To Saladin, she whispered, "Aye, a fine golden knight. Then marriage would not seem such a displeasing prospect."

Groping inside her tunic Maria drew forth a carrot and fed it to her pet. "*Amo, amas, amat.* I wonder if Father Eustace will condemn me forever to hell if I cannot remember what verb comes after?"

Saladin contentedly crunched the carrot. "If Father Eustace does not lecture me," Maria said gloomily, "mother certainly will." She looked about the bailey, where not an hour ago Henrietta had returned from a hawking expedition with Hugh, Maria's father. Maria hated everything connected with hawking. Unlike the maimed rabbits she cared for, hawks were totally lacking in either loyalty or affection. Occasionally she'd gone hawking, but when she saw the mangled corpses of the birds' helpless victims, her sensitive stomach rebelled. How could anyone consider falconry "sport"?

The mews was located twenty feet from Maria's rabbit hutch. She noticed Stephen the Falconer patiently working with Fordwich's newest addition, a huge speckled gyrfalcon. Queen had only recently been weathered and her eyes unsealed, and now Stephen was teaching her to hunt crane. For the past two afternoons he'd practiced with Queen in a meadow outside the castle curtain, using a stuffed rabbit pelt baited with meat as a lure.

"Hello, Stephen," Maria called out. "Have you yet trained Queen or is she as stupid as the rest of your birds?"

With his free hand Stephen waved. "Mind your tongue now, miss, or you'll hurt me lady's feelings." He removed Queen's hood to reexamine a troublesome sore near her beak. Satisfied that it was healing properly, he returned to Maria with a grin. "And you'd best quit overfeeding those mange-ridden pets of yours, miss, afore they grow so fat you canna lift them."

She giggled. "Is that right, Saladin?" She held her rabbit out at arm's length, then cuddled his velvet nose and face against her cheek. "Pay no attention to Stephen. He is just mean natured because of the company he keeps."

From inside Fordwich's dog kennels, built flush against the castle curtain, came a noisome snarling and snapping. The entire male pack had been wrangling over Slops, a greyhound bitch in heat. Wearied by their incessant attentions, Slops suddenly lashed out at Blue-Eye, a particularly bothersome alaunt. Her fangs laid open to the bone his lower left hind leg. Blue-Eye howled.

"Stop it!" Maria yelled. "You'll frighten Saladin."

The entire kennel erupted.

A terrified Saladin leapt from Maria's arms and hopped toward the barking hounds. Midway he froze.

"Come back, Saladin!" Maria called. He seemed hypnotized by the frenzied, leaping dogs. She ran for him, but just as she reached to scoop him up Saladin turned and darted between her legs. His crippled forepaw slowed him little as he scrambled back in the direction of the mews.

"Stop, Saladin!" Maria cried. "Stephen, get Queen!"

Before the falconer could jerk short the creance attached to his hand or pull down Queen's hood, the hawk attacked. Saladin's bandaged forepaw blurred white; Queen's spread wings blurred black. Razor-sharp talons pinned the struggling rabbit to the ground, tore at the soft underbelly. Saladin went limp.

Stephen jerked Queen's creance. The bird squawked and only reluctantly returned to her master. Thrusting the hawk inside the mews he dropped the door-bar, then turned to a stunned Maria. "I am so sorry, miss," he said. His plain face was transformed by unhappiness. "I would rather cut out my heart than hurt your pet, do you not know?"

Mutely, Maria nodded. She stared down at the flesh and fur and bone that had been her pet. Of what consequence is one mere rabbit? she told herself. None, mother will say. Death is a common occurrence, so why do I feel like crying?

Bending down, Stephen carefully lifted Saladin's bloody

remains. "I'll give him a proper burial down by the River Stour, miss, if 'twould please you."

Maria gagged. Hand to her mouth, she fled across the bailey toward the keep and stumbled up the stairs to the great hall. She would go to her chamber, conjugate her Latin, work her embroidery, or even read one of her father's romances. Anything to take her mind off her dead pet, those dreadful hawks.

Near the doorway Clarice, the tiring maid, turned from her conversation with Piers the Cook to watch Maria. "Why, sweeting, is something wrong? Your face looks green as the lily pads in the well ditch."

Shaking her head, Maria ascended the stairway and approached her room, which was located next to her parents' solar.

"Maria, is that you?"

She paused reluctantly. "Aye."

"Come here, please. I would speak with you."

Maria entered the gracefully proportioned but shabby solar, where Henrietta and Hugh were seated in the window seat with a chessboard of inlaid wood between them. Hugh's shortened right leg, which often pained him, was propped on a pile of pillows. Looking up from the chess game, Hugh's homely face wrinkled in a welcoming smile.

"Have you yet conjugated your Latin?" Henrietta's wide blue eyes remained fixed on the board. Even in relaxation, her well-shaped back remained straight, her slender white hands correctly folded in her lap.

"What is wrong, poppet?" Hugh's close-set eyes viewed Maria with concern. "Did you take a spill from Baillet?"

Maria shook her head. "Queen killed Saladin." Her voice was barely audible.

"Now tell me, poppet," Hugh said, reaching out to draw her close to him. "Just who might this Saladin be?"

Henrietta's eyes swept Maria. "One of her rabbits." Picking

up a rock of whalebone, she tapped it speculatively against the mahogany edge of the chessboard. "Her hutch is filled with them."

"Oh, well." Hugh held Maria at arm's length. "Now listen to me for a moment. You must not be overupset with your Saladin's death. He was just a pet rabbit, and though you enjoyed him, 'tis just one of life's unfortunate occurrences, like my leg here." Hugh's leg had been injured in the last Scottish campaign of 1307, the year the old king, Edward I, had died.

When Maria looked unconvinced, he continued, "Life is filled with predator and prey, remember that."

Her lower lip quivered. "But Saladin was mine, and he was crippled with only me to care for him. That—Queen just tore him to shreds." Despite her best efforts, she felt hot tears slip down her cheeks.

"Killing is the way of the hawk," Henrietta said matter-of-factly. "Queen was only doing what a falcon is trained to do." Thick coils of auburn hair framed her flawless profile as she once again bent over the chessboard. "The woods are filled with rabbits, daughter. Tomorrow why do you not just take a pair of your father's hounds and fetch another?"

"I hate your birds!" Maria cried, losing control. "You are always complaining about how poor we are and yet you buy those silly birds. I wish . . ."

In an elaborately patient voice, Henrietta reasoned, "You are near fourteen years old, daughter. At your age I was already betrothed. I can understand your unhappiness, but you are too old to be playing with rabbits, anyway."

"I am not and—"

"Enough!" Henrietta interrupted. "No more arguing. Your rabbit is dead and there is naught you can do about it. Go to your chamber and meditate on your unwomanly behavior." Grimly, she pushed a bishop diagonally two squares.

Maria glared. Her hands balled in tight fists; her fingernails dug into her palms. "But I—"

"I said go to your room!" Henrietta yelled.

Alone in her chamber Maria buried her face in the wolf coverlet on her bed. As she brushed her fingers through the long fur, near as soft as Saladin's, her mind whirled with resentment. Her mother didn't understand. She never did. Henrietta didn't care about anything save her murderous hawks and turning Maria into a marketable marriage piece.

I wish the mews still stood empty," Maria whispered. Her hands paused midstroke. "Empty," she repeated, and in her mind a plan began to form.

By the slant of the full moon Maria knew it was well past the witching hour. The castle was quiet. Eleanora didn't even stir when she eased from the bed they shared. In near total darkness Maria groped for her clothes, but by the time she entered the inner bailey, the moon and an occasional wall torch provided sufficient light. This night, specifically, would be perfect for her plan.

She tiptoed past the laundress's trough and the ruins of the family chapel, which had been destroyed by fire three years before. Two charred and jagged beams thrust upward like fangs. Scooting past the rubble, she paused beside the communal oven, still warm from the day's baking. Beyond she saw the hutch. When she reached it, she peeked inside. Jerusalem the Runt and Lionheart were nosing about their dinner scraps.

Maria peered into the shadows. Nothing moved. Even the kenneled hounds remained silent. Overhead, along the upper curtain, she heard a scuffling. Soon the knight, Jack Straw, passed, walking his post. His bald head, long missing the wild thatch that had earned him his nickname, gleamed. Whistling a tavern song, he disappeared into the darkness.

To Maria's left stood the stables, beside it the blacksmith's shop. Both were cloaked in shadow. Quiet. Not even the yowling of a bailey cat or a cough from the knights' barracks above the stables disturbed the stillness. The mews stood to the right of the stables. Around its door were several inverted cone-shaped blocks upon which new birds were weathered. Tonight the blocks looked like squat, ugly dwarfs.

Maria darted for the mews. Even though straw covered the cobblestones, her steps sounded louder to her than an entire hawking party. She was certain Stephen would momentarily appear from his pallet in the stable storeroom to check on the noise. The falconer's ears were keen enough to detect his birds' tinkling bells out in Oldridge Woods; he'd surely hear her tromping about. She held her breath until she was certain he would not appear. Then she inched the bar from the door, eased it open, and stepped inside. A window in the back of the cage provided enough illumination to see. Holding her nose against the foul smells of droppings and raw meat, she approached Queen, who was the largest of six hawks roosting on perches of various heights.

"Stupid Queen," Maria whispered, as she began untying the gyrfalcon. "Do not make a squawk." Carefully, she worked around the bells tied to the bird's feet. After Queen's leather ties were loosed, she freed the merlins, kestrels, and short-winged goshawks and sparrow hawks that were positioned closest to the gravel floor.

Quickly she backed out the mews, scooped up a handful of gravel, and tossed it inside the open door.

"There, miserable birds," she whispered, as they began a frightened fluttering and squawking. "Go do your killing in the woods where God intended." Lifting her skirts, Maria turned and fled back to the castle.

"But m'lord, I checked me birds afore I made for the George and Dragon in Fordwich town," Stephen the Falconer said. "And I was back afore matins, I swear, and everything was fine. But then this morn, with the doors wide open and me birds gone . . ." He stared unhappily into the interior of the mews as if expecting them to momentarily materialize. Hugh and Henrietta stared too, but they saw nothing save empty perches, dangling leashes, and a great amount of feathers due to the molting season.

Maria was frightened by her mother's face, which was white as the wimple framing it. Hugh limped back and forth before them in an awkward pacing.

"Poor Stephen," Eleanora whispered. "Is he not a piteous sight, sister?"

He was indeed. Stephen's plain face had collapsed; his bright blue eyes blinked rapidly in an effort to hold back tears. His unruly thatch of golden hair, trademark of his natural father, the knight Jack Straw, stuck out in all directions.

What have I done, she worried. Never in a thousand years did I think Stephen would be blamed. Never did I think at all, it seems. Maria kept her eyes downcast, on a patch of cobblestones peeping through the bailey straw. When she looked at Stephen's stricken face her conscience nagged most uncomfortably.

"M'lord, someone on purpose loosed them," he said. "I had them leashed, I swear by St. George, and I know I bolted the door after I put the salve on Queen's sore. I remember pushing down the bar, clear as you stand afore me. Only after did I go to Fordwich town, as God is my witness."

"All my birds gone," Henrietta said tonelessly.

Hugh ceased his pacing. "You'll have to be punished, Stephen, you realize that, do you not? You must leave Fordwich, and not in all England will you ever be allowed work as a falconer. Furthermore . . ."

"But I love me birds." Stephen burst into tears and he, who, with his slow, deliberate manner, had seemed to Maria a man, became just a frightened boy.

It doesn't matter what happens to him, she reasoned. He is partly responsible for Saladin's death after all. She pressed her hands together to keep them from shaking. He's but a peasant, and he did leave his birds to go drinking. But Stephen was always kind to her and made her laugh. Sometimes, when everyone else was too busy, he'd even toss balls or play her a game of guilles, though his eyes were so sharp he'd usually knock down all the pins on his first throw of the stick.

"You'll wish you'd not been born." Henrietta's eyes were cobalt chips set in a carefully controlled face.

Stephen lifted his hands to shield his tears. Those same hands had deftly administered headache and cold remedies to ailing birds; those same hands had cradled Saladin.

"Go pack your things." Hugh's harsh voice was totally unlike his usual pleasant tone. "Be at the stables in an hour and . . ."

"No, papa, I did it!" Maria cried. As she approached her astonished parents her legs felt unsteady as a babe's. "I set them loose because they killed Saladin."

"You set free my birds because of a crippled rabbit?" Henrietta shook her head in disbelief. "Did you not care how I cherished my birds, what their presence meant to me?"

"I. . . I did not think." Maria looked to her father, but his cold eyes offered no comfort. She looked down at her scuffed slippers and wished herself miles away. "'Twould not be right for Stephen to suffer because of my misdeed."

"I agree." Henrietta glared at Maria before continuing in a carefully measured voice, "Go to your chamber. Stay there until I tell you otherwise. I must have time to decide your proper punishment."

A familiar blast of trumpets announced the even meal. When the door to her small chamber opened, Maria looked up from the bed upon which she'd been sitting. She'd spent the afternoon ostensibly working a tapestry but in reality worrying over her possible punishment and assuring herself it would not be too severe. Eleanora, not Henrietta, beckoned.

"Where is mother?" Maria asked, as they hurried down the passageway to the great hall. "Think she forgot all about me?"

Eleanora shot her an exasperated look but did not answer until she'd washed her hands in the basin at the entrance to the room. While Maria dipped the tips of her fingers and dried them on the skirt, her twin said, "'Tis a certain bet mother hasn't forgotten you. You know she loved her birds."

"I suppose it does not matter that I loved Saladin, does it?" Maria's voice quavered; her stomach began tightening in troublesome knots. "It was foolish of me to loose the hawks, was it not?"

"Aye, sister, it was." They entered the hall.

"I wish I could be more like you," Maria said as she noticed her parents already seated at the dais. "You would never have done such a childish thing."

"At least you told the truth about Stephen," Eleanora said as they approached their places at table. "If you had not, I would have."

Maria turned on her in surprise. "But how did you know? Did you see it in a dream?" Eleanora's "sight" never ceased to fascinate her.

"I need not visions to understand a bit of human nature—especially yours."

As Maria swung her legs over the bench beside Hugh, he squeezed her knee in encouragement. The gesture elicited nearer dread than comfort. Throughout grace, she tried to study her mother, to ascertain from her stony expression what punishment might be forthcoming. Maria's stomach began to hurt.

The pantler and butler had finished performing their services. Pages carried in the main dishes.

Addressing a lad carrying a huge steaming bowl, Henrietta spoke for the first time. "Serve my daughter, Maria, first."

In Maria's trencher the page plunked a vinegary smelling sauce, thick with onions and big chunks of meat. Even the pungent spices could not disguise the meat's unique smell. Disbelieving, she turned to her mother, who calmly picked up her silver spoon.

"Rabbits are for eating, daughter. Eat your rabbit stew."

Maria stared at the trencher. She raised her eyes to the salt dish, which suddenly blurred.

Henrietta dipped her spoon into the stew.

Jumping up from the bench, Maria bolted from the great hall, out to the inner bailey. Her rabbit hutch stood empty. Disbelieving, she raced back inside. Stumbling to the dais, she faced her mother. "Where are my rabbits?" she cried.

"I told you." Henrietta calmly sipped her broth. "Rabbits are for eating."

"Not my rabbits." Maria's voice cracked. "They are my pets and . . ."

"Daughter, rabbits were not put on this earth to be coddled and stroked. God placed them here to provide food for all manner of animals. 'Tis the nature of things. You must learn not to disrupt Our Father's plan, whether by keeping rabbits or loosing my birds. Understand?"

"Nay, I do not." Tears spilled down Maria's cheeks. "All I know is that you are eating Jerusalem and Lionheart and they were my friends."

"'Tis time you found new friends then. Male friends." Henrietta eyed her as she always did when readying to deliver her familiar lecture on duty, marriage, and men. "Your behavior has convinced me that I've allowed you too free a hand. You are no longer a child, Maria, whether you would pretend or no. 'Tis time we found you a husband. Next year we will hold the grandest Cherry Fair ever and pray we can find someone foolish and rich enough to wish you for a bride."

"Nay. You'll force me to wed someone I hate and . . ."

"Enough of this!" Hugh slammed his silver mazer down on the table. "I have had an abundance of this bickering. You both wrangle so it hurts my head.

"Daughter, you did a childish, irresponsible thing by loosing those hawks, and your mother had a duty to punish you in whatever manner she chose. And 'tis time you gave thought to marriage. Life is made up of duty, not pleasure. Now sit still and eat your stew."

Maria sat. She stared at the now congealing sauce, the chunks of meat marbled with fat. I'll never marry, she thought, as she picked up her spoon. Not if you threaten me until Christ's Second Coming. And never will I forgive either of you for killing my rabbits.

TWO

bove the jagged line of Cheshire's Wirral Forest the morning sky colored red as a hart's blood. At the edge of the trees, Richard Plantagenet, earl of Sussex, reined in his gray Percheron. The other members of his hunting party followed suit. As Richard dismounted, Rolf the Huntsman plunged deeper into the forest, still dark shadowed and cold with the lingering breath of night. Handlers followed, skillfully controlling the lymers, brachets, and greyhounds straining at their leashes.

"A perfect spot to break fast." Lady Constance de Clarke smiled, displaying oversize yellow teeth. After motioning her servants to spread cloths and lay forth meat, wine, and bread, Lady Constance moved toward Richard. The earl turned his back. More pleasant to face a screaming battalion of Scots than Constance de Clarke so early of a summer morn.

A triumphant baying emerged from the Wirral's interior.

"The hounds must have found the deer's spoor, m'lord." Phillip Rendell, the Herefordshire knight, stood beside Richard. The two men were similarly matched in physique, though Phillip's hair was black, while Richard's was as golden as the royal lion gracing his tunic.

"Sit with me, will you not, Sir Rendell?" Richard asked. He

found Phillip's unobtrusive manner pleasing. Richard felt he'd known his vassal all his twenty-one years, rather than a scant fortnight. Besides, Phillip could provide relief from the constant Constance, who had attached herself to Richard's right. Saints protect him from the woman. Unwed, exceedingly wealthy, and exceedingly ambitious. The possibilities were frightening.

As the meal proceeded, Phillip, at least, ate without unnecessary conversation. Constance, however, gossiped about the guests at yestereve's banquet, Richard's forthcoming meeting at Berwick Castle with his half brother, King Edward, and Edward's queen, whom the lady had never met. Her braying laugh shattered the hour's softness. Who could hear the shy trill of a mockingbird, the forest stirrings over Constance's ear-wrenching voice? If one deer remained in all of Wirral Forest, it must be deaf as Margarite, the queen mother.

Lady Constance licked her stubby, beringed fingers, sticky with venison juice. "I hope when you ride north to battle the heathen Scots, sire, you send their leader to the block. I can think of no finer sight than to see Robert the Bruce's head stuck atop a pike."

Richard's eyes met Phillip's. The glimmer of a smile danced across the baron's full mouth.

"Aye," Constance continued, "I hope to see the Bruce brought as low as that grasping, greedy Piers Gaveston. 'Twas a great day for England when Thomas Lancaster divested the favorite's pretty head from his body."

The hand bringing Richard's wine cup to his mouth froze. His eyebrows met in an angry line.

"You forget to whom you speak, lady. You would do well to keep your opinion of His Majesty's friends to yourself." Richard turned away, fighting to control his temper. He had not liked the avaricious Gaveston either, had chafed at his cavalier use of England's Great Seal, his arrogance and insatiable appetite for property. But Edward had loved Piers, and his grief over his favorite's death had been terrible to witness. Gaveston's sins might have been great, but so had been his fall.

From the forest, Rolf the Huntsman emerged and strode toward Richard. He bowed.

"What have you found, Rolf?" Richard stood and tossed the dregs of his wine onto the dew-damp grass. Droplets splashed on Constance's green supertunic. "Is the stag of a good size?"

"I measured his tracks with me fingers, m'lord, and the velvet of his antlers left on the tree trunks, and I think he is a stout stag and worthy." Rolf thrust a hunting horn in Richard's face. "I gathered a bit of his fumes, sire, if you would care to judge for yourself."

Richard firmly pushed away the huntsman's hand. "That is unnecessary, Rolf. I'll trust your judgment." The earl had no desire to poke about deer droppings, no matter what their contents might reveal.

"Then I might take the dogs, sire?"

"Aye."

Smoothing her velvet tunic over her thick waist, Lady Constance flicked at the drying splash of wine. "Oh, I cannot wait for the hunt," she bubbled, casting a sidelong glance at Richard. "There is nothing quite so exhilarating as seeing a fine stag brought to bay, is there, m'lord Sussex?"

Richard could think of all manner of unchivalrous replies. Instead, he ignored her. Undeterred, Constance slipped her arm through his. He firmly replaced it at her side. The woman annoyed Richard to distraction. Perhaps he would leave for Berwick Castle and his half brother, the king, earlier than planned. Say, immediately after the hunt.

As they remounted, Richard turned to Phillip. "When the time comes, would you care to kill the stag?"

A smile lightened Phillip's dark features. "I would consider it a great honor, m'lord."

Such a little thing to please Phillip, Richard thought, as he removed his ivory oliphant from its saddle strap. Would that all my vassals were so easily pleased.

*   *   *

The fallow stag careened toward Richard's hunting party. Its yellow coat, spotted with white, was wet and roughened with sweat. Behind it ran a howling pack of dogs.

After raising the oliphant to his lips, Richard hesitated. His signal would bring the deer to bay, end its life. A magnificent stag, one of the largest he'd ever seen—graceful, dignified, even in panicked flight. Richard blew a series of harsh monotonic notes, alerting the pursuing hounds. As the dogs closed the distance to the rapidly tiring stag, Constance loudly thanked St. Martin and a plethora of hunters' saints. Her voice pierced above even the baying, the blast of the horn.

The hounds drove the stag past the party, toward a huge outcropping of sandstone, a silver sliver of stream. Spreading out across the buttercup-blanketed meadow, the riders followed.

The stag splashed across the stream; the hounds guided it toward the rock, trapped it. The stag tried to leap above the boulders; its hooves struck granite. Tumbling to the ground, it landed on its side. The dogs closed in. Struggling to its feet, the stag faced the hounds. Head lowered, antlers menacing, the deer's ribs bellowed in and out. Foam mixed with blood dripped from its nostrils and mouth.

Misjudging the separating distance, a greyhound ran too close. The stag lunged, impaling the dog on its rack, then dipped its head, jerking upward. Flying through the air the hound crashed, slamming against the gravelly edge of the stream. A second dog fell victim to the stag's cloven hooves, but the deer was obviously exhausted, its movements floundering. If the huntsman gave the signal, the hounds would move in for the kill.

Rolf turned to Richard, a pleased grin splitting his coarse features.

"A fine stag, is it not, m'lord? Just as I told you!"

Richard's gaze remained on the deer's frightened eyes, showing white. Fine dark eyes, intelligent eyes. Richard's

[17]

mouth tasted sour. Turning to Phillip, he nodded. Phillip flung his left leg over his saddle and, lance in hand, dismounted.

Sunlight glinted off the tip of Phillip's poised spear. He circled to the stag's right, to the exposed shoulder that was dusted with white spots as well as sweat. Phillip raised the spear, tensed. The shaft hurtled through the air, above the heads of the leaping dogs. Steel met muscle, penetrated. Blood spurted outward, staining the stag's coat, turning the white spots scarlet. The lance quivered with the force of impact, the sudden tremble of the stag's body. The animal's legs buckled. It fell forward, sinking on its forelegs, shook its great head—as if clearing death from its vision—then toppled onto its side. Racing forward, Phillip removed the dagger from his belt. Leaping upon the stag's shoulder, immediately above the lance, he grasped its antlers, curved its neck backward. His dagger slashed toward the animal's jugular.

Watching, Richard's hands tightened on the pommel. He forced himself to look into the stag's clouding eyes—no longer brimmed with pain or terror, but merely focused on a great distance. Phillip's knife jerked across the jugular. Blood spilled onto the blue wolf's head sewn on the baron's tunic, his fingers. After placing the animal's head on the ground, Phillip stood and walked to the stream where he washed his knife blade, the blood from his hands and forearms.

Face conveying no more than casual interest, Richard watched the entire procedure. From earliest childhood he had accompanied his father or half brother on hunting expeditions, had brought a hundred stags to bay, personally braved the tusks of countless boars. And hated every moment.

Richard edged away from Constance, snoring softly on her side of the canopied bed. Pulling back the bed curtains, he reached for his chausses, his every movement careful. Blessed Christ help him should the lady awaken. Richard was in no mood to further feast of her charms.

Bending over he slipped on his cordovan leather boots. Tomorrow he would confess his fornication to Father Andre' and resolve never to commit such sin again. At least not with Constance de Clarke.

She snorted. Richard turned, startled, but Constance settled her head more firmly against a raft of pillows. One arm was positioned across her large breasts; the bed linens draped about her hips. Constance's figure reminded Richard of a food trencher—thick, shapeless. Her hair, yellow as the flame from the night light beside her bed, snaked about her shoulders. Richard was certain nature had not bestowed on the woman that golden shade. Since convention decreed that blond hair was most desirable, both sexes often used saffron to achieve what nature had not.

After closing the bed curtains and dressing, Richard tiptoed from the room.

In Wirral Castle's great hall, he searched among the knights palleted there until he found Phillip. Bending down, he touched the baron's shoulder.

Phillip sat up, immediately awake. "M'lord?"

"Would you ride with me? I feel a need to be away."

Phillip stood, still fully dressed. "I would be honored to ride with you, sire."

Richard's gray stallion, Excalibur, stretched beneath him. The earl bent forward, enjoying the night wind pummeling his face, blowing away the lingering scent and feel of Constance. A full moon raced overhead, keeping pace. The dirt road stretched toward the city of Chester near the border of Wales. He and Phillip reined in and dismounted at the stone bridge spanning the River Dee. Trading ships were moored near the city wall along Bridgegate, one of the entrances to the city.

The two men stood on the bridge. Richard looked down at

the water slipping by; Phillip's gaze fastened overhead on the Milky Way. Richard relaxed, grateful that Phillip did not question or chatter.

"You are not married, Phillip?"

Phillip shook his head. "My older brother constantly laments my state. Humphrey would have me marry a rich heiress to add to the family demesne." His mouth twisted. "But what heiress would settle for a second son?"

"If you desire property and a good marriage, I could arrange both."

Phillip turned in surprise. "Sire, I was not asking . . ."

"Aye. That's why I offered."

Phillip returned his gaze to the heavens. He did not speak for a time. "I am twenty-seven years old. If I had wanted to marry I could have, but it does not interest me. Nor does land. I would rather roam freely about the world than be tied to a few acres of dust. Humphrey says travel is my mistress. Perhaps my brother is right."

"At one time I'd also thought not to marry." Richard's voice was low pitched with reflection. "At one time I'd thought to be a Knight Templar, to fight in another crusade, to devote myself to being a true knight in the service of the Lord."

"Did not the Templars take vows of chastity?"

Richard grinned. "Perhaps 'tis best my brother had them disbanded and imprisoned. I fear I would have broken that vow a hundred times over."

"At least you would not have been forced to endure the Lady Constance."

Richard laughed. "The monks say it well. Such as she is an insatiable beast, a house of Tempest, a curse upon mankind."

Scooping a stone from the ground, Phillip tossed it in the River Dee. "After the Scottish campaign I'll be bound for Venice, where a friend and I will travel to the Holy Land. I've promised my brother I'll marry when I return." He paused. "I think I'll not see England again."

* * *

Richard and Phillip entered the sprawling stable area of Berwick Castle, perched on the border of Scotland. King Edward had recently returned from hawking and was now relating a bawdy joke to an attentive circle of knights.

Stopping behind his brother, Richard waited patiently for an ending he'd already heard a dozen times. Even if Edward had not been king, Richard would not have interrupted. Joke telling gave Edward a measure of happiness—rare since Piers Gaveston's death.

As Edward finished and the knights broke into coarse guffaws, Richard glanced at Phillip, whose smile appeared more polite than amused. Crude as a London shit-raker, Edward had never achieved wit or subtlety in his stories.

The king turned to Richard, a pleased grin lighting his regular features. "What is it, brother?" Never one to stand on formality, Edward waved aside the customary obeisance and flung a muscular arm around his half brother's shoulders.

"I have news, Your Majesty." Richard glanced at the knights, still hovering about. All battle-hardened veterans and most had fought with the late King Edward. But Edward II had little in common with Edward I save blood, and one could no longer be certain of loyalties. "I think 'tis best, sire, that we speak in private. In your chamber, perhaps."

"Oh. Aye, well . . ." Edward turned from the knights with a vague wave of the hand. He was still wearing a silver-threaded hawking glove. "Return to your dice, men, and do not forget to send for me during the cock fights."

The three men crossed Berwick's inner ward to the hall. At Edward's chamber, Phillip hesitated, but Richard motioned him inside saying, "I have no secrets from you." Richard was growing increasingly dependent on his vassal. If Phillip were not absolutely determined to be off for Venice, Richard would find him a permanent position within the Sussex household.

Trustworthiness was as rare a quality in a man as compatibility.

"Aye, Sir Rendell, do come in," Edward said amiably. He tossed his hawking glove on a mahogany-colored table beside a wooden model of a sailing ship. "Pour us all some wine. My throat feels as sour as a drunkard's following May Day revels." The king motioned to a filigree folding table upon which sat a silver tray and goblets.

As Phillip poured, Edward held up to the narrow chamber window his half-finished model, a delicately proportioned galley. At thirty years of age Edward of Caernarvon moved with the easy grace of a man delighting in physical exercise. Though he and Richard were matched in size, Edward had reached the pinnacle of manhood, while his half brother was approaching it. Yet, in Richard the sometimes overnarrow and long Plantagenet features had been ennobled. Edward might look the part of athlete, but Richard looked the part of king.

Phillip handed them each a goblet of vernage. Richard waited for Edward to speak. Sooner or later, his brother would address the business at hand. When he could no longer avoid it.

Edward replaced his miniature galley on the table, tossed off his wine, handed it to Phillip for a refill, and wiped his mouth with the back of his hand. "Now, brother, what would you tell me?"

"Twenty-one thousand foot soldiers have assembled from the northern counties and Wales." In the spring of the year, 1314, His Majesty had issued a summons calling for an army to meet the continuing threat of Robert the Bruce. Finally, in early June, his army was coming together.

"Twenty-one thousand!" Edward grinned, his face suddenly boyish. "Even father was not able to raise so vast a force!"

Richard did not comment. Their father, Edward I, had been born a soldier. Two men or two hundred thousand—it would have made no difference. His very nickname, Longshanks, struck terror into the heart of the stoutest Scot. Richard

doubted a similar reaction at mention of Edward Caernarvon—
or himself. But then this campaign would be his very first.

The king drained a second cup of vernage. "And how large an
army has Robert the Bruce gathered?"

"Our best guess is seven thousand. With five hundred
knights."

"Christ's cross! Such numbers ring sweet to my ears. We'll
send those demon-bastards back to their hills!" Picking up the
detached mast to his ship model, Edward twirled it between his
fingers. "Father knew how to deal with them. Crush them, run
them to the ground like mad dogs. And I shall not allow them
their freedom again, ever."

The earl glanced at Phillip, who was studying the king with
unfeigned interest. Edward sounded like an undersize boy
bragging about his prowess. Richard hoped Phillip would not
notice. Braggadocio was not a pleasing characteristic in a king.

"And now the Bruce and Black Douglas are taking back all
my castles, save Stirling," Edward continued. "And Stirling, too,
if I do not hie me north. Why cannot everyone just leave me in
peace?"

"Lord Mowbray has agreed to turn over Stirling to the Bruce
if we do not help him," Richard reminded him. "'Twould
appear the Scots have thrown down the gauntlet."

"And England will have to pick it up." The words were
uttered without enthusiasm. Not that Edward was a coward.
Richard had seen him face a wild boar with nothing more than
a knife in hand. But Edward had not the head for war, nor the
tenacity. Neither had Richard—though he'd long pretended
otherwise. For their father, who'd been so disappointed by his
legitimate son's martial ineptitude—as well as his other weaknesses.

"What about my barons?" Edward continued. "Have they all
arrived?" Though his manner was casual, the question was not.

"Most have, sire."

"Who yet stays away?"

"Warenne, Warwick, and Arundel, though they sent troops."

All named had been involved in Gaveston's death.

Edward's brow furrowed. "And what about Cousin Lancaster? Has he shown his viper's face?"

"Nay."

The ship mast snapped between Edward's blunt fingers. He tossed the pieces to the rush-strewn floor. "Dear Cousin Tom."

Richard moved beside Phillip, who stood in front of the folding table. The earl busied himself straightening the silver tray, wiping up a minuscule wine stain. He could not bear to view his brother's face, and yet he knew Edward was no longer at Berwick Castle, but miles away and two years past. At Blacklow Hill with Lancaster and Piers Gaveston. Viewing with his mind's eye the broadsword that ran through Piers, that severed his curly head from his slender body.

"Would you like more wine, Ned?" Unconsciously, Richard reverted to Edward's childhood nickname. "I've still a bit of a thirst."

"Cousin Thomas will pay," Edward muttered, his eyes focused on an arras hanging from the chamber's north wall. Then he shuddered, raised his gaze to them both, and forced a smile.

"Sir Phillip, you look like you can well handle seven thousand Scots. Are you looking forward to a bit of bloodletting?"

"I am looking forward to serving my king," Phillip said diplomatically.

"Then you are one of the few." Edward's smile contained more sadness than mirth.

The English vanguard, under the dual command of the earls of Gloucester and Hereford, followed the Carse Road, which wound into a hunting ground reserved for Scottish kings. Richard rode immediately behind the two constables, who were even now wrangling over how they should proceed. A scouting party of Scots had been recently spotted, and both Gloucester and Hereford had agreed to engage them—though they could not agree on anything further. Taking a deep breath, Richard licked his cracked lips, trying to ignore the constables' bickering, his incessant thirst, and the uncomfortably heavy armor. St. George be thanked that the June afternoon was at least mild. If the day were hot, hell would be cooler.

Row after well-ordered row of knights, astride high-stepping Flemish chargers, continued forward, silent save for the creaking of saddle leather or occasional ring of steel striking steel.

"The Scots have picked their ground well," Richard commented to Phillip, who rode beside him.

Phillip nodded as he surveyed the terrain. "If we do not seize the Carse, our main army will never be able to pass through."

Richard's gaze swept past the River Forth and slow-running Burn of Bannock, across the flat Carse to the heavily forested Gillies and Coxet hills. Phillip was right. Edward's army, which yet struggled miles behind, would be hemmed in on both sides.

"Strike hard and early," Richard said half to himself. Edward I's credo. But the knights had already marched twenty miles and the Scots, besides being rested, had enjoyed days in which to map out strategy and position. An unchivalrous way to fight—but effective.

When they reached the Carse, Gilbert of Gloucester signaled a halt. A strong corps of Scots was positioned at the far edge of the open field. As Richard viewed the enemies' ragged line, stunted Highland horses, and mismatched armor, his gaze riveted to one knight positioned in the middle of the formation. It was not the man's armor—little better than average—that Richard noticed, nor the helm, but what was fastened above the helm. A golden crown.

Richard pointed to the knight. "Robert the Bruce!"

The knight's identity blazed through the English ranks. Stiffening in his saddle, Richard attempted for a better glimpse of the wily king who'd so plagued Edward I.

Ahead, Henry de Bohun yelped like a goaded dog at a bear

baiting. "What luck! The Bruce himself, and with no more than a handful of vermin to guard him."

Richard did not share de Bohun's enthusiasm. "I think they would not leave their king so ill guarded," he said to Phillip.

"I agree." Phillip flipped down his visor. "I smell treachery."

As Gloucester and Hereford argued over the possible meaning of the king's appearance and how to exploit this apparent opportunity, Henry de Bohun broke rank and rode toward the Scottish line.

"Christ's wounds!" Phillip swore. "Henry will be split upon the Bruce's claymore ere the hour's out."

Across the yellow field patched with the emerald of swampy mosses and dotted with gnarled trees, Henry de Bohun galloped. With his multicolored jupon, painted lance positioned at rest, his burnished armor, de Bohun looked the very epitome of knighthood. His voice, challenging Robert the Bruce to single combat, carried far in the sudden stillness.

"If de Bohun kills their king," Phillip observed, "the Scots will rout."

"Aye," Richard agreed. "And Bruce knows that well as any man.

Accepting the challenge, Robert the Bruce cantered forward astride his shaggy gray pony. From his saddle bow he removed a battle-ax.

Not a man stirred along either line. Richard held his breath, his eyes on the brilliant de Bohun. The young knight raised his lance and charged. The spear tip bore toward Bruce's chest. Bruce did not flinch, but waited. When de Bohun appeared in easy grasp of victory, Bruce jerked an armored knee into his gray's ribs. The mount sidestepped just as de Bohun thundered past. Rising in his stirrups, Bruce crashed the ax down on de Bohun's head. The blade sliced through helm, past the skull beneath, cleaving de Bohun's head in two. Blood and bone exploded into the air. The blow knocked de Bohun backward, over his destrier's rump.

The English army looked on, stunned. De Bohun's horse, glossy withers bespattered with its master's brain, kicked and bucked, trying to rid itself of the clinging corpse; de Bohun's steel boots remained caught in the stirrups. His body bounced across the rough Carse, slamming into trees. The crazed horse careened toward the Scots, then disappeared into the forest.

After a stunned moment of disbelieving silence, the entire English troop erupted. Battle cries shattered the stillness. Lance, sword, and battle-ax were brought to battle ready, and of one accord, the calvary galloped toward the Scots. Richard and Phillip rode side by side.

The first line engaged the enemy. They fell back. The English pursued. Swinging his broadsword, Richard had little time to notice anything save the warriors in front of him. But one thing he knew. There were too many to be a mere scouting party. Though the Scots fought, they gave ground. Too easily? The English line pressed forward. Destriers reeled and plunged, men screamed.

"Pits!" someone yelled. The Scots had indeed picked their spot well, and with plenty of time to dig their traps. Richard tried to jerk Excalibur to the right even as a forward knight plunged into a hole and was impaled on the pointed poles within. He jerked harder. Excalibur careened toward a second destrier, struggling to veer away from the holes. Behind, an English knight slammed into them; Excalibur stumbled. Richard was nearly unhorsed and flung into the abyss, now filling with riders. Excalibur righted himself. The line behind seemed to slacken and he struggled toward an opening. Finally he broke free and Richard guided him around the treacherous maze. He glimpsed Phillip ahead, swinging his mace over his head. To Richard's left, a claymore flashed. Reacting instinctively, he swung his blade, lopped off a man's head, which flew toward the pit. One for Henry de Bohun.

The earl of Gloucester's herald suddenly called retreat. Richard was more relieved than surprised. The troop began their withdrawal. The English would meet their enemy on the field of Bannock again on the morrow. God grant this time they would be better prepared.

Soon after dawn on the morning of June 24, Richard had made full private confession, readying himself for the forth-coming battle. Who would God listen to this day? Richard stared at his brother's broad back, covered by a magnificent jeweled tabard. The English outnumbered the Scots three to one, possessed far superior weapons, as well as baggage support trains that stretched twenty miles to the rear. How could they fail?

Richard's eyes swept the circle of barons kneeling for a priest's final blessing—Bartholomew Badlesmere, a veteran of the dead king's Welsh campaigns, silent Hugh Despenser, and the dark Roger Mortimer of Wigmore, who'd brought with him a troop of Irishmen. All of England's barons save for Thomas Lancaster, who remained safely hidden away in his castle at Pontefract, would fight at Bannockburn.

Following the benediction, King Edward inspected his troops, his manner as nervously buoyant as his high-stepping white charger. Sensing easy victory, he laughed and joked, continually belittling the enemy. "We'll rout them in an hour!" he boasted.

"Be wary of their schiltron," Roger Mortimer warned. He was a marcher lord from the border counties and known to be a deadly fighter. "'Tis a wicked formation. And if they possess only a handful of cavalry they will use their pikemen."

Edward waved a negligent hand, dismissing with his gesture the martial prowess of an entire nation. "A legion of pikemen are no match for one knight. Besides, I've planned it all. We cannot fail." Because of the narrow area in which the English had to maneuver, Edward had divided his troops in three lines, called battles. One battle would follow another. Gilbert of

Gloucester had been picked to lead the first wave.

The king motioned to a waiting herald. "My Lord Gloucester is ready. Send forth the summons."

The sun was low, the air still edged with night's chill, when the earl of Gloucester galloped across the Carse. He led a well-ordered cavalry whose horses' heads were protected by steel chamfrons from the wicked Scottish spikes. Behind the knights marched line after line of foot soldiers. Up the rough Carse toward the Scots who were positioned in several schiltrons—circular formations with pikes to the fore and ready reserves in the center.

"A St. George! God wills it!" the English knights cried as they thundered forward, toward the waiting pikes with their pointed metal heads. Suddenly, portions of ground collapsed, plunging knights and chargers into cleverly hidden pits. Others met iron caltraps, concealed in the grass. Spikes pierced the vulnerable center of stallions' hooves, ripping into the frogs' exposed flesh. Racing on, the main battle slammed against the Scottish line, which held. Gloucester fell back, reformed, charged again.

Watching from the sidelines, Richard felt as if worms gnawed his stomach. Today was his first real battle, and fear warred with eagerness. Beside him, King Edward shifted impatiently in his saddle. His gauntleted right hand bounced on the pommel in nervous rhythm; his blue eyes swept the chaotic field, willing Gloucester to break through the line.

"Our archers!" His Grace turned to Richard. "They'll provide Gloucester with the victory." He motioned to a herald. "Send the order round. My archers are to cross the Pelstream burn and hit Bruce's flank."

After the bowmen moved to obey, Edward signaled his second battle forward. Most of the lords, including Phillip and Richard, were part of this wave. The battle moved out, with Edward keeping well to the back. A king must be well protected, Richard thought. His position makes sense. But their father had always ridden in the lead, never asking his troops to do and risk what he would not. Richard himself rode to the fore, though his every instinct cried for the far safer position an entire line could provide. He glanced over his shoulder at Phillip. At least Phillip, who was a veteran of many battles, would be near and would look to his safety more effectively than his squires.

As the second battle moved slowly forward, rivulets of nervous sweat coursed down Richard's chest, back, and arms, causing his inner gambeson to stick to his underclothes. Gloucester's troops still had not penetrated the Scottish schiltrons, and if the second English line continued they would meet, not Scots, but Edward's own foot soldiers. Richard's throat felt dry from fear as well as billowing dust. He licked cracked lips and tasted blood.

Gloucester's cavalry struggled forward. Suddenly the line surged. The English had penetrated the schiltrons! A cheer rose from the second wave and accelerated when His Majesty gave the order to engage.

Moving beside Richard, Phillip jerked his arm, pointed down field. The third line was moving forward.

Phillip leaned close, shouting above the din. "They've already been ordered up. We'll be caught between the third battle and Gloucester's men."

A chill hand squeezed Richard's heart. Already he could see the faces of the foot soldiers leading the third wave. If the forward battles did not successfully push into the Scottish ranks, all of them would inevitably be trapped like rabbits in a snare. Richard's eyes met Phillip's. Phillip shook his head as if to say, What can be done? He was right. If death awaited them on the field of Bannock, they had no choice but to ride forth and embrace it.

Scots clung to Richard like leeches to a wound. On all sides, screaming, wielding claymore and battle-ax. The earl swung his sword with relentless precision, acting and reacting on an instinctive level instilled by years of training. Encased in a steel tomb, his helm providing limited peripheral vision, Richard's battlefield extended directly in front, a few feet to either side. He was totally blind to the back. Thank God for Phillip.

The line struggled slowly forward, England's cavalry as much in danger of killing one another as their enemy. Ahead, Richard glimpsed Gloucester, suddenly down, an ax through his cuirass. His maddened destrier trampled him beneath, then was itself felled by a stray arrow.

Shouting off to the flank, where Edward had ordered his archers. "On them! On them!" the Scots yelled as they attacked the bowmen from behind. A rain of arrows dropped English foot soldiers like meadow grass before a windstorm. English arrows dropping English troops. Shafts thudded into Richard's padded surcoat. Men began to panic, searching for a place to hide. But where? Hills encased them on either side, as did the burn of Bannock, now filling with the morning tide. Scots ahead, English behind. Trapped in the middle, Richard could not have run, even if he would. He glimpsed Edward on the line's edge, more spectator than participant.

The shower of arrows ceased. Shouting. "Bruce has routed our archers! We are done for." Scots emerged from all directions, materializing from the ground, multiplying a hundredfold. Bruce, who'd been holding back his reserves, had thrown them into action, leading them through gaps in the schiltrons. With Gloucester dead and the ranks badly depleted, the line slowly, inexorably gave ground. A swell of corpses hampered their retreat. Horses stumbled over slopes slippery with blood; foot soldiers slid on guts and dismembered limbs. Bodies floated in the pulling tide of Bannock; wounded soldiers floundered and drowned. The Scots pushed relentlessly, a river of silver swelling and breaking over the English ranks.

The second battle fell into the third. The entire line began to waver. Richard felt it even before he saw it; and more, sensed the change in himself. From a measure of confidence, to rising panic that threatened to totally paralyze him. He wanted to throw down his sword, turn, and flee all the way back to London. Bannockburn was lost, and Richard knew they were lost with it.

Glimpsing Edward's jeweled tabard, he tried to edge Excalibur toward his brother. The line was buckling; the Bruce and his men pressed harder. Richard saw Phillip behind him, surcoat studded with arrows. He pointed with his sword toward Edward. Nodding, Phillip spurred his horse. Forcing a path toward the king, Richard moved against the tide of retreating Englishmen. Edward, surrounded by his earls, was well protected.

An arrow pierced Richard's thigh. He jerked the shaft upward, his brain exploding with agony. Shaking his head he forced his mind beyond the pain, his eyes to the mild June sky, to silent Gillies Hill. Richard stared at the hill, suddenly alive with Scottish reinforcements, scrambling from the forest toward the English flank, toward the king himself. With the latest screaming Scottish wave, Edward's entire army collapsed like a rotten drawbridge.

Jerking his reins, Richard wheeled Excalibur to a halt. Phillip was off to his right, eyes also on the Scottish reinforcements. Richard pointed. The Scots, those who had turned Bannockburn into a complete debacle, were not worthy knights, but camp followers. Fletchers, cooks, wagoners—men and women waving, not banners and pikes, but broken pike handles, broomsticks, and crutches topped with petticoats, clouts, and tattered cloaks.

"Sweet Christ! I do not believe it!"

Phillip's and Richard's eyes locked. Then, as of one mind, they closed the gap between themselves and the king. Edward's earls were already leading him from the field. Hugh Despenser held his charger's reins.

"Father would not have left," Edward said to no one in particular. He sounded more bemused than angry.

Furious with his brother's incompetence, the entire folly, himself, Richard shouted, "But you are not father. Now get yourself to Stirling Castle before you are captured and of no good to anyone."

Edward's eyes flew to his face. Richard read hurt there, but was too angry to care. Shame burned in him like poison. England would never live down this tragedy, and Edward was responsible. He was Edward's brother. If he'd fought harder, if he'd not been afraid.

Richard turned. His gaze swept Bannock's field—the trampled English banners, men struggling and drowning in the burn, the sea of bodies. He slammed his gauntleted hand on the pommel of his saddle. Bannockburn. The name would be spit like a curse at him and Edward. It would haunt their children's children. He knew it. Richard felt like crying. Instead he spurred his horse and, with Phillip at his side, followed his brother from the field.

Edward and his royal guard of five hundred fled toward Stirling Castle as if Satan and all his legions nipped at their heels. They had detoured to the left of the Scottish line and then north toward Stirling, hoping to pass unnoticed. It proved a vain hope. Scots engaged them several times, troops led by Robert the Bruce's brother, Edward. Riding at the tag end of the line, Richard and Phillip bore the brunt of the attacks. Richard felt as if he'd been fighting forever, as if he'd died and gone to hell and his eternal punishment would be endless skirmishes.

Seemingly from nowhere, Edward Bruce appeared, cutting off the route to freedom, riding down on the English king surrounded by exhausted troops. Hugh Despenser and several other knights formed a ring around Edward, repelling several charges. Edward, too, fought, expertly wielding his mace, but an English knight fell and the Scots struggled forward toward him. Richard raced to close the iron ring, but he was too late. One Scot was already grabbing for the king's reins, another for Edward himself. He beat furiously at the Scot reaching for his bridle. The line broke and the king fled toward Stirling Castle. Immediately, the Scots were after him.

Richard felt he had not the strength to follow, or raise his sword another time. He looked over his shoulder, seeking Phillip. Riding toward Richard was a Scot, dressed all in black, without identifying surcoat or mark of any sort. He sat astride a destrier black as his armor. Richard's limbs were suddenly paralyzed. He could not tear his eyes from the faceless knight. Death, bearing down on him. Death, raising its sword to smite him. Yelling a warning, Phillip spurred his horse, trying to cut off the Scot. Life returned to Richard's limbs. He jerked Excalibur to the left. Too late. The claymore whistled past Richard's exposed head, hit his cuirass. He felt searing pain along his chest. The blade shimmied over the breastplate, sliced into Excalibur's arched neck. The gray collapsed. Struggling from the saddle, Richard tried to leap, stumbled. His body would not properly respond. Wetness spread through his inner gambeson along with white hot pain.

Wheeling his horse, the black knight returned for the kill but Phillip intercepted. Knee to knee, the two hacked and parried. Phillip's destrier attacked with hooves and bared teeth. The Scot's horse panicked and Phillip's sword dispatched the black knight to heaven or hell. Not Death at all; he bled as copiously as any man.

Spurring his destrier toward Richard, Phillip held out his arm. "Grab hold!"

Strength draining with his blood, Richard tried unsuccessfully to pull himself up.

"Hurry!" Phillip urged. Those remaining Scots who were not otherwise engaged with stragglers from Edward's royal guard were already looking to them. Realizing Richard's weakness, Phillip leapt from his horse and helped him mount.

The earl was in the saddle. Phillip whirled to face two oncoming Scots. "Go!" he shouted to Richard. But Richard could not. Far in the distance he heard Phillip's voice. He shook his head, trying to bring the world back to clarity. Where was he? What was happening? A gauntleted hand reached up, grabbed the pommel of the saddle, and Richard's world went black.

A cooling wetness trailed along the burning line of Richard's wound, which snaked around his right pectoral muscle. Though it was much easier to keep his eyes closed, to hover in a vague netherworld, he forced them open to a patch of deepening sky. The wetness relieved the burning sensation. Phillip was cleaning his wound with an undershirt. Once white, the material now showed scarlet. Scarlet like the blood of the hart they'd killed at Wirral Forest. Only this was not an animal's blood but his own. Richard attempted to raise his arm. His limbs, though relieved of their armor, felt like sacks of grain. His thigh, where it had been pierced by an arrow, throbbed relentlessly.

Phillip looked up, his grim expression easing. "The wound is clean, m'lord. 'Twill leave a magnificent scar for some woman to remark upon."

Phillip used his helm to bring Richard water. Raising the earl's head, Phillip eased a trickle down his throat. Richard swallowed, coughed. Phillip wiped the water from around his mouth.

"We are near the road to Stirling Castle, m'lord," he said. "'Tis but half a league away. I'll take you there."

Richard nodded, or thought he did. What was at Stirling Castle? His father? No, father was dead. "Boil the flesh from my bones," he'd said before he died. "And carry them before you into battle." They had not done that, had they? And they had lost the battle and Piers Gaveston had been recalled . . .

"I did not allow His Majesty entrance to Stirling," Lord Mowbray said. "And I regret I cannot help you either. Stirling

Castle belongs to the Scots now, as was agreed before the battle. To the victor the spoils, sir."

Mowbray's booted feet were planted on the drawbridge in a truculent pose. He was angry that Edward had lost Bannockburn, angry that he was now forced to such an unenviable position. Spitting into the moat below the bridge, Mowbray wiped his mouth with the back of a hairy hand. "This entire business leaves a sorry taste in my mouth, I can tell you that."

Phillip turned from Mowbray to Richard, positioned on the litter. Above the mantle that covered him, the earl's face was white, his mouth set in a painful line. Though the mantle was heavy, the June afternoon mild, Richard was beginning to shake.

"His Majesty rode for Dunbar. Perhaps you could catch up with him," Mowbray pressed.

"He would die before we lost sight of the castle," Phillip said. He studied the baron's lined face. A plain face without guile, incapable of subterfuge. "You have a physician here. You must see to m'lord's needs." Was that the sound of horses riding up the winding road toward Stirling? Was the Bruce even now coming to claim his prize?

"The Bruce would not murder the king's own brother, would he?" Phillip asked abruptly, as a plan began to form.

"I do not understand, sir."

"If Richard of Sussex should perchance fall into the Bruce's hands he would be held for ransom, would he not? And what a fine ransom would be paid."

"I suppose so, but . . ."

"If the Bruce would find Sussex already at Stirling, would he not see that my lord receives the best of care? He would be worth much more to the Bruce alive than dead." Phillip fell silent, considering. If he left Richard he would be well cared for, and he could ride for safety. Phillip had no fear of falling into the hands of the enemy. One man could hide forever in Scotland's hills.

Richard's breathing was shallow and rapid; blood seeped through the woolen mantle. Phillip turned back to Mowbray. "Take him inside Stirling, sir, and care for him. M'lord is generous. When he recovers you will be properly rewarded."

"But what about you?" Mowbray asked. "What will you do?"

If Phillip stayed, he would also be ransomed. The Scots, so everlastingly poor, would be eager to enrich Scotland's coffers. No, Phillip would not be risking death—at least not death by a sword. But imprisoned in a dungeon without sky to see and roads to travel, would that not be another kind of death?

"Well, sir? Will you stay or go?"

Phillip looked down at Richard, then raised his eyes to Mowbray. "I'll stay with my lord," he said.

THREE

ordwich Castle contained the most celebrated cherry orchard in the south of England. A grand sight it was during Eastertide, with row after row of cherry trees exploding in brilliant white blossoms and the spring air heavy with their fragrance. When Hugh and Henrietta had married they had held their wedding feast in the orchard, and the surrounding festivities had been dubbed the Cherry Fair. Henrietta had enjoyed the event so much that it had soon evolved into an annual affair, lasting a fortnight and attracting celebrated knights for the jousting, as well as members of England's most powerful houses. Edward II had even once stopped overnight while en route to Dover, but he disliked tourneys, saying they were but an excuse for his barons to gather and plot against him.

In conjunction with Fordwich's activities, nearby Chilham Castle, owned by the powerful Lord Bartholomew Badlesmere, conducted a fair that sold everything from bolts of cloth and Venetian cut glass to the pewter and vests and cambricks of traveling peddlers. As the festival grew in extravagance, however, it created an alarming drain upon the d'Ardernes' already precarious finances. In addition to all other expenses, costly gifts must be distributed to every important guest, and the floods, rotting crops, and famines so characteristic of the winters of 1315–16 had hit Fordwich Castle as brutally as any demesne. To finance the current Cherry Fair, which Henrietta had vowed would be the finest ever, Hugh had been forced to sell their townhouse in Sturry, the Leopard's Head, to St. Augustine's Abbey.

Maria had always looked forward to the excitement of the fair. She truly loved the joust, and the fortnight provided a welcome respite from Henrietta's strident lessons, which spanned such boring topics as the art of making spiced wine or keeping a bed forever free of fleas. This year, however, she dreaded every moment of every day. I am to be the grand prize, she thought, as she was submitted to endless introductions and strained conversations with any widower or bachelor possessing proper marriage credentials. Henrietta was particularly determined to impress one man—Sir Edmund Leybourne, earl of Wessex. Though the family was currently out of royal favor for a cousin's part in the murder of Piers Gaveston, the Leybournes possessed enough money and lineage to nullify their temporary fall from grace. But a dozen earldoms and London townhouses could not reconcile me to Lord Leybourne, Maria thought, as they readied for his arrival. A tall man with a drooping belly, Edmund walked with a cane to ease his gouty leg. Most of his teeth had long ago fallen out, causing the lower half of his face to crumble into ruin. Of necessity his main foods consisted of gruel and mashed vegetables. It was Sir Edmund's manner, however, that most grated. Though he was not a shy man, he seemed overwhelmed by Maria's presence, constantly referring to her beauty and treating her as if she were a precious relic from Walsingham or one of England's other shrines.

"Lord Leybourne is besotted with you," Henrietta said as she scrutinized her daughter's dress. "We must use his foolishness to best advantage. If the Cherry Fair does not produce a richer suitor we will settle on him."

Since the incident of the hawks three years past, Maria seldom openly rebelled against her mother. She was never certain how malicious Henrietta would be and dreaded the misplaced word or act that could impel Henrietta to wed her from spite. But I cannot marry Leybourne, she thought, as they waited in the inner bailey for word of his arrival. And though the next several days would be taken up in dozens of different activities, she knew she could not forever avoid his attentions. Between mother's ambition and Edmund's infatuation, Maria worried, I'll not survive the Cherry Fair unbetrothed.

"Lord Leybourne is a better match than you deserve." Henrietta held out her hand to examine the rings gracing her slender fingers. "He has more earldoms than anyone save Thomas Lancaster, as well as a glorious past. Was he not one of our old king's most trusted advisers?"

"Edward the First has been dead ten years now," Maria countered. "Lord Leybourne's glories are in the past."

"But his money is not," Henrietta said, putting an end to the conversation.

Trumpets blasted in the outer bailey, announcing Edmund Leybourne's arrival. Henrietta ran her hand absentmindedly along the scarlet velvet of her surcoat, then critically examined her daughter. "'Twill not do," she said, though Maria had already twice changed her dress. "Go put on your Cyprus silk, the blue one that shows off your breasts." She glanced up at the sky, where storm clouds were beginning to gather in the direction of Canterbury. "God's teeth! All we need is a storm to ruin the banquet—and my gown."

After Henrietta left to greet Edmund, Maria made her way back toward the keep. Servants in various liveries swarmed the inner bailey as well as lords and ladies readying for riding or hawking expeditions. Anticipating her forthcoming meeting with Leybourne, panic squeezed her heart. Upon impulse she detoured to the stables where Baillet, her mare, was kept. Through the window opening she glimpsed Sir Edmund's arrival. I cannot face him, Maria thought, at least not now. I'll ride into Canterbury, just for a time, and I will be so polite upon my return mother will not even care.

She turned to Wat the Stableboy. "Saddle Baillet. And be quick about it."

On the road approaching Canterbury, Maria encountered St. Augustine's abbot, John Fyndunne. He was trailed by a meinie of squires, carters, porters, grooms, and kitchen servants, and along with dozens of other travelers she detoured to the clearing alongside the highway to allow the train's passage. John Fyndunne had negotiated the recent purchase of the Leopard's Head and had returned Maria's resentment with an equal measure of dislike. But this day he wore a distant air, and though he continually blessed the pilgrims lined along either side of the road, the monotonous sameness of their dusty brown robes, flopping hats, and iron-tipped staffs designed to pin down the devil obviously bored him.

Canterbury's Northgate was crowded with beggars who clutched at Maria's leg and cried for money or called out lewd suggestions. "Have you not a penny for a poor man, pretty lady?"

"I would pay you for the pleasure of your company, sweetheart!" another beggar said with a leer.

Though she was becoming increasingly uneasy, Maria did not yet have the courage to return to Fordwich and face Edmund Leybourne. Somehow, she thought, as she rode along Palace Street, I must convince mother that I cannot marry him. But Maria also realized Henrietta was not asking for something out of the ordinary. Wives were not expected to love their husbands, and monetary considerations were always of prime importance. "But love should matter most," she whispered, as she maneuvered Baillet along busy Palace Street.

Christchurch Cathedral, constructed of honey-colored caen stone, dominated the thriving town of Canterbury. Around the cathedral gates clerics, professional palmers, friars, and false pardoners loudly peddled phony indulgences and obscure relics to the afflicted. Along Mercery Lane vendors did a brisk business in the sacred relics and signs plastering their wooden stalls.

The afternoon air was humid and close, with drooping clouds threatening a spring shower. A jag of lightning escaped from the darkness; thunder boomed above Canterbury's steep pitched buildings. Another crack and the storm broke wild, slashing directly in Maria's face, attacking her exposed hands, the light material of her dress. The wind whipped her hair about her face, lashing at her eyes and cheeks. Desperately, she peered into the stinging rain, seeking any available shelter. Finally she spotted the blurred outline of St. Mildred's Church, where escaping prisoners from the nearby royal prison of Canterbury Castle often fled for sanctuary. Once into the yard, Maria leapt from Baillet's back and scrambled inside. Slamming the door against the howling wind, she collapsed against it. Looking down at her mud-caked dress clinging to her body, she moaned. "Ruined! Mother will have me on the rack for this."

"'Tis a brutish storm, is it not, damoiselle?"

Maria whirled toward the voice. A knight stepped from the shadows. He was tall, with black hair and finely chiseled features. On his tunic was displayed a blue wolf's head.

"Pardon, my lord," she stammered. "I thought I was alone."

"Nearly. Just myself and my squire." The man smiled and Maria's immediate positive reaction was intensified. He was easily the most striking man she'd ever seen—tall, well formed, with a muscular torso that tapered to narrow hips, belted about by a sword. Even in the dimness of St. Mildred's, his face appeared as deeply tanned as the Spaniards who unloaded cargo from the painted galleys docked along the River Stour. The darkness of his skin only heightened the blueness of his eyes.

Rain rattled on the tiled roof, but already with less fury than when she'd entered. "'Twould appear the storm will soon be over," he said.

The knight had a most unsettling way of looking at Maria—

pleasantly unsettling. Common sense told her she should not be alone with any stranger, let alone speak with him. Yet Henrietta's lectures had never covered this exact situation and she was so instantly smitten, she could have stayed at St. Mildred's forever. Or at least until this stranger departed.

"Have you a name, damoiselle?"

"Maria d'Arderne." She found her voice and even managed an awkward curtsy. "From Fordwich Castle."

"Ah, the Cherry Fair!" His eyes swept her length, taking in the clinging gown, the lustrous hair beginning to dry and frame her face, the straight nose and long-lashed eyes.

Maria felt her face flush red. Such a look from another man would have left her annoyed or unmoved; yet now her head swam as if from an overabundance of wine. "You've heard of our fair, Lord . . ."

"Rendell. Phillip Rendell."

"You are not the knight of whom minstrels sing? The knight who saved our lord Sussex's life and was personally ransomed by His Majesty?" From the minstrel's descriptions Maria had formed a certain image of Phillip Rendell, but her imaginings had never prepared her for the man before her.

"I would not know what minstrels say of me or anyone else, damoiselle. I've not been in England these past three years."

A feeble ray of sunlight struggled through the narrow windows of St. Mildred's as the storm slackened. Scattered drops of rain slithered down tiny panes to pool in the corners.

"'Tis past," Phillip said.

"What? Your travels?"

He smiled. "Those too. But I meant the storm." Phillip turned to his squire and Maria saw that his cheekbones were high, his profile virtually flawless. "Bring the horses round, Gilbert. I'll be along."

When Gilbert moved to obey, Phillip turned back to her. "I think this is a stroke of luck for both of us, damoiselle. 'Twould appear you are in need of proper escort and I am in need of direction."

"Direction, my lord?"

"Aye. I have heard much of the Cherry Fair's tourney and I'd thought to try my fortune there." Philip smiled into Maria's eyes, thinking how large they were, how blue. "Perhaps 'twas not luck at all that brought us together, damoiselle, but fate."

Rows of tables—spread with linen tablecloths and topped with silver salt cellars, covered dishes, and serving trays heaped with food—had been placed in a U shape in the center of Fordwich's cherry orchard. Though some diners had already left the banquet to dance or roll a game of bowls beneath the trees, most guests remained at table to finish the last of six courses, consisting of copious varieties of fish and meat and topped with pastries and sweetmeats. At the dais, Piers the Cook had placed his triumph, an enormous sugar-and-paste *soltelte* fashioned in the shape of two mounted knights facing each other with lances at ready. Behind the *soltelte* the diners were partially hidden from view, but Maria glimpsed Edmund Leybourne and the empty seat next to him.

"'Tis fine," Phillip breathed, enchanted by his first view of the Cherry Fair. The brilliance of the costumed lords and ladies heightened the beauty of the trees surrounding them. Clouds of white blossoms bowed the limbs to earth and the smooth petals seemed to shimmer in the afternoon heat. The air, freshened after the shower, was redolent with their smell, intoxicating in its intensity. Near as intoxicating as the girl beside him, Phillip thought, risking another glance at Maria. She was truly a lovely young woman: slender yet curvaceous, with skin free from any blemish and hair the color of burnished mahogany. But he found most intriguing the unconscious sensuality of her movements and proud lift to her chin.

A woman bustled from the dais toward them. Her resemblance to Maria was unmistakable, though Phillip thought her thin as a rack of ribs and with a hysterical edge to her mouth and eyes.

"Where have you been, daughter?" Henrietta's eyes swept Phillip. "And who might you be, sir?"

Phillip bowed. "Lord Phillip Rendell, m'lady."

"He is the Herefordshire knight," Maria interjected, nervously twisting her hands together. "The one who saved our lord Sussex at Bannockburn."

Henrietta wrinkled her nose. "Aye, we've all heard the tale of how you refused Lord Sussex's gift of a demesne near the size of Wales to indulge your wanderlust. 'Twould appear what you enjoy in chivalry, Lord Rendell, you lack in common sense." Grabbing Maria by the arm, Henrietta pulled her roughly toward the dais.

"By the rood, my lord," Phillip's squire, Gilbert, swore. "I pity that poor girl. Her mother is a veritable dragon."

"I have not yet slain a dragon," Phillip said, as he watched Maria obediently take her place beside Lord Leybourne. "Perhaps 'tis time I did."

"You've grown even more lovely, Damoiselle Maria, than when last we met." If Edmund had been angered by her absence he gave no sign. His rheumy eyes continually wandered from her face, probing the cleft between her breasts. Maria itched to slap him until his teeth rattled. Only Sir Edmund had no teeth—and his beard, filled with particles of food, was in need of a good trimming. When he was not ogling her he sopped a pastry in gravy, gummed it, belched, and swilled it down with wine.

Ignoring him, she sought Phillip and found him seated at a lower table. Pretending interest in the various jugglers, tumblers, and strolling minstrels, she actually watched only the Herefordshire knight.

"Daughter," Henrietta said sharply, "Lord Leybourne was speaking to you."

"Where is your head this day, poppet," Hugh said, frowning into his wine cup. He'd already drunk far too much. Now he wanted only to sneak away to find some quiet place where he could fall asleep and momentarily forget how much this year's Cherry Fair was costing him.

Edmund leaned toward her. "I merely requested most humbly, damoiselle, that you honor me with a stroll about the orchard."

When Maria hesitated, Henrietta answered for her. "She would be delighted. Would you not, daughter?"

Resentment seethed inside. Though Maria feared her mother, docility did not come easily. And the revulsion she felt for Edmund Leybourne made obedience that much the harder.

"I have something to discuss with you, dear heart." His broad smile displayed an amazing expanse of gum.

Reluctantly, Maria accepted. As was customary, she rested a hand atop his as they walked, but rather than talk to him she watched the bare-chested young men at the orchard's edge hurl lances, throw stones, and wrestle.

"Damoiselle, I have formally asked your parents for your hand in marriage." Edmund's words were slurred with wine, but she heard them well enough. "An earl's wife you'll be, with a fine manor house in Wessex and all the clothes, horses, and jewelry you could ever desire. I have a fine townhouse in London and when our family returns to court we can spend all our time there, if 'twould please you."

"I have never wanted to go to court," Maria said softly. While Edmund rambled on, she fought back an overwhelming urge to cry. Life was not turning out at all as she'd expected. Though she'd always known her duty was to marry well and produce children, she'd not expected to be caretaker for an old man while time and happiness passed her by.

"I have outlived three wives, damoiselle," Edmund continued. "I've sired sons off the lot of them, not to mention a mistress or two." He chuckled, a wheezing sound like a defective bellows. "But in all my years I've not had a woman lovely as you. Oh, we will make fine sons together."

Maria jerked away her hand. I'd sooner spend an eternity in

hell, she thought. They approached a group of dancers who were caroling to the music of viols and harps provided by jongleurs. Though Maria loved to dance, she silently thanked the saints for Edmund's gouty leg.

"Might I have the pleasure of this dance?" Seemingly out of nowhere, Phillip Rendell bowed before her.

"Oh, aye!" Before Edmund could protest, Maria allowed him to lead her away.

"Thank you, my lord," she said as they joined the other dancers. Though most were dancing in a circle, by unspoken consent they drifted off by themselves. "You truly rescued me from an unpleasant situation."

"The Leybourne name is fine and old," Phillip said. "Your mother, I think, has reached high."

"I would not care if he were the king himself—I'll have no part of him." Defiance was easy enough with Phillip as her audience. Aware of the intimacy of her words and manner, she flushed and fell silent. As she tried to concentrate on the intricate steps of the dance, she became increasingly aware of the pressure of his fingers, the nearness of his body, which was as intoxicating as the fragrance wafting from the cherry blossoms.

"I have seen sights in my time," Phillip said, gazing at the surrounding trees. "But never have I seen anything any lovelier."

Maria looked past him to the overladen branches. Already petals were beginning to drop free and litter the ground. "I no longer find the Cherry Fair beautiful."

"Because of your mother?"

She was startled by the impertinence of the question, but answered truthfully. "Partially, I suppose. But in a sermon once Father Eustace said something that has stayed with me, and I cannot even look at the trees without feeling sadness."

"What could a priest possibly say that would so spoil such a sight?"

"'Life though pleasant is transitory,' Father Eustace said,

'even as is the Cherry Fair.' Now when I even smell their fragrance I cannot help but think of time's passing."

"Or of duty and obligation, of things we should have done and things we never will." Phillip's eyes saddened.

"Duty means marriage to Edmund Leybourne. I had always known I must marry but I had thought my husband would be . . . different." Like you, Maria amended silently. Why did I meet you when 'tis too late? Their eyes locked and she felt her legs turn to water, he every coherent thought flee.

"Marry me," she blurted.

"Pardon, damoiselle?"

Maria's face flushed crimson. She'd not even realized she'd spoken.

"That is enough dancing for the day." Henrietta stood before them, her widely plucked brows drawn in an angry frown. "I have taught you better than to be rude to your guests." As Maria reluctantly returned to her suitor, Henrietta turned on Phillip. "This even my husband and I will announce our daughter's engagement to Lord Leybourne. Maria needs not the likes of you to confuse her, and I trust that in the future you'll have the good sense to leave her be."

On the morning of the betrothal Henrietta dressed Maria in a silky golden kirtle topped by a red supertunic and left her hair to fall free down her back. She also adjusted Maria's bodice to reveal a larger portion of breast, but as soon as her mother's back was turned Maria tugged the material back. Soon they would ride into Fordwich town, and at the church of St. Mary the Virgin, Maria and Edmund would recite the traditional betrothal vows. Though the vows were not binding, they were blessed by the church and a great scandal would occur should they be broken.

"You will make a beautiful bride," Eleanora said as she watched a maid sprinkle gold dust in her sister's hair.

Silent tears slipped down Maria's cheeks. "I do not want to

marry Edmund," she whispered. "If only I could gainsay mother."

Her sister shrugged. "'Tis necessary to restore Fordwich to true prosperity. 'Tis a certain bet that with my sight and meager looks mother will not have another chance to gain such an advantageous marriage match."

Maria twisted the betrothal ring around her finger. She hated it, so large and cumbersome. "He is so old, older even than papa. And the way he looks at me. If I have to share a marriage bed with him, I swear I will kill myself."

"Do not look so miserable." Eleanora pushed a strand of hair away from Maria's face. Moving as if to hug her, she whispered against Maria's ear, "You'll not marry Edmund Leybourne, of that I am certain."

Maria gasped. "You've seen something?"

After a glance at her mother, who was discussing her own betrothal with several of her ladies, Eleanora nodded.

"Who then?" She immediately thought of Phillip Rendell. Though she'd not privately spoken with him since the dancing, he was constantly in her thoughts.

As if reading her mind her sister shook her head. "'Tis always the same face I see, the face of the golden knight."

"But I do not want some stranger," Maria cried. "I want . . . someone else."

The betrothal ceremony did not take long. Following a few short prayers, Edmund, resplendent in jewelry and a tunic trimmed in ermine said, "I will take thee for my wife." Maria could scarce choke out her response. 'Tis not binding because I did not mean it and God can see my true heart, she silently assured herself. After her parents and Edmund's sons added their consent, they all swore on a sliver of the true cross presented by Father Eustace. But Maria did not actually touch the jewel neath which the sliver rested. She told herself she yet had no obligation to Edmund, though the defiant façade no longer fooled even herself. She only dared rebel in her mind, and that did her no good at all.

Following the betrothal, everyone rode to Chilham Castle, where a fair was already in progress. Tomorrow the jousting would begin. And four days following, Maria thought, staring down at her betrothal ring, I will be Lady Maria Leybourne.

Chilham Castle was situated atop a gentle hill clustered with gaily striped pavilions and overlooking a valley lush with fields and forest. The fair took place just beyond the castle curtain, which closely surrounded the small dun-colored eight-sided keep. Buffoons, jugglers, gleemen, and trained monkeys provided entertainment for the ever-increasing crowd. Loud, buoyant music vied with peddlers pushing their wares; pickpockets and prostitutes worked the crowd. Among them Maria noticed Meg Smythe, the Sturry Prostitute. The woman forever frequented such events. 'Twas rumored Meg was the daughter of Thomas d'Arderne, Hugh's elder brother, who had been killed in a long-ago tournament. Maria did not know whether the rumor was true, but many said she favored Meg in looks, and papa sometimes hinted at the prostitute's origins.

Hugh and the others had drifted off to view a horse market so Henrietta, chattering constantly, walked with Edmund and Maria. Never had Maria seen her mother so excited. Victory intoxicates you, she thought sourly, as well as the prospect of money.

Near the herbalists, who'd spread their drug-laden cloths upon the green, Henrietta spotted a pair of tiny white dogs dancing on their hind legs. She laughed and clapped her hands over their antics. "Are they not darling?"

Maria had never heard her mother refer to anything as darling, and she'd always maintained small dogs were useless for anything but distributing fleas.

"Would you like them, my lady?" Edmund asked. "'Twould please me greatly to present one to you and one to my beautiful fiancée." He leered at Maria. Since the betrothal his manner was quickly shifting from deference to open possessiveness.

While Edmund bickered with the herbalist over the price, Maria drifted away, ostensibly to watch a bear baiting; in reality to be free of both her fiancé and her mother. As she viewed the black bear swiping at its canine tormentors, her heart leapt suddenly to her throat. Phillip Rendell stood amidst the shouting, laughing crowd—watching her.

The rises around Fordwich were thick with common people, some of whom were perched upon favorably situated branches of the numerous white-flowering horse chestnuts. At the beginning of Fordwich's tourney, they'd arrived barefoot, with their new shoes slung over their shoulders to save the thin soles, and wearing courtepys, a poor man's imitation of the knightly tabard. They'd already enjoyed liberal quantities of food and ale—courtesy of Lord and Lady d'Arderne. Maria knew the cost had been dear. With every shilling spent, her parents became more indebted to Edmund Leybourne.

The galleries were bright with the dress of the noblewomen— Brussels scarlet, brocades, Damascus silks, and fine linens from Rheims, all trimmed with miniver, ermine, or, most expensive of all, sable. This final day of the tourney Henrietta wore sable. As Queen of Beauty and Love, Maria was seated in the place of honor beneath a striped canopy. Her mother was situated nearby. She spent as much time criticizing Maria's behavior as studying the action on the field. Whenever Phillip jousted, Henrietta's tongue dripped venom. Never had Maria heard such sarcasm, and she grew ever more resentful. It never occurred to her that part of Henrietta's malevolence might be inspired by fear.

During the tourney the crowds had enjoyed many acts of skill but no deaths, a blessing. The church labeled such deaths suicide, which automatically excommunicated the offender and doomed him to hell. Phillip had acquitted himself especially well, besting four who had ridden against him and enriching himself with the resultant ransoms. Each time he jousted Maria felt pride in his skill—despite her mother's diatribes—but also dread. Each passing hour brought her that much closer to her marriage. By the closing afternoon of the tourney she could not even concentrate on the activities. In her mind's eye, she saw a naked Edmund Leybourne approaching their marriage bed, reaching out to caress her. What will it be like, she wondered, to kiss a man who has not teeth?

"Look!" Eleanora, who sat to her right, poked her in the ribs. "Your knight is at the head of the lists."

Emerging from her unhappy vision, Maria shaded her eyes and surveyed the field.

Phillip's pursuivant, dressed gaudily—as were all pursuivants—in particolored mantle and bliaut, stepped forward. After waving the crowd to silence, he challenged all comers. From the opposite end a second pursuivant finally answered the challenge. His lord was Bartholomew Badlesmere, whom Phillip had unseated on the first pass two days previous.

Before taking their places, the two knights circled the lists. Men cheered; ladies threw garlands of flowers, streamers, gloves, and other favors. Three days of jousting had led to a certain sameness, and Phillip's challenge had instilled a new excitement into the activities. The winner of this contest would be declared victor of the tournament. Though other prizes would be presented, to him would go the most coveted award, a gold and emerald chaplet.

When the knights took their position on opposite ends, the spectators hushed. Waving a wand, a marshal stepped forward to shout, "In the name of God and St. George, do battle!"

The two men charged. The first pass was fairly met, but upon the second, Bartholomew Badlesmere's lance aimed too high, and Phillip momentarily swooned in the saddle. Only the saddle's high ridge and his own horsemanship kept him righted. Maria's nails dug into her palms. She sent a dozen prayers heavenward.

On the third pass Phillip lifted Bartholomew Badlesmere from his seat as effortlessly as he might pluck a cherry from a tree. The crowd roared its approval. From the barricades someone shouted, "Philip Rendell!" Immediately, everyone began chanting his name.

While his squires carried the unconscious Badlesmere from the field, Phillip triumphantly circled the lists.

'Tis just like in the romances, Maria thought, watching him with shining eyes. And you are just like the fabled knights papa always told me about—Arthur, Roland, Bohemund the Mighty.

Below the canopy under which Maria was seated Phillip drew rein. As Queen of Beauty and Love, it was her duty to present him his prize. He removed his helm. Phillip's hair was matted, his face streaked with dirt and sweat, and the smile he bestowed upon her took her breath away. In her memory Maria registered every plane, every line of his face and form. If I am wedded to Edmund Leybourne a thousand years, she thought, if I never see you again, I'll never forget how you looked this moment.

With the chaplet in hand, Maria descended the tiers to where Phillip awaited. When she bent over to place the circlet atop his head, she inhaled the scent of him—a pleasant combination of leather, sweat, and sandalwood.

"Meet me tonight." Phillip's lips were but inches from her own. "In Fordwich town, down at your family's warehouses."

Stunned by the request, she drew back and searched his face. "You know I cannot."

"If you will but come, we will run away. I would marry thee, Maria."

She felt suddenly light-headed. "'Tis impossible. I am already betrothed."

"I have made up my mind. Tonight. Be there." He kissed her hard on the lips. As Phillip galloped toward the exit to the lists

his chaplet reflected the light from the lengthening sun in
blinding flashes.

I would give the world if our marriage could be so, Maria
thought, blinking back tears. But 'tis too late.

"You've disgraced us all, you and that bastard spawn,"
Henrietta cried, cracking Maria across the mouth. "I could not
believe your actions. Nor could Lord Leybourne, who was
horrified, and rightly so. Have you no care for his public
humiliation?"

"I am not the first woman to be kissed at a tourney, mother.
It did no harm."

Henrietta cracked her again, snapping her head back. "He
has spoiled everything, your fine knight. Why could he not have
been killed in some godforsaken part of the earth before
ruining my life?" She began pacing the room. "Phillip Rendell is
naught but a second son with no inheritance to speak of and no
prospects, and I'll not have him ruining my plans."

"He is Richard of Sussex's friend, mother. If Phillip and I
should marry . . ."

"Do not say another word," Henrietta shrieked. "You are
going to marry Edmund Leybourne—and that is the end of it."
She inhaled deeply, striving for calm. "I am going down to the
banquet now. Clarice will dress you in your blue velvet. When
you are presentable you will come down, apologize to Sir
Edmund, and reassure him that on the morrow you will be his
wife. And if Phillip Rendell ever enters Fordwich again I will
have him forcibly removed, that I promise you." Slamming the
wooden door behind her, she left the solar.

From the off chamber Clarice and Eleanora emerged. The
tiring maid removed Maria's blue dress from a wall peg, draped
it across the canopied bed, and began inspecting it for spots or
tears.

"Are you all right?" Eleanora peered at her. "Your jaw is
starting to swell."

"'Tis nothing. I just have a fearsome headache." Maria's lower lip quivered. She swallowed hard, trying unsuccessfully to keep the tears inside. "I cannot marry Leybourne, I cannot. Tell me, what am I going to do?"

Eleanora patted her on the shoulder. "You have no choice." She sympathized with Maria, but was not her sister marrying well? Little matter that Edmund Leybourne was not a knight from the romances, what man truly was? "He will take good care of you—of all of us."

"You said yourself that I would not marry him. You said you saw it in a dream."

"My dreams are not always truthful, and in this case, at least, 'twould seem I was wrong."

"Nay," Maria whispered, "you were right." Filled with sudden resolve she turned to Clarice. "Would you mix for me some root of peony and oil of roses for my headache?"

"Aye, miss. And I'll bring you something for your jaw. 'Tis turning an ugly color."

After Clarice left, Maria scooped her heavy woolen mantle off a wall peg.

"What are you doing?"

"I'm running away."

Eleanora laughed. "You cannot do that. The roads are filled with brigands and you have no place to go or anyone to escort you."

"I have Phillip."

Seeing that she was serious, Eleanora scurried to her. "You cannot. Blessed Mary, but mother would never forgive you the scandal." She grabbed Maria's arm. "I would have to tell her, you know I would. You'd not get beyond the drawbridge."

Maria shook off her hand. "Do not tell her, I implore you. 'Tis my only chance for happiness—and I must take it."

"We are not supposed to worry about happiness, but duty, and 'tis your duty to—"

"Do not speak to me of that," Maria interrupted. "Mother has pounded such things into my head until I cannot think for myself. But this time I'll not be dissuaded." She grasped Eleanora by the shoulders. "Please, when Clarice returns, make an excuse, anything, just to give me a measure of time."

She shook her head. "'Tis madness."

"When Phillip and I marry, you can come live with us. I will find you a proper husband and—"

Eleanora laid her fingers atop Maria's lips. "Never mind. I am weary of arguing, and you and mother have been at odds so long that tonight was probably inevitable. Though I'm certain I'll rue my action. I'll do what I can."

Maria hugged her. "I must hurry now before Clarice returns."

"I will pray for you, but be careful." Eleanora's eyes glittered strangely and Maria felt a sudden chill.

"Have you had another dream, sister?" When she did not reply, Maria persisted. "What have you seen, tell me?"

"Death, standing beside you."

FOUR

uted light from the shuttered cottages of
Fordwich town eased the darkness as Maria
turned down Well Lane. The smells of cabbage,
bacon, and woodsmoke lingered in the still night
as she approached Fordwich's quay. Repeatedly
she twisted around to see whether a troop of knights raced
after her. Or Death. Shivering, she kept her eyes to the road,
toward the crane that loomed above the family warehouses. If
Death is in the air it will be mine, she thought, as she dismounted. For mother will kill me when she catches me.

Rows of long, low warehouses stood at right angles to the
River Stour. The quay was eerie in its emptiness. Fordwich
provided the sole outport for Canterbury, and during the day
French ships, their holds weighted with blocks of caen stone,
maneuvered up to the docks; exotically dressed Spaniards
wrestled with casks of wine and cumbersome bolts of cloth,
while cursing Normans unloaded iron and spices. Now only
anchored galleys bumped against the dock, their naked masts
silhouetted against a velvety night pricked with stars. A pale
half moon shimmered off the water, onto the gray stones of the
quay. From Fordwich's inn, the George and Dragon, drifted the
muted chorus of a tavern song. From atop one of the many tuns
of wine, a cat yowled.

"Phillip?" For the first time Maria saw his squire, Gilbert, in the shadows by the cranehouse. Then Phillip himself appeared and pulled her inside, out of the moonlight.

"Mother and I had a fearsome fight." Her body began an uncontrollable trembling; she struggled to keep from crying. "I've run away."

"You've not run far enough," he said, drawing her close. She did not protest the intimacy but rather pressed against him.

"I think 'tis time your mother discovered that fate can change the most certain of plans." His arms tightened around her waist. "You and I together, we will give them all a fine chase."

Maria looked up, trying to decipher his expression in the darkness. "You truly meant to marry me? No matter that I am betrothed?"

"A betrothal is not marriage. Not even the church will disapprove if we are married proper. Besides, Edmund Leybourne may be powerful, but our lord is even more so. We will ride for Rockingham Castle and Richard of Sussex will marry us."

"What if they capture us before?" The enormity of what they were contemplating was beginning to penetrate defiance. "Our family names will be forever disgraced. Jesu! I will end up in a nunnery."

"They'll be looking for us at my family's manor of Winchcomb, not Rockingham. And England is large enough to conceal three people, if they desire not to be found."

The England Maria and Phillip passed through in early May of 1317 was poorer than it had ever been during Edward I's time. Years of increasingly unstable weather had ruined croplands. Many previously prosperous manors now were abandoned and nature once again encroached on what had previously been cleared pasturage. On existing acreage crop yields had fallen because the soil itself was depleted. During the famines and floods of 1315–16, wheat had sold for forty pence a bushel in London, while in Northumbria people had resorted to eating dogs and horses. Along the Pilgrim's Way, bodies had been stacked like cords of firewood. Near Rochester, starving brigands had cut corpses from the gallows and eaten the rotting flesh. Many of the homeless had taken to the roads and still roamed in lawless bands. The Welsh conducted raids from the hills into borderlands, while the Scots had penetrated as far south as Lancashire. Robert the Bruce's brother, Edward, had conquered much of Ireland.

In the vicinity of Phillip's home, thieves haunted the dense Alton Forest and from headquarters there swept outward to ravage Berkshire, Wiltshire, and Hampshire. Robbers, extortionists, pickpockets, and kidnappers plagued towns across the breadth of England. The growing shortage of good pastureland and restrictions on silver exports had forced up prices, and King Edward had mercilessly raised taxes, further emptying purses and forcing the desperate to a life of crime. Sheltered as she'd been in Fordwich, Maria had only known how the bad times had affected her family. The shortages had meant less extravagance, but never starvation.

Phillip and Maria rode all the first night and did not stop until dark of the second. In East Anglia they found an abandoned leper, or lazar, house, one of a multitude throughout England. On the morrow they would reach Rockingham, located in the Midlands.

Saddle sore and exhausted, Maria stumbled from her horse while Gilbert gathered peat for a fire and Phillip set off to find supper. Walking over the swampy moorlands he sniffed out cooking herbs of wild thyme, bog myrtle, and dried sage to flavor his discovery of wild bird eggs and the heron he'd uncovered nesting in the marshes.

With each passing hour Maria found herself more in awe of Phillip and his capabilities. In her seventeen years she'd never traveled more than a half day from Fordwich. Nothing had prepared her for such primitive conditions. Without Phillip she was certain she would have already been prey for robbers or the wolves howling in the forests. Phillip, however, seemed to thrive in land that was as unfamiliar to him as to Maria. When streams could not be found for water he uncovered pits and ponds used by sheep or cattle. Using a bow and arrow he shot down waterfowl, devised a snare for rabbits, or with a fishing line made of horsehair caught a meal of fish. He never appeared uncertain about anything. And if he ever doubted the rightness of their running away or the possible repercussions he never voiced these doubts.

As she washed herself in a creek murmuring past the lazar house, Maria surreptitiously watched him readying their meal. You will take care of everything, she thought, from my hunger to my mother and Edmund Leybourne, should he indeed be following us. At Fordwich she'd thought Phillip the incarnation of all the minstrel's romances. She'd not found reason to change her mind.

The aromas from the burning peat and the cooking bird drifted to her upon the wind. The winds were as natural a part of East Anglia as the marshlands and fens from which men, using no more than basins and wooden shovels, wrested fertile land.

She approached the campfire. Looking up from the heron he was turning on a spit, Phillip smiled. His smile warmed Maria as a mere fire never could. Tomorrow 'twill all be over, she thought as she sat beside him. I'll have a bed to sleep in and a regular bath and wine to drink. And I shall miss this. Then I'll have to share you with others. Then we'll have to face the reality of what we've done.

After they finished their meal, Phillip banked the fire, stretched out, and, resting on one elbow, studied the slow ascent of the golden moon that edged above the monotonous horizon. Gilbert whittled and Maria sat with her legs drawn up, watching her beloved.

"The most beautiful moon I've seen," Phillip said, "was in Venice, I think. Would you say so, Gilbert?"

His squire looked up from the horse he was carving. "I would think Jerusalem, sire."

"You were more enamored there of the women, I'll wager."
Gilbert grinned and returned to his whittling.

"Tell me about Venice," Maria urged. The few times he'd spoken of his travels his natural reticence had been replaced by eloquence. She loved to listen to him talk—as much for the timbre of his voice and the animation of his face as the words.

"'Twas at St. Mark's Piazza, where I was gawking at the ships," he said. "Through a patch of clouds the moon suddenly appeared like an enormous scarlet ball just hanging against the sky. The galleys were to harbor, their sails rolled up and angled against the night, and 'twas so still and beautiful I thought heaven could not be finer."

Maria had seen ships down at Fordwich's quay thousands of times, but never had she viewed them as things of beauty or witnessed a similar scene. "You've seen so much. You must have been to near every place in God's world."

He shook his head. "Not even a half of it, and 'tis the sights I've not seen that seem most intriguing. There is a cape called Bojader, I'm told, where men come so close to the sun their skins roast black. And near there a sea so shallow it boils away to a stinking slime crawling with sea monsters."

"Monsters?" Maria's eyes widened. "Have you ever seen a sea monster?"

"Nay. But I have slain a dragon." He slid a glance at Gilbert, who grinned.

"A dragon? Jesu! You are totally fearless."

"Hardly." Phillip was amused and flattered by Maria's obvious hero worship, though she was wrong, of course. As all knights did, he feared being crippled in war, but he also feared something deeper, something he could not even explain to himself. Was it the routine, the way of life others of his class so unquestioningly embraced?

"Tell me more about your travels," Maria urged. "I want to hear it all. The pilgrims who come to Fordwich with their endless tales of shrines are all cut from the same cloth and bear stories cut from the same. I never dreamed traveling could be other than drudgery and crawling from one holy relic to another."

"There are hills out there, they say, made from a lodestone that draws the metal fastening from ships' planking and lures sailors to their doom." He gazed at the moon, beginning to fade in the immense expanse of heaven, the brilliance of a billion emerging stars. "And the Garden of Eden is out there somewhere, too—far to the east, somewhere atop a mountain so high, 'tis told, it pierces the moon. There is a palace in Eden, of crystal and jasper columns, and streams bedded with jewels." Phillip sat up and hugged his knees. "I looked for the Garden. If it is truly there I cannot find it."

"Perhaps you will." Maria was certain he could do anything.

He shook his head. "I am thirty years old. 'Tis time to settle down. And I would settle down with you, Maria, no one else."

As she lifted her gaze to the glittering darkness Maria's heart soared. When they'd first met she had thought him as inaccessible as the moon. Sometimes she still sensed a remoteness in him. But I have done the impossible, she thought. I have ensnared the moon and soon it will belong to me.

Rockingham Castle had originally been built by William the Conqueror on the elevated site of an ancient British fortress commanding the valley of the River Welland. It remained a royal residence. Kings used it both as an administrative center in the Midlands and as a hunting lodge for Rockingham Forest, which covered most of Northamptonshire.

Maria and Phillip reached Rockingham just as the sky was beginning to turn with the scarlet colors of sunset.

"God is with us!" Phillip said, pointing to the standards flying above one of two square towers framing Rockingham's portcullis. "Not only is Lord Sussex in residence, but also His Grace."

"Our king?" Maria was dismayed. It would be frightening enough to meet King Edward under the most ordinary circumstances, but as a runaway? She could imagine now the royal disapproval. Like her mother's, only a thousand times more terrible.

In one of the few physical gestures of their journey, Phillip patted her arm. "Do not look so frightened. His Grace hates the Leybournes. Their cousin, Guy of Warwick, was one of those who murdered Piers Gaveston, and the family openly applauded Warwick's deed. King Edward will approve our marriage on that basis alone."

"His Majesty is not overmean?"

Phillip smiled. "He is kind and generous." And petulant and hot tempered when crossed, he silently added as they picked their way up the rutted road to Rockingham Castle. But generally only to his enemies.

They passed beneath the portcullis without more than a rudimentary challenge from the porter. Rockingham's outer bailey consisted of the great wall, chapel, and various domestic offices. The courtyard itself appeared deserted.

As Maria dismounted her legs began shaking, from fear as well as fatigue. "I'll not have to meet our lord and . . . everyone, will I? Not just yet, anyway? I am so bedraggled from our traveling. Will not His Grace and Lord Sussex disapprove of me?"

Before Phillip could reassure her, a stocky knight with deep-set brown eyes emerged from one of Rockingham's two towers and strode toward them.

"Lord Rendell?" he asked.

When Phillip nodded, the man introduced himself as Michael Hallam, squire to the earl of Sussex. "My lord asked that I await your possible arrival. This morning he received a missive from Fordwich detailing . . . events and enlisting his help in the matter. My lord thought mayhaps you would ride for Rockingham." Michael Hallam's fierce eyes swept Maria, seeking in her a clue to Phillip's bizarre behavior. She looked no different from any other woman to him, and he found the entire affair, as related by the lady's parents, incomprehensible.

What true knight would risk disgrace over a mere woman? In the two years since Michael had become Richard's squire he'd guarded his lord with fanatic loyalty; he sensed trouble here.

"Then my lord is expecting us?" Phillip asked.

Michael nodded. "They are dining in the great hall."

"The king and queen also?" Maria asked. When Michael nodded, her frightened eyes sought Phillip. "I could not possibly meet them in my state."

Though Michael's face remained impassive, inwardly he was annoyed. Women's preoccupation with fashion and cleanliness was foolishness and vanity, nothing more. "My lord bade me tell him should you arrive. If you prefer you can wait for him here."

When Michael returned, Maria at first thought King Edward strode beside him. The man was tall and powerfully built, with a regal carriage, hair more sun streaked than true blond, and a strong handsome face.

"Our very king!" she whispered, overcome by awe and fear.

"Not our king," Phillip said. "Our lord."

He left her side to greet Richard. Maria was surprised at the intensity of the reunion. Obviously, the bonds of friendship ran deep between these two men. But why should they not? Richard owed Phillip his life.

Nervously Maria anticipated their forthcoming introduction. Even now Phillip was relating to Richard their plight. *What will he think of me? Will he call me foolish, irresponsible?* The nails of her hands, which were clenched together, dug into her flesh. *Will he send me back under armed escort to Fordwich and Edmund Leybourne?*

When Richard finally approached her, Maria sank to a curtsy, made awkward by nervousness and the weariness of the ride. As she rose she stumbled. Richard caught her arm to steady her.

"Damoiselle d'Arderne, 'tis honored I am to meet you." He smiled into her eyes. "I can well understand that Phillip would risk much for you." Richard's first impression was that Maria looked very young and frightened. Touched by her vulnerability, he quickly sought to allay her fears.

"Though I am your parents' lord as well as Phillip's, you must know where my sympathies lie. Edmund Leybourne is not a friend of my brother's, and I think Edward will take much pleasure in thwarting him."

"Thwarting him, my lord?" Increasingly overwhelmed by events, Maria had trouble comprehending his meaning.

"Aye, damoiselle. Phillip and I have decided that you should be married. Tonight."

Maria and Phillip's wedding was scheduled to take place in the dead of night, at the hour of matins. As Queen Isabella's maids scurried about attempting to properly ready Maria, Richard summoned the bishop of Ely, who was staying nearby at Thorney Abbey. The bishop was Edward's man and Richard was certain that if a large enough donation was promised to his favorite priory, His Excellency would overlook Maria's previous betrothal. Haste was of the essence. Should Edmund Leybourne be of a mind to press the matter, which the d'Arderne missive suggested was the case, he could do little once Maria and Phillip were married and their union consummated. Wars had been fought, however, over similar affairs. Recently John, earl of Warenne, had abducted Thomas Lancaster's very wife. In response Lancaster had ordered his troops to ravage Warenne's Yorkshire lands and had laid siege to the earl's castles at Conisborough and Sandal. In present-day England even the mildest spark could ignite to a civil war capable of spreading far beyond its original boundaries. Richard prayed Phillip's indiscretion would not end so bloodily.

"Edmund is so ancient I think he could not properly sit a horse, let alone ride it for any length of time," Richard said to Phillip as they privately discussed the situation. "I'll wager he'll bluster about a bit, but I do not think he'll risk armed confrontation."

"'Twould be his right," Phillip replied. All through their journey to Rockingham he'd expected to be pursued by the earl's troops. Maria, after all, was more Leybourne's property than his own. In addition, Edmund was a great lord, while he was only an insignificant baron. "I owe you a great debt for helping us, sire. Not everyone would be so sympathetic to our plight."

Richard waved away his words. "The scar on my chest daily reminds me that I owe you the largest debt of all."

As Richard and Phillip met with the bishop of Ely, Maria bathed and readied for her forthcoming wedding in Rockingham's lone bedroom. The tiny chamber, built into the eaves of the great hall by Edward I for his queen, was the only private place in the castle. Surrounded as she was by strangers and overwhelmed by events, Maria remained totally befuddled. Easier to count the number of snowflakes in a storm or the stars in the sky than comprehend what was happening. Only Queen Isabella's infrequent presence jerked her from her daze. Though Isabella was as palely beautiful as Henrietta was dark, Maria found their resemblance eerie. Or was it just that Isabella seemed as openly disapproving of her as was her mother?

"'Tis a troublesome thing you've done, Damoiselle d'Arderne," the queen had said upon their meeting. Isabella believed strongly in duty and propriety. Noblewomen did as they were told, not as they pleased. "You have broken your vows, traveled without proper escort, and are entering marriage with less care than a peasant."

Later, as Isabella watched her maids lightly rouge Maria's cheeks with cochineal paste, darken her lashes, and help her into a borrowed blue gown, she relented of her harshness. The girl's bewildered expression reminded the queen of her five-year-old son, Prince Edward, following an overharsh scolding.

"I do wish you happiness," she said as she presented a gold girdle set with various good-luck stones. Maria's gratitude was so unfeigned that Isabella even felt moved to kiss her on the cheek.

Watching a maid position a golden circlet atop her veil, the queen observed, "I was thirteen when I first met Edward in the cathedral at Boulogne. I was dressed in blue and gold, just as you are, and His Grace wore a fine satin jacket and a jeweled cloak. I was as enamored of him as you are of your knight." Unconsciously she twisted her marriage ring. "But I am no longer a child."

Isabella swept from the room in a rustle of brocade and Cyprus silk. Only the lingering scent of violets from her perfume remained in the close air of the bedroom.

The bishop of Ely performed the mass of the Trinity and wedding ceremony in hushed, hurried tones. Repeatedly he looked beyond Maria and Phillip, as if fearing Edmund Leybourne or the d'Ardernes' imminent arrival. The lateness of the hour also lent a certain furtiveness to the atmosphere, as did Rockingham's chapel, which was lighted only by a pair of candelabra. Much of the altar and nave were swathed in shadow, as if too much light might expose things better left hidden. Edward and Isabella attended, however, lending a certain air of propriety to the proceedings.

For Maria little of the ceremony registered, nor the guests, save for the royal couple and Richard. Phillip remained calm throughout, and a measure of his strength began to penetrate, soothing her nervousness.

After the bishop pronounced the traditional blessing and Phillip slipped on Maria's finger the customary gold marriage ring set with a lone ruby, the mass ended. As the Agnus Dei was chanted, Phillip advanced to the altar and received from His Excellency the kiss of peace. Then he turned to Maria. Raising from her face her lace veil he took her in her arms. Even through his tunic she felt the heat from his body, his pounding heart, his muscles knot as their embrace tightened. His parted lips met hers in their first marriage kiss. When he finally released her, Maria was breathless.

Outside Rockingham's chapel, they were congratulated first by the king, whose brocade finery surpassed even his wife's. Leaning over, Edward smacked Maria wetly on the mouth. "Lady Rendell, you are as beautiful a bride as I've seen. Save for you, dear heart," he said, grinning at his wife.

Isabella's lips tightened. Her husband was free with pretty words, which she'd long ago decided meant little. He'd also had too much to drink. Not until Richard of Sussex's approach did she even acknowledge Edward's compliment, and that was as much to avoid speaking with the earl as to converse with her spouse. Never had Isabella liked the Bastard. Not only did she find him arrogant but she had often overheard him denigrating her porcelain beauty. For revenge she badgered him about his heredity, a subject about which Richard was most sensitive.

"'Tis your turn, brother, to kiss the bride," Edward said, pushing Richard toward Maria.

Dutifully, the earl kissed her on both cheeks. "I pray that God will bless your marriage bed and give you many years of happiness." He turned to Phillip. "You chose well, my friend. I envy you." Such compliments were commonplace at weddings, and though Richard found Maria attractive, he already regarded her as an extension of Phillip rather than an individual.

"With the earl of Warenne running off with Thomas Lancaster's wife, 'twould appear abductions are all the fashion," commented Hugh Despenser, lord steward of the royal household. He placed himself squarely between Edward and Queen Isabella, who glowered at him. Ignoring her, Despenser proceeded to draw the others into a political discussion. As always the earl of Lancaster was the focal point. Following Bannockburn, Thomas had rammed through Parliament a series of ordinances greatly curbing Edward's power and causing England to be, in effect, jointly ruled by himself and the king. Lancaster's influence resulted from his five earldoms, an army equivalent to Edward's, and his royal lineage. But though Lancaster was adept at thwarting the king's desires, he had proven himself totally inept at governing. Mention of his name usually meant hours of indignant rehashing over his latest actions, but this night Isabella, at least, would have none of it.

"A wedding is not the proper place to discuss the earl of Lancaster," she said coldly. Thomas Lancaster was related to her as well as to Edward, and because of his part in Piers Gaveston's death she yet counted him an ally. Besides, Isabella seized every opportunity to contradict or chastise Hugh Despenser in front of her husband. She found their deepening friendship distressing. Gaveston had once come between her and Edward, but she'd thought the king's "peculiarity" had died with Piers. Would Hugh Despenser prove her wrong?

As was customary, Richard and the rest of the guests led Maria and Phillip to Queen Eleanor's garden, where a pavilion had been hurriedly erected to accommodate the newlyweds. The night was warm and sweet. An intermittent breeze filled the walled enclosure with the fragrance of heliotrope, violets, lavender, gillyflowers, and a pleasant mixture of mint, fennel, dittany, and other herbs. Rose and yew hedges, shaped like elephants and mythic animals, intermittently marked the path. From the pavilion's interior, light shimmered and spilled beyond the open flap onto the grass.

A low couch, made up with silk sheets and a counterpane of cloth of gold, had been placed in the center of the room. Upon the floor were thick carpets, lounging pillows, and even a lute. A filigree tray, laden with wine, goblets, various fruits, and sweetmeats, was located near the couch. An oil lamp upon a stand provided a golden glow to the sensuous surroundings.

After blessing the marriage bed, the bishop left Maria to be disrobed by one of Isabella's maids. As she slipped naked beneath the rose-colored sheets, Maria awaited Phillip's arrival with a mixture of anticipation and fear. Living as she did in the open environs of castle life, she was not ignorant of sex or men. As strict as Henrietta had been about proper conduct, she had seen nothing amiss in herself sitting on a guest's bed while he was within and conversing with him, or even exchanging crude jokes. Such behavior was customary in most households. Maria and Eleanora had sometimes helped bathe the more exalted barons who visited Fordwich, and more than once Maria had seen a knight tumbling some doxy in the hayloft above Fordwich's stables. But a proper maid arrived at her wedding night a virgin, and love's mysteries she was expected to discover without explanation from her mother or anyone else.

From along the pebbled path outside Maria heard footsteps and a murmur of conversation. She recognized Richard of Sussex's voice and was surprised by the twinge of jealousy she experienced. Though she could not fault the earl's kindness, the ties linking the two men effectively excluded her and seemed more powerful than anything she had to offer. Yet, she thought as she stared at the pavilion's striped ceiling, billowing upward. Someday 'twill all be different.

When Phillip entered, Maria's unease immediately changed to excited anticipation. As he undressed she did not modestly look away but rather openly watched him—delighting in the play of back muscles as he removed his tunic, the narrow waist, tight buttocks, long legs. Only when he turned and approached the couch did she close her eyes.

As he slipped in beside Maria, Phillip's weight sank the cushions, rolling her toward him. The hard-muscled length of his body felt pleasantly different from her own. He stretched against her, fitting curve to curve. The hairs on his chest tickled her back. He slipped his arm over her waist and with fingertips light as a fluttering butterfly began stroking her thighs, following the path of her body downward and upward past her waist, along her rib cage, toward her breasts.

"Never had I thought to willingly embrace marriage," he

whispered. "You have proven me wrong." Twisting a handful of her hair, Phillip lifted it from her neck and kissed the uncovered flesh. "I have waited long for this moment, Maria."

Turning in his arms she faced him. "I have waited long, too, my love." Reaching up, she traced the outline of his face, his cheekbones, the bridge of his nose, his soft mouth surrounded by the harshness of beard. "'Twas worth it, running away. Not even in dreams could I have imagined such a husband."

His lips brushed the corners of her mouth. "And I hope I will not prove a poor match for you. For no man is the stuff of dreams. Certainly I am not."

As the enormity of their act, his commitment began to dawn, apprehension threatened to overwhelm Phillip's desire. Marriage! I am a married man. Forcing his mind to concentrate on the moment, he crushed Maria's body against his, and her response, combined with his increasing passion, eventually extinguished all disquiet. Phillip did not speak to her of his love but he showed Maria with his mouth, his hands, his body. This night, at least, the lovemaking alone was enough for both.

FIVE

ear Midsummer Day Phillip and Maria, accompanied by a small escort, set out for Phillip's family demesne of Winchcomb in Herefordshire. Their wedding present from Richard, Deerhurst, was located adjacent to Winchcomb, and after a short visit with Humphrey Rendell, Phillip planned to retire there. Maria was relieved to finally have time completely alone with her husband. At Rockingham she'd had to share Phillip with Richard. Sometimes Phillip seemed to prefer the earl's company to her own, which had led to a certain amount of friction between them. In addition, Maria often brooded over her family's refusal to answer her many letters or acknowledge her marriage. She knew Henrietta was behind the continued ostracism, and Maria could not completely blame her mother. If only that awful thing with Edmund Leybourne had not happened . . .

Maria and Phillip passed through the towns of Coventry and Winchester, through flat farmlands and scatterings of cattle and sheep that had escaped the previous years of devastating murrains. The Rendell lands themselves appeared neat and prosperous; Humphrey took great pleasure in farming.

As they approached the graceful turrets of Winchcomb Castle, Maria sensed a change in Phillip. Though always quiet he also appeared uneasy; yet when she questioned him he merely shrugged.

"Lady Jean is sweet as an angel, but Humphrey can be unpleasant. He has not yet forgiven me the 'scandal.'" Their running away and the subsequent tragedy was always euphemistically referred to by that term. "I would rather forgo my brother's diatribes."

With the mention of the scandal Maria lapsed into gloomy silence. She didn't blame herself or Phillip for Edmund's death—indeed she took it as a sign from God that he was displeased with the earl. Yet sometimes she doubted. The day following their flight, when Edmund had been haranguing the d'Ardernes and demanding justice, he'd suddenly toppled over and died. Maria said the hand of God had smote him, Henrietta maintained his heart had exploded with grief, and Phillip had ridden off with Richard to discuss the matter. He'd not subsequently mentioned it to Maria save for one oblique reference. "You do not think our marriage is cursed, do you?" Maria had been stunned by the question and the uncertainty implicit in the words. With the passage of time, however, she'd whittled Edmund's death and Phillip's uneasiness down to more manageable proportions. 'Twas just an unfortunate accident, she repeatedly told herself, and proceeded to shove the entire event from her mind.

When they reached Winchcomb's inner gate, Phillip rang loudly on a heavy metal gong hanging there. "Though I sent word ahead, I would not ride in unannounced. Lady Jean is of a nervous disposition that irritates my brother. I would not unnecessarily upset her."

Phillip's solicitude for another woman immediately nettled. Yet when Maria saw Lady Jean scurrying toward them, dragging a four-year-old girl and unsuccessfully attempting to keep up with her husband and son, she was ashamed of her jealousy. Jean Rendell was a tiny, washed-out creature with honey-colored hair and eyes and, Maria soon discovered, a personality as sweet.

"Saints be praised! We've been expecting you! Oh, husband, is this not grand?" She bustled forward, her face a mixture of apprehensiveness and joy. As Phillip dismounted, Jean blurted, "We've missed you so these past years," and began to cry. With much muffled sobbing, she bent over to retie a ribbon in her daughter Missy's hair.

"God's bones!" Humphrey Rendell swore. "If you are going to snivel at every visitor who comes along, I'll not allow you out in public. You have more tears inside than clouds have rain."

"But we have not seen Phillip for three years, and now with his bride . . ." Jean's voice cracked. Turning away, she blew her nose daintily on the underside of her sleeve, wiped her eyes, and struggled for composure.

As Phillip helped Maria dismount, she surreptitiously studied her new brother-in-law, whose domineering manner had immediately grated. Humphrey Rendell was shorter than Phillip and much heavier. Even as she watched he straightened the rich folds of his fustian tunic, attempting to hide his generous belly. His passing resemblance to Phillip was blurred by too many years and too much food, but Maria's main surprise was at the lavishness of his dress. Phillip cared very little for fashion, yet his brother, from his enormous trailing sleeves to the tips of his long pointed shoes, was dressed in the latest style.

"So here is my brother's fine bride." Humphrey's gaze ran over her, weighing, appraising. Maria knew immediately that he despised her.

Before he could make further comment, Lady Jean scurried forth and bussed her on the cheek. "And such a pretty bride you are. But I knew you would be, for Phillip wrote us all about you and we heard . . ." Her voice trailed away. "Well, no matter what we heard." With a wave of her hand, Jean dismissed weeks of gossip. Turning to Phillip, she continued, "I prayed so hard that you would return safely home to England and here you are looking so fine and handsome and with a worthy wife and I am just so happy!"

Before Lady Jean could again start crying, Phillip bent over and kissed her on the lips. Surely, the kiss, Phillip's entire attitude, is more than brotherly in nature, Maria thought, as she watched the embrace. Phillip and Jean had known each other for years. Had they once been childhood sweethearts? Had he given her pins and glass rings? Had they played "Pinch-Me" neath a summer moon, chased each other through Winchcomb's halls, stolen kisses following the Easter mummery?

As she struggled with her jealousy, Maria pretended great interest in the Rendell children. Missy intermittently stared at Phillip and stepped on the heels of her teenaged brother, Harry, who either swatted at her or picked at a boil alongside his nose. Humphrey Rendell glowered at them all as if suffering from a sour stomach.

After Phillip released her, Lady Jean clapped her hands. "Now we can all go into the pleasance. We had planned a feast especially to welcome you home." She slipped an arm through Maria's. "You and I will be friends, I know it. Anyone whom Phillip loves I cannot help but love also."

Humphrey rested a hand on his brother's arm. "Stay a moment, please. Now that you have finally deigned to return home after long years, we have a few things to discuss."

Immediately after Maria had disappeared into Winchcomb's great hall, he turned on Phillip in an angry rush. "Whatever possessed you to do such a thing, you fool? You've disgraced our name and, Christ's blood, the woman is worse than I feared. You needed a nice quiet little wife like my Jean, not some strumpet without scruples, who caused the death of poor old Edmund Leybourne, and who is a total mismatch. God's bones! Her hair, her eyes, her manner, everything about her is totally wrong."

Phillip moved away from his brother, toward the keep. "Maria is the woman I chose to marry. I would have no one else."

"You chose to marry her!" Humphrey hurried after him.

"Since when has a man been able to choose anything? Marriage is a delicate affair, involving months of negotiation concerning dowry and position and land and . . .

"Fordwich is a fine little manor that will someday belong to me. And do not forget Lord Sussex's wedding gift of Deerhurst. Though I care not, I'm no longer a landless knight. In fact, brother, even you should be pleased with my new status."

Humphrey spat upon the ground. "Do not dare crow about Deerhurst! 'Tis the same gift you so foolishly turned down after Bannockburn. You could have had more—"

"Aye! My lord of Sussex should have granted me all of England as well." Phillip spun around to face him. "And you would not have been satisfied until you had planted rye and barley from Northumbria to Sussex. For years you complained because I would not wed, and now because I do. I thank you, brother for this most kind welcome home."

Humphrey shook his head. The folds around his mouth waddled disapprovingly. "You refuse to understand. You always have. But hear me well. Your—that woman is naught but trouble. Someday, I promise, you'll curse the very name Maria d'Arderne."

After a strained few days at Winchcomb, Maria and Phillip left for Deerhurst. Two hours' ride from Winchcomb, Deerhurst was a sprawling demesne with crop yields and soil that even Humphrey envied. Around the small castle clustered a well-maintained kitchen, servants' quarters, stables, barns, and storehouses. The keep itself consisted only of a private bedroom and great hall which had been built in the old style— aisled like a church and with rows of stone pillars supporting the timbered roof. The chimneyed fireplaces on each wall cast a certain warmth to the soaring ceiling, boars' and stags' heads, arms and armor, and the banners cluttering the whitewashed walls. Richard of Sussex's retainers had proved competent in their administration. The outdoor seneschal, Sir Timothy

Maudelyn, knew precisely the amount of acreage sown, plowed, or ready for reaping, as well as the condition of the pasturage and the number of livestock kept and improved.

"We will be happy here," Maria said to Phillip upon their arrival. She offered silent thanks to their lord Sussex for his generosity. Lady Jean had provided her with a lady-in-waiting, Anne Perth, who was an efficient addition to the original household staff, and Maria looked forward to running Deerhurst and enjoying life as Phillip's wife. Before summer's end, however, political events dictated her husband's presence hundreds of miles to the north, and Maria found herself alone.

King Edward had ordered a muster at York against the ever-threatening Scots, to which knights from across England responded. Thomas Lancaster's retainers from Pontefract, however, barred the way to the assembling forces, stating that if the king wished to take arms against anyone he ought first to notify the steward of England. Thomas Lancaster was, of course, steward of England and worried that the king was plotting to weaken his position. Because of Lancaster's latest intransigence, civil war began to appear increasingly imminent; Thomas even contacted Robert the Bruce concerning a possible alliance against Edward.

By April of 1318 the need for conciliation was made imperative by the Scots' capture of Berwick, Harbottle, and Wark. Only in Ireland, where the most powerful baron of the Welsh march, Roger Mortimer of Wigmore, had succeeded in routing Edward Bruce, did matters look other than hopeless. While the king and Lancaster wrangled over power and the concept of "crown," the Scots burned and pillaged much of the north of England. Finally, in August 1318, a settlement—more favorable to the king than to his cousin—was reached in the Treaty of Leake. With Edward and his cousin in temporary harmony, a major campaign against the Scots was finally mounted in 1319.

Alone in Deerhurst, Maria knew little more about political affairs than that they often kept Phillip away from her.

Deerhurst, the entire surrounding area, was part of what was known as the marchland—that area of England bordering Wales. The march was strategically important but much of it was isolated, and when Phillip was gone she felt abandoned. She spent a miserable year longing for Fordwich, pondering the babe growing in her belly, and brooding over her husband's absences. It seemed Phillip would no sooner return than he would be summoned for yet another campaign. Sometimes she thought he left her too willingly, especially as the time of her delivery drew near.

Maria wrote to her family, requesting Henrietta's presence at the birthing. In the months since her marriage she'd received occasional missives from her father and Eleanora, but nothing from her mother. At first Henrietta's silence rankled and she told herself she'd not beg her mother for forgiveness. But as she herself readied for motherhood, Maria yearned to reestablish with Henrietta some sort of relationship. "If you will but come," she wrote, "I swear I will be the daughter you always wished."

Maria was delivered of her son, Thomas, with Lady Jean and her maid, Anne Perth, at her bedside. Phillip was in York with Richard. Henrietta remained at Fordwich.

The Treaty of Leake destroyed the effective unity of Lancaster's opposition. Agreement between the king and Lancaster himself, however, proved fleeting. Thomas soon retreated to his estates where he sulked over the treaty as well as the recent appointment of Lord Bartholomew Badlesmere as steward of the household—a post which Thomas, as hereditary steward of England, felt he should control. When a two-year truce was finally signed with the Scots at the end of 1319, Edward blamed Lancaster's uncooperativeness for terms he considered humiliating. Lancaster, in turn, blamed the king.

At Deerhurst, Maria anxiously awaited her husband's return. As fall deepened into winter she bundled up little Tom, now nearly a year old, climbed the stone stairs to Deerhurst's north facing battlement, and strained for the first glimpse of Phillip's banner. Her bitterness toward him for so often leaving had long ago dissolved into an aching loneliness. She wanted only to look upon his face, hear his voice, rest again in his arms, to share with him their son.

Her days now revolved around little Tom and the duties demanded by her position as chatelaine of Deerhurst. Both her indoor and outdoor seneschals were competent, but Maria periodically rode across the estate with her overseer, Timothy Maudelyn, and went over the household accounts, which ran from Michaelmas to Michaelmas, with William, the chamberlain. She politely entertained the occasional guest or traveler, supervised the household staff and her maids, including little Tom's nurse, Alice—a fat, motherly woman who also doted on her child. In her small solar Maria supervised the sewing, embroidering, and knitting, and personally executed most of the spinning, using distaff and spindle.

As she ordered the changing or freshening of floor rushes or instructed the gardener on the variety of cooking and healing herbs to plant, Maria was reminded of her mother. Sometimes she found herself using similar words and phrases or treating servants as she'd seen Henrietta do, though she did not feel like true mistress of Deerhurst. I am only playacting, she thought, like a child stumbling about in grown-up clothes. Nor did she derive much intrinsic pleasure from her duties. Perhaps 'tis because Fordwich still is home to me, she thought. Perhaps 'tis because Phillip is not here. With her husband absent, so was half her reason for existence. Little Tom provided the other half.

If angels could be seen, she was certain, they would look— and act—like her son. Maria fussed and worried over him so much that Alice chastised her for her overprotectiveness, but she did not care. Half the children born did not live to the age of five, and Maria, at the slightest sign of fever or cold, administered steaming herbal baths and calamint tea and syrup; if Tom was listless or irritable she worried he had contracted smallpox or some dread disease like St. Anthony's fire. Contrary to custom she personally breastfed him and kept him always near her in the solar, whether when playing or napping in his elaborately carved cradle—a gift from Richard of Sussex.

At Tom's baptism, Richard had also sent a dozen exquisitely detailed robes and Queen Isabella even bestowed upon the child a silk robe trimmed in ermine. Isabella had been recently delivered of her third child, Eleanor of Woodstock, so Maria attributed the queen's surprising thoughtfulness to happiness over the birth of her first daughter.

From her own mother Maria heard nothing.

St. Remigius' Day passed, and with it the end of harvest time. Rents were paid and leases fell due and fall drifted toward winter. For the past week Maria had haunted the battlements, always looking north. A feeling of foreboding weighed on her as insistently as the storm clouds concealing the horizon. Something dreadful has happened, she told herself, and because the danger remained unfocused it assumed life-shattering proportions. Phillip was dead; her family had all perished of a plague. Tom's recent cough was not minor but fatal. Though she was not prone to weeping, Maria cried herself to sleep, hugging little Tom, who slept beside her.

Finally, she spotted the troops approaching along a road white with a recent dusting of snow. The afternoon light was too uncertain for proper identification of the banners but Maria was certain Phillip had come home. Rushing to the solar she changed into her best kirtle and awakened Tom from a nap.

"Papa's home, sweetheart!" she cried as they entered the inner bailey where the troop was already dismounting. Then she halted, stunned. Upon their jupons the knights bore, not the blue of the Rendell wolf, but a red leopard's head. The man who turned to her with a glad cry was not Phillip but her father.

"Poppet!" He crushed her in a fierce embrace. "How I've missed thee." He began to cry, and when he finally drew back,

Maria saw that his face was thinner and more lined than she'd remembered. In two years' time he'd aged two dozen. "And is this my grandson?" he asked, as she led Tom forward. Hugh bent over, favoring his bad leg, and bestowed a shaky smile on his grandson.

Eleanora bustled forward to hug her. She smelled of lavender; Henrietta had used lavender perfume. "We've come to take you home."

Maria drew back and searched her sister's face. "Mother's dead, isn't she?"

Eleanora nodded.

"I knew it." Maria inhaled shakily. "When?"

"Near Michaelmas. Of a sickness to the lungs, as have so many these past months."

"Why did you not write? Why did mother not send for me when she took ill?"

Eleanora made a great show of removing her gloves.

"Did she ask for me before she died?" Maria pressed. "What did she say? Oh, I should have been there. I've known something was wrong. 'Twas mother calling out to me, begging me to return home."

Eleanora bent down and beckoned to little Tom, who stuck his thumb in his mouth and refused to obey.

"Why are you avoiding me? Why will you not tell me about mother?"

Hugh opened his arms and, when Maria went to him, enfolded her in a tight embrace. "Did she die an awful death?" Maria swallowed down an anguished sob. "Did she forgive me for Edmund, and did she miss me very much?"

Hugh could not meet her eyes. "She passed so quick she had not time really to mourn for anyone."

Something was not right here. Hugh and Eleanora were not behaving as they should. Maria's mind began whirling with all manner of possible events concerning Henrietta, all involving her in culpability. "You do not blame me, papa, do you? Do you think mama died of a broken heart because of me?"

"Stop it!" Eleanora cried. Tears slid down her face, but they were more of anger than grief. "Mother did not die because of you or anyone. She died of a murrain, that's all. And from the hour of Edmund Leybourne's death she never once mentioned your name, so do not torture yourself with fantasies of what might have been and never was."

When Eleanora's meaning registered, Maria's sorrow began to harden until she felt dead inside—as dead as her mother. Henrietta had used her as a marriage pawn and when her usefulness had ended, obliterated the very thought of her. Henrietta had not anguished over their estrangement; she'd given it no thought at all. Maria raised her eyes to the darkening sky, to the snowflakes beginning to drift to the hay-glutted earth of Deerhurst's bailey. "Now I know," she whispered. "I think I've always known."

SIX

he winter of 1320 proved the severest since the years immediately following Bannockburn. Leaving Deerhurst in the competent hands of Timothy Maudelyn, Maria and Phillip had returned to Fordwich and it was here they passed the brutal months. Snow climbed halfway up Fordwich Castle's outer curtain and drifted against the portcullis and outer gatehouse. Violent winds blasted through drafty passageways, flapping wall tapestries and extinguishing struggling wall torches. Chillblains were a universal affliction, as were perpetually aching extremities. Maria was certain she'd never again be warm.

During the past year Phillip had stayed to Fordwich and proven himself a competent administrator. He'd also been prescient enough to have the castle's dungeon storerooms filled with wheat and other necessities, but elsewhere Englishmen went hungry, especially the poor. Poaching became commonplace. Hunting in the forests was reserved for nobility, but with the worsening food shortages, peasants dared sneak an occasional hare or hart. By royal edict, death was ordered for any villein caught hunting in King Edward's private preserves, or those of his barons.

By choice, His Majesty remained isolated from his subjects'

problems. The meals Edward enjoyed were often sumptuous affairs, containing a variety of dishes lesser folk could only dream about. At Edward's side sat his now inseparable companion, Hugh Despenser, who had risen to a position of favor unparalleled since Piers Gaveston, dead now seven years. As chamberlain of the royal household, Hugh the Younger enjoyed constant personal contact with Edward, and as his hold over the king tightened, his own greed and that of his father, Hugh the Elder, surfaced in an alarming manner. Both Despensers coveted land—anyone's land—and they proceeded to obtain it by lawful means or no. Resentful and frightened, England's noblemen, led by the increasingly bitter Thomas of Lancaster, laid plans to thwart the favorite's ever-increasing power.

"If it comes to force of arms," Roger Mortimer of Wigmore said, "we'll wield a sword to protect our lands. I'll not suffer lightly anyone trying to carve up marcher property to his own desires or to reach higher than he should." Strange words coming from a man known for his ambitions, but as the Despensers' actions became ever more outrageous, other magnates openly agreed. It was not long before Hugh the Younger provoked them beyond endurance.

Hugh Despenser had married His Majesty's niece, Eleanor. Eleanor was the eldest daughter of the last earl of Gloucester, Gilbert, who had died in the first ill-fated charge at Bannock-burn. Hugh's marriage made him coheir to the great Clare estates, which suited his ambition of becoming a member of the highest aristocracy. Since Bannockburn, death had depleted the ranks of the earls from fifteen to six. Fresh blood was needed at the top, and Hugh was determined to provide that blood. Wishing to base his future greatness upon a marcher principality in south Wales, Despenser moved to concentrate all the Clares' territories, as well as any other available land, in his hands. Declaring that Hugh had "despised the laws and customs of the march," a coalition of marcher lords rose against him. It was led by Roger Mortimer of Wigmore and his nephew, Roger of Chirk. Behind the confederation stood Thomas of Lancaster.

In April of 1321, the marcher barons, wearing a special green uniform with a yellow sleeve on the right arm, torched the lands of both Hughs. Phillip rode with them. Not only were his brother Humphrey's lands threatened but at one time the favorites had even expressed interest in Deerhurst—an interest soon thwarted, Phillip was certain, by Richard of Sussex. Across the Clare estates he and the Mortimers and the other lords rode, putting to torch thousands of acres and hundreds of manors, slaughtering or robbing the Despensers of tens of thousands of sheep, oxen, cattle, hogs, and horses. The night sky pulsated as flames annihilated acre after acre, driving animals and people before their wrath, destroying manor houses and outbuildings as well as food, furniture, gold, and silver valued in the hundreds of thousands of pounds. Over brutal mountain areas and gentle farmland the marchers raced—into the Wye Valley with its lofty cliffs and snaking river, across forests planted to pen in sheep—burning all they saw. An effluvium of smoke, the stench of roasting animals, replaced the fragrance of meadow grass, fresh water, new-turned earth; cinders raced the night wind, a glowing mirror of the stars beyond.

As Phillip executed the swift strikes he experienced a fierce joy. He felt himself one with the darkness, an anonymous bearer of the flame. He was exhilarated by the pounding vibration of his running horse between his thighs, the hot wind, the flames clawing upward into the night. When the pillaging was over, he and the Roger Mortimers and the other marcher lords withdrew to their castles to await the Hugh Despensers' next move. But Thomas Lancaster acted first. He called barons and clergymen to Pontefract and in July, accompanied by an unprecedented number of magnates, marched on London. With him rode a large army that encamped in the villages to the north of the city. The time had come. Edward must either give up his favorites or give up his crown.

*　　　*　　　*

Royal Westminster, the seat of England's government, was located just beyond London's walls and adjacent to the River Thames. Westminster Abbey, founded by Edward the Confessor, and its palace comprised the major buildings. Two throughfares serviced Westminster, and it was from the north, along King Street, that Thomas Lancaster and England's barons rode on August 14, 1321. Knowing he had no choice, King Edward had hastily convened Parliament to deal with the matter of the Hugh Despensers. His barons were in no mood to compromise. To signify their unity they wore on their arms a white band; already the convocation was being referred to as the Parliament of the White Bands.

In Westminster Hall, King Edward studied the determined faces of the lords assembled in the gallery. Though an inner fury raged, he also realized his helplessness, for he no longer possessed the power to force his will. England's entire peerage stood against him. Someday, he thought, balling his fists, I will make you all pay. He hated his barons—always carping at him and blathering about "Nephew Hugh's" influence, when Hugh Despenser was worth the lot of them. But for now Edward knew he had no choice. He must either banish the Despensers and return all their property or risk losing his throne.

From the hall's gallery, rising twenty feet from the floor, the lords clustered in small groups, their eyes constantly straying toward the entrance through which Thomas Lancaster would momentarily arrive. The marcher lords were still dressed in the dramatic green and yellow that they had worn during their raids. I hate you most of all, Edward thought. You arrogant marcher lords who think you owe not allegiance to any man. You who think just because you patrol the Welsh border you can make your own laws and create your own principalities without regard to a king's sovereign rights. His gaze came to rest on the most powerful marcher of them all, Roger Mortimer of Wigmore. Descended from the legendary William Marshal as well as Welsh princes, Mortimer was dangerous, ambitious, and, following his successful campaign in Ireland against the Scots, the only military hero of Edward's reign. The king was beginning to fear as well as despise him.

A blast of trumpets announced the arrival of Thomas Lancaster. As the earl approached Edward, the king noted that Thomas's bearing was as regal as if 'twas he who ruled England. He was also wearing near as many jewels as belonged to the crown. Lancaster's scarlet and vermilion riding cloak swirled about his narrow shoulders, displaying beneath a purple and gold supertunic. No wonder my Piers nicknamed Thomas "The Fiddler," Edward thought. Not even a Frenchman would attire himself so garishly.

Westminster was so silent that Lancaster's footsteps echoed off the cavernous roof supported by wooden columns clear as the ringing of St. Martin's at curfew. The earl obviously enjoyed being the center of attention. Neath his liripiped and plumed hat, his small mouth curved in a half smile. Lancaster had reason to smile. He had reemerged from the Treaty of Leake and his period of isolation as still the most powerful man in England, next to the king.

As the earl swaggered to a stop before him, Edward squeezed the arms of his throne until his knuckles whitened. For a moment he thought Lancaster would not bend his knee to him. He took his own most gracious time—and made the obeisance appear contemptuous.

The two men exchanged stiff greetings. Thomas then nodded to Richard, standing behind Edward, and took his place among his supporters in Westminster's gallery.

The Parliament of the White Bands had officially begun.

Long shadows crept across the barnlike expanse of Westminster's hall, crawling across its two-hundred-forty-foot length to Edward, slumped in his gilt-edged chair. After seemingly endless wrangling and threats, Edward had agreed on this day of August 19, 1321, to sign a decree without parallel in English history. Though members of the nobility had previously been banished—witness Piers Gaveston—all had been foreign born. Never before had a true Englishman been formally exiled. Until today.

Edward's hand hesitated over the document. He tugged nervously at his reddish-gold beard, then turned to Richard. A look passed between them. Richard bent near, his tawny head appearing even darker contrasted to Edward's bright curls, topped by a jeweled crown. Thomas Lancaster shifted impatiently in his seat. His hand edged to his dagger. Roger Mortimer looked to the entrance, as if momentarily expecting Edward's royal guard to break through.

"Treachery," someone hissed.

Richard straightened. Edward looked down at the document, then back up to Richard as if he were king. The papers rattled in his hands.

Richard nodded. Edward's sigh echoed in the expectant silence. Leaning forward he signed the decree banishing from England the Hugh Despensers, who, the document stated, were "false and evil councilors, seducers, conspirators, disinheritors of the crown, enemies of the king and his kingdom."

The Palace of Westminster had been the monarch's residence from the time of King Canute early in the eleventh century. Tonight, following the signing of the decree, Edward had retreated to the Painted Chamber. Richard occupied the prince's chamber, parallel to his brother's. Only yards away the River Thames slipped past, and sometimes early of a summer morn, when the palace was asleep and London's ships were to dock, Richard imagined he could hear the water whispering past. Often Edward and Hugh Despenser had enjoyed the royal barge or stood upon the quay tossing tidbits to the royal swans, and talking.

The chamber's once-blazing fire, lighted to take the chill off the night, had burned down to scarlet embers, partially hiding the brilliant wall frescoes. The battle and biblical scenes done in backgrounds of ultramarine and vermilion and riotous with greens, purples, blues, crimsons, whites, blacks, and golds were hardly restful. Across from the earl, with a folding table between, sat Phillip Rendell. Richard's squire, Michael Hallam, kept silent watch beside the door. A flask of wine, nearly empty, sat upon the table. During the past hours he and Phillip had caught up with their months of separation, but repeatedly the conversation had returned to the present crisis.

"The Despensers brought their banishment upon themselves." Richard stretched his legs toward the hearth. Phillip, who had been studying the fire's embers, swirled in his cup the last dregs of wine. "They refused access to Edward unless a bribe was offered or one of them hovered nearby like a wet-nurse after her charge. They answered petitions as they pleased, replaced good officials with corrupt, appointed justices who were ignorant of the law of the land, and used false jurors to pervert that same law."

Phillip nodded. "And any who displeased them or whose lands they coveted they finagled into prison. A murrain on the both of them."

"Aye, but why do I not feel jubilant about their exile? Even if Thomas Lancaster triumphed, 'tis also best for England. And yet I cannot rejoice."

"His Majesty loves them both and you love your brother. His pain is your pain."

Richard slumped in the uncomfortable wooden-backed chair, suddenly weary to the core of his being. A plethora of unrelated images crowded his benumbed brain. Queen Isabella kneeling before her husband, pleading for him to banish the Despensers . . . If only she loved Edward more, perhaps she could prevent his unnatural attachments . . . Thomas Lancaster's triumphant smile . . . Edward's shaking hands . . . Sometimes when events weighed heavy, Richard slipped at midnight to Westminster Abbey and listened to the monastic horarium. As the monks recited hour after hour of psalms and texts he would relax with the rhythm of their voices and drink in the visual beauty of Edward the Confessor's shrine, located on a low platform behind the high altar. In the dancing candle flame the golden, bejeweled shrine atop its marble and mosaic base, decorated with images of kings and saints, emanated peace as well as beauty. The monks' voices blended with echoes from ceremonies long past and Richard felt a communion with his saintly forebear, a soaring of the spirit that left him refreshed, at least momentarily. I need that now, he thought. Edward needs that now.

"'Twould be so much simpler," he said aloud, "if we could choose whom we love. But we cannot."

Phillip stared into the fire. "Or how best to love them." He refilled his cup with the last of the wine. "I have a son whom I love. And a wife that any man would desire."

Richard was surprised at the personal turn of the conversation. Phillip usually kept such matters to himself. "But 'tis not enough?" He vaguely remembered Phillip's wife— auburn hair, a pleasant face and quiet manner. But a son, would not that bring contentment? "You have what every man strives for."

Phillip ran his hand distractedly through his hair. "I have presided over so many manor courts they invade my dreams. I've passed judgment over trespassing pigs and wandering sheep, the amount of shillings owed me or my father-in-law for rents, pretended interest in a dozen stolen eggs and assessed just fines when Tom defames Jack's corn so that no one will purchase it. I have inspected more granaries, storehouses, cattle byres, and slaughterhouses than England has shrines. I know more about crop yields than my brother Humphrey, by the cross! 'Tis to a low state I've fallen."

Richard laughed. "You make our lives sound dull indeed."

"If I had not the Scots and the treachery of the Despensers or Thomas Lancaster to get me away at times, I would go mad."

"If a good crusade was being fought, or you had committed some great sin so that you could haunt every shrine from here to Jerusalem, your life, I think, would improve. Mayhaps my brother could start a war with France or Spain or even the Moslems. I do not think it would be too difficult to arrange. He has alienated everyone else."

Phillip's mouth twisted in a rueful smile. "We have become as wedded to our land as our villeins. A hundred years from now you'll not be able to tell us apart." He sighed. "I am no longer a child. Why must I still chase the dreams of children?"

"What is it exactly that you want?"

"To fly," Phillip whispered. "To be free and unencumbered, to go where I please when I please and not be chained to routine and society and 'shoulds' and 'musts.'"

"I would fly, too," Richard said. Reaching across the table, he rested a hand upon Phillip's shoulder. "But I think the difference between us, my friend, is that I know 'tis impossible."

SEVEN

eeds Castle was located in Kent's Maidstone district, which was famous for its apples and cherries. In October of 1321 the entire area was awash with the rusts, golds, and reds of an unusually glorious fall. Leeds was a dower castle belonging to Queen Isabella, and when the queen undertook a pilgrimage to Canterbury she detoured to Leeds in order to break her journey. She was accompanied by a retinue that included banner-bearing monks as well as a group of armed knights led by Richard of Sussex. Currently Richard and his squire had detoured to Boxley Abbey, and Isabella counted herself lucky to be even temporarily rid of him. Richard often reminded her of what her husband might have been without his weaknesses, and she misliked the reminder. Sometimes she wondered whether England might not have been better served if Edward I had not indulged in an uncommon lapse of morality between marriages, or Richard had been firstborn. An accident of birth. It made Isabella hate him all the more.

The castellan of Leeds was Bartholomew Badlesmere. As they began the last mile of their journey, Isabella sent ahead a marshal to announce to Lord Badlesmere her arrival.

Beneath a protective canopy borne by four knights, Isabella approached Leeds. Leeds had been a favorite residence of Edward I's first wife, Eleanora. Isabella could well understand why, for it was an exquisite place. The keep nestled like an enormous jewel in the midst of a placid lake formed by a natural hollow of the River Len. Today the contrast between the castle's honey-colored walls, brilliant water, and the riotous colors of the surrounding woods was especially breathtaking. Children fished for pike off the castle drawbridge; swans glided among the trailing water lilies while geese and pigeons pecked along the lake's edge. The pastoral scene was marred only by the sight of Isabella's marshal racing back toward her across an open meadow.

The knight jerked his horse to a stop. "The Lady Badlesmere has refused us entrance to Leeds, Your Grace."

Isabella stared at him uncomprehendingly. Margaret Badlesmere was infamous for her viper's tongue and obnoxious personality, but still the marshal's words made no sense. "She cannot refuse me entrance to my own castle."

"She said that her lord Badlesmere rode for London and left her in charge during his absence. He ordered her to admit no one without specific letters from him."

"There must be some mistake," Isabella said. "Lady Badlesmere must have misunderstood. Did you not tell her that 'twas her very queen asking entrance?"

The marshal's mouth tightened. "I think the bitch Badlesmere does not care."

"Then 'tis up to me to make her change her mind," Isabella said crisply. With her retinue trailing behind, the queen approached Leeds. On the battlements, Margaret Badlesmere appeared. Her dark cloak whipped about her in a sudden wind; her hair snaked about her head.

"As you can see, Lady Badlesmere, your true queen stands before you," Isabella called. "Without further ado I ask entrance for myself and my people. We are all tired and hungry."

Margaret Badlesmere's face appeared set in granite; her jaw jutted pugnaciously. "I open to neither queen nor peasant without orders from my lord. Spend the eve at Boxley Abbey or in the woods, it matters not to me, but you will not be welcomed here."

Isabella was momentarily shocked into speechlessness. In all her twenty-nine years no one had ever spoken to her so rudely. "I am your queen," she finally shrieked, "and I command you . . ."

Stepping back, Lady Margaret signaled to several sentinels who immediately came forward to the embrasure. They let loose, not with the usual cheers and rose petals, but a volley of arrows aimed straight at the queen and her train. Arrows whizzed past Isabella, thudded into horses and unprotected monks. Isabella's women began screaming, men began falling. A second rain of arrows showered upon them. One of her knights grabbed at her jennet's bridle and led the frightened animal out of the path of fire. When the shooting finally ceased, six of Isabella's subjects sprawled dead upon the meadow grass.

Queen Isabella retreated to Leeds Priory, and there, with her retinue and twenty canons of the Order of St. Augustine, spent the night. The priory was one of the richest in all Kent, and had for hundreds of years given hospitality to pilgrims on their way to Canterbury. Richard the Lionheart had spent a night of vigil here in this peaceful place on his way to the crusades—but Isabella was not thinking of ancient history, this October night.

Her first coherent act was to send for Richard of Sussex. Upon his arrival she heaped upon his head hysterical invectives.

"While my life was being threatened you were chatting with your friends and gaping at some foolish relic out of Boxley Abbey. You have been completely remiss in your duty to me and your brother, who entrusted me to your care."

"And a marvelous relic the Rood of Grace is, madam," Richard said conversationally. "When I approached the statue it came to life and raised its hands in benediction. That is a kinder reception than it has given some."

"Stop it!" Isabella stomped her slippered foot. "Six of my men have just been killed, I was almost killed, and you prattle on about some relic of no importance. Spare me your religious devotion, Lord Sussex. The ecstasies you desire lie between the legs of some slut and not upon Christ's cross."

Distractedly knotting a rosary of Hansa amber in her hands, the queen paced the small room. "Oh, I knew the woman was a traitorous bitch, but I would not think anyone capable of this!" Isabella's pale eyes snapped; her delicate brows drew together in an ugly line. "I will have that creature's head and Badlesmere's, too, if his hand was truly in this. And you, my ever devout brother-in-law, will execute my vengeance. Do you understand?"

Richard risked an amused glance at his squire, Michael Hallam, who stood guard at the door. Though Lady Badlesmere had committed an unpardonable act, he did not find Isabella's personal humiliation totally reprehensible.

"We will march on Leeds tomorrow," she continued. "I'll see that bitch and everyone inside Leeds hanging from the gibbet ere nightfall."

"That would not be wise, madam. If we handle this matter properly, perhaps we could turn it into some sort of victory for His Majesty."

"Edward? What has he to do with this? He is enjoying the Isle of Thanet with dear 'Nephew Hugh.' What a fine joke banishment has proven to be. I see less of Edward now than before. Perhaps he will take to pirating, as Hugh has done. He obviously finds any diversion preferable to governing his country."

"Nevertheless, madam, I was thinking as I rode over that Edward might use this incident to good cause."

"I do not want to wait on my husband," Isabella shrieked, shaking her fist at him. "The glorious victor of Bannockburn? Jesu! Edward is incapable of finding the front of an army, let alone leading it. Nay, I want Margaret Badlesmere's head now, and if you are too afraid I'll find someone else to do my bidding."

Though remaining outwardly indifferent, Richard felt like leaping upon the queen and throttling her. He misliked Isabella's implications concerning his bravery as well as her remarks concerning his brother. A dragon would provide more pleasant companionship. Aloud, he continued, "I can hardly be frightened of a madwoman, madam, not when I am daily surrounded by such. But His Grace is in need of a popular cause. I am not."

"Why would she fire on me, her own queen?" Isabella's voice cracked.

I can think of a thousand reasons, Richard thought, glancing once more at Michael Hallam. "'Tis obvious that Bartholomew Badlesmere has totally thrown in his lot with the marchers and Cousin Lancaster, who are behind this mess, I'll warrant. But if the bitch thinks our Thomas will ride to save her scrawny neck she'll have a long wait. Tom might be riding high, but he hates Badlesmere and still cannot make up his mind to arise from bed of a morning, let alone start civil war."

Isabella ceased her pacing. "I cannot truly believe Lord Badlesmere would do this—he who has eaten the king's salt and broken his bread. He has been politically a moderate and his family always supported the crown."

"Many things are hard to understand since the Parliament of the White Bands." Richard's manner softened. "I think we have all been recently confused at the odd twists to events."

Isabella sighed. "What would you have me do, then?"

"Ride on to Canterbury—complete your pilgrimage. I will post Michael with a few men here to see that the bitch does not slip away, and I'll ride to my brother. Your subjects love you well. Edward will have no trouble raising an army to avenge your humiliation. And when he is seen riding at its head perhaps the people will look more tolerantly on his past— indiscretions."

Isabella nodded. Crossing to a leaded window she gazed outside. It was too dark to see, but Isabella was looking into her past, to the first time she'd met Edward. At the cathedral of Boulogne. She'd been thirteen and she'd thought her fiancé, with his height and fine clothes, the handsomest man in all the world. But Edward had acted coarse as a peasant and when they'd landed at Dover he'd fallen on Piers Gaveston, crying "Brother, brother!" Then Isabella's heart had frozen. Nor had it thawed.

"My lord Sussex?"

"Madam?"

"Edward did not manufacture an incident, did he? He would not have sent me to Leeds knowing I might be fired upon, would he?"

"Of course not. You are the mother of his children and his wife. He would not willingly expose you to danger." Richard spoke with more conviction than he felt, for he did not know. Following the Despensers' banishment Edward had openly vowed to destroy all those who had stood against him. Because neither his financial nor military position allowed him to destroy his enemies simultaneously, he'd sought the weakest first. Lord Badlesmere, who'd long walked a tightrope between kinship alliances among the marchers and loyalty to the crown, had been a logical first target. Leeds Castle, his chief residence, was easily isolated from the rest of England and was surrounded by estates royal to His Majesty. Had Edward sent Isabella to Leeds hoping to enter it without the expense and risk of a military campaign? Richard could not say. Since the Despensers' banishment, his brother spent an increasing amount of time alone, brooding and scheming to accomplish his favorites' return. 'Twas impossible to know what Edward might think or do.

When Richard related the event to his sovereign, his first reaction was to write an angry letter to Bartholomew

Badlesmere, who was staying at Stowe Park with his nephew, the bishop of Lincoln. Now that the time had come for action, Edward vacillated.

"Letter writing is not quite the strongest response I had in mind," Richard remarked. "Not when we know that Badlesmere has gone over to the marchers and Lancaster."

Edward stared into the distance, a small frown between his brows, then motioned for a scribe. "Perhaps we can obtain Leeds without bloodshed. Perhaps if I write to Badlesmere he will willingly order his wife to surrender Leeds. I mislike sieges. They are boring."

Bartholomew Badlesmere's reply, however, threw Edward into a rage. Not only did the baron refuse to apologize for his wife's behavior but he openly approved her attack on the queen.

"I will have that whoreson's head!" Edward cried, smashing his fist into the palm of his hand. Calling once again for a scribe, the king issued a proclamation. "The sheriffs of Hampshire, Surrey, and Sussex must assemble every man between sixteen and sixty before Leeds Castle by Friday, October twenty-third. I will brook no delays or excuses. I will show my barons that they do ill to thwart my will."

"Do not forget our own citizens here in London," Richard said. "They love Isabella and will flock to your standard."

Thousands answered Edward's call. Mounted knights, trained bands of townspeople, yeomen, and ordinary folk assembled at Leeds. Wavering lords rallied to the king and in the marcher countries, the lords sent word to Bartholomew Badlesmere that they'd not assist him. Thomas Lancaster did not even reply to his pleas.

Leeds fell within a week. Edward's subsequent justice was swift and merciless. He ordered the castellan of Leeds, Walter Culpepper, tied to the tail of a horse, dragged from the castle, and hanged from its drawbridge alongside a dozen other garrison leaders. Then, leading a triumphant army, the king returned to London. Lady Badlesmere and her family rode with him and upon arrival were packed off to the Tower of London. Appealing again to Thomas Lancaster and Roger Mortimer, Bartholomew Badlesmere tried unsuccessfully to raise a force against his king.

Edward's magnates were astonished by his uncharacteristic brutality at Leeds. This was the first application of martial law to internal discord, and the implications were terrifying. Opposition to a king might no longer culminate in the chance to at least be heard in a court of law but rather in the immediate loss of one's head. Baronial strength was now so divided that Edward was certain he could obtain enough support to do as he pleased, and he moved swiftly to take advantage of his unaccustomed position of strength. Now he was certain it was just a matter of time before he would once again gaze into the face of his beloved "Nephew Hugh."

EIGHT

fter issuing a warrant for Bartholomew Badlesmere's arrest and the arrests of the leading marcher barons, King Edward traveled west. He was accompanied by many of the lords who'd rallied to his side at Leeds. Richard stayed in Kent to oversee Badlesmere's lands, currently in the hands of royal keepers. He was appointed constable of Dover Castle and traveled to Chilham Castle, where he set up primary residence. Chilham was Badlesmere's birthplace and had been granted to him by the king in 1312, but Badlesmere was an outlaw now.

Richard enjoyed Chilham Castle, not only because of its peaceful atmosphere but for its proximity to Phillip Rendell. Phillip's quiet companionship provided a calming influence, and these days Richard was often in need of calming. On December 8 his brother had ruled the decree banishing the Despensers invalid and officially recalled them to England. The marcher lords, led by Roger Mortimer, immediately hurried north to Thomas Lancaster, seeking active support against Edward's treachery. Lancaster accused the Despensers of piracy and the king of supporting them. He gave his royal cousin until December 20 to respond to his accusations, but Edward was done with negotiating. Sensing that their sovereign's star was in the ascendancy, several of his former marcher enemies rode to Cirencester, where Edward resided, and officially submitted to him. Lancaster's knights and bannerets, increasingly upset over Thomas's treatment of their king, also began deserting him. Well pleased with events, Edward made plans for Christmas, and afterward, for a final confrontation with his nemesis.

Angry and hurt over his brother's actions, Richard endeavored to stay as far removed from political events as possible. He took to spending much time at Fordwich, where spiced malmsey and laughter flowed freely and the machinations of Edward could temporarily be forgotten. Hugh d'Arderne, with his knowledge of everything from alchemy and philosophy to travel, proved an interesting conversationalist; the burgeoning relationship between Michael Hallam and Eleanora provided secret amusement, and little Tom was an enjoyable substitute for the royal princes, whom he missed. Only Maria Rendell caused Richard a measure of disquiet. She had grown into a true beauty, with a lushness to her face and form that made Richard think of bed sport, though her innocence was as apparent. This rare mixture of sensuality and unaffectedness accounted for Maria's appeal, but he forced himself not to dwell on her. Surrounded as he was by servants, courtiers, and sycophants who desired his company only for the material gain it might bring them, Richard knew how dearly bought was true friendship. Only two men would he completely trust with his life or his love—Michael Hallam and Phillip. No woman, no matter how desirable, could be worth the price of a friendship.

On the afternoon of December 21, Maria bundled up little Tom and rode to Fordwich town. Phillip was trying to finish Tom's Christmas gift, a set of wooden weapons, and found it impossible with Tom relentlessly trailing him.

Hoping to please her husband, Maria had suggested the excursion. "Today is also the feast day of Tom's namesake, Thomas the apostle, so I might surprise him with a visit to

Fordwich's quay and the George and Dragon for a pork pasty."

Phillip rewarded her with a smile, and Maria left Fordwich Castle in an ebullient mood. Sometimes she sensed in her husband a distancing, even a disapproval of her, which made her strive ever harder to earn his love. Since Richard of Sussex's nightly visits, the withdrawal seemed even more pronounced. Is it because Lord Sussex is usurping my position, she wondered, or because their frequent blathering about the wonders of travel is making Phillip restless? Maria could only surmise and worry. Not knowing what, if anything, was truly wrong made trying to please her husband as frustrating as tilting at shadows.

Tom chattered all the way into Fordwich town, his normally quiet nature disappearing in the holiday excitement. He pointed and questioned and bounced about in Maria's arms until he stood in danger of falling off Facebelle, a dainty gray mare she'd received from Phillip on their fourth wedding anniversary.

"Now once we get to town, sweetheart, we must stop at Dame Dane's for a beaver hat to warm grandpere's ears. Then we must see Sara the Churchkeeper, for she makes sewing gloves just the way Aunt Eleanora likes."

"And what shall I get for m-my saint's day, mama?" Whenever Tom was excited he tended to stutter.

"You'll just have to wait, darlin'. If I tell you now 'twill spoil the surprise."

The road was muddy and framed with piles of rust-colored snow. On either side of Moat and Well Lane spread tracts of farmland belonging to St. Augustine's Abbey, land that had once belonged to the d'Ardernes. Every time Maria passed the land or thought of the Leopard's Head in Sturry, which had been sold to Abbot Fyndunne, she remembered her mother. Maria misliked thinking of Henrietta, for it dredged up all sorts of ambivalent feelings. How could a mother not love her child? she wondered, as she glanced down at Tom's curly head. 'Tis as impossible to comprehend as the majesty of God.

Fordwich town was in a festive mood. Pine wreaths laced with ribbons hung on front doors, as did clusters of mistletoe, and when they reached Sara the Churchkeeper's on King Street a group of children gathered neath the widow's window were singing:

> Wassail, wassail through the town,
> If you've got any apples throw them down.
> Up with the stocking and down with the shoe,
> If you've got no apples, money will do!

Dame Sara flung open her shutters and, laughing, dropped fruit into each outstretched bag. A chorus of thank you's, and the children continued on toward Father Langeley's.

"C-can I do that, mama?" Tom cried as they dismounted at the corner of King and High Streets. "What exactly are they doing?"

"They are going mumping." Bending down, Maria pulled her son's mantle closer about his neck against the cold. "Children go mumping, poppet, in honor of your saint. Thomas is the finest saint in all the world, as you are the finest son." She kissed the top of his head.

"Look, mama! M-might I have one of those?" He pointed behind her to three ancient women hobbling past Watergate House toward them. They carried baskets lined with evergreens and flowers and filled with crude Advent images shaped in the form of Christ and the Virgin.

"May I have one, m-mama, may I?"

"But we have no presents to give the women in return and 'tis traditional to . . ."

"Please, mama. For my feast day."

Maria could not resist his pleading. Motioning to the women, who immediately stopped and began exclaiming over Tom, she rummaged in her coin purse and handed her son three pennies. Toothless grins greeted the coins Tom carefully placed in each palm. The ladies then handed him an Advent image, as well as a sprig of evergreen to prevent toothache. After they sang "The Seven Joys of Mary," Maria invited them to Fordwich Castle, as was customary, for such women brought good luck.

"Was that not nice?" she asked, after they departed. Leaning over, she pretended to minutely inspect the roughly carved statues. "We'll place them neath the cross above your bed."

"Good afternoon, Lady Maria." Richard of Sussex reined in his white palfrey before them. He was dressed in deep blue, edged with red, and Maria's first involuntary thought was how masculine, how vividly alive he looked contrasted to the drab sky and gray day. A chill wind tugged at his hair; his beard lent an arrogant cast to his face. She suddenly thought of Eleanora's reaction upon first viewing their lord. "He is the golden knight of my dreams," she'd said. When Maria thought on her sister's words, she felt a thrill of foreboding. What has Richard to do with me? she wondered. And why in his presence did she sometimes feel slightly breathless?

Crossing his hands across the pommel of his saddle, Richard studied her with more familiarity than during his nightly visits. Away from Fordwich and Phillip he felt more free to enjoy Maria's presence, to openly admire her beauty. In the middle of a busy street what harm could come of it? "'Tis a pleasant surprise to meet you so unexpectedly, m'lady."

"Good day, my lord." A cart rumbled past, followed by a yapping dog. She pulled her son closer to Fordwich's Watergate House, away from the road and the curious stares that the earl's presence always created. The Sturry Prostitute, Meg Smythe, passed on her way to the George and Dragon. Maria saw Richard's startled look as he noticed the prostitute. He will mark on my resemblance to her, Maria thought, feeling increasingly uncomfortable. Instead Richard exchanged a look with Michael Hallam, who shook his head and turned away, a glum expression on his face.

"'Tis my feast day, sire, did you know?" Tom piped. "Mama brought me to town for treats."

Following a last glance after the prostitute, Richard dismounted and bent down to Tom's level. "Why 'tis so, Tommy-trot. And what a grand saint Thomas was." During the past weeks a special bond had developed between the earl and Tom. Even Maria, who resented Richard's visits, had to admit he treated her son with touching gentleness.

"Now, Tommy-trot, tell me about your patron saint." The hem of Richard's tunic brushed the muddy road.

"He built buildings, he did. Fine ones. M-mama told me all about them. And one time a king in a far-off land asked him to build a beautiful palace, so Thomas agreed, and the king gave him a castle full of gold."

Laughing, Richard glanced up at Maria. His manner was friendly without being overintimate, though she found it difficult to respond in a totally natural way.

"And what did St. Thomas do with all the king's gold, Tommy-trot?"

"He spent it on the poor and the king had him killed."

"What a smart lad you are!" Richard ruffled his hair, then stood. Reaching inside his tunic he withdrew his coin purse. "I have not with me a castle filled with gold, but I hope this will please you."

He placed in Tom's hand several coins, which the boy studied with wide-eyed delight.

"Thank you, sire. You've pleased him greatly." Maria made an elaborate ritual of removing the now forgotten Advent images from Tom's other hand. The directness of Richard's gaze unnerved her and made conversation near impossible. "Now, darlin', we must be getting to Dame Sara's for Eleanora's sewing gloves. Thank Sir Richard and then . . ."

"And what would you desire from me, Lady Rendell?"

Stunned by the question, Maria was even more unprepared for the challenge in Richard's voice. Or did she imagine it?

"What would you have from your liege lord this Christmas?" Richard was near as surprised as she that he had spoken so boldly. "'Tis customary that I present gifts to my vassals," he quickly added, "and you all have pleased me greatly these past weeks."

Tom tugged at her hand. The sounds of festive singing crescendoed from the nearby Give-ale House.

Maria's eyes searched Richard's face. He was right, of course. A man's greatness was partially determined by his extravagance to those about him. She groped about for some innocuous reply, but her mind remained blank. A priest passed and, after a curious stare, disappeared inside Watergate House. Abbot Fyndunne sometimes stayed at Watergate. "I want the Leopard's Head," she blurted.

"And what might the Leopard's Head be?"

"A manor house in Sturry. It belonged to our family for a hundred years. Papa had to sell it to Abbot Fyndunne and the Canterbury monks."

Though a smile curved Richard's lips, he studied her intently. "I know Abbot Fyndunne well. We dine together whene'er I visit Sturry."

Probably at our house, Maria thought. Aloud, "I want the Leopard's Head back."

She was not even sure why she asked. Since her marriage, the fortunes of Fordwich had improved somewhat. Am I trying to prove something to mother? she wondered. That I need not marriage to an old man to prosper? Why should Henrietta's approval matter, and why after nearly five years should Maria be thinking of Edmund Leybourne? Both dead. A sudden shiver, which had naught to do with the wind, raced through her.

"You surprise me," Richard said. "Phillip told me you were without ambitions."

She was stung by the implied criticism. She did sound bold and grasping—as grasping as the Despensers. And the entire idea was ridiculous.

Tom tugged at her arm. "Hurry, mama, so I can show my gold to papa."

She wanted to tell Richard she'd changed her mind, to ask

for something sensible like a mantle or bracelet or ear bobs—or better yet nothing at all. Instead she allowed Tom to pull her past him, up the street. What a fool you must find me, she thought. Though I care not.

On Christmas Eve Richard arrived at Fordwich like the magi, bearing gifts. As Richard strode into the great hall he was followed by Michael Hallam, whose arms were burdened with presents wrapped in blue cloth edged in gold.

Eleanora's cheeks flushed a becoming pink. Unconsciously she smoothed the folds of her kirtle and, as she took the presents from Michael, smiled up at him. More surprisingly, to Maria at least, Michael smiled back. Richard's squire possessed a fierceness of face and manner that belied any of the softer virtues. 'Twill take a wilder nature than yours, sister, Maria thought, to tame that one.

"Has the weather cleared?" Hugh asked as he took Richard's mantle. "This morning the snow looked as if 'twould last a week."

"'Tis a beautiful night." Richard stomped the snow clinging to his boots. "I'll wager 'twas on just such an even that our Blessed Savior was born.

After they left the hall for the more cozy solar and settled in around its fire, Hugh dipped them each a bowl of wassail from the cauldron bubbling over the flames. Richard then proceeded to hand them their gifts, all save Maria. Stung by the affront, she pretended great interest in Tom's present, a miniature wooden army. As her son carefully inspected each tiny knight in helm and hauberk astride his painted warhorse, she felt a twinge of anger. Not only was Richard being rude but the gloves and cap she'd so painstakingly fashioned for Tom would never provoke such excitement as this army.

"Look here, daughter." Hugh hobbled over to her. "My lord Sussex gave me a copy of Walter Henley's *Stewardship*.

Another book! Is that not grand?" Hugh loved to read, but books were so expensive his library contained only two other manuscripts.

Maria tried to muster the appropriate enthusiasm as she did over Eleanora's carved sewing box, crammed with everything from needles to fine scissors of Toledo steel. In a removable compartment lay a dozen sewing gloves.

"They are from Dame Sara's. I heard you well liked her gloves." For the first time Richard looked at Maria. She looked away. Soon his slight would be apparent. Not even a man of Richard's stature could buy from Mother Church what was not for sale. Besides, Maria was certain he had not even tried. Soon the questions would begin and she would have to explain the brazen cupidity of her request. Would Phillip, too, react as Richard had done? *I thought you were without ambition, wife. I see I am mistaken.*

Phillip stood before the fireplace inspecting a palm-size globe. The world's countries, outlined in silver and gold, shimmered in the light from the flames. *You've never gazed at me with such delight,* Maria thought, watching him, *not even when we are making love.*

"The countries you've visited I had outlined in silver," Richard said.

"There is more gold than silver here." Phillip's fingers traced the boundaries of nations.

"Aye," Richard said. "'Twould seem you still have a bit of traveling to do." He then turned to Maria.

"You have not yet received your present, Lady Rendell. I've saved the best for last."

Reluctantly she accepted from him a package shaped like a book. Whatever its contents she felt like throwing it—along with Phillip's globe—into the fire.

"Thank you, sire." She made no move to open it.

"Come along, daughter," Hugh said. "Let us all see what our lord has given you."

Reluctantly, she removed the cloth, which revealed an

unadorned leather-bound document. Aye, a book.

"Look inside, m'lady," Richard said.

A folded parchment nestled within. A deed. With trembling fingers she removed the ribbon, but she did not need to read the ornate Latin script to know its contents. "You did it," she whispered. "I had not thought such a thing possible."

"There are always ways."

Phillip moved closer. "What has our lord given you, wife?"

"The deed for the Leopard's Head. My lord and I were talking . . . 'twas a stupid request I should not have made. But you actually did it." She grinned. "Jesu, I'll wager Abbot Fyndunne was most displeased!"

"I have seen happier men."

"I had not known you two had discussed this matter." Phillip's manner was wary, like a stag alert to a sudden change in the wind.

"We did not, really," Richard said. "'Twas just something mentioned in passing." He bent to help little Tom set a knight properly astride his destrier.

Phillip turned his back to both Richard and his wife. Forgotten globe still in hand, he stared into the fire.

After a tipsy Hugh was helped to bed, and Phillip carried a sleepy Tom to his chamber, they set off for midnight mass at St. Mary the Virgin. The night was beautiful. By mutual agreement, they left the horses stabled and walked into Fordwich town. Nearly six inches of fresh snow covered the ground. The moonlight, reflected off its pristine mantle, caused the surrounding area to appear bright as a new day. Piles of snow banked the road and stretched unbroken to Oldridge Wood.

Fordwich lay hidden by a low-hanging haze of smoke. Cracks of light leaked through shuttered windows, an anemic match for the brilliant stars powdering the heavens. On nearby Tancrey Island a huge plume of smoke hung suspended in the air, frozen against the cobalt sky.

"Look, Eleanora. I'll wager the de Marinis family is out ice-skating. Perhaps after mass we might visit."

Maria's sister walked ahead, escorted on one arm by the earl, the other his squire. "Aye. This very moment Dickon is probably hanging a cauldron of wassail over the fire." She laughed. Around Richard and Michael Hallam she felt witty and happy and as pretty as her sister. As they reminisced about childhood Christmases she found herself conversing with both of them as effortlessly as she might address her maids or her family.

"My Christmases were sometimes other than pleasant," Richard said, as they turned on Moat Lane. "Not only was father busy with his second family and affairs of state I believe he often perceived my presence as an embarrassment better left in the background."

"And though we were landed folk," Michael said, "we were poor as the meanest villein. Christmas was just another day of struggle for us."

"And how were your Christmases, my love?" Maria turned to Phillip, who had joined in little of the conversation. She sensed from him a disapproval that she assured herself must be imagined. He had no true reason to be displeased with her.

Her husband was gazing up at the stars, an awed expression softening his features. Maria followed his eyes but saw only a half moon surrounded by a sprinkling of stars. What was he looking at, what was he thinking? Was he deliberately ignoring her?

"Don't you ponder what the stars are like?" His voice was husky with wonder. "Whether they are hot or cold, smooth like glass or made similar to our earth?"

Maria's grip tightened on his arm. He wasn't thinking of her at all.

"Sometimes," Phillip continued, "I wish I had wings so I could fly up to them. Mayhaps they are populated, too, with people just like us."

At one time Maria had not found such wonderings annoying or threatening. But we are no longer children, she thought. We cannot forever be stargazers. "Since our earth is the center of the universe," she began reasonably. "and Christ died for man's sins, I think 'tis proof enough we are unique."

"But 'tis such a vast space," Phillip persisted. "Don't you sometimes wonder at what is out there? Once in Constantinople I met an astronomer, and the wondrous things he knew! He told me . . ."

"I thank the Lord you have no way of reaching the stars," Maria interrupted. "Or you'd soon be planning a journey there." She removed her arm from his and completed the walk alone, silently berating both her husband and Richard. If you had not presented Phillip with that globe, perhaps he'd not now be yearning to soar to the stars. If only I could physically squeeze all such thoughts from your head, she thought, and replace them with contentment. Maria sighed. Increasingly she felt she knew her husband not at all.

The church of St. Mary the Virgin was festive with wreaths, boughs, and a multitude of garlands. Pine branches as well as red and gold ribbons were wrapped round the banners of St. Christopher and St. George. While the church had long condemned such artifices as heathen, they remained popular. Even the Fordwich Stone, reputed to be the tomb of St. Augustine, was covered with mistletoe, the tree from which Christ's crucifix had been fashioned.

Father Langleye, who had recently replaced ailing Father Eustace, elevated the communion host. Maria thought of the Leopard's Head and looked to her mother's tomb topped by a marble effigy, also elaborately decorated. You would be pleased with me, mother. I am turning into your daughter after all.

The mass continued, and as she joined the other celebrants in song, Maria became aware of Richard's voice rising pure above the rest. The earl stood beside Eleanora and, in contrast to her drabness, blazed like a torch. No wonder all eyes are drawn to you, she thought. He seemed oblivious to the stares and nudges of the villagers, however, and appeared totally absorbed by the mass. He sang the long responses with an emotion that seemed to Maria quite out of character with the man she believed him to be. One would believe Richard devout and most certainly moved, this Christmas Eve.

What manner of man are you? she wondered, studying the earl through lowered lashes. Earlier he'd given to Mayor Knyght for Fordwich's poor; he'd given the Leopard's Head to her. Richard of Sussex wore a multitude of conflicting faces—under which resided the real earl?

"Drink Heil!"

"Wassail!"

"Jesu!" Maria said as she downed a second bowl of steaming wassail. "You've made this, Dickon, stout enough to revive a dead man." Her world was beginning to appear fuzzy around the edges.

After mass, they'd walked to Tancrey Island to visit the de Marinis family, and liberally toast Christmas morn. Eleanora was also feeling the wassail's effect, for she leaned against Michael Hallam for support. Maria's own eyelids felt heavy, her body warm and tingly. Her heart overflowed with holiday cheer, though Richard, for one, appeared glum this night. The earl stood apart from everyone, tossing snowballs into the fire, watching their disintegration with apparent fascination. Without warning he lifted his eyes from the fire to Maria. She raised her bowl in a mock toast before collapsing against a portion of rock wall. Closing her eyes, she listened to the laughter and shouts of skaters who gracefully maneuvered on the ice with bones tied to their feet. Phillip was talking with Dickon, something about the de Marinis apiaries. Tancrey Island possessed the finest honey for miles around—and Phillip's voice made no more sense to Maria than that of a droning bee.

Placing her half-filled bowl in one of the bee boles that had been cut at right angles into the wall, she approached Richard. The earl's head appeared crowned by the flames in a golden halo; his face remained half hidden in shadow.

"You are looking a bit sour for Christmas morn, my lord."

Richard shrugged. "'Tis my usual state these days." He looked beyond Maria to the darkness. The Leopard's Head had been a foolish mistake. He should never have wrangled it from Abbot Fyndunne, for he was certain the whole incident would cause naught but trouble. He had allowed his attraction to a woman to cloud his judgment and possibly harm his relationship with a friend. At this moment Richard hated Maria.

"I should have spent Christmas at Cirencester, I think," he said softly.

"Are you bored with our humble pleasures, sire? I thought you and my husband were the best of friends."

"If I am bored, m'lady, 'tis not because of Phillip."

She was stung by the remark, which she interpreted as a thinly veiled jibe against herself. "Then why do you not join your brother?"

"Perhaps my purposes have been better suited hereabouts," he replied. "But you presume much when you dare question me." His look sent chills down Maria's spine. "You'd do well, Lady Rendell, never to presume where Richard the Bastard is concerned."

NINE

fter Christmas, King Edward moved north in a
final campaign to crush Thomas Lancaster and
all those who had stood against him.

Roger Mortimer and his lords, lacking money,
troops, and after waiting in vain for Lancaster's
promised help, surrendered to the king on January 23, 1322.
Under heavy guard Mortimer was packed off to the Tower of
London. The imprisonment of the fiercest marcher lord
frightened most of the other rebels into surrender. Castles
began to fall, knights to desert. The remaining marchers fled
north to Pontefract, where Thomas Lancaster sat as if
paralyzed, allowing his allies to be captured and Edward to
march north virtually unimpeded. After only token resistance
the earl's great castles of Kenilworth and Tutbury fell. Rumors
of Lancaster's involvement with the Scots had long circulated
and his retainers bore little allegiance to a lord who made
secret agreements with their enemy. At Tutbury, Edward
uncovered evidence that confirmed those rumors and marked
Lancaster as traitor—correspondence with Scotland's king,
Robert the Bruce.

Finally, Thomas had no choice but to bolt for his northern-
most castle of Dunstanburgh. On March 16 he and a troop of
seven hundred men reached Boroughbridge in Yorkshire. On
the north bank of the River Ure, spanned by a bridge so narrow

an armor-clad knight could scarce cross, awaited Edward's troops. They were jointly commanded by Andrew Harclay, governor of Carlisle, and Richard of Sussex. Since January Richard had traveled with Edward, but when the Despensers had rejoined him at Lichfield a fortnight past he had ridden north. For now, at least, Richard and his brother must remain united; now Thomas Lancaster was within their grasp.

On March 17, 1322, following a battle in which most of his commanders had been killed, Thomas of Lancaster crossed Boroughbridge and, under a flag of truce, surrendered. Richard accepted his cousin's sword with an emotion approaching disbelief. These past years, as England had been torn with internal strife, the cause of that strife had become embodied in Richard's mind by one man. Thomas Lancaster had gradually metamorphosed from flesh and blood to an evil, brooding presence, lurking in the bleakness of the Yorkshire moors, awaiting the proper moment to sweep south and annihilate his enemies. This day, however, Richard saw a hesitant man with slightly stooped shoulders, gray in his beard, and weary eyes—eyes in color not unlike his own. Richard almost felt sorry for him.

King Edward sat in the middle of Pontefract's great hall, surrounded by clerks and courtiers, and to his right, Hugh Despenser the Younger. Before them with head bowed and hands tied behind his back stood Thomas of Lancaster, steward of England. Thomas had just emerged from several days in Pontefract's Swillington Tower and looked nearer dead than living. Today, March 22, the earl of Lancaster stood before his peers no longer as their equal, but as a condemned criminal. In the past he'd broken bread with each of the barons—young Edmund Plantagenet, earl of Kent and Edward's legitimate half brother, the earls of Pembroke, Sturry, Arundel, and Richard of Sussex. Nine months ago, he'd entered Westminster in triumph, during the Parliament of the White Bands. Now he would not even be able to offer a defense for the charges put before him. Like Lucifer when driven from heaven, Thomas Lancaster had fallen far.

A young clerk read the summation of charges, a long list containing only one truly treasonable offense—his alliance with the Scots. Seated with the other barons, Richard found his attention wandering. Never would he understand his cousin's love of Pontefract, which was a gloomy, graceless place. One of the strongest inland garrisons in the kingdom, the eight-towered castle perched atop eight acres of rock, beneath which existed many natural subterranean chambers. From a rectangular stained and leaded window, light streamed onto the stone floor in shimmering patches, partially alleviating the interior's murkiness. Today was one of those rare spring days that would be unmarred by rain. Would it be better to die on such a day or in dreary winter, Richard wondered, when the world is cloaked in gray and the cold seeps into the bones so that no fire could bake it out? If I could choose the day to die . . .

The clerk, reading the document that would cost Lancaster his life, was obviously bored. "With banners displayed," he recited in a singsong manner, "as in open war, in a hostile manner resisted . . . and hindered our sovereign lord the king . . . for three whole days so that they could not pass over the bridge of Burton-upon-Trent . . . and there feloniously slew some of the king's men."

Richard looked at Thomas's brother, Henry, seated in the shadows. Henry was obviously in torment over his brother, as well as the shame that had befallen the House of Lancaster. I must see that Henry does not pay for Thomas's sin, Richard thought. If his fate is left up to Edward, he'll die of neglect.

Not until the clerk referred to Piers Gaveston and his death did the king, who had feigned indifference throughout the entire proceedings, even look at Lancaster. Now his body went rigid, his expression became suffused with hatred. 'Tis not really any "understanding" with the Scots or thwarting of the king's dictates that has sealed Thomas's fate, Richard thought, but his part in Piers's death, nearly a decade past.

"This is a powerful court and great in authority." Thomas cried out, speaking for the first time, "where no answer is heard or given."

His Majesty fixed Thomas with a contemptuous smile. "This is the usual summary process of martial law, as you must know, cousin. A defendant is not allowed to make a defense once his offenses have been recognized by witnesses."

Richard ran a hand across his brow and sat up straighter, trying to shake off his fatigue. He'd not had a full night's sleep since the Despensers' arrival at Lichfield. Edward's open hatred bothered him. Should not hatred, no matter how justified, be tempered with justice, if not mercy? Was it true that men of Edward's proclivities were vengeful creatures, or just that human love knew no reason? Besides, Lancaster had touched on something that worried Richard. There were those who said that the entire trial was illegal because martial law had not been in effect at the time of Tom's capture. The courts had been sitting so it could not be definable as "time of war." Nor had Edward ever unfurled his banners, a second requirement. When he'd been readying to do so he'd been stopped by Nephew Hugh who feared that if time of war were declared and Edward lost the last battle he and his father would immediately lose their heads.

"Wherefore our sovereign lord," droned the clerk, picking at a tear in his tunic, ". . . having duly weighed the great enormities and offenses . . . has no manner of reason to show any mercy . . ."

Richard stifled a yawn. A man will today lose his life, history is being made, and I cannot even stay awake. He arched his back, uncomfortable because of the backless bench. If I could but whisk you back to happier times I would do that for you, Tom, or rush you past your judgment to when you are moldering in your grave and will not care. But I cannot. The world will not pause, the clerk will not cease worrying his tear, and time will not wait, even for one moment—not for you, Thomas, nor me, nor any other man.

The final verdict was delivered by the royal justice. "Because you are most highly and nobly descended," the official read, "you shall not be drawn and hanged but execution shall be done upon you by beheading."

"You cannot do this," Thomas cried out. "You cannot execute someone of royal blood. 'Tis without precedent. You might dispossess me, but you cannot murder me."

Two knights rushed forward. One held Thomas while a second jerked a hood over his face.

"I can do anything I please, cousin!" Edward called after him as he was dragged out of the hall. He turned to Hugh Despenser and grinned as if he'd just related the ending to a favorite joke.

Thomas might have been weak and foolish, Richard thought, turning away from his brother's triumph, but he is not alone. It was not only the lack of sleep that made him so bone weary.

While the sun was yet high and the day mild, Thomas of Lancaster was taken to St. Thomas Hill. He made the journey on the back of a gray pony and was pelted with stones and offal by subjects who'd previously cheered him.

"King Arthur," some shouted, in obvious reference to the *nom de plume* he'd used in his correspondence with Robert the Bruce, "where are your knights to help you now?"

Richard, who rode behind, turned to Michael Hallam. "Good Englishmen all, are they not? Their loyalty does not extend past these last several minutes."

Michael looked gloomier than ever. "Aye, m'lord. Their favor, as well as their stench, shifts with the wind."

At that moment Lancaster, who'd been silent, swayed in his saddle and called out, "King of heaven, grant me Thy mercy, for the king of earth has forsaken me!"

Atop St. Thomas Hill the executioner's block was ready. The

trembling earl, flanked on either side by Sussex and Hallam and several others, dismounted from the pony and knelt beside the block, facing east.

Two more minutes and your world will be ended, Richard thought. What does it matter now that you are a traitor when you will lose you life? No more will you breathe the sweet English air, see the wispy clouds crossing the sky, track a starling, hold a woman, hear the voices of your children . . .

Though his thoughts were his own, he addressed Thomas in a flat emotionless voice. "Place your traitorous head not to the east but toward the north, cousin. Look you in the direction of your friends, the Scots."

Richard closed his eyes when the ax fell.

The Parliament of York met in May. Clergy, barons, and commons were represented, but few barons attended. Some, like Phillip Rendell, had chosen to stay away; others were dead or imprisoned. The missing magnates made Edward's will that much easier to execute. The subsequent Statute of York left the king virtually free to do as he pleased. Nor was anything done about the matters that had originally sparked his barons' rebellion. The Hugh Despensers took active part in all matters. At Parliament's end Hugh the Elder was made earl of Winchester, though fear of the marcher lords, even in prison, withheld from the younger Hugh the title—if not the authority—of the earl of Gloucester.

To Richard the titles were the last outrage in an increasing list of acts that ranged from bizarre to truly dangerous. As he awaited his brother's arrival from a late night of gambling with Nephew Hugh, Richard crossed to a window in the small chamber of York Castle. A sudden gust of wind rattled the window shutters. He felt a cold blast of evening air, heard a low rumbling of thunder. The threatening storm well matched his mood.

"Pour us both some wine, Michael," he said and, as his

squire moved to obey, stared unseeing into the night. The world had gone awry, was spiraling downward into madness. Edward's revenge had careened beyond the bounds of reason. He and Hugh had ignored the laws of the land and the results were nightmarish. Not only did England's magnates tremble over his actions but ordinary people as well. And I am frightened, too, Richard thought, accepting the wine goblet from Michael. Horrible precedents were daily being set. Edward would be remembered not only for Bannockburn but also the atrocities that were being committed in the wake of Thomas Lancaster's execution. On the same day as the earl's death, a group of northern retainers had been hanged. At Bristol, Gloucester, Windsor, Cambridge, Wales, and Cardiff multiple executions had occurred. To terrify the rebels' vassals Edward had ordered the executions to take place where they held their lordship, a novel, albeit ghoulish, idea. Though in the past hanging, drawing, and quartering had been limited, with two exceptions, to foreign rebels, multiple Englishmen had already suffered the same fate.

A jagged bolt of lightning came to ground seemingly in York's courtyard. In the fireplace a log crumbled; flames shot upward. Richard stared into the darkness as a scattering of rain rattled on the roof tiles. Never had he felt such bleakness. 'Twas as if he'd glimpsed into Edward's soul and found there a blackness as yawning and infinite as the night. In Kent, Bartholomew Badlesmere had been dragged by his horse though Canterbury to the crossroads at Bleen. There he'd been hanged though not dropped and allowed to nearly strangle before being revived with vinegar. Then his belly had been cut open, his entrails drawn out and burnt before him. Finally Badlesmere had been beheaded and his body cut into quarters. As a silent reminder of Edward's justice, his head had been stuck on Canterbury's Burgate. Bartholomew's fate had been repeated elsewhere, indiscriminately it seemed, and the randomness of the punishment frightened Richard, everyone, as much as the manner of death. Sixty-two barons were imprisoned in obscure castles, but worse, wives, children, even elderly relatives were also incarcerated. Such acts were not only ludicrously petty but previously unheard of.

The rain began an intermittent patter, gradually increasing in intensity. Opening the window attached by hinges, Richard leaned out over the sill, breathing in the cool night, the moisture, the purity of new falling rain. Night and day still appear, he told himself, and rain and sunshine as they should. Crops are growing in the fields and ewes dropping their lambs. 'Tis only man that has gone awry.

At that moment Edward entered, his face flushed with wine and good cheer. "Close that window, brother. You'll be soaked with rain. And 'tis a fine storm we'll be having, will it not?" He motioned for Michael to pour him some wine. His manner was nervously ebullient, for he was certain Richard would do naught but berate him this night. Increasingly their time together consisted of verbal bickering, as tedious as his quarrels with Isabella, and he had taken to avoiding his brother. If he wanted criticism he could recall Parliament.

Blue-white lightning forked across a boiling sky. The wall torches sputtered, danced, and dimmed. Richard closed the window and turned to him.

"I am leaving court, sire. I am going south, to Chilham and Dover. I have business there."

"What business?" Lifting a poker from the hearth, Edward thrust it at the blazing fire. "You did not tell me."

"I cannot countenance what is happening with you. You no longer listen to me and I will not watch you destroy yourself and your kingdom."

The king turned to him with a nervous laugh. "Do not be dramatic, Richard. It ill becomes you. You just want to criticize me over Parliament or my friends, and I'll not listen. You are unfair to me and Hugh also. He only wished to govern well by making my administration more efficient, by helping me bring more money into England's treasury. What harm is there in that?"

"Aye," Richard said bitterly. "Hugh is a true champion of the people."

"Did not we invite representatives of the commons in north and south Wales to Parliament so they might speak on behalf of their region, where all these accursed troubles began? That was Hugh's idea."

"And what about these barbaric executions? Are they Hugh's idea, also?"

"They were my enemies," Edward said sullenly.

"Englishmen are not hanged, drawn, and quartered. Englishmen are not imprisoned as it pleases you, or their wives and children. You even imprisoned Roger Mortimer's poor mother, by the rood, and she is near seventy years old. You cannot rule by tyranny, brother, for the people's hatred will someday overwhelm their fear. You must cease these executions, listen to the voice of Parliament, and . . ."

"Parliament!" Edward waved his hand. "'Tis useful only for raising taxes. Otherwise 'tis just a troublesome device used to thwart my rule at every turn. I can govern more peaceably without my barons always yapping at my heels like a pack of pesky dogs. I need not them to tell me how to run England."

"Nay, and how can they? Most of them no longer possess heads from which to voice their protests."

Edward poured himself a second cup of wine from the table near the fireplace. Outside the storm approached a crescendo, howling around corners, beating with angry fists against shutters and window, demanding entrance. I would prefer the storm outside to that within, he thought, gulping down his wine. Why cannot even Richard understand?

"My subjects will not soon forget what it means to rise against their rightful sovereign." The king's voice was little more than a whisper, hard to catch above the pounding rain. "No longer will I attempt to be loved, to be reasonable and just, for I'll not win their love anyway. They loved father, not me. Why? His rule was one continually of war. He left England's treasury so empty I've had to spend my reign like a beggar, living from hand to mouth, supplicating my barons, my bankers. This war, especially, proved humiliating beyond endurance. I could not pay my way. I was decried throughout the country and had to exist on whatever driblets of revenue the exchequer could send. Foreign bankers would not extend me credit; only the Bardis would lend me a few hundred marks or pounds here and there." He clenched his fist. "I'll no longer beg. I have the captured estates of my enemies and I will soon have England's treasury full to bursting, which is something father could never do."

"Do not dare bring up father," Richard cried, his restraint disappearing in a rush of anger. Though there were things that must never be said, especially between brothers, he was past the point of caring. "Tell me what you did on father's death."

Edward slammed his cup down on the table. "I will not talk about that."

"I was there when father was dying, just as you were, when he requested of you three things."

"Enough, I warn you," Edward doubled his fist. "Do not continue. You have no right to dig up things that best remain buried."

Richard faced him across the folding table. "'Do not recall Piers Gaveston without consent of Parliament,' father told you. Do you remember? 'Send one hundred knights to the Holy Land carrying my heart,' he said, and 'Wrap my bones in a hammock so that you can carry them before you to victory in battle.'"

"Aye, I'll not forget," Edward cried. "Even in death father thought himself superior to me." He began to pace the narrow room. "I hated him, I did—always lecturing me, filling my head with shoulds and should nots, and criticizing me because I could never measure up."

[123]

"You did not even try. There was no trip to the Holy Land, no bones, and Piers was recalled before father was cold in his grave. No wonder your reign is cursed."

Edward wheeled on him, his face white. "What did you say?"

"Listen well to the wind outside, brother. Mayhaps 'tis not the wind at all, but father crying for justice."

"Such nonsense!" Edward snapped, but he glanced beyond Richard to the rain-streaked window. "It seems you have forgotten to whom you speak. I am king of England, dear brother, and what are you? Some bastard pup that father begat between the legs of a serving maid."

They faced each other, their breathing ragged in the ugly silence.

Striving for calm, Richard inhaled deeply, then motioned to Michael Hallam. "My men are awaiting me at the outskirts of York, Your Majesty. I request your permission to join them."

Edward spread his hands in supplication. "Let us not fight, please. I hate it when we bicker. I did not mean what I said."

"But I did." Without waiting to be dismissed, Richard left York Castle and his brother the king.

TEN

ichard spent the next months in Kent. Deliberately he remained detached from events involving his brother. No reason to become upset over Edward's actions when he was helpless to change them. Better not to know. After his initial anger had faded, however, Richard found that he missed Edward and often toyed with attempting a reconciliation. But Edward seemed content with the company of Nephew Hugh and in planning another Scottish campaign to take place in the fall of 1322, so Richard busied himself at Chilham. Recently he'd been approached by several lords concerning a possible marriage alliance with Thomas Lancaster's wealthy niece, Beatrice. A marriage uniting Lancaster's house with the royalist cause seemed a possible way of healing some of England's still festering wounds. Dead, Thomas Lancaster was proving himself a more powerful adversary than in life. So many miracles had been reported at his tomb that Edward had ordered the entrance sealed. Many who'd once castigated Thomas now openly spoke of him as a saint and invoked his name in every conversation critical of the king and his policies.

To the talk of marriage, Richard said very little. Throughout his life, he'd been involved in dozens of similar negotiations, but all had come to naught. He was not adverse to the idea. A man in his position had not the luxury of marrying for love or staying a bachelor, and Richard did not question the fact that he must someday wed. A part of him even embraced it. Perhaps married, he thought, I'll forget Maria Rendell.

Since his return to Chilham Richard often hawked, hunted, or rode with Phillip, but he seldom went to Fordwich. He wanted no chance encounters with Maria that might lead to further foolish acts like those of last Christmas. He assured himself that his feelings for Maria were purely physical, a passing fancy, and events seemed to bear out that belief. He'd become involved with Meg Smythe, the Sturry Prostitute. Though initially Richard had found her resemblance to Maria intriguing, the prostitute's considerable physical charms kept him returning.

"Meg is no surrogate lover," he said to Michael Hallam, who stood guard during Richard's frequent visits to Meg's cottage.

"If you keep telling me, my lord, perhaps someday 'twill be so," Michael said glumly "but I doubt it." Victim of an unhappy marriage which he preferred to keep secret, Michael had little use for most women. Eleanora, however, at least possessed a measure of sense and no false airs. His lord's attraction to Lady Rendell could lead to naught but tragedy, of that he was certain. Though Michael also knew his lord would never intentionally hurt Phillip, women had a most unpleasant way of making men forget all about duty, obligation—and friendship.

As muster for Edward's Scottish campaign neared, Maria silently watched her husband readying his armor, his lance of ashwood, his mace, and a new shield made of hide and wood and painted with a blue wolf's head. Botulph the Smithy meticulously sharpened the edges of St. Michael, Phillip's sword. The very idea of another campaign, another leave-taking, terrified Maria, but when she sought reassurance, Phillip merely shrugged off her feelings or made light of her fears.

And I am a mass of fears, she thought as she followed her

husband to the stable area. She felt so distanced from him—
from everyone—so lost and alone. Michael Hallam spent more
time with Eleanora than Phillip did with her. Even little Tom
preferred riding with his father and Richard or talking with the
knights in Fordwich's barracks to spending a quiet moment
with her.

"I am naught but a glorified nurse," she griped to Eleanora.
"Tom only comes to me when he falls down or is out of sorts or
hungry. For anything else my own son does not even want me
around."

Eleanora merely laughed. "What boy prefers the company of
women? And what mother would truly want him to?"

Maria was annoyed that her sister treated the matter so
lightly and annoyed at her perpetually sunny mood. Mayhaps
you think Michael Hallam will marry you, she thought sourly.
But he is too devoted to Richard to make anyone a proper
husband. Not that Maria was any longer certain exactly what a
proper husband should be, or a proper wife for that matter. She
sensed in her marital relationship a steady deterioration, but
though she could not pinpoint the exact cause she blamed
Phillip.

If you would but speak to me, she thought as she watched
him lead out his destrier, Merlin, for inspection. Tell me you
love me, that you want nothing or no one but me and we would
be happy forever—for you are all I want. Increasingly she found
herself pushing him for reassurance, for the one phrase that
would cloak her in the security she needed and dissolve all her
doubts about his love. The more she pressed him, however, the
more pronounced his withdrawal. It seemed an endless circle.

You care more for your destrier than me, she thought, as she
watched Phillip run his hands along Merlin's broad crupper
and question the groom about the fit of the animal's chamfron.

"Hello, husband." When Phillip turned from the groom to
her, Maria thought she detected a measure of annoyance in his
eyes. "Are you so busy that you cannot spare me a moment?"

"What is wrong? Has something happened to Tom?"

"No, nothing is wrong with Tom. I would just spend time with you, since you are always off with Lord Sussex or someone, doing things that involve everyone but your wife."

His hand idly caressed Merlin's glossy neck. "I am busy, Maria. We can chat later." Phillip's voice possessed the same patient edge as when their son pestered overlong.

"'Tis obvious you take more pleasure in the company of your horse than me."

After glancing at the groom, who quickly bent to inspect the stirrups on Merlin's gilded saddle, Phillip faced her. "My life might soon depend on my horse. And I am not readying for battle because it pleases me, but because it is my duty, as you well know. A peasant's duty is to tend the fields, the clergy to tend men's souls, and a knight's to protect them all."

"I need not a lecture on duties," Maria retorted, "though often you do. You are eager enough to neglect a husband's duties when it suits you."

The groom moved away and pretended great interest in the bridles hanging upon the stable wall.

"I would say I know well enough my duties, wife. You seem to have forgotten yours, however. Your conduct is unseemly."

"I am weary to death of you men and the wars you so eagerly anticipate. Why cannot you do like papa? He paid a scutage so he would not have to serve and risk his brains being mashed to gruel by the Scots."

"Your father is old and crippled. He is not able to fight even if he would."

"I hate you," Maria cried, losing control. "Soon you'll go off and leave me without a thought to how I'll fare. You can prattle on forever about obligations, but you've always hidden behind it to do exactly as you please."

"Enough!" Phillip clenched his fist. Though he had never struck her, a husband had a perfect right to hit his wife whenever she displeased him. "You are turning into a shrew, Maria. I would rather spend my time fighting a battalion of Scots than be cut to ribbons by your tongue."

* * *

Following her quarrel with Phillip, Maria rode to the Leopard's Head. As her relationship with her husband worsened, she spent an increasing amount of time there. She found the quiet house with its memories of childhood more pleasant than current reality.

The Leopard's Head was located at the outskirts of Sturry Court above the River Stour. The court, owned by St. Augustine's Abbey, was a placid place. Chickens and geese scratched about the farmyard, milk cows peeked from the stables, a white-robed monk passed from the brew house to the lavatories while a handful of others clustered near the hall and abbot's chamber. Pleasant smells emanated from the bakehouse and kitchen. Beyond the stake-and-brushwood fence surrounding the court, tenant farmers worked the surrounding fields, harvesting grain to turn over to His Majesty's officials, who were securing such goods for the impending campaign by right of purveyance.

Dismounting, Maria handed Facebelle's reins to a waiting groom. The Leopard's Head, at least, was old and familiar, from the ivy gracing its wattle-and-daub walls to its roof shingles of oak tile and the carved leopard finials gracing the gable ends. As a child Maria had skipped through its narrow halls and played tag with Eleanora among the great boxes, tuns, and casks stored on ground level. During warm summer evenings they had tossed rocks into the nearby Stour from the window of their third-story garret room. It was here, in her childhood bedroom, where Maria spent most of her visits. Sinking down upon a bench positioned neath a narrow window, she looked out upon Sturry Court's buildings of flint and stone dressing, the golden fields of the tenant farmers, the yellow and white lilies glutting the water ditches. Though she had once found the stillness restrictive, like being too long in church, now Maria craved the quiet, so unlike her own turbulent thoughts.

"So much is wrong," she whispered. Her unhappiness

revolved around Phillip, of course. How could anything be right when the man she loved was indifferent to her? Were we ever close? she wondered. Or was I so besotted I did not long ago see your apathy? Only when they made love did she feel a measure of closeness, but the lovemaking itself provided a problem. If their union was blessed, why had they not conceived a second child? Tom was four years old now and she'd not even once been late with her monthly flux. She'd talked to Father Langleye but he'd only made her more confused. "A chaste marriage, like that of Mary and Joseph, is what God truly desires," he'd said. "But barring that, sex for procreation is not a sin. 'Tis only natural that you desire intercourse with your husband, for we know that the female, being imperfect, desires to be united with perfection, which is male. You must not make your husband desire you too greatly, however," he finished. "That would be committing adultery, which would displease God most heartily."

Sometimes Maria wondered whether their problems were not rooted in an event even more basic. Had Edmund Leybourne's death cursed their marriage? She'd wrestled with that possibility a hundred times, always discarding it, always returning to it. If I had obeyed mother, if I had not run away, would I be now blessed with more children?

"But I would not have Phillip," she whispered. "And without him, life would hold no meaning at all."

"Whore!"

A Dominican, who had approached from Sturry Court, stood in front of an astonished Maria. She had just left the interior of the Leopard's Head for the stables when the priest blocked her path. "What are you doing here, so near to sacred ground and dressed as a respectable woman—not the vermin you truly are?" The Dominican thrust his narrow face close to hers; his dark features were twisted with hatred. "Where are your stripes, creature, your hood of scarlet rey?"

"Father, I beg your pardon. I do not understand." Maria was bewildered and hurt by the man's words, his unprovoked rancor. "I . . . this is my property and I was just . . ."

Grabbing her arm, the Dominican dug his broken nails into her flesh. "You will burn in hell for your corruption, you and the Bastard both. Do not think that you have fooled me or Him." He pointed a grimy finger heavenward. "We have seen you, pressing putrid flesh to putrid flesh, and our wrathful Father will sentence you both to an eternity of torment for your sins."

"I do not know of what you speak. Please, just leave me in peace." Maria tried unsuccessfully to twist away from him. He smelled so strongly of sweat, garlic, and stale food her stomach turned. Holy men often disdained such physical comforts as bathing in order to mortify their flesh. "Are you mad, father? If you do not let go of me I will call for help, I swear."

Late afternoon shadows crawled across the road along which three riders were approaching. The bells from Sturry's church began booming out vespers. The priest raised his voice to an oratorical pitch. "You think I have not seen the Bastard leaving your brothel at all hours? Jesu, no wonder England is cursed, with such as he . . ."

"Leave go of her, priest, or I will slit your gullet."

Before the priest could respond, Richard of Sussex, who with Meg Smythe and Michael Hallam had been out riding, reined in his horse and hurriedly dismounted.

"There you are!" the Dominican cried. He stretched his corded neck at Richard until he looked like an angry rooster. "Fornicator! Blasphemer! Murderer! 'Tis corrupt whoresons such as you who have led our country from the path of righteousness. I have seen it all in a vision. The king's court is worse than Sodom and Gomorrah, and God will not long be mocked. Everyone knows you are the murderer of the sainted Thomas Lancaster and the rapist of his widow afterward."

Richard had often seen the Mad Dominican about and had even politely listened to his impassioned sermons on Richard's sins. He was one of the reasons Michael Hallam guarded Meg

Smythe's door. The priest had the unpleasant habit of appearing at the most inopportune times. Though Richard had tried to treat him with the deference his position deserved, he could not forgive the man's treatment of Maria. "Father Pieter, you may be holy but you are also mad, I think. 'Tis one thing to berate me for your fantasies concerning my political actions but quite another to accost a respectable woman and subject her to your ravings."

Michael Hallam withdrew his sword and advanced toward the priest. "I have listened to your ravings long enough on other nights. Your ill treatment of Lady Rendell gives me good cause to do what I have long dreamed of doing." Michael smacked the priest's bony buttocks with the flat of his sword.

Father Pieter yelped.

"Now be along with you," Richard said, "before my squire really becomes angry. You've tormented him often enough when he was not in the mood for sermons, and he would fancy a measure of revenge."

"You'll not be rid of me so easily," the Dominican cried. "Do you think I am an idiot when I have eyes to see? This creature is no proper woman, no matter what you say."

A loud laugh cut above the priest's diatribe. For the first time Maria noticed Meg Smythe, still astride her mare and surveying the scene with high amusement. Father Pieter's words suddenly fell into place. Maria knew well enough whom the priest had thought her to be.

The Dominican gaped from Meg to Maria. "I beg pardon, m'lady," he finally managed, addressing Maria. "I see clearly now that you could not be . . ."

"'Twill be the last error you make for a time, father," Michael Hallam interrupted. "At least around my lord." He raised his sword and the priest scurried out of his way. Gathering his cassock, Father Pieter scooted toward the gate leading to Sturry Court with Michael at his heels.

Meg Smythe's laugh jarred the ensuing silence. "God's balls! What a fool!"

"Did he hurt you, m'lady?" As Richard gazed into Maria's stricken face he forgot all about Meg. "'Tis all a silly misunderstanding, as you can see, and I would not have subjected you to his ravings. I promise you the Mad Dominican will be dealt with harshly if you would so desire."

Maria's gaze shifted from him to the grinning prostitute. She shook her head. "It does not matter." She began suddenly to shake. She stiffened her arms at her side in an effort to stop the trembling, but could not. She was certain she was going to start crying and, like a wounded animal, craved privacy. She stumbled back toward the Leopard's Head, but Richard soon caught up with her.

"'Twas a mistake," he said, placing his hands on her shoulders. "All of it." The rose fragrance of her perfume tantalized his nostrils. "I hope you will forgive the priest, and myself, for I would not hurt you, Maria, I hope you know."

Almost imperceptibly she nodded. She felt the warmth of his fingers through her tunic, sensed him behind her. She felt an overwhelming urge to whirl around, burrow against his chest, and pour out her unhappiness over her husband, the priest, even Meg. She willed herself to remain rigid until the urge passed.

She turned around to face him. "I know 'tis just a mistake, my lord, and a bit of a surprise as well. I would not have thought a man such as you would have to consort with prostitutes."

Richard lifted her chin with his fingertips. Her nearness was so intoxicating that his good judgment, his carefully constructed resolutions were swiftly crumbling. "And what sort of man do you believe me to be, Maria?"

His touch caused confusion and a trembling that had naught to do with fraught nerves. Maria gazed into his face, so strong and pleasing, and her heart gave a sudden leap.

"Do you think on me sometimes," Richard whispered, "as I think on you?"

Maria opened her mouth to deny the question. But she did

think on him, more often than was necessary, and in a manner more intimate than a lady for her lord. A conflicting plethora of emotions overwhelmed her. She loved Phillip with every fiber of her being, and yet she was so drawn to Richard. How long had she felt this way? Since last Christmas certainly. Maria realized it now that Richard stood before her. "'Tis wrong," she whispered. "It cannot be." Breaking away she ran for the stable.

Before Richard could follow he was blocked by Michael Hallam. "Nay, sire." Michael placed a restraining hand on his lord's arm. "Do not start what cannot be stopped."

Richard looked beyond his squire to the stable, from which Maria was now emerging astride Facebelle. It took great effort for him to turn and walk away, back toward Meg.

In Meg Smythe's large but ill-kept cottage, Richard stood before the window, unshuttered to allow in the crisp evening air. The cottage smelled of woodsmoke and fish. In the center of its one room burned a hearthfire above which hung a huge cauldron of water from a chain. Meg's companion, a halfwit who also plied the trade, was pouring steaming water into a large wooden tub.

"My lord."

Richard turned. Meg stood naked beside the tub. Flames caressed her naked body, strong calves, generous hips, the chestnut hair tumbling to a tapering waist. Looking at him neath half-lowered lashes, Meg tossed her head provocatively. "Would you join me, sire?"

"Nay, Meg. Tonight I'll watch."

She pointed to the tub. "I am using the rose soap, my lord, just like you said."

"Fine, Meg."

"I like to please you, sire." She eased herself into the tub. "Do I please you?"

Richard nodded, then returned to his post at the window. As his thoughts filled with his earlier encounter with Maria he promptly forgot Meg. Alternately he berated himself for being so weak, or relived Maria's every expression, word, and act. Richard closed his eyes. This must stop. I must stop it. He heard the prostitute splashing in the tub, humming a bawdy tavern song as she washed herself. Why cannot Meg be enough? he wondered. Behind her loomed no complex friendship. She was near as lovely as Maria and more seductive. Meg openly flaunted her charms, whereas Maria appeared almost apologetic for hers. If not Meg, why not Beatrice or Constance de Clarke or any woman? Why must it be Maria Rendell?

Meg's wet body pressed against him, her arms encircled his chest. He turned. Her small mouth parted, her eyes narrowed to slits. Her hands slid downward, around his tunic, unlacing his chausses. Abruptly Richard pushed her away.

"Get dressed, Meg. This night I'm not in the mood."

"What is wrong, my lord? Have I displeased thee?"

Shaking his head, Richard turned back toward the window, to cold chips of stars scattered across a cloudless, moonless sky. Wind buffeted through his tunic, raising goosebumps. To his left sprawled the muted lights of Sturry Court.

"'Tis Lady Rendell, is it not?"

"Do not say such a thing. 'Tis too ludicrous to even think upon."

"You have never turned me aside before." Meg reached for her chemise. "Nor have you ever looked at me the way you looked at her."

"Do not speak to me of her." His voice lowered in warning.

Meg had hoped that Richard would set her up in a fine house, perhaps even take her to court. Such things sometimes happened. She saw all her ambitions evaporating like dew in the morning sun, and because she knew their relationship was ending, could afford to speak truthfully. "'Tis no doubt that you are besotted with her, my lord, so why not just bed her and be done with it?"

Richard was horrified. "Maria is wife to my friend as well as my vassal. How dare you even suggest—"

"It happens all the time." Picking up a comb, Meg began pulling it through her wet hair. "More than one lord would be pleased to trade his wife's favor for a higher position at court."

"Phillip would not."

"No man is without ambition. Even Sir Rendell, I'm certain, has a price, which you should know better than anyone." She began inspecting her face in a hand mirror. Mirrors were rare and costly things; this one was a gift from Richard. She would miss him, and not just for his generosity. "Life is too short, my lord, not to take what you want."

"I cannot. No woman is worth the price of a friendship." Richard balled his fists. "Not even Maria."

ELEVEN

s twenty-two thousand men gathered at Newcastle-upon-Tyne to campaign against the Scots, Richard rode for Conway Castle in Wales. He'd received a summons from Edward to meet him there. Richard had been born at Conway and it remained his favorite of the several border castles constructed by his father to contain the Welsh people. The king preferred Caernarvon, which Edward I had also built and where he had originally presented the baby prince to the Welsh. During the week-long journey, Richard had plenty of time to ponder whether his brother's choice of Conway had been a conciliatory one. Edward's message had given little clue to his frame of mind, but Richard's anger had long ago dissipated to regret over their parting and a longing for reconciliation. He hoped Edward had acted out of similar desires.

The roads upon which Richard, Phillip, and their knights traveled were extremely dangerous. Long ago, private wars between great subjects had been ruled illegal, thus setting England apart from much of the continent. Beginning with the death of Piers Gaveston, however, internal feuds and criminal brigandage had become the rule, contributing in large measure to the country's slide toward anarchy. Since Thomas Lancaster's execution many of the rebels, or contrariants as they were sometimes called, had become hunted fugitives with estates open to plunder. Vast quantities of jewels, money, plate, furniture, animals, and grain had been stolen from their estates by former tenants, neighbors, and officials. Other contrariants, unable or unwilling to flee into exile, had enlisted the help of local sympathizers to carry on guerrilla activities, especially in the Welsh march where the Despensers' lands were most concentrated. From the forests or castles of allies they terrorized the surrounding countryside and any who dared trespass. Knowing that the mere sight of his standard might cause enmity, Richard and his men stayed on the alert, but they were plagued more by September rains than robbers. They reached Conway Castle without mishap and Richard settled in to await his brother, who had not yet arrived.

"If only Edward will not bring with him Hugh Despenser," he said to Phillip, "As much as I would not fight, I'd as soon slit 'Nephew Hugh's' throat as look at him."

Phillip nodded. "You and the rest of England."

Conway Castle, with its white lime-washed walls topped by a jumble of conical roofs, looked like a furtive ghost against a blanket of dense fog.

This third day following Richard's arrival he could barely even see his standard drooping from one of Conway's eight matching towers. As he urged his horse up the hill from the town, a mizzling rain clung to his face. The River Conway flowed past the castle curtain gray as the rolling fog obliterating the river's opposite shoreline and distant ships. Only the mournful call of circling sea gulls penetrated the clouds. Perhaps Edward will already be waiting for me, Richard thought, as he approached the ramp to the drawbridge. 'Twould be an awkward way to renew our relationship. Silently he cursed the Welsh who though conquered would never be tamed. The Welsh lord of the north, Gruffydd Llwyd, had proven a trustworthy ally during the Lancaster uprising, but the people themselves remained surly. Daily it seemed Richard had to mediate quarrels between his men and the villagers. Now, when he should be readying to properly welcome his brother, he'd been wrangling with merchants at the marketplace over a stolen chicken.

Crossing Conway's drawbridge he passed through the west barbican to the outer ward.

"Has my brother yet arrived?" he called out to Phillip, who stood by the mews talking to one of the cadge boys.

"Nay, sire. And with the fog, let us hope he is well on his way."

A sentry hailed Richard from the southwest tower, the tower in which Richard had been born. Lady Diane had not been allowed in the royal privy chamber or the king's tower, but had been relegated to the outer ward, reserved for Conway's household. Which was what Richard's mother had been, a member of the domestic household. Edward I had already been blessed with a legitimate male heir, but he had at least arrived at Christmas 1294, and, after the birthing, had held Richard and proclaimed him a worthy son. Had he given his royal approval because Lady Diane was even then spilling her life blood onto bespoiled sheets? Out of guilt for his rare lapse from conventional morality? Or because his father really did love him, as Richard believed, if in a casual and occasional way. Ghosts at Conway, just as his mother had given her ghost to the winds.

Shaking off the memories, Richard dismounted and strode toward the east barbican, where he would meet his brother. On the wall-walk he studied the vague outlines of ships, but the king's galley did not yet number among them. Approaching by way of the river, Edward would arrive privately. Richard began pacing between the stockhouse and chapel towers. The waiting was the hardest, and he was nervous. What if the reunion goes poorly? he worried. Or if Hugh Despenser has engineered the meeting to manipulate a total break between us? I'll not let him, he silently vowed. No provocation is worth fighting with

Edward. There had always been too much quarreling among the Plantagenets. Richard had no wish to end up like his namesake, the Lionheart, wrangling with his father and brother as quickly over the length of a candle stub as the fate of England.

The fog seemed to settle in Richard's lungs. An unpleasant mixture of smells from the bakehouse, kitchen, and brewhouse also rested sluggish, making breathing a conscious effort. He heard voices and various noises from the outer ward where the household was readying the night's feast. Save for Michael Hallam, he was alone on this part of the wall-walk. He wanted a measure of privacy for his meeting, away from gaping courtiers who would interpret every word for good or ill.

A crashing. Richard spun around. Michael's sword flashed. Then, seeing the source of the noise, he laughed. "A piece from the roof."

Michael sheathed his sword. "'Tis more dangerous to reside at Conway than fight the Scots."

Conway, as were all the border castles, was prone to leaking roofs and blocked gutters, which, when left untended, threatened the entire structure. Vast sums were required to keep the border castles in good repair and an increasingly parsimonious Edward preferred to allow revenues to stack up in the treasury, no matter how pressing the need to spend them.

"'Tis amazing how something so indestructible is also so delicate," Richard commented.

"Like a warhorse," Michael agreed.

"Or a woman." He thought suddenly of Maria Rendell and brutally shoved the thought from his mind.

From the river a huge shape loomed against the fog, maneuvered up to the dock. His brother had arrived.

Hurrying down the vice, Richard awaited Edward in the east barbican. Richard had played in the barbican garden as a child, and here his brother had presented him with a painted wooden castle that had been Edward's own in years past. Master John Brodeye, cook, had built the castle for the prince when he'd

been ten years old. "Here, Dickon," Edward had said, taking
Richard's hand and leading him along a secluded pathway to
the turreted castle complete with a maze of wings. "I found it
in a storeroom at Caernarvon. I've real castles to play with
now."

Should I have met you at the water's edge? Richard
wondered. Will you think I'm slighting you? Did you bring
Despenser? Will you be petulant? He heard his brother's
laughter. Edward had the sort of laugh that made others feel
good just listening. At least it pleases me, Richard thought, as
the king appeared framed by the opening of the watergate. As if
expecting to be met by an empty garden, His Majesty looked
quickly about. Richard was relieved to see that Edward's right
was occupied, not by Hugh Despenser, but by their younger
brother, Edmund of Kent.

As Richard knelt before the king, he sensed the jockeying for
position, the lords straining to hear every word, witness every
gesture. His enemies, as surely there were even in his brother's
household, would mull over every inflection of the voice, give it
political interpretation, all to his detriment—just as did
Edward's foes. If we could just be left alone, he thought, to be
allowed to love and cry and pass a measure of our days in
private, to enjoy a simple life like ordinary people.

"Do not kneel to me." Edward touched Richard's shoulder.
"I did not come here to gain obeisance from a subject, but
regain the companionship of my brother."

When Richard rose they embraced. As he gazed into his
brother's eyes he told himself that no matter what Edward did
or whom he loved, Richard would never again publicly break
with him.

In Conway's palatial great hall with its plastered walls, airy
stained-glass windows, and high, raftered ceiling, Richard sat
between Phillip and the king. The wine and pimento flowed as
freely as it had fifteen years past, during Edward's coronation.

Eyes bright, face flushed, Edward turned to him. He, all of them, had drunk immodest amounts of the spicy pimento. His Majesty had already repeatedly regaled the assemblage with bawdy tales, and though Richard usually considered joke telling a waste of time, he could think of no better way to spend this evening than listening to his brother's rich voice and laughter, rising above Robin the Minstrel's eerie rebec.

"Did you know that I've sentenced that traitor Roger Mortimer to death?" Edward propped an elbow against the table for better stability. "I've decided that the tower is too fine a place for a traitor. I would rather see his head stuck atop London's bridge."

Richard nodded. Edward had told him at least twice earlier about his grisly plans for the marcher baron, and he had been informed by others of the death sentence weeks ago. The pimento was beginning to wreak its vengeance on them all.

Edward fell silent. Perhaps he was connecting Roger Mortimer with the Despensers' banishment, and the Parliament of the White Bands. Such memories were better left for other times. Richard swirled his wine in his cup and succeeded in spilling it over the rim onto his fingers. Across from him, his half brother, Edmund of Kent, nodded amiably to one and all. Edmund was an agreeable lad whose head would soon be lolling in his mazer.

Leaning across Richard, Edward began discussing with Phillip the forthcoming Scottish campaign. "Robert the Bruce, they say is suffering from leprosy—the 'mickle ail' as the barbarians call it. 'Tis strange, but they seem often to suffer from that affliction. Perhaps 'tis the uncivilized way they live; perhaps 'tis punishment for their sins. But by the time I'm through with them this time they'll prefer leprosy to my vengeance."

Richard stared at the swirling smoke, his eyes traversing each curve of the eight-raftered ceiling, the light from the large stained-glass windows adding to the room's palatial feeling. Bannockburn! He looked at Phillip and knew his thoughts had also reeled eight years past, to that ignominious battle.

"Men from all over England are arriving with sixteen days' supply of food, and those who do not come willingly I will demand," Edward continued. "My army will have all the supplies they need by purveyance and the people will not complain because for a handful of grain or a scraggly milk cow we will soon be forever free of the Scots."

Richard no longer felt drunk, but rather clear headed—and wary. "You well know, Your Majesty, that Robert the Bruce is neither a fool nor a weakling. Our forces might be large, but would we not fare better if we used his own tactics—riding swift and light, striking where least expected, then disappearing into the hills? A million men will not stop the Scots if we cannot find them."

"They are barbarians with no civilized way of fighting. This time I will crush them, as father never could do." Edward waved to Robin the Minstrel, his favorite. "Sing of Bannock-burn, and England's glory."

Obligingly, the flaxen-haired lad launched into an account of the debacle that bore no resemblance to the reality of that June day. Edward II emerged a true hero, personally responsible for hundreds of dead Scots. Only through treachery had the Bruce managed to gain the upper hand and then England had left the field in an orderly manner, leaving behind more dead Scots than English. If Bannockburn hadn't been the greatest triumph in England's history, it certainly had not been a disaster. Richard tried to shut out the minstrel's voice, tried to shut out the lies. Reality was Henry de Bohun galloping to meet the Bruce and having his skull cleaved in two; Gilbert of Gloucester breaking through the schiltrons, racing to his death. Reality was the paralysis in Richard's limbs when the Scot had ridden toward him, the blade of a Scottish claymore slicing into his chest. Richard closed his eyes. So many lives lost, and for what? So that minstrels could make up glorious stories. As always when he heard or thought of Bannockburn, Richard felt a creeping shame of defeat, of cowardice. Hadn't he been terrified? Had he fought his hardest, or had he been so fearful for his life that he'd stayed to the background?

Richard looked to his brother, who was listening to Robin with a pleased smile on his face. As if Bannockburn had really happened so. Why can I not believe that? he wondered. Why do I feel that, despite propaganda to the contrary or the glorious tales told before Edward's court, our people utter my name and his with the same contempt as they do Bannockburn? We have been found out, my brother and I. We've been weighed and dissected and found to be hollow inside, made of dross instead of gold.

"I cannot take this," Richard muttered to Phillip. He motioned to the minstrel, who came forward, his aesthetic face lit by an expectant smile. But if Robin expected compliments, he was disappointed. "Sing of something else," Richard said.

"But, sire, His Grace . . ."

Richard glanced to Edward, who was waving for his goblet to be refilled.

"I do not think my brother will even notice, and I assure you, good Robin, that I will."

As Edward and his troops traveled north to engage the Scots, they passed through a devastated countryside bearing little physical resemblance to the land in more peaceful times. Peel towers—smaller versions of a magnate's castle—had been erected throughout the area. At first sight of the enemy, tocsins clamored warning and unprotected families hurriedly gathered behind the peel's rock walls. Manor houses were a relic from the past, for they were too easily destroyed. Peasants were reduced to living in the woods or in hastily constructed shanties that the raiders repeatedly burned during their raids. Most of the agricultural fields, so patiently carved out of the recalcitrant land, had been totally abandoned to nature. Before His Majesty's arrival, Robert the Bruce, with his commanders

Moray and Black Douglas, had spent three weeks raiding as far south as Preston near the Irish Sea. Every open town they'd set to torch, and in places such as Cartmel and Lancaster only the monastic buildings had been spared to stand forlornly amidst the rubble.

Richard's heart was saddened by the gaunt faces of the refugees, the children who no longer cried, the women whose tragedies shone in the blankness of their eyes, the bloated bodies strewn along the route, stripped of clothing and valuables and left to scavenging animals. Few men walked the roads; those who had not been killed or enlisted in the campaign had been carried away as hostages. Livestock was also a rarity. The murrain of 1321 had devastated the cattle herds, and what remained were either driven into Scotland along with sheep and domestic pigs or slaughtered on the spot. Without meat or grain, the people starved and fell prey to epidemics that had annihilated ten percent of the population. Truth to tell, King Edward's policies shared partial blame for the north's devastation. That much Richard knew, though he kept such thoughts to himself. The direct taxes His Majesty had imposed during the famines of 1315–16, as well as the famines themselves, had caused such hardship that Edward complained the entire area was worthless as a source of revenue. Also, his Welsh and Irish troops often looted with as much rapacity as the Scots.

Richard saw the hopeless faces in his dreams and sent heavenward a thousand prayers and questions to a God who appeared oblivious to his people's pain. "This time we will rid you of the Bruce," he told a woman cradling an infant to her breast and flanked by two whose shriveled faces were already stamped with death. He gave her his daily ration of food, which would at best only postpone the inevitable. Nor did Richard truly believe that the current campaign would be successful, no matter how well Edward maintained he'd planned in advance. They were deficient in cavalry and their leaders were in the main inexperienced. Most of Edward's battle-hardened generals had been executed, imprisoned, or were members of the outlawed contrariants.

As King Edward penetrated Scotland, Robert the Bruce prudently withdrew. Edward unsuccessfully besieged Berwick Castle and laid waste to Lothian, but the Scots refused to meet him in open combat. At Leith he was told that no more supplies could reach him from the sea, due to raids by Flemish pirates and storms that had destroyed fourteen English ships. Faced with a hungry army whose ranks were decimated by desertion and epidemic, Edward decided to turn back. Crossing Alcrum Moor in Roxburghshire, he arrived at the border where he had many services offered in thanksgiving for his safe return. The entire expedition had lasted sixteen days; six Scots had been taken prisoner. Immediately Edward began dispersing his troops, though he spoke of spending the winter on the border, "the better to discomfort our enemy."

Richard knew the falseness of his brother's words. *We will all go back to London and forget about the starving children, the raped women, and the mutilated men.* Edward will commission a minstrel to sing of his prowess, the brave deeds he executed, and will count himself a fine monarch. Richard felt disgusted, as well as impotent, for what really could be done? The logical thing, aside from engaging the Scots in real battle, would be to negotiate a settlement, but unless Edward himself decided on this course, events would continue as before and more people would die.

On their last night together, Richard and Phillip bedded down near a stand of oak and birch. Richard had made plans to travel to his earldom in Sussex where he would continue marriage negotiations with emissaries of Lady Beatrice. As Edward's ineptness became increasingly apparent, the alliance assumed greater importance, to Richard at least. Phillip, in turn, talked of visiting Winchcomb and Deerhurst before returning to Fordwich. Throughout the campaign, he had turned increasingly inward and Richard sensed in his friend a change, though he could not pinpoint the cause.

The sharp night air smelled of woodsmoke, fallen leaves, and decaying earth. A madonna moon tinged a bloody red rose above the hills and forest; wispy clouds suffused the moon's light, lessening the chill of stars. It was a calm night when sound drifted unnaturally far—the neighing of a tethered horse, the murmur of conversation, the coughing and moans of sick men. Several of the remaining infantry had died this day from the sickness that had plagued the entire campaign. Throughout, Edward had been too fearful of the Bruce to allow time for proper burial, and English dead were scattered among the broad valleys and narrow lakes of the Lake District, the heather-covered moorlands and white limestone gorges of the Peak District, the bogs, moors, caves, and waterfalls of the Yorkshire Dales. Perhaps it was the ghosts of all those people who had died unshriven that caused Richard such disquiet. Always he had misliked the north, which seemed to him not a true part of England, but an alien, hostile land.

Beside him, Phillip inhaled deeply of the cold pungent air. Placing his hands behind his head he stared at the rising moon. He loved Yorkshire, felt a kindred spirit with the bleak moors and tumbling streams, gorges and jagged rocks, the huge tracts of untamed and unexplored land. As he'd traveled throughout this wild region, the restlessness, the longing to be free, had settled upon him with a brutal, unshakable intensity.

"The Garden of Eden, they say, lies atop a mountain touching the moon," Phillip said quietly. "I met a man once who claimed to have been there. He showed me a ruby he swore he'd smuggled from Paradise itself."

Richard leaned on his elbow, his gaze also on the moon. Within its circle a golden madonna and her babe appeared imprisoned. "Did the man say where Paradise might be?"

"To the east somewhere. He did not specify. But it is out there waiting." A shooting star arced across the heavens. An evil omen? Phillip wondered. But he'd seen dozens in his time, above the sugarcake turrets of the Church of Santa della Pisa, the doge's palace in Manila, over Jerusalem.

"There is a wall in China," he continued, "that stretches six million paces. Marco Polo walked it. Remember when he returned with his tales? And when he spoke of the Gobi Desert and sirens who sing songs that lure travelers to their death?"

"They are just tales we've heard thirdhand and embellished by the tellers," Richard said. "Marco Polo is most probably a liar and braggart. We are too old to believe such fantasies."

"I think I'll never be too old." Phillip was certain the world contained sights and wonders more beautiful, more stirring, more exotic than any he'd yet beheld. When he'd been in the Holy Land he'd heard marvelous tales of a place called Afghanistan, which housed the roof of the world. The Pamir Range soared so high, 'twas said, that a man could not differentiate its snow-covered peaks from the clouds. From their summit men were known to have reached out and touched heaven itself. What would it be like to touch the sky? he wondered. Would it be hard and impenetrable or just a colored vapor? Evil spirits also lived in the Pamir Range, and the rumble of their laughter triggered avalanches that collapsed entire mountains. Monks capable of levitation resided there in lamaseries where they worshiped dragon statues gilded in gold, with bulging eyes and ripping teeth. And beyond Afghanistan were more wonders, some that Phillip was certain no man's eyes had ever before beheld. He need not journey to the Gobi Desert to hear his own siren song. "If I could have been born anyone, 'twould have been Marco Polo," he said aloud. "In his twenty-four years of travel he saw things that most of mankind has not seen in as many centuries."

"Marco Polo had not a wife and son. He was a merchant, not a knight. Merchants can do as they please and no one cares." Richard sympathized with Phillip's longings, but if he'd been blessed with Maria he'd not be chasing chimeras.

Sitting up Phillip brought his knees to his chest, rested his head upon his knees. All about, the camp settled into sleep; knights and yeomen stretched upon their mantles as quietly as clouds drifting across the face of the moon. "I am thirty-five years old. Yesterday I was a child, tomorrow I'll be a doddering old man. Our time on earth is but a passing whisper, and yet never once have I had a glimmering as to what is the point of our lives."

"The point is to prepare ourselves for death, then our eternal reward or punishment. For me that is the easy part." Richard groped for the proper words. "'Tis harder to behave as though we would die tomorrow and not live forever." He thought of Maria, of the sin he committed every time he could not control those thoughts, of the other sins for which God would some-day hold him accountable—lust, avarice, cruelty, impatience, pride, treachery.

"I want Paradise," Phillip whispered, "though I do not even know what it is."

Richard knew well enough what Paradise would be for him. "You cannot leave your wife," he blurted, as the full impact of Phillip's words began to penetrate.

Turning his eyes from the moon, Phillip studied his face. "The sea is ever changing while a woman's mystery, even Maria's, remains basically one and the same. 'Tis not enough for me."

Richard returned his gaze. "'Twould be enough for me."

Maria knew Phillip's leavetaking would be just a matter of time. She had known it since his return from Deerhurst, a fortnight past. How will you tell me? she wondered. What excuse will you use or will you not even bestir yourself to offer one? Phillip could do as he pleased, and while many knights were bound to their lands and content to stay there, he was not and would no longer pretend, of that she was certain. He did not speak of his plans, but sometimes he stared at her and little Tom as if storing their faces, their very action in his memory— like a squirrel gathering nuts for the winter. If possible he grew even more withdrawn and absentminded about manor affairs, leaving them almost totally to Hugh. He was seldom mean or short-tempered with Maria but rather indifferent, as if she were a casual acquaintance whom he found mildly enjoyable.

You have the mark of Cain upon you, she often thought. Unlike Cain, who was doomed to roam the earth without a home, however, 'tis your choice to wander and I'll shed no more tears for you. A thousand times she thus vowed and a thousand times she gainsaid that vow. If she could harden herself to him, not care when he went or stayed, she would. Yet when Maria looked at him her heart still caught in her throat, as if it were six years past and she was seeing him for the first time. Phillip still seemed a stranger, like the heroes in the minstrel's tales—handsome, brave, and powerful but as mysterious as the dark side of the moon. Yet he was flesh and blood and when he touched her, she still responded. She hated herself for her weakness but her body continually betrayed her, seeking in his caresses the closeness she so desperately needed. But 'tis a false closeness, she told herself afterward, as he slept beside her and she stared into the darkness. And each time you make love to me it only highlights my weakness and your control. I would that I did not still desire you, that I could turn from you cold and indifferent, that my senses ceased to quicken at the very thought of you. Someday 'twill be so, she thought as the silent tears slipped down her cheeks . . . I just pray to God that day will soon arrive.

Phillip's leavetaking appeared in the form of a Venetian, Niccolo Dia. On a previous trip to the Holy Land, Niccolo had been Phillip's companion. He had visited Deerhurst and, after a discreet amount of time, followed Phillip to Fordwich. Maria knew his appearance was not coincidence.

Niccolo spoke rapid-fire French with an abysmal Italian accent, as well as a dozen other languages, or so he maintained. The man was never still. As he chattered, Niccolo jumped about, paced, bounced his legs, cracked his knuckles, or pulled at his long nose. Hugh and Eleanora vowed they found him and his multitudinous tales captivating. Maria had hated him on sight. Night after night, as he and Phillip shared their memories, she felt increasingly the outsider, a starving beggar peering in at a banquet.

She took to retiring earlier. Alone in their bed, she tossed, or moved to the unshuttered window where she stared into the long spring evenings. Eastertime of 1323 had arrived, a time of pageantry and passion plays, the time once again of the cherry blossoms. She could see the orchard from her window, the pale flowers shimmering in the moonlight. She had met Phillip during the Cherry Fair, and now he would leave her.

"Is not Niccolo a wonderful man?" Phillip said later, as he removed his supertunic and placed it on a wall peg. "The knowledge stored in his brain, the sights his eyes have seen, that is what makes life bearable, to see and learn, to view the wonders God created for man." Crossing to the washstand he cleaned his teeth with a woolen cloth, then washed himself with warm water and scented soap. From their bed where she sat hugging her knees Maria forced herself to look away from the play of muscles across his naked torso.

Approaching the bed, Phillip looked down on her. "'Tis time we talked, Maria."

Her heart began a frantic pounding. The moment she'd dreaded, the moment for which she'd so carefully rehearsed was at hand. "I do not want to talk. I already know what you are going to say." She tried to pick her words carefully but her planned calmness slipped away in a rash of fear. "Cannot England be enough for one man? Cornwall has wild cliffs and oceans and you told me yourself that Yorkshire has high mountains and forests no man has yet entered and probably animals no man has looked upon. There are shrines scattered the breadth of the country and miracles and fairies, and London's Smithfield Fair, they say, contains a multitude of freaks. Why go to India or Persia or any of those awful places with their three-hundred-foot-long snakes and Amazons and frightening creatures, where people die and are never heard from again?"

Phillip's eyes were soft with compassion. He lifted a strand of her hair and rubbed it gently between his fingers. "How can I expect you to understand what I do not myself?"

Slipping into bed he forced her back so that she rested stiffly in his arms. "I told you once, Maria, that I would prove a poor match for you."

The tears she vowed she would not shed began to fall. She balled her fists, trying to control her trembling.

"I have not been a good husband to you; you've deserved better." He kissed the top of her head. "But I do love you and Tom, in my own fashion, whether you believe me or not."

A choked laugh emerged from her throat. "I've seen little evidence of that."

"Other men leave their wives; 'tis not as if I am the only one."

"They leave because they are obligated to, whether because of their sins or duties to their country. Not because it suits their fancy."

He had no answer for that, for what she said was true. He'd dreaded this encounter, postponed it as long as possible. He did not want to hurt Maria and he did not know the words that would ease the blow, justify his act to her—or himself. "Niccolo and I will leave from the Cinque Port of Dover. We'll spend time in Europe, I think, then go to the Holy Land. Perhaps beyond."

"How long will you be gone?" Her nails dug into the palms of her clenched fists. No matter how she'd counted herself prepared for this moment, she'd not been able to guard against its pain.

"I cannot say. Three years, perhaps more."

"Three years?" She twisted in his arms. "Nay, do not. I could not live without you. I know that I have not been a good wife, that my nagging has distanced us, but I will do better, I promise, but please do not leave. Life is so transitory, and if something should happen to you, my life, too, would be over. Oh, do not do this to us!"

"'Tis no lack in you that has brought this about. You are everything a man could want in a wife. There is something inside of me that has always tormented me, a restlessness that does not afflict other men. I would that I could be different, but I cannot."

"You do not love me—you never did." She began to sob uncontrollably. "But I do love you and I am begging you, do not leave."

Phillip put his arm around her shoulder. She jerked away. He hated to see her like this, she who was usually sensible and controlled. He had no idea how to placate her or make her cease her crying. "When I am gone, if you should need anything, our lord Sussex will be there for you. He has promised me."

"Richard? When will he have time for me? He is to be married within the month."

"We have already discussed it. You need but ask him . . ."

"Oh, aye, ask him when he will play me false just as you've done."

Phillip's expression was peculiar. "'Tis his obligation as our liege lord to care for us. I was not speaking on a more personal level."

Bolting from the bed, Maria shook her fist in his face. "I hate you. I wish we'd never married. And if you leave me do not ever bother to come back, for we are finished as man and wife."

"Do not spout nonsense." He was shocked at the venom of her words. "You cannot mean such a thing, and 'tis foolish to make idle threats. Now come back to bed. I would not part with such harshness between us."

Maria jerked out of his reach. "'Tis not a threat. As God is my witness if you leave me I will bar you forever from my bed and my life."

TWELVE

ood morrow, Lady Rendell! I have not seen you since Rockingham, is that not right? Windsor Castle is lovely this time of year, is it not? And I must admit that Lord Sussex has outdone himself on his wedding festivities."

Maria looked up from her position near the gallery steps surrounding Windsor's lists. Queen Isabella, dazzling in purple velvet, smiled down at her. Flustered, Maria managed to curtsy in the confined space. Beyond, the grand melee, which included all tourney combatants, was readying to begin. Today was the last day of the joust. Richard and Lady Beatrice were scheduled to be married two days later, on Whitsunday, the first Sunday in June.

"Your Grace, I would not think you'd remember me," Maria stammered. Since her arrival for Richard's wedding celebration a week past, Maria had been introduced to a multitude of people, most of whom she could not remember a moment past the initial greeting. She could not fathom how Queen Isabella would recall her from a time six years past.

Isabella smiled indulgently. "I have a memory for faces, Lady Rendell. How fares your son Thomas? He is the same age as my Eleanor, is he not?"

After exchanging a few more pleasantries, Queen Isabella continued to her seat beneath a gilded canopy. Sitting down sedately, she folded her hands in her lap and pretended interest in the joust, though she could concentrate on nothing but the

[154]

current joyous news. Last night Roger Mortimer had escaped the Tower of London! She could scarcely hide her elation. Since the uprisings that had culminated in Thomas Lancaster's death, the most powerful of the marcher barons had been imprisoned in the appallingly mean confines of Lantern Tower. But 'twould take more than bars to hold that one, Isabella thought, hiding her smile behind a fan. Roger had escaped the tower and was now on his way to safety, in Normandy. Isabella was certain of that, because she, along with several others, had engineered Mortimer's escape.

On Windsor's field, trumpets blew, destriers thundered toward each other, barons broke lances and knocked out teeth or spilled blood, but the queen was lost in her last conversation with Mortimer. When she'd told him the escape was scheduled for August 1, the Feast of St. Peter and Vincula, the look in Roger's eyes had been exciting to behold.

"Someday I will repay you for your favor," he had said, and she knew he meant not in money. The very thought of the marcher baron made Isabella's heart race. From his many months of imprisonment he was romantically gaunt, and even jail could not lighten his swarthy complexion. Mortimer possessed such a confidently masculine air that the queen felt pleasantly dominated by his very nearness. Like so many of the marcher lords he was arrogant and supremely self-assured—a marvelous change from a husband who was more ineffectual than most women. Roger Mortimer is all male, Isabella thought. He looks at me as Edward never has and no other man would dare. When her fourth child, Joan of the Tower, had been born, she had been housed in the Tower of London's royal apartments and it was during this time she came into more intimate contact with Mortimer. Isabella found herself irresistibly attracted to him, and she had ultimately allowed herself to be drawn into his escape plan. It was not only infatuation with Roger Mortimer that caused her to act, however. Increasingly the Despensers terrified her. She counted them capable of any cruelty. Though her husband's coffers were overflowing he allowed his favorites to treat her as poorly as any serving maid. Her royal apartments in the Tower of London had been abominable—rat infested and with a leaking roof through which rain had dripped upon her poor newborn babe. Repeatedly both Despensers attempted to cut back her allowance while simultaneously adding to their own multifarious holdings. Whenever Isabella thought on the Despensers of her parsimonious husband, she fumed with impotent fury. But not today. Today Roger Mortimer was free of the tower and life looked sweeter than it had in years.

Maria and Eleanora shared quarters in Windsor's upper ward, where the domestic quarters and king's offices were located. They were jammed in a small room with a dozen other ladies, for Windsor was packed from storeroom to tower with guests. In the lower ward, harried pages scurried in and out of the king's ceremonial apartments; an endless stream of food carts was unloaded before Windsor's several kitchens. Hawking and hunting parties vied for space with noble ladies and their entourages, minstrels, musicians, various clergymen—concentrated in the cloisters and chapel—and with armored knights returning from the lists.

The press of people and various activities still could not ease Maria's heart. Her parting with Phillip had been so acrimonious that she was certain he would never return to England. She found that the thought of Richard's wedding also disturbed her. 'Tis just that he has not the time for me, she assured herself. 'Tis a selfish feeling on my part and has naught to do with the marriage itself. Since her arrival, they'd only spoken once. Immediately after Richard had inquired after her health and Phillip's leavetaking, he'd been whisked off by Lady Beatrice, who threw Maria a haughty look. Maria decided she hated the woman, who was short, dumpy, much older than Richard, and possessed a laugh like a donkey's bray.

Windsor Castle overlooked a verdant valley checkered with

fields and meadows, currently thick with tents and pavilions. At the meadow's edge, the River Thames glided past. Sometimes Maria and Eleanora rode a barge along the Thames, or she and her father rode into the wooded Chiltern Hills, which guarded Windsor's rear. Since William the Conqueror's time, the area had been a favorite royal reserve and was flush with game. Maria had to admit that if she could have picked her place of marriage she would have chosen Windsor. Legend told that King Arthur and his knights had once walked its halls, and with its round tower, sprawling wings, colorful pennants, the castle appeared a proper home for mythical kings. Was it a tribute to Richard's nature or his feelings for Beatrice that he had chosen such a romantic setting for their marriage?

On the evening following the grand melee, Maria entered Windsor's great hall with Hugh and Eleanora for another evening of feasting and dancing. She had long ago been sated by food that in its variety and abundance confounded belief, and had previously begged off the dancing, as she intended to do this night. I will be glad when I can return to Fordwich, she thought, as she searched for a place to sit. There I can be miserable without interruption.

She heard her name called out and was dismayed to see Humphrey Rendell and his wife coming toward her. "Do come and sit near us." Lady Jean slipped her arm through Maria's. Throughout the past several days Maria had often encountered her in-laws, but while Jean remained perpetually sweet, Humphrey Rendell eyed her as if she were afflicted with a loathsome pestilence.

"You look so lovely tonight," Lady Jean continued. "I've not seen a caul of seed pearls so intricately worked before. And the green of your kirtle well becomes you. Does not Maria look breathtaking, husband?"

"Indeed." Humphrey contemptuously noted the cut of her gown, the lushness of her figure. "You do not appear to be suffering overmuch from my brother's leaving."

She flushed. "'Tis a private matter, sir. I handle it in my own way." Feeling hurt and resentful, she walked away and found a seat as far from her obnoxious brother-in-law as possible.

Across from her, Eleanora sat with Michael Hallam, and their father next to the recently widowed Lady Katherine Gower. Lady Gower chattered incessantly, but Hugh rather enjoyed her and whenever she fell silent long enough to shovel in a mouthful of lark, cream of almond, stewed potage, or another of the endless dishes, he asked her questions to which she responded at interminable length. Currently Lady Gower was elaborating on Lady Beatrice's "exquisite" dress of cloth of gold and Tripoli silk and the king's ransom worth of presents Richard had already bestowed upon the wedding guests.

Unbidden, Maria raised her eyes to the high table. The king and queen, all those seated at the dais, appeared to be exquisite creatures from another world. The placement of candles flattered their faces, highlighted the dazzling hues of their clothing, and sparkled off their crowns and jewelry. Even Richard, who had inherited his father's plain taste in clothes, wore a rich blue velvet, a gold coronet on his head, and several rings upon his fingers. Though always handsome, tonight he seemed as breathtaking, but alien, as a mythical god. Maria could scarce connect the dazzling suitor whispering in the ear of his beloved with the man she'd known.

"Does not our queen look ravishing this even?" Her dinner companion, Geoffrey Marchaut, had mistaken the object of Maria's interest. "But His Majesty looks a bit glum, for he's not recovered form Roger Morimer's escape. He is sending troops to Mortimer's marcher properties to recapture him. I hold out little hope of his success, however, for Mortimer is as sly as he is dangerous."

"I know little about political matters." She accepted a drink of wine from Lord Marchaut but shook her head when he urged her to eat. "I have no appetite."

"I have not seen you at court before, my lady. It has been my loss." Sir Geoffrey's eyes kindled as he looked at her. Increasingly, his gaze lingered on her bosom.

"I am but a simple country maid, sire. I am more comfortable at Fordwich than at court, I assure you." She turned away. Her head was beginning to ache. I want to be gone from here, she thought. Unaccountably, tears pricked her eyes. Here, surrounded by people, she had never felt so alone.

Near the dais, Robin, the king's favorite minstrel, was just finishing the last of a dozen love ballads dedicated to the Lady Beatrice. He was replaced by several jesters who kept up a steady banter of ribald jokes aimed at Richard and his lady. The jests were pointed and often crude, but the two were hardly novices at love.

Following the banquet's end, pages removed the tables to allow dancing. Maria stood to leave. Geoffrey caught her arm. "Would you stay a while, my lady? Just one dance with me?" Geoffrey was a pleasant-looking young man, with eyes dark and dancing as a gypsy's. His unruly hair reminded her of Phillip's.

When she hesitated, he pressed. "You are such a lovely woman, Lady Rendell. Surely, you are the most beautiful woman at Windsor, nay, in all of England."

Maria laughed aloud. Geoffrey was obviously so enthralled with the notion of courtly love that his natural good sense had been replaced by hyperbole.

He flushed and appeared so crestfallen by her response that Maria relented. What harm could a measure of kindness cause? "I would be delighted to dance with you, Sir Geoffrey."

"You are looking especially lovely this evening, Lady Maria. No wonder Lord Marchaut and a host of others cannot keep their eyes from you."

Maria looked up in surprise. She'd been concentrating so intently on the intricate steps of this particular carole she'd not even noticed her partner. Being in such sudden close proximity to Richard left her short of breath.

"My lord Sussex." She looked quickly down at her feet. She

was aware of the warmth of his hand, his body as his tunic brushed her arm.

"I have been seeking opportunity to speak more privately with you since your arrival, but my time has not been my own. Who would have thought marriage would prove so complicated?"

"You have no idea how complicated, my lord." She thought of Phillip, their harsh parting, the resultant emptiness. "Your . . . the Lady Beatrice is really quite . . . lovely." Maria had trouble vocalizing the lie, especially when she found the woman as unappealing as the pox. "I am truly happy for you." She concentrated on the floor rushes, the hem of her gown, the velvet slippers peeking forth.

"And unhappy for yourself? How are you faring without Phillip? Have you had a need for my help?"

Maria's hand trembled in Richard's. Aye, she thought. If you could have been near to ease the parting, if you had not also betrayed me . . . Unnerved by the dangerous turn to her thoughts, she shook her head. When she could trust her voice she said, "Phillip and I quarreled. I said certain things I should not have. I do not think he'll ever return."

Before Richard could further question, the lilting sounds from the minstrel's gallery signaled a change in partners. Maria searched for a way of gracefully exiting the hall. She had no wish to speak further with Richard. His presence was too disturbing, and her mind threatened to betray her at every turn.

Mumbling an excuse to her dancing partner, Maria hurried from Windsor, out into the pleasance.

The night was lovely, cool and quiet after the noise inside. Several couples shared the garden, either strolling the pebbled paths or sitting on the many stone benches, but all sought privacy. Breathing in the evening air, Maria looked up to the inky darkness, sprinkled by a million radiant stars. Darkness always brought out such strange emotions—sadness and longings and desires she could not understand. Darkness reminded her of Phillip. She hugged her arms together. And Richard also? In two days he would be married. The prospect pains me not at all, she told herself. But if only something would remain constant.

"Maria." Richard stood silhouetted in the light from the banquet hall.

Her heart leapt. "You should not have come. You will be missed." A part of her was glad he'd followed, despite the words.

"I made the appropriate excuses. My guests can spare me for a few moments."

He crossed to her, stopping when less than a hand's length separated them. He breathed deeply of the fragrant air. "'Tis a beautiful night. I think such a night does not well suit my mood."

"Why, sire?" Her sleeve brushed his tunic.

"These past weeks have been taxing. I have never been one for much ceremony." He paused. "And sometimes I doubt the rightness of this marriage."

"Why? Lady Beatrice is a fine match. Everyone says."

"And what do you say, Maria. How do you feel?"

Maria felt as if they were standing on the edge of a precipice. She groped for the proper words. "I only know with you married I will be even more lonely. I'll feel somehow I've lost you."

"You will always have me, Maria. That will never change."

The words could be interpreted in so many ways—in friendship, or in love. She studied his expression, trying to decipher the meaning. "I wish it were so. I wish that something or someone would remain constant. With Phillip gone and you marrying I feel so . . . empty."

"I never knew my getting married would affect you at all."

"Aye. You've been a friend to me as well as my lord and . . ."

"A murrain on your friendship," Richard interrupted. "I don't want it. I never have."

Maria looked him full in the face. She'd known it in so many diverse moods—the face of a king, the face of a bastard, Richard's face. Her heart leapt. "What have you wanted from me, my lord?"

He looked past her to the moon. "I've wanted you, Maria. That's all." His head bent to her; his lips hovered inches above her own. "I know 'tis wrong of me to think it, let alone say it. But tonight I do not care." His mouth brushed the corners of her own, then settled over its fullness.

Through her surprise, Maria found herself responding—even as she'd responded to Phillip. The intensity of her feelings frightened her. She pushed against his chest. "Nay. We must not." She must flee Richard and the confusing wave of emotions crashing over her, threatening to drown her. She bolted past him. The moon, caught in a twisted snarl of branches, broke free to follow her flight along a pebbled path, past couples lounging on stone benches.

She'd reached her apartment in Windsor's upper ward before she was aware that Richard was immediately behind her. She ran blindly on until he jerked her arm and spun her around to face him.

"You should not have followed me. You must go back . . ."

Richard's lips crushed hers in a brutalizing kiss. Maria struggled against him. "'Tis wrong," she gasped, twisting away. He caught her again. Her mouth opened under the onslaught of his kisses. He forced her back against the doorway to the ceremonial apartments, where he resided.

"Please do not. When you kiss me so, I cannot think."

His breath was hot against her ear. "Let me make love to thee, Maria. Just this once."

Not only desire marked Richard's face, but a yearning she'd never before seen—not with Phillip, not with any man. She felt her resolve melt away, and as his lips brushed her forehead, cheeks, the hollow neath her eyelids, the tip of her nose, the corners of her mouth, flames of desire leapt outward from the pit of her stomach. Richard whispered her name until she was light-headed and felt as if she were floating. If he loosed her she was certain she would rise past Windsor's apartments to the moon hovering among the stars.

Maria's arms crept around his neck; her fingers closed in the soft thick hair curling at the nape of his neck. Richard's hand reached up to cup her left breast. His right hand slid down her rib cage, searing through the velvet of her kirtle. His hand trailed upward to her right breast, teasing, tantalizing with its deliberateness.

"For more than a year now," he whispered, "I've dreamed of naught but this moment."

Maria's mouth opened under the delicious assault of Richard's lips. As they tasted and explored each other, her limbs lightened to water. He bunched the folds of her skirt, hiking it past her calves. Intoxicating sensations coursed through her like heady wine, even though her mind counseled caution. She ignored the warnings. Maria no longer cared to listen to what was right or wrong, to weigh the consequences of her act. Now, this moment, was enough.

Sweeping her into his arms Richard carried her through the doorway of the apartments, up the stairs to his chamber. When he released her, he kissed the hollow of her neck, then caught her right earlobe gently with his teeth. His tongue traveled a light pathway along her jaw line, up to her mouth, outlined, teased, and trailed to her left ear. Maria swayed against him, pressing ever closer. Slipping her hands neath his tunic and shirt she felt bare skin. His muscles jumped upon contact.

Swiftly Richard removed his clothing until he was clad only in form-fitting chausses. He moved to take her in his arms, but Maria shook her head.

"Just for a moment, let me look at thee." 'Twas against convention to behave so boldly, but was not everything about this night contrary to her upbringing? Besides, Maria could not help but exult in the sheer magnificence of Richard's body. How could poets and minstrels praise womens' anemic charms when their softness could never match the true beauty of a knight's physique? Moonlight silhouetted every hard curve and swelling line of Richard's massive chest and arms, the shadow of his chest hair against the surrounding skin. A jagged scar followed the outline of his left pectoral, slashing past his nipple.

"Bannockburn?"

"Aye."

Bannockburn meant Phillip. Maria shoved all thought of her husband from her mind. With her lips she traced the uneven course of Richard's scar, feeling the ridges of puckered tissue, as well as the slamming of his heart.

"Please, Maria, have you no idea what you are doing to me?"

Pulling her upright, he worked her skirt even higher. Before she was even certain what was happening, her outer garments lay at her feet. Nothing save the flimsy length of chemise now separated them. Richard's fingers caught the delicate strap, ripping the material to her waist. His gaze burned a trail along the contours of her body, but Maria saw something more mixed with desire—that unsettling tenderness. More than lust, the tenderness sealed for Maria the rightness of their act. "I think this moment was inevitable," she whispered, "from the very first."

Richard carried her to his bed and settled atop her. Though her body moved with a will of its own, Maria's thoughts remained coherent. Richard would make love to her. They would commit the ultimate sin and repent of it the rest of their lives. But it did not matter. For this moment Richard of Sussex belonged to her. The world did not exist beyond this room—not Windsor Castle, nor Phillip, nor the morrow . . .

"I love thee, Maria," Richard whispered as he entered her. "Until death parts us I will love no one else."

Maria crossed to an unshuttered window. Lights from Windsor's banquet hall, situated higher than the lower ward, radiated into the night, piercing even the darkness of Richard's chamber. Occasionally she heard a shriek of laughter, the murmur of voices. The outer world, with its responsibilities, was beginning to intrude.

Coming up behind her, Richard slipped his arms around her naked waist. She leaned against him, closing her eyes. Nothing has changed, she thought. When we leave this room, Richard will return to Beatrice, I will return to a Fordwich without Phillip, and we will both have to beg the church's forgiveness for our sins.

"Let us pretend that 'tis just you and me," Maria whispered, "and that we have forever."

"But we don't." Richard buried his lips in her fragrant hair. "Not even love can make time stand still."

He turned her around to face him. "And I do love thee, Maria."

She reached up to smooth the tangle of hair tumbling across his forehead. Their parting had already begun and she could not even echo his declaration. 'Twas true that no woman could be in love with two men and she loved Phillip, but she felt such a tenderness toward Richard. Is this then the true wage of sin? she wondered. Not death, as the priests preach, but the emptiness accompanying the deed? Nay. The emptiness has naught to do with the sin, but rather the knowledge of its ending. Is it sin at all? she thought. Does God really begrudge us our fleeting moment together? If I were God I would be too busy admiring my handiwork, counting and rearranging the stars in my heaven, studying the face of the man in the moon to worry over the actions of two lonely people . . .

"You know 'tis over, do you not, Maria?"

She closed her eyes. "Aye."

"Because of Phillip." Richard's voice caught on his name. "I have betrayed him and betrayed him willingly, and I must live with that. But it cannot happen again."

"He will never know. And if he did he would not care. Phillip does not love me. He never did." Easier to justify her adultery by believing in her husband's indifference.

"You know him not at all, or you would not say that. Phillip is driven by demands and desires we cannot know. And he does love you, but love is not the end all, Maria. There are other things."

She covered her face, trying unsuccessfully to hold back tears that were accompanied by rasping sobs. Taking her in his arms, Richard stroked her hair until she quieted. "You are wed to Phillip and your duty and love belong with him," he said softly. "The past cannot be changed, nor should it be. But a measure of my future, at least, will not come to pass. I have decided I cannot wed the Lady Beatrice."

"Jesu!" Maria breathed. "You must. The scandal would be dreadful."

Richard smiled. "You once braved something similar and survived nicely. Besides, by the morrow all of Windsor will know what we have done. I will have to put a fine face on the broken engagement and enlist Edward's help with some appropriate excuse. Mayhaps the Scots will suddenly break the truce so recently signed, or I will be called west to search for Roger Mortimer. Whatever, we will think of something. After you, I'll have no other woman."

"I almost wish we had not made love, for it makes the very thought of parting unbearable." Maria pressed against him. "Phillip will be gone such a long time, Richard, and I will be so lonely for you both. Will you not just visit sometimes at Fordwich? Papa and Eleanora and Tom also enjoy your company and . . ."

"Nay, lovely. I'll not disgrace your family by bedding you within their very house."

"It wouldn't have to be that way. Not if we were careful."

"But I would not want to be. Just looking at you I would be remembering tonight." He shook his head. "'Tis best that I just send your father someone to help manage Fordwich until Phillip's return and maintain a distant interest—as I do with most of my vassals."

They heard footsteps on the stair outside, the murmur of

female voices. Queen Isabella and two of her maids were returning from the banquet.

Maria thought suddenly of the saying from the Cherry Fair, "Life though pleasant is transitory . . ."

Richard wrapped her in a bone-crushing embrace. "I love thee always," he whispered against her ear.

And if I do not love you, Maria wondered, then why does our parting hurt so?

THIRTEEN

t Fordwich the next two and a half years passed in monotonous routine. To Maria nothing seemed to vary from day to day—a squabble with Piers the Cook, a ride to the Leopard's Head, Tom falling from his pony, or a letter from Phillip. Only her daughter, Blanche, born eight months after Phillip's leaving, provided true change; only she and Tom gave Maria a true measure of pleasure. Blanche was nearing two and was a stout-legged girl with curling auburn hair, mischievous eyes, and chubby hands that constantly darted about, touching and poking all manner of forbidden things. Blanche's birthing had been easy enough, and with her babe at her breast Maria had experienced a contentment that had long eluded her. In her arms she held someone who loved and depended on her completely. Looking down at that fuzzy head, the bright dark eyes, tiny mouth groping for her breast, Maria's heart swelled.

"I'll not abandon thee," she'd whispered. "I'll always be here when you need me, that I promise." It sometimes surprised her when she thought that Phillip did not even know he had a daughter—if Blanche truly were Phillip's daughter. Maria did not like to think about the possibility that Richard might have sired her babe, but she could not say yea or nay for certainty. The timing was too nebulous to really know. And though Blanche was as dark haired as her father and brother, sometimes Maria fancied she saw Richard's expression, or a shared mannerism. She kept such thoughts to herself, and was sometimes glad she did not truly know. Often she pretended Blanche had been sired by both men, and loved her all the more.

Richard had arrived at Fordwich following Blanche's birth, to participate in her baptism. Before her birthing, Maria had written, requesting that he act as godfather. The earl had readily agreed. Richard presented his godchild with a dozen exquisite robes of silk and ermine, tiny dolls carved from unicorn horns, and a cream-colored pony. Though he seemed in good spirits, even resuming nightly conversations with Hugh, their few private moments were strained.

He seemed afraid to touch Blanche, though Maria was certain he had not the slightest inkling about her possible parentage. Nor would he allow himself to even look at Maria.

"How is Phillip?" he asked the one time they were alone. "I had word from him months ago, at Rouen, but nothing since. Where is he now? When will he return?"

Maria waved her hand to the small wooden box atop her bedstand. Nine letters rested inside, one for each month of Phillip's leaving. "I know not. I've not opened his letters."

"But you must, Maria." He looked genuinely shocked. "And write to him, 'Tis your duty."

"I am tired of duty." She longed to reach out, trace Richard's profile with her finger, press her lips to his, nestle in his arms. She had so much to tell him—about her feelings for him, her loneliness since his departure, the nights when she'd awaken from a fitful sleep with the taste of his kisses fresh and alive, the days when she thought of naught but him—even her wondering, about Blanche, though that, at least, must always remain hidden. In all matters she kept her silence and when Richard left Fordwich, she counted it a relief. During the ensuing months, she cuddled Blanche closer to her, spent more time with little Tom, and told herself her children were enough.

Tom was seven now, and he was the one she worried about.

He had reached the age where boys left home for the castles of other lords who would begin them on their long apprenticeship toward knighthood.

"When can I go, m-mama?" he asked repeatedly. Was it her imagination or was his stutter becoming more pronounced?

Maria touched his cheek, still rounded like a babe's, and shook her head. "When papa returns. Before, I would miss you too much. Who would look after me?"

"Sir Richard would, m-mama. Would you write him and ask him to find a place for me in someone's house? How can I grow to be a real knight if I n-never leave home?"

"But you are just a babe, Tom. You are growing too fast as it is. Won't you stay with your mama just a while longer, until I become used to your leaving? Who will protect me with you gone?"

"Grandpere can. Or papa's knights or anyone, but I can't, m-mama, if all I have is a wooden sword."

She stared into that angelic face and her heart wrenched. The entire practice of rushing off children to strange castles was totally uncivilized, she decided. If custom decreed sons must leave home, then custom was wrong and should be changed. There had been too much leavetaking in her life. To think of her precious child shoveling manure, currying horses, cleaning armor for an impatient squire, serving at table where one misstep would earn him a box on the ears was more than Maria could bear. He was barely out of swaddling bands. Though tall and thin for his age, Tom's face still retained its baby softness; his huge blue eyes yet viewed the world with untarnished innocence. He was so vulnerable—quiet, shy. When he was embarrassed he walked with a stiff sort of gait, his head cocked awkwardly to the side. Maria found this idiosyncracy endearing; she knew others would ridicule him. More aggressive pages would tease him until Tom would replace that tender walk with a mannered swagger, his sensitivity with obnoxious bravado. Not yet, she told herself. I need you near.

Tom increasingly reminded her of Phillip. His mannerisms and actions brought Phillip back to her with a sometimes painful freshness. Maria swore she would not think of her husband and month after month allowed his letters to pile up inside the chest by her bed. Gradually, however, Phillip's letters began to draw her like a lodestone and she eventually took them out, starting with the first one from Calais and progressing to the latest one from Rome. The contents were a surprise. She'd expected a travelogue, and he did mention his journey, but the overwhelming portions spoke of his desire and yearning for her. Maria was stunned. This Phillip bore little resemblance to the aloof man she'd married.

"I am not good at words," he'd written from Calais, where he and Niccolo had stayed with pilgrims and other travelers at one of the innumerable maisonettes throughout the city. "I regret our parting. I would not hurt thee, no matter what you think. I would not leave you bitter. I love you too much for that."

From Amiens, which along with Constantinople claimed to possess the true head of John the Baptist, Phillip wrote again. "'Tis different this time. The places have not changed; perhaps I have. I visit Chartres and think of you. In Paris I saw Queen Isabella's entrance and remembered back to our wedding and longed once again to make love to you. 'Tis like I've left behind the best part of me."

In his last letter he wrote, "We will be at Niccolo's in Venice through All Hallow's Eve. From there we'll sail for Jerusalem. Write to me there, Maria. Tell me about your days and about Tom. Tell me you still love me, for I love you and need you more than life itself."

"If you love me so much," she whispered, "why did you leave? Why do you not return?" She smoothed her hands over the cramped handwriting, the rolling ends of parchment, and stared into space, her mind whirling. The Phillip in these letters was not the man she'd known—or thought she'd known. Phillip had always been so miserly with spoken words of affection, yet this Phillip wrote the words Richard had verbalized. Could Phillip really love her? Richard said he did. Phillip said he did. Might it be so?

"You are the one constant in my life," he'd written. "Do not take that away from me."

How peculiar, she thought, rerolling the parchment. Why would Phillip say such a thing? And do not I feel Richard is my constant? An odd choice of words. Was Phillip unsure because he knew about Richard and herself? In Paris if he mingled with Isabella's court he might hear all sorts of gossip. Could that account for his uncertainty?

Maria pressed the letters to her heart. And how constant would you think me if you knew I'd committed adultery? How could I have so betrayed you? If I could but erase that night with Richard . . . She hesitated. Would I? Would I willingly live my life without ever knowing Richard's love, give it all up to spare Phillip? The answer took her breath away. She'd face death rather than have her husband ever discover her adultery, to shield him from the truth—but the truth itself? Nay. And if I am not sorry for having lain with Richard, she wondered, what are my true feelings for him? Staring into the shadowy corners of Fordwich's solar, Maria examined her heart. 'Tis impossible to love two men, I know that. But somehow it does not seem as impossible as it did twenty-eight months ago.

FOURTEEN

ueen Isabella flung open the hinged diamond-paned window. The small apartment she had inhabited these past few months was located on the third story of an unremarkable half-timbered dwelling. Like so many others in this part of Paris's Right Bank, the apartment cantilevered over the story below and leaned out above a narrow street cluttered by business signs shaped like the products they advertised.

Sighing contentedly, Isabella gazed out at the darkened city of her childhood. After the nightly Angelus signaled bedtime, Paris plunged into darkness. Only around its eleven crossroads or in grottoes dedicated to patron saints did candles or an occasional lamp provide light. The smell of rotting garbage wafted upward from the deserted lane. While Paris's main streets were paved and wide enough to accommodate two passing chariots, the city's more than three hundred fifty side-streets were topped by mud and offal.

The Right Bank, located beyond the old walls, was the area of commerce, industry, and the luxury trades. Wealthy residences also clustered here, and from their elaborately ornamented belvederes watchmen maintained vigilance. As a child Isabella had enjoyed her occasional outings to the public markets, which were largely serviced by riverboats traveling the River Seine. Soapmakers, fishmongers, hatters, cabinetmakers, potters, furriers, barbers, and apothecaries with rows of strange-smelling potions packed in peculiar-shaped bottles all inhabited the Right Bank. Traffic jams were a way of life, with basket-laden pack mules struggling for space against street vendors or porters bearing bundles of wood or charcoal. In the plazas jongleurs performed acrobatic stunts and feats of magic or recited satiric tales, and when the king's vintage was readied, public criers cried the royal wine.

Hearing movement from behind, childhood memories fled. "I will have to be returning to the Louvre," the queen said. "Charles may have a reputation as a philanderer but he would frown on his sister's indiscreet behavior." She stretched languidly but made no move to dress. Isabella was content here and hated to return to the royal palace, where decorum must once more be put on as firmly as the crown atop her head.

A tentative dawn began inching across the eastern sky. An assistant public crier, extolling the virtues of Paris's twenty-six public bathhouses, called through the streets:

> *Calling you to bathe, messire,*
> *And steam yourself without delay*
> *Our water's hot and that's no lie.*

Isabella smiled. Master criers and their assistants announced marriages, births, taxes, official decrees, fairs, and in May of this year, 1325, they had proclaimed throughout Paris her imminent entrance into the city.

How tumultuously her countrymen had greeted her, waving and cheering so loudly they'd drowned out the ringing of the city's fifteen churchbells. Parisians had strewn flowers along her route and as she passed reached out to kiss the hem of her skirt. Their welcome had provided soothing balm to a self-esteem sorely wounded these past years. The quarrel over Gascony, England's foreign province, had worsened until Isabella's brother, Charles IV, had confiscated the duchy. Edward had blamed Isabella, and ceased coming to her bed. Small loss, she thought, her mouth twisting, but his coldness

[174]

had triggered rumors that his emissaries were traveling to Rome to seek a divorce.

The very idea of such an act made her grind her teeth in rage. That Edward should seek to rid himself of me, she thought, when he is the one guilty of unpardonable sin! The situation with the Despensers had degenerated so badly that in September of 1324 Hugh the Younger had openly confiscated all her estates and imprisoned her servants, dispatching them to religious houses throughout England. The worsening conflict in Gascony had provided for Isabella an unexpected relief.

"Perhaps I myself should travel to France," she'd suggested to Edward. "Charles has always doted on me. I think he'd listen to England's side if 'twas properly presented."

Reluctantly he had agreed and in March of 1325 the queen had crossed the channel to her homeland. Her gripple miser of a husband, seeking to make a good impression, had even loosened the royal purse strings enough to allow her a new wardrobe. During her early years of marriage Isabella had managed to stay abreast of French fashion, spurning the English styles, which were dowdy and unimaginative. Recently, however, she'd been forced to fight for every penny in her household budget, and clothes had faded in significance. Thanks to Edward's unaccustomed largess she had entered Paris regally attired in a black velvet so voluminous and long that only the tips of her white checkered leather riding boots peeked from beneath the hem. Her pale hair had been left unplaited and held on either side of her head by cases of gold fretwork. As she'd ridden to the royal palace, smiling and waving to children and shopkeepers, her thoughts had been on her forthcoming meeting with her brother the king and one other—Roger Mortimer.

Will I still find him captivating? she'd wondered. Does he yet even reside at the French court? Has he found a younger woman whose charms he prefers? Isabella might have been queen of England but Mortimer made her feel as vulnerable as a girl suffering her first crush. Remembering her uncertainty, Isabella smiled. Such doubts now seemed foolish.

Her gaze swept the Paris skyline. In the Île de la Cité, surrounded by the River Seine, the spire of Notre Dame soared above the rest of the buildings. No English church could favorably compare with Notre Dame, which contained room enough for nine thousand worshipers. Near the cathedral stood the queen's temporary residence, the royal palace. In the fauborgs, where houses possessed gardens and on Sundays the bourgeoisie promenaded, windmills labored in the damp November air. Amid harvested vineyards, abbeys etched against the lightening sky.

As Paris rumbled awake, shutters began slamming, dogs barking, roosters crowing. From the house of a toothdrawer a servant carrying an empty bucket stumbled toward a nearby public fountain, one of many servicing Paris by aqueducts located in the northeastern hills.

Calloused hands slid around Isabella's naked waist. She leaned back, into the arms of Roger Mortimer. "I love it here," she whispered. "'Tis like I never left."

"I hate it," Mortimer said decisively. "On the Left Bank those university students are as plenteous as rats. They prattle about reason and philosophy and other matters of no consequence, and the booksellers around Notre Dame are so numerous I cannot move without stepping on one of the weasels. The shouts of the muleteers, the stench of the butchers and tanners around the Chatelet, the moneychangers on the Grand Pont who have robbed me of my money as truly as a bandit—I despise all of it."

"My wild marcher lord," Isabella laughed. "You just hate to be imprisoned by any city."

"There is no place like the march and I will not rest until I once again race across its hills." The earl's powerful fingers tightened around her waist, but he was not thinking of lovemaking. Roger Mortimer approached all of life, not only sex, with an intensity that was as overwhelming as it was intriguing.

His dynamism and self-confidence had long ago convinced the queen that he was capable of deeds other men only dreamed of. In this case the intimation behind his words frightened her.

Other exiled Englishmen, including members of the contrariants, had gathered at the French royal palace and were plotting all manner of disturbing things. So far Isabella had refrained from becoming involved in their schemes. I could stay in Paris forever and never give another thought to England, she told herself, as she slipped away from her lover and reached for her clothing. Indeed she had written Edward, who had recently begun badgering her about coming home, that she would not return until the Despensers were banished. Yet the wild talk of Mortimer and some of the contrariants, their hatred of her husband, disturbed her. Edward was a fool and a weakling but he was the father of her children, after all. Recently their eldest son, Prince Edward, under his newly bestowed titles of duke of Aquitaine and count of Ponthieu, had arrived to do homage in lieu of his sire for the Gascony provinces. Isabella had found the prince so much like Edward—without the perversions and weaknesses—that she'd wept for what might have been.

Silently, she reached for her crimson kirtle. Crimson, green, and particolored clothes were so expensive only nobles, prelates, and magnates could afford them—and some clergy so long as their gowns were long and buttoned. The queen busied herself with such mundane thoughts rather than dwelling upon the forthcoming parting with her lover. Though she and Roger saw each other at court, they had to maintain at least a perfunctory façade—and she found each private leavetaking almost impossibly painful.

Looking up, she saw Mortimer staring at her, and as always at the intensity reflected in the black depths of his eyes, Isabella's very bones seemed to melt. She who had dutifully accepted her aberrant husband, her political and domestic position, who placed responsibility above personal happiness, had fallen hopelessly in love. If Edward had been a normal husband, she thought, returning Roger's look, I would still have become your thrall.

"My gentle Mortimer," she breathed.

He laughed and moved confidently toward her. "You did not call me gentle last night," he said, crushing her against him. Roger was indeed a wild lover, but after the indifference of Edward she found his lustiness exciting beyond endurance. To Edward she had been a duty, but to Mortimer she was a woman.

"Stay awhile yet, madam." He leaned back, his manner mocking. "We have matters to discuss."

"Is that an invitation or a command?" Though she loved his dominance, sometimes his lack of respect for her position nettled.

"Take it as you will, sweetheart." Mortimer swept her in his powerful arms, carried her to his narrow bed, and as he positioned himself atop her, Isabella forgot about duty, about everything save the delight of her lover's embrace.

FIFTEEN

he Lady Katherine Gower has invited us to London for Christmas, daughter." Hugh sat down beside Maria on the bed in Fordwich's solar. "Would it please you to spend Christmas at Westminster?"

Maria shrugged. "I care not, papa."

"It might take your mind off other matters. I hate to see you looking so gloomy." When Maria did not reply he reached out and patted her knee. "Letters do have a way of getting lost, you know, poppet. You'll soon hear from Phillip, I am certain."

Looking down at her hands balled in her lap, Maria did not reply. For three months she'd not had word from her husband. His last letter, written from Egypt, had spoken of its great granaries, which rose like mountains from the desert floor, of animals called crocodiles, giraffes, and elephants with long snouts through which terrible noises emerged. The missive had been stiff and formal, including little of a personal nature.

"Why did you not write me when I was in Acre?" he'd asked. I want to hear about Tom and the babe you wrote me about. You should not deny me, Maria." That was all. When she'd first read the letter, she'd felt like tossing it across the room. Her husband was the one who'd abandoned her, yet he was trying to make her feel guilty. And she had written—to both Venice and Acre.

"I will send word to Lady Gower that we will attend," Hugh said. "You will enjoy London, I promise. 'Tis a city like no other." He no longer knew what to make of his moody daughter. He'd heard occasional snatches of disturbing gossip about her and Richard of Sussex, which he'd summarily dismissed. He'd seen no evidence of the earl's rumored infatuation for Maria, especially not during his last visit. Richard loved Phillip; he'd not so betray his vassal. But sometimes Hugh sensed a nagging undercurrent, a tension between his daughter and their lord that he did not understand. Easier to overlook it, however, than probe too deeply. Besides a great lord's favor could prove quite financially rewarding. On her first birthday Richard had granted Blanche one thousand acres near Canterbury and Tom a manor adjoining Deerhurst. Hugh blocked out such mercenary thoughts. For now he'd concentrate on shaking his daughter from her malaise by persuading her to enjoy Christmas at Westminster.

Westminster was in a festive mood and decorated for Christmas, but Maria could not fully enter into the merriment. Nor did she enjoy London, which was a sprawling, dirty, and very confusing city. The first morning there, Hugh had her out as early as the servants of great houses who did their market shopping from midnight to dawn. She shared narrow streets with eggmen shouldering woven baskets of eggs, with drapers, poulterers, and bakers who bore steaming loaves of bread toward Pannier Alley. Dogs yapped, geese honked, merchants quarreled, bulls being led to slaughter in the stinking East Cheap bellowed—and Maria wished herself back at Fordwich.

Hugh took her neath the houses atop London Bridge, past St. Paul's Cathedral, and by Tower Hill, where perched the Tower of London.

"Praise God," he said, gesturing toward its forbidding whitewashed walls, "that the moat is currently frozen over. In summer its smells near knock passers-by from their mounts."

"Indeed." Maria gazed up at the white tower, made of caen stone and soaring ninety feet. She felt small and insignificant. London's noise, jumbled buildings, garbage-strewn streets, shouting merchants, was intimidating. She'd imagined the city differently. She wasn't disappointed exactly, but she felt out of place, a gawking country maid.

Soon after Hugh took her past the tower, Maria pleaded a headache and they returned to their apartments near Westminster. Hugh spent the next several days drinking and exchanging yarns with old friends and visiting Lady Gower at her residence located at Little Tower Hill, outside London's walls. Left on her own, Maria generally stayed to her room. I should have stayed home like Eleanora, she thought. She longed for her children and the peacefulness of Fordwich. I am not cut out for court life, she told herself glumly. No matter for how short a time.

On Christmas Eve, Maria took her place at table in the Palace of Westminster along with hundreds of others. The huge yule log had already been dragged into the great hall and placed atop the old one burning in the fireplace. Following ancient custom, King Edward himself had rekindled the log. As flames crackled and roared up the chimney, onlookers cheered, for such was considered a promise for good luck and long feasting during the coming year. His Grace anticipated 1326 with a mixture of apprehension and hope. Though his wife's continued absence nagged at him, he did not personally miss Isabella. Life was much simpler without her disapproving presence. There are problems yet throughout England, Edward thought, but the raiding, banditry, gang warfare, and murders are no worse than in years past. Richard, especially, blamed the Despensers for the lawlessness, and while it was true much of

the trouble was based on their continued fighting with
followers of that accursed Thomas Lancaster, both Hughs were
justified in their actions. Edward was glad Richard was
currently absent from court. Whenever his brother was about,
the king sensed his relentless disapproval and found himself
forever apologizing for acts he secretly agreed with.

Sighing, Edward took his place at the dais, next to Hugh the
Younger, and motioned for more wassail. A sudden wave of
melancholy overcame him. He was certain his people would
never fully accept him, and even after eighteen years of rule
their condemnation rankled. The march especially remained a
constant headache. Two agents of that blackguard Roger
Mortimer had recently been caught plotting to kill both himself
and the Despensers. In Coventry a necromancer had been
convicted of using black magic in an effort to kill him and
Hugh and several other royal officials. 'Twas told that the
necromancer had plunged a pin into the heart of a waxen
image, which had resulted in the death of the official whom the
likeness represented. Edward had dismissed the very idea as
ludicrous, but Hugh had written the pope concerning such
heathen arts. Whether the tale was true or not, Edward
thought, guzzling his drink, the plotters were all executed. That
effectively ended their treason, whether magical or not. Wiping
his mouth with the back of a beringed hand, His Grace called
for the mummers to begin their entertaining and the master
cook to make ready his entrance.

Maria barely listened to the chatter of the others around her.
She had ingested enough wassail to make her feel all fuzzy
inside, but at least when she thought of Phillip and Richard the
pain was gone. Now both men seemed but golden, meaningless
memories.

A blast of trumpets announced the entrance of the master
cook, who bore a huge silver platter that he placed before the
king. On it was the customary boar's head, garlanded with
sprigs of laurel and rosemary. As the rest of the hall rose to sing

"The Boar's Head Song," the elegant Despenser leaned across Edward's arm, retrieved the roasted apple from the pig's open mouth, and popped it into his own.

And I pray you my masters be merry,
Quot estis in convivio!

Maria sang along but felt detached from everything taking place. When they sat down to the twelve-course dinner she ate little—though many revelers were already stumbling off to the garderobe to ingest salt and water or some other emetic, so they might vomit up what they'd just eaten. Then they would return to feast once more.

Maria was shaken from her peculiar detachment by various snatches of overheard conversation. Was it her imagination or was half the court discussing Richard? When she really listened it seemed his name was a whisper on everyone's lips, just below the level of laughter and light talk. She put her hand to her forehead. 'Tis but wishful thinking, she told herself. His Majesty earlier mentioned Richard was spending the holidays at Conway.

Maria looked to the dais and the king, who, wearing a garnache of gold tissue emblazoned with the royal leopards and a crown set in sapphires, was an especially magnificent sight. There was something distasteful about him, however, a certain vacuity to his features that she had never noticed before. Watching Edward absently toy with one of several gold rings she felt a sudden fear of his weaknesses. Someday will you bring about your brother's ruin? Blaming her melancholy on the wine, she forced thoughts of Richard and the king to disappear like the bubbles in her drink.

After every guest had eaten his or her fill, the banquet tables were removed and Edward motioned for the entertainment to begin. Earlier, the king had chosen a Lord of Misrule, who now capered about dressed in fantastic garb, spouting nonsense Maria could not understand. Bored, she wandered about.

Maybe I should follow papa's example and be off to bed, she thought. A victim of too many free-flowing spirits, Hugh had retired hours past.

From the corner of her eye, Maria saw the Lord of Misrule pinching the cheek and then the breast of a giggling countess. He seemed to be causing much laughter with his antics, but Maria intended to stay far away from him. She had no desire to end up the butt of some misplaced joke.

Sir Ralph Cromford, her dinner partner, caught up with her. Ralph was filled with wine and idle chatter, but Maria had no wish for a companion and searched for a polite way to tell him so. "Have you heard," Cromford said, "that the Bastard is back?" Wide-eyed, she turned to question him, but he was speaking to a second man.

"I say 'tis the talk of fools," said Ralph's companion.

Ralph tugged at his beard. He was the Despensers' man and misliked Richard and his endless carping. "If the Bastard is near, treachery is afoot, of that I am certain."

"I believe it not. Just yestermorn I heard he was in France and today in Wales."

Ralph laughed. "'Twould take a hundred earls to be everywhere he's claimed to be. I'll warrant even the Bastard is not that clever."

"Aye. His enemies see him everywhere. The time to worry is when there is no word at all."

Angered at the knights' remarks, Maria moved away, toward the Lord of Misrule, who was jumping about the king. Amused by the jester's banter, the king flashed his even teeth, slapped his thigh, and threw his arm around the less exuberant Despenser. The jester then bounced from the king to a group of ladies.

"Ah, Lady de Vere, and does your husband know he wears horns?" He bantered to an aging countess who fluttered her charcoal-darkened lashes and giggled.

To another: "Your breasts are twin mounds of beauty, my dear. Near as fine as the mound of Venus between your legs."

The women rolled their eyes and simpered. Turning her back in disgust, Maria concentrated on a small group bobbing for apples, another playing forfeits, a third hunt-the-slipper.

Behind her she heard a loud jingling of bells signifying the presence of the Lord of Misrule. "Ho, Burst-Belly!" After greeting a rotund courtier, he scooted around to face her. She feigned overwhelming interest in several pages who were carrying into the hall enormous bowls of raisins to be used in the game of snapdragon.

The jester bowed before her. Maria stiffly inclined her head. She almost believed the man was deliberately tracking her, though that was nonsense, of course.

"Well, what have we here?" he asked the gathering crowd, which included a laughing Edward whose arm remained looped around Despenser.

The Lord of Misrule thrust his painted face at Maria and shouted something about the soft, sweet underbelly of the lion. She did not understand the comment, but the audience seemed to find it amusing. Even a smile softened Hugh Despenser's sculpturesque features.

Maria stepped back but the jester pressed forward. Without warning he pirouetted and, flourishing a long plume, tickled the cleft between her breasts.

"Leave me be!" Snatching the feather from his hand, Maria snapped it in two.

Pretending fear, the Lord of Misrule threw his hands to his face and executed an awkward back flip, landing near the king and his favorite. He stumbled, then regained his balance. "Well-a-day, what is wrong?" As he waved his arms, the bells on his cap jangled. "Are you a virtuous lady loath to feel a man's touch?" He turned around with an exaggerated wink to the spectators. "Beautiful lady, please grant a fool your favors. You've been known to favor other fools."

Was he referring to Phillip? Maria cursed her slow country wit. The jester's actions not only angered but puzzled her. Intent on getting away, she spun on her heel. Quick as a cat upon a mouse, the Lord of Misrule jerked her around and crushed her in an embrace. His moist mouth groped for hers; his tongue snaked between her teeth.

The court ladies gaped and giggled. His Majesty laughed and whispered something in Despenser's ear while the men called out encouragement.

Maria slapped him, knocking off his jester's cap and sending him sprawling.

"Bitch!" he cried, his face red with wine and anger. He struggled to his feet, his hand holding the side of his face.

"No wonder the Bastard lusts for her." Hugh Despenser spoke for the first time. He possessed a caressing voice that slid above the laughter like oil over water. "The Bitch and the Bastard. A perfect mating!"

Stunned, Maria stared at the favorite, whose dark eyes shone with malevolent delight. Edward smiled nervously; the merriment died on other's faces. Some openly glared at Despenser. Maria felt her cheeks flush crimson. Turning from the now uncomfortable crowd she pushed her way toward the exit. Near the dais someone shouted for the candles to be extinguished, and even as she approached the archway leading from the hall, the area was plunged in darkness.

"Let the game of snapdragon begin!" announced a chorus of pages. Throughout the room flames of fire leapt from huge bowls as brandy was poured over raisins and ignited.

Waiting for her eyes to adjust to the darkness, Maria paused. White tongues jumped from the bowls, illuminating the surrounding disembodied faces. Hands without arms plunged in to retrieve raisins. Involuntarily, she shivered. From earliest childhood she'd misliked snapdragon. The eerie dancing flames cast even familiar faces in a sinister light, reminiscent of wandering souls or evil spirits. Goosebumps rose on her arm. Something in the darkness was watching her, she knew it. Turning, she bumped into someone.

"Pardon," Maria could scarce manage an apology for the tightness in her throat. She stepped aside, only to be pulled back by two strong hands. Forceful fingers tipped her chin in a heart-stoppingly familiar gesture. Before she could form Richard's name his mouth closed over hers, stopping all sound. His encircling arms tightened. Hungry lips searched her neck, the lobe of her ear, the hollow between her breasts.

Disbelieving, she touched Richard's hair and face. "My lord, I cannot believe it. Is it really you?"

"'Tis said memories will play you false," he whispered against her ear, "but in your case time has been most kind."

"But I thought you at Conway. I heard . . ."

"Westminster has many vantage points, where one can watch without being observed. It has been a pleasure watching you, looking so bored and haughty, even when surrounded by many would-be admirers." Richard laughed low in his throat. "Though I think you were a bit harsh with the Lord of Misrule!"

The rushlights and candelabra were being relit. Pulling her along the passageway, Richard led her away from the great hall. "Come, let us be away before people see us together. I had not planned on announcing my presence until the morrow. I would not have an untimely announcement mar some's Christmas Eve."

They passed a handful of servants and a drunken knight sprawled across the floor. The knight was mumbling a phrase from an earlier mummer's production of *St. George and the Dragon*, something about "the itch, the stitch, the pox . . ." Maria tripped over him and would have fallen, had Richard not caught her. Looking up, the knight blinked in surprise.

Opening a door, Richard pushed her inside. "I must have been mad," he said, turning to her. "Within an hour, all of Westminster will know we were together."

Richard looked about, as if to ascertain the room was empty. A thousand pairs of staring eyes looked down upon them, for they had entered the king's bedroom, the Painted Chamber. Every inch of wall space was filled with a confusing mixture of battle and biblical scenes, symbolic figures and inscriptions painted in a brilliant melange of colors. Though a hearth fire burned in the fireplace, the room appeared deserted.

Maria took a step toward Richard, caressing his face with her eyes. She'd forgotten how handsome he was, how virile. Even dreams had dimmed his appeal.

Holding her at arm's length, however, he shook his head. "It has been such a long time and I have missed you so, but it was a mistake to have given into my desires and kissed you. You are like a sickness in my blood, Maria. I doubt I'll ever succeed in purging you."

"Then I've also the sickness. For neither have I purged you." Reaching up, she smoothed a strand of hair away from his forehead, pressed her palm against his cheek, the roughness of beard. "You've no idea these past months how I've longed for you. Aye, and ached for you."

"It has been the same for me. Every moment of every day." Richard's eyes narrowed. He tore his gaze from her to the scene of the coronation of Edward the Confessor painted above his brother's bed. "'Tis a dangerous game we are playing, Maria."

"I care not." Her arms crept round his neck, her fingers curled in his hair. "Do not leave me again, Richard. Please. Let the world, even the pope himself, condemn us, but please do not leave me. Without you I am not whole."

He drew back. "We must not let passion further override our judgment. Nothing has changed. There is still Phillip, and he will return someday."

"Aye, and I love him, Richard, I do. But I love you also."

His eyes dissected her face, probing for the lie. "'Tis just the wassail talking," he finally managed.

She shook her head. "I've wrestled with it these past two years. Nay, since that first Christmas, I think." Her fingers brushed his lips, the bridge of his nose. She could not keep from touching him. "I know it cannot be, not you and Phillip both, but I do love you, Richard, and God help me, my heart cannot tell me whom I love the more."

He expelled his breath on a trembling sigh. "If we come together again, this time I'll not let you go. Not even for Phillip."

They gazed into each other's eyes. Their union might be forbidden and doomed from the outset, but they would think about that tomorrow. And tomorrow would never come. . . .

"I love thee, Richard," Maria whispered, as his tawny head bent to her. "And that is all that matters."

SIXTEEN

aria spent her days inside one of the stone buildings situated atop London Bridge. Her apartment, which Richard, for appearance' sake, had deeded over to her family, was positioned near the bridge's great wooden drawbridge. Throughout the day the drawbridge was continually raised and lowered to accommodate cargo ships passing below on the River Thames, London's life blood. The creak and pops of turning wheels, the shouts of the attendants and sailors provided a welcome alternative to the tomb-silent apartment. Save for the household servants who glided through the low-ceilinged rooms, Maria was totally alone. She missed her children and felt guilty about not returning home to them. Sometimes she contemplated having them brought to her, but London would be only a temporary residence and it was not healthful to drag children around the country, especially in winter. Besides, she did not want them to know that she was living with Richard.

When a lord took a mistress it was not uncommon to have children with a mixture of heredity sharing the same household, but Maria could not bring herself to be so brazen. Richard maintained the pretense of residing at Westminster, though whether they really fooled anyone she did not know. I have made my choice, she thought, settling down in the bay window located in the fourth story's sitting room where she spent most of her time. And I'll involve as few others as possible. Besides, she had no idea how long their liaison would last. Someday Phillip might return; someday events might tear her and Richard apart. For now, she told herself, I will live for today and whatever happiness it brings. I will not think of Phillip or anyone. The consequences I'll face later.

As the setting sun turned crimson the perpetual haze hovering above the city, Maria readied for Richard's return. After ringing for her bath, she watched Joanna, the chambermaid Richard had provided, enter the master bedroom followed by pages bearing a wooden tub. Joanna supervised the subsequent preparations with an efficient flurry of hand movements. The chambermaid had been struck dumb, 'twas told, after Bannockburn, when she'd heard of the death of her father and two brothers. While Maria would have preferred someone who could have at least provided a measure of companionship, Richard disagreed. "In London, where gossip rides the air like a foul wind, a servant who cannot spread tales is a gift from God." He had never trusted Londoners and was eager to leave a city long known for its hostility to its sovereigns—including Edward II. Constant frictions occurred between the king and various factions over conflicting boundaries regarding royal and civil rights. Some of Edward's men had even been murdered, robbed, or kidnapped without redress. While Richard did not wish to alarm Maria, he stressed the fact that she must never go out alone in London.

As Joanna laid out her clothes, Maria relaxed in the tub of steaming, rose-scented water. In the two weeks she'd been atop the bridge Richard had managed for her an entire wardrobe of rich velvets, sendal silks, and samites, favoring for her as unostentatious a style of clothing as he did for himself. The dresses she was grateful for, but when he began presenting her with expensive jewelry she'd returned most of it.

"I am not comfortable with such treasures. You should not feel you must buy a love I've freely offered." She often contemplated how her mother would have approved of Richard's generosity—if not the method of attainment.

"I enjoy giving you things," he'd responded. "I would present you all of England if 'twould make you happy."

Not all of England, yet. But enough to make her uncomfortable. Besides the bridge apartment, he'd granted her Leeds Castle, which he'd obtained following Bartholomew Badlesmere's execution.

"I know these places would give you pleasure," he'd said when she'd protested the extravagance. "And I have enough other properties. Will you not accept a small gift from me?"

"Do not people hate the Despensers for this very reason, because Edward showers them with similar favors?"

"I would hardly call a few properties excessive generosity."

When her father had returned to Fordwich, Richard had also sent along men whose sole function was to seek out proper workmen to repair and enhance Fordwich Castle. Maria's leavetaking from her father was another thing she misliked thinking about. "I will stay over in London to supervise some remodeling to the bridge apartment," she'd said by way of explaining her actions. Of course papa had not been fooled. He tried several times to bring up duty and obligation, as well as Henrietta's memory, but when Maria changed the subject he did not pursue it. Better to return to Fordwich, where ignorance was easier to maintain, and pray his daughter would soon come to her senses than to confront her in an unpleasant scene that would settle nothing.

After Maria finished her bath and dried her hair, Joanna helped her into a kirtle of blue and gold, the colors of Richard's coat of arms. Every fiber of Maria's being now strained toward the first sound of her lover's booted foot upon the stair. Restlessly, she returned to the bay window in the sitting room. Bars of ice upon the Thames caught the sun's last scarlet rays; the wharf of Queenhithe, with its stacks of wine, wool, hides, corn, and firewood, jutted into the river. When Piers Gaveston had been alive, Edward had presented his wife with the rents from Queenhithe. The king and his favorites . . . Where is Richard? she wondered. Has something happened at

Westminster? From her apartment she could see the severed heads of traitors placed above London Bridge's storehouse. Though Maria ordinarily avoided looking at the pikes, tonight she did not. Silhouetted against the bloody evening sky five new heads had been placed. Carrion crows circled, then glided to rest atop hair-covered skulls. Shuddering, Maria moved away from the window, back to the warmth of the room's roaring fire.

As lights began to bloom from Newgate to Aldersgate, close by the Church of St. Botolph, she heard the long-awaited arrival of her lover. But when she ran to the door she was greeted, not by Richard, but Michael Hallam.

"Where is my lord?" Michael's presence did nothing to lighten Maria's mood.

"He'll be a bit late. He asked that I relay the message."

Maria always felt uncomfortable around Michael. He seemed perpetually so silent and gloomy. His strong profile, the dark growth of beard, jutting chin, menacing air might make him intriguing were he not as cold as the ice glutting the Thames.

"What is happening at Westminster? Why has Edward ordered more people executed?"

"'Tis none of your concern," Michael replied, crossing to spread his hands before the fire. "Leave questions of politics to men. They have the heads for such things."

Maria began to find Michael's rudeness amusing. She could not imagine him being so brusque with Eleanora— but then she and her twin were totally different. "You mislike me, do you not, Sir Michael?"

His gaze flickered over her. "'Tis not my place to feel anything about you. I just do not want anyone to hurt my lord." Which was true. Before becoming Richard's squire, Michael's life had been brutally poor. He'd possessed no lands and few prospects, and his private life had been unhappy beyond endurance. Mere loyalty could not begin to repay his lord for his change in fortune.

"Do you think I would ever hurt Richard?"

"You already have. And you will again. 'Tis inevitable." Was not pain always the ultimate way with women? No wonder priests blamed them for man's fall and most of the world's evils.

"I would rather die than hurt Richard," Maria said softly. "I love him."

Seeing the tears glisten in her eyes, Michael softened. Rather than risk beguilement by such womanly wiles he assumed his fiercest expression. "'Tis not for me to judge your heart. But I know my lord's, and whomever he loves I'll guard with my life."

"Do you think I need protection?" she asked, startled by his words.

"We might all soon be in need of protection."

Maria leaned closer to the fire, as if its cheery warmth could belie the implication of his words. She did not question the squire further concerning their meaning, however. Better not to know.

A log in the fireplace crumbled to coals; sparks flew and popped. Entering with a handful of chemises, Joanna disappeared into the master bedroom.

Michael crossed to the bay window. He pretended to be concentrating on London's skyline, which was dominated by St. Paul's Cathedral, whose three-hundred-foot spire was the world's tallest. He cleared his throat. "How is your sister? Why did she not come to Westminster for Christmas?"

"She is busy at Fordwich. Eleanora has never been one to enjoy prolonged celebration."

"If . . . when you return to Fordwich," he said, staring out the window, "tell her I inquired as to her health."

"Why do you not visit Fordwich and tell her yourself? If you have a liking for my sister, why do you not ask her to marry you? Neither one of you is attached to another, and I'm certain Eleanora would be happy to wed."

Michael's jaw clenched. "That can never be." The words

erupted from him as scornfully as if he were cursing the God who'd made him. "In the eyes of the church I am already a married man!"

Maria's hand flew to her mouth. "I did not know, Michael, I swear. No one ever told me. I am sorry if I have offended you."

"'Tis my marriage that is the offense." He struggled to maintain control, reassuring himself that the past could no longer hurt him, unless he desired a relationship with another woman, which he did not. Save for Eleanora. "My wife and I see very little of each other. I found early on she prefers the company of other women."

"I do not understand. What is wrong with having friends?"

"I think you misunderstand, Lady Rendell." Michael fixed her with an enigmatic look. "Have you ever thought why the queen hates her husband, or why His Grace is so close with 'Nephew Hugh'?"

She frowned, for he seemed to be speaking in riddles. "I suppose . . . I know the king and Despenser seem to be inseparable—in much the same way as you and Richard, I suppose."

His mouth twisted. "'Tis a far different relationship, m'lady."

The trend of conversation was beginning to make her uneasy. She had no desire to be privy to royal secrets, if such Michael was about to impart. "'Tis not my place to wonder about such things. I am not certain it is always safe to question."

"You are right. And I hope you will always be able to stay in the sheltered world you've erected round yourself."

At that moment Maria heard Richard's step on the stair. As Michael discreetly withdrew, she forgot all about him and their peculiar conversation. When Richard opened the door, she wrapped her arms around him, feeling once again secure, loved—and happy.

"I thank you for your enthusiastic welcome." As he returned her embrace he breathed in the fragrance of her hair and perfume, felt the sweetness of her body pressed against him. "How I've missed thee." Leading her to the window seat, he pulled her onto his lap. "I leave Westminster wanting to pull my hair in frustration over the never-never land my brother and Despenser inhabit, but by the time I reach London Bridge I am soaring. The very thought of you makes it all worthwhile."

When Maria slid from his lap to remove his cordovan leather boots, he rested his fingertips atop her head, light as thistle-down, and continued, "How I survived without you these past months I cannot think."

"Nor I without you." She smiled up at him. The newness of their relationship, its possible brevity, made each shared moment that much more special. Noting the tired lines around his mouth, the fatigue in his movements, she silently berated the king and his favorites for causing Richard such difficulty.

Leaning back against a pillow he closed his eyes. When he spoke, weariness thickened his voice. "Edward rants on about the queen and her refusal to leave France and I think of you. Despenser plots how to further weaken England's laws and poison my brother's mind, and I wonder how you are spending your day, if you miss me, or no longer love me at all."

Settling once again in his arms, she smoothed his hair from his forehead, brushed his lips with hers. "That you need never worry about," she whispered. "Easier to cease breathing than to stop loving you."

Richard cradled her face in his hands. "Just a few more days. Then we can head for Dover, where 'twill be much safer and you won't have to be locked away like a criminal. In London even the walls have ears. Here at least we must be discreet."

"Aye, discreet, though I would shout my love from atop the Tower of London."

"Events are at a dangerous crossroads now," he continued. "I would not needlessly worry you, but perhaps you should know. Isabella has taken Robert Mortimer as a lover, and together they are plotting an invasion of England."

"What?" Maria gasped. She struggled up to face him. "I do not believe it! We are a civilized people. Such a thing could not happen."

Richard smiled grimly. "With Roger Mortimer plotting behind the scenes, anything is possible. If my brother does not act, he is in danger of losing his kingdom."

Seeing the terrified look on her face, Richard pulled her back down against him. "Do not fret, lovely. Edward is well aware of that fact and at this very moment is mulling various options." And will choose nothing, he silently added, but he would not further worry Maria. He stroked her until he felt the fear and tension recede, and her body relax. With her beside him, Richard soon forgot all about politics and his brother.

"I do believe I love thee, Maria, more than any man has ever loved a woman."

Eyes filling, she burrowed against his neck. She remembered Michael Hallam's prediction that she would hurt Richard—and she would. When Phillip came home, there would be hurt enough to last forever.

Lifting her in his arms, Richard carried her into their bedroom, laid her atop the silken counterpane. The dinner bell jangled but he shook his head. Spreading atop her, he sank them both into the soft feather mattresses. "Love cannot wait," he whispered, as his hands and body began moving over her.

SEVENTEEN

he morning of Maria and Richard's arrival at Dover began dull and gray, though by midday the clouds had lifted until only a wispy haze clung to the narrow road. The gentle farmland that covered so much of Kent gradually gave way to treacherous terrain unlike any Maria had ever seen. Thickly forested hills, unbroken by fields or towns, surrounded the pack train, which struggled up a highway breathtaking in its steepness.

With each passing mile Maria felt more isolated from her family. Upon their return from London she and Richard had stopped at Fordwich to pick up Tom, who was going to begin his apprenticeship at Walmer Castle, near Dover. Her visit with Hugh and Eleanora had been unbearably strained. Though Fordwich was a leisurely day's ride from Dover, Maria knew they would never visit and a part of her was relieved.

"'Tis my life to do with as I please," she'd told Eleanora when her twin had broached the subject. Her sister's disapproving remarks and looks not only made Maria uncomfortable but awakened feelings of guilt she was determined to ignore. "I am merely going to escort Tom to Walmer Castle. What is sinful about that?"

"Where did you ever get such foolish notions?" Eleanora pursed her mouth disapprovingly—a mannerism shared with their mother. "No one can do as he pleases, certainly not a woman. Show me the law that gives us such a right."

"I am not interested in laws," Maria said stubbornly, "or custom or duty or the church's teachings. 'Tis not as if I am the only woman who has ever been part of a lord's household."

"Aye. But introduce me to Richard's wife whom you would serve or his children whom you would care for. Tell me your legitimate title, sister." When Maria did not respond, Eleanora shook her head. "The only title you'll be known by is leman to the earl of Sussex."

I will not think of Eleanora or anyone, Maria thought as they neared Dover Castle. Richard promised to send soon for Blanche, and Tom rides beside me, and I'll ask for nothing more. Covertly, she studied her son. Throughout the trip he'd tried to act grown and unimpressed, but as he looked at the alien hills, rattled off questions to anyone within range, or cared for the stocky black palfrey Richard had given him, his face shone with excitement and happiness.

"I am going to be a great knight, mother," he assured her repeatedly. "You and p-papa will be so proud of me."

"I am already proud of you," she said, "and I'm certain papa will be, too." When she'd returned from London, no new letters had been awaiting her. Whether he was dead or alive, in Jerusalem or China, she did not know. Save for Tom and Blanche, I would not even care, she assured herself, but she did not probe that thought too deeply.

Richard had arranged for Tom to begin his apprenticeship for knighthood at Walmer Castle, home of one of his childhood friends, Lord Gilbert Hawes. Until the age of fifteen Tom would remain a page; then until knighthood, approximately seven years later, he would be a squire. "God willing you shall complete your training under my care," Richard had told him. "I could think of no greater honor than to have the son of such a fine father in my household."

Richard made it a point to treat Tom with deference and respect, as if addressing an equal. Maria was grateful for the earl's kindness and discretion. Neither by word nor deed did he betray their intimate relationship, and if Tom overheard or surmised that she and Richard were other than friends, he gave no indication. He was too busy commenting on the trip, asking questions about his new home, and prodding Richard for bloodthirsty tales of war to worry about anything so uninteresting as his mother. Hugh had spent much time preparing his grandson for his forthcoming training, as had Richard, but they were no substitute for a true father, and when Maria's heart softened toward her husband she hardened it with the knowledge of his neglect. It had been Hugh, not Phillip, who had taught Tom to read and write, who had helped him struggle through the Arthurian tales, the Trojan War, and Julius Caesar, all of which were combined in Hugh's book of romances. His grandfather had taught him checkers, chess, and backgammon, and it was his lord, not his father, who was teaching him how to play the lute and the art of fencing with a blunted sword. Richard had also stressed the importance of daily mass, and Tom's manner had changed from indifference to a touching devoutness.

"God is our ultimate lord, Thomas, and we must strive to serve Him as honorably as we do our earthly king," Richard had told him. "Remember that honor is the most important attribute a knight can possess, and his word the most solemn oath he can give. All is lost without honor." The earl's words near stuck in his throat. What right have I to prattle about honor, he wondered, when I have broken faith with Tom's father and continue to break it, when I am sleeping with Tom's very mother and usurping Phillip's place as a father? Such questions increasingly plagued his thoughts, bringing such unhappiness and self-loathing they sometimes threatened to overshadow his love for Maria. But now as he approached Dover Richard's only thought was to share with Tom and his mother his pride in Dover Castle, which was his favorite residence.

The Sussex train began its steep ascent up Castle Hill. Once

Facebelle stumbled and nearly fell to her knees, for the road was poorly traveled and scarred by deep ruts from runoffs. On either side forests menaced. Maria found the atmosphere disturbing.

"Round the bend you'll catch sight of the castle," Richard said, pointing. "'Tis a picture I promise you'll not forget."

The trees alongside the road abruptly ended; the land on either side fell away. Jutting above a low-hanging mist stood Dover Castle. Above its square massive keep Richard's banner snapped in the wind blowing off the Strait of Dover.

"Look, Tom!" Maria reined in Facebelle to better view the castle's forbidding majesty. Every powerful line, every thrusting tower mutely proclaimed its military function. 'Twas not just a fanciful phrase that declared Dover to be "Key of England." Thirty miles across the sea lay France—visible on a clear day. From Roman times some sort of fortress had guarded the channel from the troublesome French and a host of other enemies.

"'Tis fine, mama, is it not?" Tom stood in his stirrups. Excitement, as well as cold, flushed his cheeks.

"Aye." Neither saint nor sinner, nor all of Satan's legions, she was certain, could ever bring this mighty fortress to its knees.

"I thought you would be well impressed." Richard smiled at Tom. "Come along. 'Tis eager I am to give you both a closer look."

Pulling her cloak tighter around her shoulders, Maria shivered against the chill from the sea. Dutifully she kicked Facebelle and they began the last steep ascent up Castle Hill.

Dover Castle had been built for war, not love or comfort. Its brown gray walls of Kentish rag were in some places twenty-one feet thick; its four angle towers topping the keep afforded an excellent view of the small town and port, as well as the sea and surrounding countryside.

The keep's lower area was used as a barracks for Richard's

soldiers. The upper level contained a small chapel, as well as a gracefully proportioned banquet hall and great hall. Both were encircled by mural galleries that provided a second tier of lighting. Off the great hall were two adjoining bedrooms, which Richard had ordered completely redone. Though they were small and by nature rustic, the rough stone walls and floors had been softened and warmed by tapestries; fireplaces had also been added. Maria's chamber was known as "the queen's bedroom." For appearance' sake she nightly retired there, but as soon as the castle quieted, the noise ceased from the barracks below, she slipped next door to Richard. Groping past the velvet outer drapes and inner curtain of yellow brocade, she slipped into his waiting arms, and told herself 'twas all worthwhile.

Rumors of impending invasions either by Isabella or France itself were so constant that after the initial fear Maria learned to ignore them. Dover seemed a second court, with royal messengers forever arriving and leaving and magnates closeting themselves with Richard for hours on end, but Maria knew very little about official business.

"If 'tis important I will tell you," the earl assured her. "Otherwise I would not needlessly worry or bore you." Events seemed to totter back and forth, with nothing really changing. Because of increased communication between the exiled rebels and his subjects, Edward had ordered a general commission, covering England's most important ports, to stop the flow of correspondence in and out of the country. Though some rebel letters were confiscated, many more reached their destinations in bales of cloth, the false bottoms of barrels, or even by bribery of Edward's officials. In France, Isabella's affair with Roger Mortimer had become so flagrant that her brother had forced her to withdraw from Paris. She found refuge in the low and monotonous plains of the Netherlands, with its splendid cities made prosperous by industry. Count William of Hainault, also lord of Holland and Zealand, welcomed her to his castle near the city of Valenciennes, and there she, Mortimer, and Prince Edward enjoyed his hospitality.

When Richard was closeted with visitors or merely out hunting or hawking along Dover's cliffs, Maria spent most of her time in the castle's small chapel, which seemed the pleasantest—and warmest place—in the keep. Part of the chapel overlooked the inner entrance to the castle, and from this vantage point Maria always awaited Richard's return. It was a secret game between them. No matter how busy he was, Richard always managed a glimpse to the chapel opening, a private smile of greeting, which made the loneliness of Dover bearable.

This March day Maria ran to meet him in the narrow hall connecting Dover's chapel to the banquet hall. They embraced as passionately as if their separation had lasted years, not hours.

"Your lips are cold," she said when they parted.

He smiled and put his arm around her as they headed toward the king's room. "'Twas chilly along the cliffs. Did you miss me?" he asked as they entered his chamber, and sat down to a continuing game of backgammon.

"Aye, 'Tis lonely without you."

"I wish that we did not have to be so secretive, that I could fill Dover with people so you would never have to be alone."

Reaching out, Maria stroked the knuckles of his hand. Strange that Richard would think her lonely for others when he alone was enough to make her happy. She shivered as an odd thought struck her. Might happiness, like life itself, be transitory—even as is the Cherry Fair?

"I am pregnant, sire. I am certain of it."

Richard stared at Maria as if she were a stranger. "Pregnant?" He repeated the word as if it, too, were unknown to him. "How can that be?"

Maria smiled, though she was a bit uneased by his dazed reaction. "I think you would know how a woman conceives a child." When he did not further respond, she continued, "I could not be certain before, but now I can have no doubt, and we must discuss it. 'Tis an . . . unusual situation, and we must decide how best to approach it." She had found Richard in Dover's barracks, where his men were readying for Midsummer's activities. Some were already intoxicated, and the noise was not conducive to private conversation. Laying her hand atop Richard's arm, Maria pulled him through a round-headed archway into the lower chapel where his soldiers attended mass. Here, at least, they could talk more quietly.

Richard craned his head back toward his men, who were beginning a game of dice. "You've picked a poor time to tell me, Maria. Midsummer is supposed to be a time of pleasuring, not of mourning."

Maria stiffened. She had ambivalent feelings about her pregnancy also, but only because of the possible resultant scandal. "I think we have naught to mourn, my lord, and I only wanted to tell you now, so that we might have some time alone tonight. With the rest of Dover enjoying Midsummer, I thought 'twould be the perfect time to talk."

Richard looked down at her hand, which still rested upon his arm. He did not reply.

Dinner was a noisy affair. In anticipation of the later revels, most of Richard's men had already ingested heroic amounts of wine. Midsummer festivities would last until sunrise the following day. June 24 was the shortest night of the year, the safest time for souls who might leave sleeping bodies to wander to places where death was fated to occur. Bonfires were built throughout England and the peasants threw herbal wreaths into the flames as protection against witches and other evil spirits. A strange night, one better made for staying behind closed doors, Maria thought. She even noticed thistles about

Dover's hall; the plant was thought to provide protection
against the powers of darkness. The ruling class might scoff at
some of the peasants' more primitive superstitions, but it was
better to be safe.

Maria turned to Richard, who was engaged in conversation
with Michael Hallam. He was obviously avoiding her, and his
coldness was troubling, but they must talk. Sighing, she picked
at her blancmanger, made from a thick chicken paste blended
with rice boiled in almond milk. Recently she'd had very little
appetite, and the morning sickness had come upon her. To
herself she'd denied the possibility of pregnancy, but she could
deny it no longer. She had faced the knowledge squarely and
discovered that, despite the shame, she did not regret
conceiving Richard's child. Now if she could but convince its
father.

As the banquet hall began emptying, Maria took Richard's
arm. "Come my love, let us retire."

His eyes wandered beyond her to his exiting men. "What is
there to discuss? Words will not change reality. And I've a mind
to watch the festivities."

Maria felt suddenly weary. "I'll wait for you, as always. Please
do not forget."

All night she waited, but Richard did not come. She spent
much of the night leaning against the cold stone wall, gazing
out the window into the darkness. Bonfires blazed atop every
mountain and dotted the shoreline for as far as she could see.
Their orange flames leapt to the velvet blackness of a night
blanketed with stars. A soft night, a night made for dancing and
lovemaking. From beyond Dover's curtain drifted shouts and
laughter and merry pipes.

"Richard," she whispered, "do not forsake me now."

Tired from standing, Maria shifted position. Every babe
sapped her strength early on, and this one was no different. But
it is, she thought. 'Tis a bastard who will suffer because of the
sins of its parents. Perhaps it will be sheltered because of
Richard's power, but the stigma will still be there. With

Blanche, at least, no one could roll his eyes and count on his fingers and dismiss Phillip as father. All of England would know the heritage of this child.

Dover's keep was quiet. Only an occasional sound drifted from the barracks below. Most of the knights were probably out neath the moon, tumbling some giggling maid. And what is Richard doing?

Save for a night light set in water beside the bed, the room was dark. Outside the bonfires seemed to float above invisible mountaintops. Strange things indeed happened this night. Fairies were said to be able to speak with human tongues on Midsummer. To see them you need but gather fern seed at midnight, rub it on your eyelids, and become invisible. Shivering, Maria placed her hands across her gently swelling stomach. "You are safe within, my wee one," she whispered. "and no matter what mistakes your parents have made, we will love thee well."

Dawn streaked the eastern sky, and finally Maria went to bed. Alone.

Richard did not appear for his customary sop of wine, and Maria attended morning mass alone. She asked several people as to his whereabouts but received contradictory replies from the servants and evasive responses from his knights. By afternoon when he had not returned, she retired to her room only to find Michael Hallam and another of Richard's men, Anthony Fordun, posted on either side of her chamber door. Between them were her traveling trunks.

Maria stopped so abruptly she stumbled. Michael, who stood nearest, reached out to steady her. Shaking off his hand, she cried, "What is the meaning of this? Why are my trunks here? Where is my lord?"

Michael's brown eyes flicked over her. He forced his expression to blankness. He was here to execute his lord's will, not to feel pity for Maria, though she did indeed look a pitiful sight. "My lord asked that we bid you good-bye. We are to escort you home to Fordwich."

"Fordwich? I do not understand." Maria turned to Anthony Fordun, who was peering down at his boots. "Sir Anthony, you have always been kind to me. Will you now please further enlighten me as to what is happening?"

Anthony rubbed his blunt hands over his red beard and looked exceedingly uncomfortable. "'Tis as he says. We are to provide you escort." He raised his faded eyes to her. "We must do as our lord wishes, m'lady."

"But I cannot go home. Not now. Where is Richard?" Maria's voice rose to a shrill. "If he means to kick me out like a common whore, for no reason at all, he'll at least explain his actions."

Michael moved toward her trunks. "If we leave now we can be to Barfeston 'ere nightfall." He swung a small trunk upon his broad shoulders.

Maria's knees shook. She leaned against the wall to retain her balance. "Sir Anthony, would you please tell me where Richard is?"

"Down by the pharos," he said, coming forward to grab her arm. "Are you all right, my lady? You are as pale as whey."

She shook off his hand and, ignoring Michael's disapproving frown, left the keep for Harold's Earthwork, where the pharos was located. Walking across the green, treeless stretch, Maria reached the horseshoe-shaped promontory where sat the light-house and the church of St. Mary-in-Castro. A gentle breeze blew off the channel. The distant shoreline of France clung gray like a bank of fog. Ships edged toward the harbor, their sails billowing, their painted masts vivid against the washed-out afternoon sky. The pharos, with its rough surface of flint rubble, jutted heavenward. *What will I say to Richard?* she wondered as she approached it. *How will he explain his apparent treachery?*

She pushed open the door. "Richard?" She blinked in the dimness. The pharos, built during the time of Christ, was now used as a free-standing bell tower for St. Mary's. Pigeons, nesting in the framework, fluttered about—but nothing more.

Maria left the pharos. Her eyes swept the English Channel, the cruciform church, and to the south the stone windmill, with its slowly rotating vanes. Beyond, Richard leaned against an outer wall, gazing toward the sea. He looked so lonely; even the set of his shoulders proclaimed dejection. As Maria hurried to him her anger evaporated. No matter the reason he was acting so strangely, she could not doubt that he thought his actions right. Or that he loved her.

"My lord."

He turned. Like a curtain arrogance descended, hardening features that had been open, even yearning. "What are you doing here? You should be on the road to Fordwich by now."

"Why did you mean to cast me out, Richard? I do not understand."

The wind tugged at his hair. In the distance smoke from a still smoldering bonfire rose, then disintegrated in the breeze. "Where were you last night? I waited for you until dawn."

"I did not say I'd come. And I thought it better this way. Just to have you leave." The last was said in such a rush of agony that Maria reached out to embrace him, but he twisted aside. When he faced her his eyes were bright with unshed tears. "'Tis a fine mess we've made, is it not? A bastard begetting a bastard. God must truly mean to punish us that he would so afflict us."

"Afflict us? A babe is not a plague, Richard. And I'll grant I'd rather not bear an illegitimate child, but I am not the first woman to do so. Despite everything, 'tis our child, and I love its father more than life."

A muscle twitched in his jaw. "You talk as if love is the end all, but it is not. Love does not explain to Phillip that I have cuckolded him; love does not explain to my son why he must wear a bend sinister upon his coat of arms or to my daughter why she cannot marry as well as others beneath her in wealth. Love is but a small part of life."

"It is all I have left. If you should cast me out now I cannot return home. Think you papa and Eleanora would welcome me? If you abandon me I have nowhere to go." Maria again wrapped her arms around his waist. This time he did not pull away, but neither did he respond. "Your position is all that protects me from full shame, and I do not care. As long as you love me I will risk it all."

Richard raised her chin so that she looked into his eyes. "If you stay, you'll no longer come to my room."

Maria gasped. "What are you saying?"

"We'll not lie together. I can exercise at least that much restraint. I must. The babe is punishment, Maria, I know it. For my treachery."

Fear chilled her heart. Hurriedly, she crossed herself. "Do not say such things, Richard. They might come to pass."

Reaching out he cupped her cheek. "If only you were not so beautiful, Maria. If only I did not love you so much."

"If only I weren't Phillip's wife," she said wearily.

"Aye. If only."

EIGHTEEN

uring the summer of 1326 two papal legates from Rome slipped into Dover bearing letters from Pope John XXII. Both letters were addressed to Hugh Despenser the Younger. They enjoined him to assist in the reconciliation of Edward and Isabella, and admonished him to "abstain from provoking enmities and to study and to promote friendship."

Edward was furious over the contents of the letters, which should have been confiscated by his officials in the first place.

"Should the people get wind of that damnable cobbler's sons' hostility toward Hugh, who knows what trouble might ensue?" the king railed. "Isabella insists she'll not return until the Despensers' banishment, and the pope's blathering just gives her carpings a legitimacy they do not deserve."

After ordering Richard to imprison the papal legates, His Grace personally arrived to question them. After threatening them with death he allowed them to leave the country without announcing their commission—and prayed their message would truly remain secret.

Edward remained in Dover for several weeks, sending for his minstrels, hawks, and favorite hunting dogs, as well as many of his magnates. Upon their arrival he began drawing up a complex, and illogical, scheme of defense against a possible invasion.

For Maria, His Majesty's presence remained a source of embarrassment. She was nearly four months pregnant, and while her tunics concealed her swelling stomach, the truth would soon reveal itself. She especially hated being under the watchful eye of Edward's favorite. Nothing escaped Hugh Despenser's attention, and she dreaded the inevitable cruel comments. Like a poisonous snake he was made all the more deadly by the uncertainty of when he might strike. Her relationship with Richard also continued to deteriorate. They were polite to each other, but she had ceased sitting beside him during mealtimes, and they seldom shared a private moment together. Sometimes when she caught him looking at her his torment was so apparent that she could forgive all. Her unhappiness seemed inconsequential. She wanted only to ease his pain.

We will weather this time, she assured herself, during her daily walks along Dover's cliffs. Our love will emerge ever stronger. Soon you will accept the babe and the guilt will lessen. Phillip will never return, so there will be no true day of reckoning. She repeated this last so often that it became more a litany than a statement. As she watched passing ships drift across gray waters, she listened to the ever-present sea gulls, and their plaintive cries were matched by the loneliness in her heart.

While King Edward was in residence, huge amounts of wine were nightly consumed, and Richard was proving himself as intemperate as any man. Revelry continued into the early hours with much rowdy entertainment. Edward's jester related endless bawdy jokes to the inebriated assemblage; acrobats entertained, as did half-naked dancers who stained themselves with walnut juice and danced with knives, and the king's favorite jongleur, Robin the Minstrel, recited epic tales of war.

Robin the Minstrel especially disturbed Maria. Perhaps it was her condition, but she found the minstrel's tales, which vividly evoked blood and death, scattered brains and gore, revolting. When Robin related not the king's supposed martial exploits but Richard's, when he spoke of the earl severing a Scot's head, of plunging his hand into the chest of an enemy and yanking out the still pumping heart, she had to remind herself that such stories were always exaggerated. This was not the Richard she knew, nor cared to know. But who now exactly was her lover?

The smoke in Dover's great hall caused Richard's head to ache. His mouth was dry. He called for more wine, though his thoughts were already out of kilter. Good, perhaps he could drink until he had no thoughts at all.

Tonight Robin had ceased his blathering about imaginary battles, saints be praised, and was singing of courtly love. Every time the minstrel even indirectly referred to Bannockburn, Richard felt the eyes of everyone in the room on him. Everyone knew the real truth of Bannockburn, that Richard had been terrified, that he and Edward were responsible for parents weeping and mothers wailing for sons who would nevermore return. When I stand before my Maker, Richard thought, how many deaths will I have to atone for? And not only death— treachery as well. Bannockburn also meant Phillip.

Guzzling his wine, Richard motioned for more. Drink he needed, until his mind went dead and he could not see Phillip's accusing face. "So this is how you repay me," Phillip would say upon his return. "Thank you for comforting my wife, sire. Thank you for your bastard."

Richard knocked over his cup. Wine stained the linen table-cloth; a page scurried to blot it. "Forget that," Richard hollered. "Bring me more wine."

He looked up. Maria was watching him. What was she thinking? Did she know about Bannockburn, that the minstrel sang naught but lies? Every time she'd caressed the scar on his chest, had she thought of Phillip and remembered that save for her husband, Richard would be moldering in his grave? Phillip had saved his life and Richard had given him a bastard.

* * *

"Lord Sussex would see you." Michael Hallam stood in the doorway to Maria's chamber, glowering at her. She was causing his lord pain, just as he'd predicted. She was the cause of Richard's drinking, his solitary rides, his short temper. England was floundering and his lord's every energy was consumed by a woman. One could not expect better from King Edward, but from Richard it was disgraceful. And frightening.

"I do not understand." Maria sat up in bed, her hair spilling around her. "M'lord has not asked for me in weeks."

Michael's lips compressed in an angry line. "Well, he's asking for you now." He turned on his heel and stalked away.

Heart racing, Maria hurried next door. She knew not what Richard wanted, but perhaps this would be the night when they would finally talk, when their relationship would begin anew. Taking a deep breath, she entered the king's chamber. Richard was seated by a roaring fire that provided the only light in the room. At a nearby table pushed against the window well she noted a flagon of wine and an overturned goblet. He's been drinking again, she thought, and her optimism waned.

He turned his head. "Sit beside me." His manner was cold as the wind off the channel. Hooking with his leg a small bench he brought it close, then returned his gaze quickly to the flames. With her hair tumbling about her breasts and dressed as she was in a filmy chemise, Maria appeared as desirable as ever. More so, after the weeks of abstinence. All the vows in the world, all the confessions to Father André could not make him cease desiring her. But he must. And after the babe was born, he would provide for it and Maria and turn his energies to Phillip and restitution. But can I ever achieve Phillip's forgiveness? He looked at Maria perched on the nearby bench. And can I ever truly give you up?

After motioning for Michael Hallam to refill his goblet, Richard dismissed him. He had summoned Maria to question her about Robin the Minstrel, to ascertain whether she suspected the truth about his cowardice, but his thoughts were muddled by her presence as much as the wine. Had Robin been but an excuse? Had he really summoned Maria just to share a few private moments?

Slowly, he lifted his hand to her. He touched a tumbling mass of hair that glowed like a dying sunset in the fire's blaze. "I have missed thee so, Maria." His words were slightly slurred.

She bent toward him and he inhaled the scent of her. "And I have missed you."

"So much I wanted to say to you, to share but . . ." His voice trailed off. He'd almost added that he'd been afraid, but that was what this was all about, was it not? Fear and Bannockburn, which brought him back to Phillip. Forever and ever, like the cut of a circle. With no way out and no way in.

"I prayed he would leave, do you know that?" Richard said, vocalizing the tangled web of his thoughts. "Leave England and never return so I could have you all to myself."

Maria stiffened. She knew well enough who "he" was. "Such thoughts do no good. We've been over this endlessly, and there are no new answers, no magic way to end the pain—for anyone." Maria left the bench to kneel by his feet. "We have not been together for such a long time, let us not waste this moment." She rested her head against his knee. "Take me to bed, my love. Let me rest my ear against your chest and feel the beating of your heart. Let me fall asleep in your arms."

Richard shook his head, as much to clear it as refuse her request. Reaching for his goblet he gulped its contents, but not even drink would obliterate the voices, fears, guilt, the endless replaying of scenes. Death and love and loyalty all blurred until he had no idea what he was feeling, or where one emotion finished and another began.

He pushed Maria away so abruptly she nearly lost her balance. Leaning his elbows on the folding table, he held his face between his hands. "We are doomed, Maria, you and I."

The words were spoken without a blur of drink and in an unfamiliar tone. Not like Richard's voice at all. Fear prickled along her spine. She suppressed an urge to cross herself. "I no longer believe in prophecies." Her voice sounded much surer than she felt. "I am certain that we will only be doomed if we doom ourselves."

"And have we not done a good job of that?"

Maria had no answer. Watching him struggling with a myriad of emotions she could only guess at, she longed to comfort him though she did not know how. He had just rejected her physically and she knew not how else to reach him.

She stood up. "If you are right, what can be done about it anyway? We cannot rewrite the past or change the future, even if we would, for did not God long ago write our fate among the stars?"

"That's what frightens me," Richard whispered.

He reached for more wine. Maria returned to her room.

Save for Edward and Hugh Despenser, who had ridden to Richborough, Dover remained crowded with magnates who had gathered to plot counterschemes against the queen and her lover. Halfway through the even meal, Richard stood and, after draining his goblet, beckoned to Robin. The minstrel leapt nimbly to his feet and bowed low before his host.

"Sing to us all of Bannockburn, minstrel," Richard said. "Relate the entire battle. Begin with my unflinching bravery and end, of course, with Phillip Rendell."

Seated a discreet distance away, Maria nearly dropped her cup. She felt her face flush and was certain every guest was staring at her. She ducked her head. Richard's mention of Phillip could only call further unwanted attention to their relationship. Her pregnancy was now discernible to all but the blindest, so why was Richard so publicly humiliating her?

Before Robin had fully launched into his account, Richard loudly observed, "It seems my right is unoccupied. Is the Bastard to sup alone? Come, Lady Rendell. Break bread with me."

Maria's eyes swept the sea of faces. In the days following their midnight meeting, Richard had taken to openly taunting her, to performing verbal acts of cruelty. She did not understand this new twist to their relationship, but her pity and patience were swiftly evaporating. If he meant to wear a mental hairshirt, then so be it. But she would not don one for him or anyone.

"My lord, if 'twould please you, I am comfortable where I am at."

"Come here!" Richard roared.

As Maria approached, defiance replaced embarrassment. How dare he shame her before the entire hall?

"Sit beside me, my lady."

"I'll not."

Grabbing her hand, Richard squeezed it until the bones cracked. Maria sat.

He waved his goblet in front of her. "Will you not share with me from the loving cup?"

She bit back angry words. "Nay, my lord."

Shrugging, Richard drained the wine, then motioned Robin to begin.

Accompanied by his rebec, the minstrel launched into an epic account of Bannockburn. With each passing moment, Richard became ever more intent, leaning forward in his chair toward the minstrel. His knuckles showed white as he grasped the stem of his goblet.

When the battle neared its climax. Maria tried to stand, to break free of Richard and his madness. He grabbed her hand. She sank back down.

"And after the heathen Scot came upon the glorious earl"— Robin's voice boomed into the sudden stillness—"that brave knight, Phillip Rendell, taking no heed for his own life . . ."

Richard leapt to his feet. "Enough!" Shoving against the banquet table he sent plates crashing, food flying, guests screaming. "Get out of here, all of you, be gone from Dover. Now!"

Michael Hallam hurried forward to grab his arm, but Richard shook him off. Jerking his dagger from his belt, he pointed it at a stunned Robin, who stood amidst broken goblets and platters, streams of sauces, and half-carved haunches of venison.

"I should slit your throat. Then your voice would not sound so sweet."

Robin's face turned green as the pea sauce seeping into the floor rushes. Richard shoved him toward the exit, and the minstrel scurried away.

Then he turned to Maria. Quick as a darting fox, he spun her around until her back was against him. He pressed his dagger against her throat. Paralyzed as much by bewilderment as fear, Maria could neither move nor speak.

"Will you not plead for your life, lovedy?" Richard's hot breath seared her ear.

"Nay," she managed.

"Your courage is admirable, but only the best for the Bastard, wouldn't you agree? Never mind she belongs to someone else. Are you not lucky, Maria, to bear the seed of England's most celebrated bloodsucker?"

She shook her head in involuntary protest. The blade pressed against her throat. "Please, Richard, no more talk of blood. Just let me go . . ."

"But I want blood. Yours as well as my own." A prick; a warm trickling along Maria's neck. Richard released her and, when she turned to face him, touched the wound. Raising his hand he licked the blood from each finger.

The banquet hall careened, receded to a great distance. Maria lunged toward the knife. Richard jerked it back with such force it flew from his grasp and clattered to the floor. Doubling her fist Maria swung at him, hitting him square in the face. She leapt for the knife, found its bone handle, and plunged it toward her breast. Recovering from her blow, Richard knocked at her arm, deflecting the knife's path. The blade grazed Maria's forearm. Cursing, Richard pried loose her fingers and hurled the knife across the room.

"Fool! What would you do?"

"I would rather die than spend one more moment with you!" Maria shouted. Unconsciously, she clasped the shallow cut on her arm. "You are mad, Richard, and I hate the babe I'm carrying, for it has you as its father."

She ran from the hall back to her room and slammed down the door bar. Collapsing upon her bed, Maria buried her face in her hands. I have no one to blame but myself, she thought, even as she cried. But I have someone else to think of now. Rolling over, she touched the swell of her stomach.

"We must be gone from this hellhole," she whispered. "For your sake as well as mine. And I do not hate thee, my babe," she added. The uneasy feeling lingered, however, that her words, once spoken, would come back to haunt her. Like a curse.

At the following evening's approach, Maria decided it was time to try to escape Dover. She could not return to Fordwich, but she would be safe at Deerhurst. She planned to ride for Walmer Castle, where Tom was, and enlist an armed escort there. If Lord Hawes refused, she would rather risk danger and death on the roads than another night with Richard.

The earl had not appeared for lunch or dinner, and before the end of the even meal Maria left the banquet hall. She paused by Richard's door, listening for any sound. He'd probably passed out hours ago. Tiptoeing to her chamber, she hurried inside, lowering the wooden bar.

Richard was propped upon her bed, watching her. Save for the feverishly bright eyes he appeared sober enough, though she knew he must be drunk.

"Oh, my lord!" she gasped. "I did not think to find you here." Jesu! I've locked myself in with a madman. Searching for something to protect herself, Maria spied a log by the fire, then looked to the small candelabrum by her jewelry box. Her gaze fixed on the traveling cloak and coin purse she had earlier lain out. Even Richard in his intoxicated state would be able to deduce her plan.

Moving to block his view, she spoke. "I missed you at table, sire. Have you been ill?"

"Aye, Maria." His eyes glittered like a rat's. She suppressed a shudder. "I have been sick with an old malady. One that dates back far—perhaps even to childhood."

So, was Richard also prone to fits, to strange seizures where he swallowed his tongue? "Has the sickness passed?"

"Nay, lady, it never passes."

"Never?" His words made no sense.

Richard leaned his head back in a gesture of complete weariness. "There are things that must be said. I can no longer keep them locked inside . . ." He was silent so long he appeared to be asleep. Finally he opened his eyes and, with renewed strength finished, "I have never loved anyone as I love you, Maria. I know that, deny it as I might. So there are some things I must explain. I tried to tell you before, but I could not. 'Tis most difficult for me to speak after all these years—and I crave your indulgence."

Though she was certain all the words in the world could not soften what had passed between them, Maria nodded.

Richard doubled his fists, Rising from the bed, he turned his back to her. Slowly she inched back toward the door, intending to raise the bar and flee.

"Perhaps my behavior with Robin last night was a bit—intemperate. But he never should have come." Just as Maria reached the door, Richard turned around. "You see, he knew nothing but lies, and the lies sickened me. All his talk of glory and bravery were but products of his imaginings. Bannockburn was no victory, Maria, but a senseless slaughter. My brother was responsible for it, as he was for the murder of all those innocent northerners he left to the mercy of the Scots—but so was I, and a million pretty phrases cannot hide the blood on my hands."

"Nay, Richard, I do not believe that." Stunned by his words, Maria temporarily forgot her fear of him. "How old were you, nineteen, twenty? How could a boy have gainsaid the king of England?"

"If I had tried harder." His voice cracked. "If I had not been afraid." He looked at her as if expecting some reaction to this revelation. "Afraid, Maria, I was so afraid I could not think for the terror. I wanted to turn tail and run all the way back to London."

"But you did not. And every man is afraid before battle. How could he not be? Even your father I'll wager, must have . . ."

"Nay!" Richard's hand smashed into his palm. "Do not talk. Listen! 'Tis not just Bannockburn. From childhood, I've been afraid, though I am a consummate actor. I've had to be. But I needn't remind you of my origins. God gave me the face and form of my father and the heart of my good mother who, I'm told, was the gentlest of serving maids. What a fine jest. To look like the lion but possess the heart of a deer."

"Do not go on, Richard. This is preposterous. You . . ."

"When I was afraid, my playmates would sneer, 'What more can we expect of a bastard,' so over and over I was forced to prove I was the best and bravest, when inside all I wanted to do was run away."

"But you did not—and that is what matters." As Maria watched his tortured face and listened to his jumbled disclosures, her heart responded to his torment. He was not mad at all, but in need of compassion.

"I am no fit Plantagenet," Richard said. He raised his eyes to her. "Phillip should have let me die."

"Nay! Do not say such a thing!"

"'Twould have been so much better for everyone. I would not have mothers cursing me on the heads of their dead sons—and I would not have sown my seed in your belly."

"Will Phillip never cease haunting you? I am as much to blame as you and I am not sorry for one day of our love." That statement was true enough, but what about the guilt she often felt and just as often suppressed?

"I've hated you for making me love you, but I know ultimately I did it all of my own free will."

Maria took a step toward him. "We cannot choose whom we love."

"But we can choose to love in silence. Do you think if we were married that Phillip would so betray me?"

She placed a hand on his arm. "Phillip does not love me as much as you do." She hated discussing her husband. Though she tried to deny it, he loomed between them even when they made love.

"I wonder. Perhaps he loves you more."

"His actions proved otherwise." Drawing Richard to the bed, Maria gently pushed him against the mattress. "You look tired, my love." She bent down to loose his boots.

"When Phillip comes back . . ."

Pressing her fingers against his mouth, Maria stilled further talk. "We'll discuss that some other time. After you've slept." Besides, she thought, he might never come home. Would not that make things simpler? If Phillip never returned? Maria's eyes sought the wooden crucifix over the window well. Lord, forgive me for even thinking such a thought.

NINETEEN

n September 24, 1326, Queen Isabella, with an army of fifteen hundred men, landed on the coast of Suffolk between Oxford and Harwick. She and her followers had crossed the channel in ten fishing vessels. Their arrival was not challenged by England's eastern fleet, which was led by King Edward's younger half brother, Thomas of Brotherton.

"'Tis a good omen, is it not?" Isabella asked her lover. When Roger was at her side, Isabella felt brave and confident, but sometimes the magnitude of their act—their treason—threatened to overwhelm her. "If Edward's very kin will not come to his aid, then we cannot fail."

"The Bastard will not abandon him," Mortimer said. "But he is one against an entire country. No one else will raise a hand to save your fine husband."

Mortimer's prophecy proved accurate. When Isabella disembarked, she and her followers were greeted by enormous crowds, ringing bells, and blazing bonfires. Women and children strewed flowers in her path.

"We have come to avenge the execution of my dear cousin, Thomas of Lancaster," she told the cheering throngs, "and drive the accursed Despensers from power."

"The crowds love you, my dear," Mortimer observed, his black eyes mocking. "You tell them exactly what they want to hear."

"'Tis also true, Roger," Isabella said. Sometimes her lover's cynicism uneased her. At times she wondered whether he had approached their liaison with the same calculation he applied to all other matters. As they penetrated into England and picked up the trail of the hated Despensers, however, Isabella forgot all her doubts and concentrated on one matter, revenge.

King Edward was in the Tower of London when he heard of his wife's invasion. He immediately sent protests to Pope John XXII, as well as Isabella's brother, Charles the Fair. He also discussed the matter with members of the Council and leaders of Parliament, though he did not heed their advice. Edward had no intention of giving up the Despensers, even if that act would abort the invasion.

"I did not break the power of the barons or Cousin Lancaster to crumble at the first hint of trouble," he told them. Instead he issued a proclamation stating that all who took part in the invasion, save for Isabella and Prince Edward, would be treated as traitors. He placed a thousand-pound bounty on the head of Roger Mortimer.

Still no one rallied to his cause.

In full armor, Hugh Dispenser the elder, Earl of Winchester, stood before Isabella in the great hall at Bristol Castle. He was nearing seventy and showed his age, but gazing into that lined face Queen Isabella felt not pity but triumph—and hate, of course. Since her arrival one month past, she'd survived on hate, which had nurtured and sustained her as food never could. Now that hatred, which was like a constant blackness robbing her brain of all coherent thought, would be sated. Bristol's garrison had refused to stand by Winchester, who had sought refuge there, and yesterday, on October 26, 1326, the father of her most detested enemy had walked across the castle drawbridge and surrendered.

Isabella could barely refrain from sharing with Roger Mortimer, even by a look, her elation. Revenge was indeed proving as sweet as she'd anticipated during her years of humiliation.

"I've waited long for this moment." She addressed Hugh the Elder. "Do you recall your treatment of my cousin Thomas Lancaster, a man of royal blood, who was put to death because of your machinations?"

Hugh the Elder muttered something in reply. Most of his teeth were missing, pushing his mouth into a perpetual position of surprise. His eyes still flashed their old arrogance, however, which served to start Isabella's old hatreds churning up fresh and raw.

"You also treated me, your queen, in a shabby and insulting manner," she continued, her voice rising. "You never allowed me money and you and that whoreson you spawned poisoned my husband's mind against me."

"Your Grace . . ."

She cut him off with an imperial wave of her hand. Leaning forward in the curule chair which had been placed for her in the middle of Bristol's hall, she taunted, "Your lands are burning now, Hugh—the lands for which you schemed and robbed and which have insured your swift descent into hell. How transitory are your possessions, near as transitory as your life." Isabella's troops had plundered all of the Despensers' lands along their route of march and beyond. She had proclaimed that her supporters should take what they pleased and, after splitting it between herself and Mortimer, retain a portion for themselves.

"Ah, madam," Winchester cried. "God grant me at least an upright judge and a just sentence."

"Aye. You'll receive the same treatment you gave Thomas Lancaster." Now she smiled at Thomas's brother, Henry of Leicester, who had reached her weeks back, near Dunstable. He'd been one of the first to join her, bringing with him a large contingent of Lancastrian retainers.

William Trussell, a local judge, read the earl of Winchester's death sentence. "You shall be drawn for treason and hanged for robbery, decapitated for your crimes against the church, and your head taken to Winchester where you were earl against law and reason." Because he'd broken the laws of chivalry, Despenser was to be executed in a robe bearing his coat of chivalry, which would thereafter be permanently discarded.

Immediately following the verdict Mortimer, Leicester, and the others escorted Hugh to Bristol's bailey, where a gallows had been erected. From a window inside the castle's solar, Isabella watched the execution. While the earl was being readied, her two daughters, Eleanor and Joan, bounded in, filling the room with questions and chatter. Shutting out their voices, she absently put her arms around them. She'd been reunited with her children only yesterday, but now their presence did not even register.

As a noose was slipped around Despenser's neck Isabella's heart began a mad hammering. She was certain something or someone would momentarily appear to rob her of her prize. She could not believe that, after all this time, Hugh would not somehow escape and return to further torment her.

"My gentle Mortimer," she breathed. "Winchester is filled with the devil's very tricks. Watch him close."

When the executioner raised the rope, jerking Despenser ever higher in the air, Isabella gasped. Unconsciously her fingernails dug into her daughters' shoulders. The girls had grown very subdued and were watching the scene with open-mouthed horror. Hugh the Elder dangled in the air before beginning to twist slowly back and forth. His armor caught the rays from the sun in powerful flashes.

Suddenly five-year-old Joan screamed. "'Tis a monster," she cried. "Mother, look!" Her voice broke off in a wail. She began sobbing hysterically and was immediately joined by Eleanor, who, though three years older, was every bit as terrified.

Turning from the window, Isabella gathered her children to her breast.

"Do not cry, my wee ones. 'Tis no monster you see, but a very bad man who was mean to mother. He deserved what he got." And more, she thought. Now there were only two men left, besides her husband, with whom to deal—Hugh the Younger and Richard of Sussex. But the Bastard was only an incidental, not even worth more than a passing thought. Isabella was obsessed by Hugh Despenser, and until his capture, everything and everyone else faded to insignificance.

As her daughters clung to her, sobbing and hiccuping, Isabella thought of her husband, who had escaped from Bristol with Hugh the Younger just hours before her arrival. What will happen upon your capture? she wondered. Thinking of Edward confused her. He was weak and had been sometimes cruel as well as thoughtless, but he'd invariably been kind to their children and sometimes even loving to her. After listening to Mortimer's arguments, she had resigned herself to his deposition and Prince Edward's elevation to England's throne. She knew that Mortimer wanted to be the power behind her son. But what is wrong with that? she thought. He is powerful, decisive, and will prove an invaluable adviser until Ned reaches his majority. But she could never overcome that nagging problem—what to do about a deposed monarch. Alive her husband would prove a constant rallying point for malcontents, but at forty-three Edward was in excellent health and had many vital years left. Unless someone cut short his life. Isabella shivered. Sometimes she sensed the rebellion was assuming a life of its own—a monstrous life that could exist apart from herself, a life she could no longer control.

I must talk to Roger about it, she thought.

On October 2, King Edward set sail from Chepstow with Hugh the Younger and a handful of retainers, which were all who remained loyal to him. His destination was Lundy Island, the place from which Hugh had pirated during his brief banishment. The island had been stocked with provisions for their arrival. With Edward traveled an exchequer official, John Langton, who was in control of nearly thirty-nine thousand pounds.

Ironic, the king thought. At one time I had men but no money and now I have a fortune but no men to pay. 'Tis that she-wolf and her lover who have turned my people against me. The very thought of Isabella and Mortimer made him gnash his teeth in rage. When I am back in power they will pay for their sins. But for now I must concentrate on more immediate matters.

At his heels raced Henry of Leicester and the marcher lords, closing in as relentlessly as hounds upon a hare. Only Richard's repeated harassment had allowed Edward his continued freedom. But Richard is the only one loyal, he thought as he paced the deck of the cogship that was supposed to bear him to Lundy Island. Even the coastal winds were thwarting him. Not even repeated prayers to St. Anne had done any good. When Edward remembered his two younger brothers, Edmund and Thomas, he felt a mixture of anger and sadness. Edmund had arrived with Isabella from France and they'd landed next to Thomas's manor, where they'd spent their first night back in England. From the very outset, Edward's brothers had marched with the traitors. They had proven more rapacious than the most hardened mercenary in pillaging lands and taking plunder for their own. Someday I will deal with you all, he thought. You will rue the day you so betrayed me.

Contrary winds kept Edward and his men in the narrows of Bristol Channel. Finally, on the same day as Hugh the Elder's execution, they disembarked and rode west from Caerphilly. Everywhere he stopped, Edward issued vain summons and commissions that no one obeyed. Daily he expected to hear that Richard had been captured or killed.

On November 16, Edward left Neath, bound for Llantrissant. He was forced to travel in a torrential rain. As the water pounded against his helm like spoons upon a kitchen pot he assured himself that the rain, though miserable, would shield his band from possible enemy encounter. Riding into the slashing rain, he tried unsuccessfully to penetrate the grayness, which stretched in all directions. When he swiveled in his saddle he could not even see Simon of Reading, who was the last man in his troop.

The road soon grew impassable. The destriers, hampered by armor, sank to their knees in the sucking mud and still the rain beat upon them. Water had forced its way through junctures in Edward's hauberk and his gambeson clung to him. Where it rubbed against metal his shoulders felt raw and sore. He turned to shout a complaint to Nephew Hugh. From the gray mass to the north he glimpsed a movement, a shape like that of a man on horseback. Thinking it a trick of the atmosphere, he blinked. To his horror Edward saw not one but many figures, appearing out of the rain, riding toward him with drawn swords. The knights seemed to glide over the ground, undaunted by the mud. Watching them appear out of the rain, moving so silently and effortlessly, momentarily unnerved him. Might they be phantom soldiers, ghosts of the Welsh his father had killed during his many wars of subjugation?

Hugh the Younger unsheathed his sword.

"Do not!" Edward yelled above the hammering rain. He now realized that the riders were true flesh-and-blood and more dangerous than a dozen phantom armies. Their lack of armor accounted for the ease of movement, the badges upon their jupons attested to their identity. Henry of Leicester, and a seeming multitude of other marcher lords, bore down on them. Useless to struggle. They were outnumbered ten to one.

'Tis all over, Edward thought as Leicester rode up to accept his sword in surrender. His brain was too benumbed to know fear. Yet.

TWENTY

turbid fog rolled off the English Channel, obscuring the white cliffs of Dover. Phillip was sorry for that. The cliffs were impressive and he was eager for a first glimpse of his homeland. Instead the fog had settled upon everything like a giant slug, and though the trip from Calais was short, the sea proved sullen and uncooperative.

If I never set foot aboard ship again, Phillip thought, his eyes trying to penetrate the fog, I'll count myself blessed. He'd had enough of the heat and the stench of pilgrim ships, the passengers packed in the hold neath the rowing deck in berths eighteen inches wide and the length of a body. Light and air entered only through the hatchways; rats, lice, fleas, and maggots had proven even more of a nuisance than fellow pilgrims.

Mentally, he urged the galley ever swifter across the choppy waters. He had heard the news of Queen Isabella's invasion after docking in Venice, and had hurried north from there. Everywhere he asked the same question of Englishmen, "What news have you of King Edward? Has Richard of Sussex been captured?" He received so many conflicting answers that he could not sort truth from rumor. He knew only that Richard must need him.

As the galley maneuvered toward the dock, Phillip waited

impatiently to disembark. He was glad to be home, and not only because of political events. This time I'll never again leave, he thought. Travel had proven to be but a chimera. From the very beginning this journey had been different; his restlessness had not been assuaged by people who varied only in the cut of their clothes and the look to their faces, and events that changed only in their locale.

At Jerusalem's Church of the Holy Sepulcher, with the lights from a thousand prayer candles flickering red across stone walls, monks chanting and altar boys singing, the truth had come to Phillip with the intensity of a revelation. What he had been searching for, he'd possessed all along. Maria and his children, his land, and the love of a good friend. Now that he'd found the key, Phillip's only fear was that complacency and boredom would eventually again cloud the truth, and the pattern would repeat itself. Must happiness also prove transitory as the cherry fair?

'Twill not be so this time, he assured himself as he walked down the galley's ramp. Before I never really knew what I wanted. Now I do.

Phillip was surprised at Dover's quiet. He'd expected the port to be a cauldron of frenetic activity—of talk and worried faces, people clustered in groups rehashing the latest events and their meaning. Instead sailors went about their duties with a minimum of cursing, and brown-garbed pilgrims, using their staffs to balance themselves after the roll of the ship, stumbled toward the dock. An occasional merchant, tally book in hand, searched for the ship's captain and their promised merchandise.

The fog lifted then settled again, like a restive dragon. The knot in Phillip's stomach tightened. The scene seemed somehow unnatural. But was not everything in England unnatural, with the treason of the French queen?

As his squire, Gilbert, looked to obtaining for them proper mounts, Phillip sought the latest news. He accosted a middle-

aged tavern keeper, here to greet his brother on his return from
Rome.

"Sir, I crave from you a bit of news. What has been
happening? Has King Edward been captured yet?"

"Aye, my lord, and is imprisoned at Monmouth. Hugh the
Younger is being taken to London where he'll stand trial. Hugh
the Elder has already suffered a traitor's death." The tavernkeeper's face was arranged in impassive lines. Phillip could
read nothing of his true sympathies there.

"What about Richard of Sussex? Has he been captured also?
What have you heard of him?"

"He yet remains free, though not for long, I'll wager. Roger
Mortimer will know easy enough how to flush the Bastard out
of hiding. Just lay siege to Dover Castle, where his whore yet
resides."

"Richard was at Dover? His whore? You speak in riddles, sir."

The tavernkeeper smiled, exposing black stumps for teeth.
"You *have* been gone from England a long time, m'lord."

"Over three years."

"The Bastard took for his leman the Lady Rendell. I've not
personally seen her, but she is said to be the most beautiful
woman in all England."

Phillip stared uncomprehendingly at the tavernkeeper.
"Maria Rendell?" His knees threatened to buckle beneath him.
"Not Maria?"

"My lord, what is wrong?" He grabbed hold of the knight's
arm, as if to steady him. The man's face had blanched gray as
the fog.

"I do not believe it. There is some mistake. Richard would
not do that." Phillip's voice sounded as muffled as the tide
slapping against the piers, the hull of the galley. "She would not
do that."

He turned and walked away, his mind so benumbed it would
not function. Tendrils of breaking fog tugged at his feet. A
weak sun struggled through an outer bank of clouds, only to be

annihilated. The steep, narrow streets he wandered did not register; nor did he recognize his squire when Gilbert appeared, astride a bay palfrey and leading a second.

Gilbert swung from his horse and hurried to him. "What is wrong, sire? Have you heard bad news?"

Slowly Phillip emerged from his daze. "They betrayed me, Gilbert." One arm pressed against his stomach as if shielding a wound. "I had not dreamed they would."

Maria and Richard exited Dover's keep for Harold's Earthwork, where the Roman pharos and St. Mary-in-Castro were situated. The fog had lifted enough to reveal ships edging toward the harbor.

Richard's hand felt cold in hers. She looked at him, the new lines around his eyes, the leanness of his face and body. A new Richard had returned to her—a hunted fugitive, a man with the twin plagues of vengeance and bitterness corroding his soul.

"We will be ready to leave Dover by nightfall. Once we are safe at Conway in Wales, I will be able to rally support for my brother," Richard said. "The Welsh lords have been loyal to him."

Since his return late last night Richard had spoken of little save Edward, and the treason of Isabella. When he spoke of Roger Mortimer, his eyes turned as cold and bottomless as the English Channel itself. "Mortimer will pay," he said repeatedly. "I will not rest until that whoreson is food for the carrion crow."

Maria's hand tightened in his as they stopped near the pharos. His life consisted of kingdoms and power and loyalists crying out for him to lead them to victory. As a woman she did not possess the words that could comfort him. The only gift she could offer was the gift of acceptance. She was entering her seventh month of pregnancy and any riding would be awkward, much less a sustained journey. She dreaded the forthcoming trip, more out of fear for her child than because of Roger Mortimer. She kept her fears, however, as tightly wrapped as the mantle she clutched about her thickened form.

Soon it will all be over, Maria thought. Her eyes swept the channel, the cruciform church, and to the south Dover's windmill, its arms swishing like the blade of a giant broadsword. I will have time to bear my babe, and comfort Richard, or watch him ride from Conway, nevermore to return.

Like the bolt from a crossbow, a rider hurtled from the fog. Maria turned, watching his approach. 'Tis more tragedy, she thought, unconsciously leaning against Richard. I had thought we'd experienced it all.

The rider's horse reared as he jerked to a stop and flung himself from the saddle.

Maria looked at the rider, and her heart stopped. "Phillip?" She was not even certain at first. He wore his hair longer than she remembered, his skin was burned brown by eastern suns, and he was heavier, though he'd accumulated muscle, not fat.

"You are dead," she whispered. "You were not supposed to return." As she gaped at him, the doubts and uncertainties his presence inevitably aroused flooded over her with as much intensity as her surprise. He yet seemed to Maria like the moon—dark and distant and unreachable. I was mistaken, she silently marveled. You have not changed at all.

Phillip strode toward them; the sword at his side clinked in concert with his movements. "Who would have believed it?" He addressed Richard. "My liege lord and friend, I loved you well. I cannot think you'd repay that love by bedding with my very wife. But here you are, the both of you." His gaze swept Maria, came to rest at the protruding stomach. His eyes widened with pain and disbelief.

"No!" He shook his head.

Maria took a step toward him. "Let me explain." But as easy to explain their betrayal as the babe, and both were impossible.

Richard stepped in front of her. "We must talk, Phillip. Maria and I did not mean to hurt you, you know that, do you not?"

"How could you?" Phillip floundered, trying to collect his

thoughts, trying to react in some coherent fashion. The extent of their betrayal pounded against him like a hammer's relentless blows. Rational thought eluded him, but action did not.

He unsheathed his sword.

"I do not blame you for your anger and pain," Richard said. "I have greatly wronged you. I did not meant to fall in love with Maria, and I thought to love in silence. I would rather have died myself than hurt thee."

"Why should I be hurt?" Phillip mocked. "The two people I most loved? I would have ridden to hell for you had you asked, and never questioned the rightness of it. And you, Maria, I trusted your virtue as much as your love." His eyes flickered over her, back to Richard. "But you were truly neither woman nor wife, but a poison that corrupts the blood." He pointed his sword at Richard's chest. "And this hour I will have my blood."

Terrified, Maria stared at the three-foot-long blade. "You cannot mean to fight Richard. 'Twas my fault, I was the one. Oh, please!" She stepped toward her husband, but froze at the murder in his eyes.

"I'll not fight you," Richard said. "Your anger is justified. I would just ask that we could talk, that you might try to understand, if not forgive."

Struggling rays from the sun glanced across the flat of Phillip's broadsword. The windmill murmured and creaked; sea gulls swooped and squawked before soaring beyond Dover's cliffs out toward the sea.

"If I live to be a thousand I'll not understand, and 'tis not within me to forgive." Phillip's words were punctuated by his broadsword, which sliced down in front of Richard's face.

Maria jumped back. Richard did not flinch.

"I curse the day we met. I should have let you die at Bannockburn, but since I did not I will now rectify that error. Fight, Bastard."

Richard shook his head. "Kill me if you would, but I'll not lift my sword against a man I still would call friend. If I could have overcome my weakness, Phillip, I would have. I know you would not have treated me so shabbily."

Swift as a leaping wolf Phillip grabbed Maria and slammed her against the flint-rubble surface of the pharos. He jabbed the point of his sword into her stomach. "Fight me, or your leman and your bastard die."

Maria tensed her muscles against the unyielding steel, as if that might somehow protect her babe. Now that death was at hand, she felt little fear—for herself at least. If you kill me, she thought, at least there will be an end of it.

Richard drew his sword.

The two were evenly matched. Richard was a shade taller, Phillip heavier, but both were in superb fighting form. Phillip, however, was driven by rage while Richard's every thrust and feint measured his reluctance. From the first Phillip took the offensive, methodically forcing Richard back toward the windmill. Steel clashed and slithered along steel. The promontory reverberated with each ringing blow; their straining arms shook with each brutal contact.

Maria could not tear her eyes away from the slashing swords. With each lunge she imagined steel biting into skull, brains bursting onto the treeless plain. With each assault she held her breath, unconsciously jerking away from the path of the deadly blades.

Phillip was the first to draw blood—a ragged gash to Richard's left thigh. Richard's hauberk deflected much of the blow's power, but the rent appeared from thigh to knee.

Maria screamed, which only added to the fury of Phillip's attack. He wielded the blade like a man possessed. Only slightly slowed by the wound, Richard parried, seeming to guess Phillip's intended attack before it began. But he did not take the offensive, even when Phillip provided opening.

Phillip pushed him back toward the circling vanes of the windmill. Their swords sighed and whistled; their breathing rasped loud. Turning to gauge his distance from the vanes, Richard misstepped, and as he tried to right himself, Phillip slammed his blade down near Richard's hilt. The sword flew from his hand, beneath the windmill's arms. Off balance, Richard fell. And lay still.

Maria's breath tore her throat as Phillip raised the broadsword over his head, hesitated. The sword seemed to hang suspended for the length of a lifetime.

"No!" she screamed, shattering the moment. As the blade descended she ran toward Richard. The sword point quivered in the earth a hair's breadth from his throat.

"Aye, comfort your lover!" Phillip gasped as he struggled to regain his wind. "Do what you wish. But mark my words, wife. I will have an annulment from you, whether it takes five years or ten, whether I must sell all of Deerhurst to bribe Pope John that we share a common ancestor."

"Nay, Phillip. Please, no more. Has not enough been said and done in anger?"

"Go with the Bastard, go to hell, for that is where you both are bound." Phillip jerked his sword from the earth. "Should I meet you again, my former lord, 'twill be in the service of the white lion of Mortimer. Roger Mortimer will soon bring you to heel, and when he does I will rejoice the loudest."

After a detour to Walmer Castle, where he retrieved his son, Phillip rode for Deerhurst. Inside he nursed a cold hatred of his wife and her lover that nothing could assuage. Even his son, who shared common expressions and mannerisms with Maria, provided as much pain as pleasure. Every time he looked at Tom he saw her, and a thousand memories rushed to the surface. He'd nursed those memories during his travels. Now he vowed to kill them, every one.

Phillip arrived home just as Queen Isabella decided that Hugh Despenser the Younger must immediately be brought to trial.

The queen had long dreamed of a triumphant march into London with the fallen favorite in tow, but since his capture

Hugh had refused meat and drink and she was afraid he would soon die. Not to be denied her full measure of revenge, Isabella ordered Hugh's trial in the nearest large town, which happened to be Hereford. If not London, at least Hereford would provide enough spectators so that Despenser would be subjected to the greatest amount of public humiliation possible.

The trial took place in Hereford's episcopal palace. After judgment was privately passed upon Hugh Despenser, he was stripped of his knightly garb, dressed in black, his escutcheon reversed, and a crown of stinging nettles placed atop his head. Massive crowds, flocking from throughout the marcher lands, lined the narrow city lanes to the gallows. Phillip and his brother Humphrey numbered among the spectators. While he'd ordered little Tom to stay at Winchcomb with Lady Jean, Phillip had willingly ridden to Hereford to witness the execution. His heart no longer possessed room for any emotion save hate, and this day there would be hatred enough for all.

"My only regret is that 'tis Hugh Despenser who will die, not Richard of Sussex," he said to Humphrey. "I should have killed him at Dover when I had the chance."

The day chosen for Despenser's execution, which followed the feast of All Saints, was as ugly as the malevolent atmosphere. Storm clouds drooped low. A bruising wind cut through the warmest woolen mantles, but not even its chilly breath could blow away the animosity stamped upon the expectant sea of faces. When Hugh Despenser finally appeared, slumped atop a mange-ridden pony, the resultant noise fairly shook the surrounding jumble of shops and apartments.

Phillip was shocked by Despenser's appearance. Not only had he never seen Hugh in anything but the most elaborate clothing but the earl's eyes appeared clouded and lifeless, the skin across his cheekbones and aquiline nose was stretched to a parchment thinness that outlined the very contours of his skull. He seemed deaf to the screams, the blasts of hunting horns, the pounding of spoons upon kitchen pots that accompanied his passing. Some of the more learned ran to scrawl upon him scriptural verses denouncing arrogance and evil, others befouled his tattered gown and even his face with midden. Hugh appeared oblivious to everything. He reminded Phillip of a mortally wounded animal who wanted only to crawl off alone and die. His indifference only incited the mob to further frenzy.

"Look at him!" Humphrey Rendell bellowed. "Arrogant and unrepentant to the very last."

Phillip thought of Richard. Will you also be ridden through city streets and similarly humiliated? He pulled his mantle closer about him. I just pray I will be there to view your pain.

He could not really imagine Richard subjected to such treatment, however, Unlike Hugh he was not hated, his disapproval of the favorites had long been known, and would even the most hardened Englishman fault a brother's loyalty, no matter how undeserved?

As a rotten egg slammed against Hugh's cheek and splintered open, Phillip looked away. The feeling of anarchy, the mindless hatred, was beginning to unease him.

After Hugh Despenser reached the gallows, which Queen Isabella had ordered fashioned fifty feet high, his sentence was publicly read by William Trussell, who had also pronounced death upon his father. When the justiciary motioned for silence, the noise abruptly ceased; the sound of Hugh being dragged up the wooden steps resonated accusingly in the resultant stillness. Intermittent pellets of sleet slashed upon upturned faces and the wind blew wild from the north, but the mob's attention was focused upon the gallows platform.

"You, Hugh, are found as a thief and therefore shall be hanged, and are found as a traitor and therefore shall be drawn and quartered; for that you have been outlawed by the king and by common consent, and returned to the court without warrant, you shall be beheaded; and for that you abetted and procured discord between king and queen, and others of the realm, you shall be emboweled and your bowels burned; and so go to your judgment, attainted, wicked traitor."

Phillip's eyes turned to Hugh, whose face registered no emotion. The crown of nettles atop his dark head drooped over his forehead. Christ also wore a crown, he thought, but there the resemblance ends, for Hugh is nearer the devil. 'Tis inevitable, Phillip told himself as he pulled his beaver hat down against the sleet. Men who reach for the sun must always risk getting burned. He thought again of Richard.

"Make way for the baron of Wigmore!"

The crowd parted and Roger Mortimer rode his prancing white charger up to the steps of the gallows. He flashed a smile to the crowd, then turned to watch the favorite's execution. From the time Phillip had known his fellow marcher lord, Roger Mortimer had not failed at any task. Was he not now bending England to his will? Phillip was certain Roger was the driving force behind the queen. Without her lover, Isabella would have obediently returned to England and the rebellion would have achieved no more substance than morning mist hovering above a pond. Richard is no match for Roger Mortimer, Phillip thought, and the knowledge gave him no pleasure.

The executioner, dressed all in black and with a hood over his face, slipped a knotted noose around Hugh Despenser's neck. He jerked Hugh up higher ever higher to the gallow's arm, nearly lost in the pendent swoop of clouds. Despenser's limbs danced like a marionette's; his tattered gown flapped, then disappeared in the blackness of swirling scud. The crowd gasped as the executioner loosed the rope and Hugh plummeted to the ground.

Grabbing a butcher knife, the executioner bent over Hugh and cut open his stomach. As he withdrew white coils of intestine, Despenser groaned but did not cry out. Taking a proferred torch the executioner thrust the fire into his bowels. The resultant smell was blown toward the spectators on the howling wind. Hugh slumped in the arms of the knight who was propping him up and his eyes glazed over, but he did not die. The knight then lifted him by his arms and dragged him to a wooden block. Hugh's entrails snaked beside him. The executioner positioned the favorite's head precisely in the wooden hollow. He raised his ax heavenward. When the blade plummeted and Despenser's head thudded to the platform, the crowd cheered and resumed thumping on their pots.

"I am leaving," Phillip said to Humphrey.

"Do you not want to stay to see Despenser quartered? Four horses will be used instead of the usual two."

"What does it matter?" Phillip snapped.

He rode back to Winchcomb, where his son was staying. Phillip was glad for the time alone, without the blathering of his brother or the hysteria of the crowds. He needed time to think, to assimilate what he had just seen and his conflicting feelings. The hatred was still there, certainly, but its intensity was fading. Other emotions were crying now for their turn.

The sleet changed to a thick falling snow, covering the fields, the backs of cattle not yet herded to their byres, the tracks made by Phillip's palfrey along the flat stretch of highway. He squinted his eyes against the huge flakes that clung to his face before trailing downward like tears. "I denied you a warrior's death for that of a traitor's. Even I cannot wish for you such a fate."

TWENTY-ONE

xhausted from four days of hard riding, Maria nearly fell from her horse's saddle. She and Richard were bound for Conway Castle, which lay yet another three days north. Conway meant safety, though their journey north was extremely dangerous. The most direct route lay by way of London, which was crawling with rebels, so they swung through marcher country. The threat of Roger Mortimer remained constant as a heartbeat. His white lion seemed to be everywhere, and Richard's troop of fifteen knights was pitifully small. They kept to the back roads, well away from populated areas and arteries, and did not directly encounter his men, though Maria was beginning to believe that Roger Mortimer was as omnipresent—and omnipotent—as God.

They rode through the poor lands of Surrey, the fertile fields of Berkshire and Oxfordshire. Near evening of the fourth day, they wound down into a beautiful valley called the Vale of Evesham. Before them spread a panoramic view of trees, hedge-covered fields, and flocks of sheep whose bleating cries reverberated through the crisp winter air. In the vale they discovered a long deserted milking shed, as well as the remnants of a farmer's cottage and, for the first time since leaving Dover, enjoyed shelter from the elements. After fishing from the River Avon, they risked a fire, also for the first time, and baked their catch in the coals. Later, Maria and Richard withdrew to the dilapidated cottage, where she rested as snug against him as her babe would allow. Her bulk made riding especially awkward, and as the days progressed, she repeatedly experienced stabbing pains in her legs as well as contractions. Always she feared that she would miscarry, for what child could endure such unaccustomed agony? She did not complain, however, and whenever Richard questioned her she maintained she felt fine. She spent her time in the saddle shifting about, seeking unsuccessfully for a degree of comfort, and praying she would survive just another moment, let alone an hour. This night, blessed by the shelter of a roof, Maria slept the sleep of the dead. Before she would have counted it possible, Richard was shaking her shoulder and whispering, "Time."

The other knights were already mounted. Attempting a stretch, Maria winced and limped to Baucent, the destrier Richard had provided. He had feared Facebelle would prove too delicate for such a difficult journey and could not risk a horse going lame or straggling too far behind. Clenching her teeth against her protesting muscles, Maria struggled into the saddle and awaited the earl's signal to move out. They were now in Herefordshire. She recognized much of the terrain from her days at Deerhurst. Deerhurst meant Phillip. But I will think about him later, she thought. I cannot now, though he was ever lurking in a part of her mind—as was Roger Mortimer.

It was on this, their fifth day, that they encountered their first foul weather. Fresh snow blanketed the ground; thin layers of ice skimmed the surface of ponds. An intermittent sleet soon intensified into a howling blizzard. They rode directly into the storm, braving snow that stung their faces and clung to beards, eyebrows, and lashes.

They followed the snaking River Severn to a known bridge, only to discover the ropes had been cut. The bridge's remains bobbed in the ice-glutted water. Michael Hallam looked to his lord; Richard shook his head. His eyes swept the swirling horizon, as if searching for the perpetrators of the deed. It was not lost on him that his brother had been captured in similar weather. Had the bridge been destroyed to slow them? Was Mortimer even now watching them?

"We must attempt a crossing," he said to his men. "But keep a sharp lookout."

The Severn, while not overdeep, was freezing cold. After fording it, Maria's wet clothes hung stiff and unyielding, without any warmth at all.

As they rode into the deepening storm and her limbs began to ache against the relentless onslaught, Maria lost heart. Not only will I lose my babe but we will never reach Wales, she despaired. Her extremities had lost all feeling; her face hurt so from the slashing snow that she began crying, but the tears froze. The beards on the knights' faces had also turned to ice.

I would almost risk capture by Roger Mortimer rather than another moment of this, she thought, as she peered at the men hunched over their mounts, shapeless mounds in the gray swirling mass. Either by Mortimer's black hand or God's, we are all going to die.

The following morning the sky cleared and by midday sparkled a dazzling blue. In places the snow brushed the horses' saddle girths, but as they approached the border to Wales the troop's optimism returned.

"We'll be safe in Wales," Richard said. "And by this time tomorrow, God willing, we'll be enjoying a warm fire and steaming bath at Conway."

The terrain grew increasingly hilly, but the piles of snow lessened. Questioning their good fortune, the earl's gaze continually probed the horizon and surrounding stands of trees. Wigmore Abbey was not far from here; they were now in the heart of Roger Mortimer's domain. Mortimer is probably in London by now, Richard assured himself, though he could not shake his unease.

They entered a narrow valley surrounded by sharp rises and

clusters of towering pines. Feeling revitalized, Maria breathed in the crisp air. *We survived yesterday's storm and sleeping in hollowed-out snow caves,* she thought, confident that the saints were finally with them. *Mayhaps our luck will hold.*

Snow nestled in the spreading branches of pines and occasionally fell with a rolling thump to pock the smooth expanse below. From a stand to their right darted a stag. It careened toward them before bounding away over a hill. Richard raised his hand and the men halted. For a long moment it seemed that the earth made no sound but held its breath along with the knights. Images burned Maria's brain— the dazzling sky, wispy clouds, black pines straining upward, their snow-weighted branches sparkling—like sunlight off a sword.

"To arms!" Richard shouted. The silence was shattered by battle cries as enemy knights hurled from either side of the valley. The area was a sudden mass of churning hooves, rearing horses, flashing swords and maces, struggling men. Steel clashed upon steel, mace against metal. Maria saw that they were far outnumbered, that Richard's knights had not time to group into the protection of a circle. Next to her, Michael Hallam was fighting a knight bearing Mortimer's badge upon his sleeve. Michael smashed his battle-ax into the knight's chest, but after the man fell a half dozen more rushed to take his place.

The press of battle continued around Maria. Crouching over her destrier she tried to maneuver Baucent to the area's outer perimeter. If she could break free, perhaps she could ride for help. Spying an opening, she kicked her destrier, who plunged toward it, swerving around fallen bodies. The mutilated snow showed red with mud and blood. She glimpsed Richard, fighting furiously, his sword a silver blur. Mortimer's men fell back, then re-formed, surrounding him. Maria broke free.

Stretching out, Baucent plunged through the snowdrifts. As Maria bent awkwardly over the charger's neck, her page's cap flew off, revealing her unbound hair, which whipped behind.

"Faster!" she urged the struggling stallion. Baucent responded, the white socks for which he was named pumping frantically in the crusted surface. Risking a glance over her shoulder, Maria saw that several of Richard's men were already disarmed and standing off to the side, guarded by Mortimer's troops. At that moment a knight broke from the pack and raced toward her.

She dug her heels frantically into Baucent's belly. The grunting of the enemy's warhorse, the *thud-dump* of its hooves sounded increasingly louder. Snow from Baucent's hooves shot upward, stinging her face. He was swiftly tiring, his movements becoming increasingly labored. With a triumphant shout, the knight closed the separating distance. Momentarily Maria expected to feel the bite of his broadsword into her backbone, slicing it—and her—in two.

They rode neck and neck; the man's armored calf slammed against her. Baucent shied away. He followed. Maria glimpsed a leathery face, grizzled beard, a jupon splattered with mud and blood. The knight maneuvered so that her destrier was forced to slow and grabbed for the reins. Baucent struggled to a halt.

Maria grabbed for her dagger.

"Do not, lady." The knight bared his teeth. "I would not like to kill the Bastard's whore. You are one of the day's finest prizes." He led her back to the battlefield. Knights littered the muddy snow, grotesquely contorted in death. She counted three of Richard's men, a half score of Mortimer's. Richard had inflicted more damage than he'd received, but it had not been enough. Seeking his face among the captives, she was relieved to see that he looked angry but otherwise unhurt.

A knight rode from the pack and approached her. He had a swarthy complexion and night-black hair, as well as a beard that crawled across his cheeks to end near his eyes. The darkness of hair and skin cast his blunt features in an unholy light. She did not need an introduction to recognize Roger Mortimer.

"Welcome, Lady Rendell!" Mortimer's teeth flashed white in

the expanse of beard. His shrewd eyes perused her length. Her dress, that of a male page, tended to accentuate her stomach. Watching his gleeful reaction, Maria felt a wave of revulsion. How could Isabella ever share such a creature's bed? 'Twould be like crawling between the sheets with Satan himself.

"'Tis honored I am to meet England's most celebrated whore."

His flat black eyes continued their insulting examination. Maria's revulsion quickly escalated to fear. Mother Mary protect us! she thought, remembering the fate of the Despensers. I think you would be capable of any atrocity.

Mortimer maneuvered his mount until their thighs touched. "The reports of your beauty, Lady Rendell, do not do you justice. Though I did not hear tell of your current condition. 'Twould appear that, at least in bed, the Bastard is not impotent." He looked past her to Richard, who did not outwardly react to the taunt.

"Your brother was no match for me, Bastard," he continued, "and neither are you. I picked this spot with loving care. I know the peaks and valleys of this country as well as you know your whore's charms. 'Twas foolish of you to think that you could outwit me in my own territory."

He returned his attention to Maria. Leaning across the pommel of his saddle, he lifted a strand of her auburn hair. "Though I usually enjoy the charms of fairer—and less plump—women, I look forward to sampling yours." His eyes narrowed. "And if you should make trouble for me, bitch, after I have my pleasure with you, I may just slice off your nipples. Was not that Edward's own punishment for adulteresses—and in this instance I would relish obeying our former monarch!"

They rode until sunset and stopped a few miles beyond the city of Worcester. Maria's wrists had been bound hours ago, which made dismounting difficult. She was helped by Ranulf Leybourne, the eldest son of her one-time fiancé, Edmund. The men from her past were coming back to haunt her thoughts. Edmund's son, and Phillip, whose manor was no more than five miles southwest of their camp. *Are you trying to remind me, Lord, of my many sins?* she thought. She needed no remembrance. Tonight might be her last night on earth, surely her most horrible, but she could not truly believe her forthcoming fate. *Something will happen,* she assured herself as Ranulf tied her to a tree. *But did the Despensers believe they, too, would be spared? If neither God, nor the devil would save the two most powerful men in England, who will concern himself with me?*

With the coming night the air had turned chill. Maria's chausses were wet, her fingers numb with cold. Her stomach was like a leaden weight before her, without movement. "Do not be frightened," she whispered. "Somehow we'll muddle through. We must. But first I must figure a way to free myself of these ropes."

Maria shivered as a blast of air cut through her. She looked longingly at the bonfire around which Mortimer and his men had gathered. The captors were grouped closer to the warmth than she, but Mortimer was little inclined to share either it or his food and drink. Standing before Richard, the marcher lord raised a measure of ale in mock salute.

"I have much reason to celebrate, Bastard. All my queen's enemies are dead or imprisoned, and England will be the better for that." Mortimer wasn't certain that the country was really better served, but he knew he was.

As night deepened and the drinking increased, Mortimer eyed Maria with increasing interest, though the others remained uneasy about raping a pregnant woman.

After talking it over among themselves, Ranulf Leybourne and several others approached their lord with their misgivings. "'Tis wrong in the sight of God to thus violate a woman," Ranulf said. "Her only sin is that she is the Bastard's leman. I think we should take her to London and imprison her, if need be, but nothing more."

Mortimer looked at the chorus of bearded faces, all nodding in agreement with Ranulf. Throwing back his head, Mortimer barked out a loud laugh. "You are as useless as a bunch of mewling, psalm-singing churchmen. But so be it. You stay away from her if you fear God's wrath. But Roger Mortimer fears neither God nor man, and pregnant or no, I intend to take my pleasure of this whore."

When Mortimer ordered the remaining scraps of food distributed among the captives, Ranulf brought Maria a cold slab of pork and enough ale to wet her lips.

After glancing at his lord, who was again unsuccessfully needling Richard, he spoke softly. "I would have you know, Lady Rendell, that I do not wish you any animosity. And I will try to divert my lord's attention to other matters so that he'll leave you in peace."

"But Richard, what about him?"

"Lord Mortimer has assured me that the earl will receive a fair trial in London."

"Do you really believe he will keep his word?"

"I do not know, my lady. Things are happening so fast . . ."

"Come away from the whore," Mortimer shouted. When he reached them, he knocked Ranulf on the shoulder. "You are not man enough for her, so leave her be." After Leybourne stepped away. Mortimer yanked Maria to her feet. Still tied to the tree her wrists and back scraped against the rough bark. He kissed her; one hand squeezed her breast, the other swept downward over her stomach, to her crotch. He thrust upward.

Though her every instinct was to jerk away, Maria did not cry out or flinch, but willed her body to remain passive. As she met Mortimer's black eyes, anger surged though her. "What a fine man you are, my lord, bullying a woman who is not only pregnant but defenseless. If this is a sampling of your prowess, then God help England—for you'll soon prove a poor master."

Mortimer's eyes narrowed, but the grin remained on his face.

"Is this how you trapped our rightful king? Did you creep up on him in sleep, or when he was alone and you armed with thousands?" she taunted. "If you fear one woman so much you must keep her tied, how you must have trembled before our King Edward."

Mortimer removed his dagger from its sheath. "Your tongue flaps uselessly, whore. How would you like me to cut it out?" Before Maria could react, Mortimer leapt on her. He slammed her against the tree trunk and reached behind to slash the ropes.

"Does that feel better, bitch?" Seeing the terror in her eyes, he laughed. "You really thought I would mutilate you before I enjoyed my fill? What a fool you are." He half turned away, then spun around, hitting Maria square on the jaw. She struggled to her knees, then, only semiconscious, collapsed.

Mortimer loomed above her. "Your time has come. You will soon rue your every word, that I promise you." He strode back to his watching men.

Senses reeling, Maria remained sprawled on the snow-covered ground. She heard him jesting concerning her immediate future but could not react. Shaking her head to clear it, she rose to take measure of her surroundings. Her hands were no longer tied. That at least provided hope, though how she might escape two score of men she could not think. The bonfire was thirty feet in front; the forest behind was only half that distance. Should she bolt for the trees she knew she could never outrun her captors.

But perhaps I can trick them, Maria thought, easing herself up. 'Tis dark in the woods and the pines are stout and close together . . .

Mortimer's back was to her, as were the backs of the men guarding Richard. Most of the others were preoccupied with the ale or fire. She edged past the tree where she'd been tied. Once she reached the shadowed meadow, Maria crouched and dashed for the woods. Just as she gained the forest, someone shouted. As she plunged inward, the whole camp erupted. The more alert had already grabbed their weapons, but though they made their way over the crusty snow toward the trees, their movements were not as swift as they might have been.

Maria struggled up a tall pine. Her pregnancy made climbing difficult. She grabbed desperately into the darkness, seeking leverage. Pine needles scratched her hands and upturned face; bark scraped against her stomach. Her breath came in labored gasps, betraying her position. If they catch me now, she thought as she struggled for control, Mortimer will kill me within the moment.

Maria had barely climbed eight feet before the first knight entered the forest. Others soon followed, occasionally making obscene jests and vowing loudly to find her. But they milled about in a small area, and their boots obliterated her tracks.

Men thrashed past her, heading deeper into the forest. Directly below two knights paused. She recognized Roger Mortimer's voice and that of Ranulf Leybourne. Heart hammering in her ears, Maria clung to the tree, pressing against the bark until her exposed skin began to bleed. A clump of snow fell from a branch beneath her, thudding to the ground at their feet. Ranulf scanned the tree. She froze, certain she had been discovered.

"The whore will die slow," Mortimer said. "I mislike having to traipse about the woods when I had other pleasures in mind."

"She could not have gone far," Ranulf said. "But we'll not find her standing here. I am going on." He moved deeper into the trees.

Mortimer followed. Weak with relief, Maria relaxed her iron grip upon the furrowed bark and inched upward, seeking more secure shelter.

Shadows again passed, this time heading back toward camp. Soon the knights returned, trailing torches that tore apart the darkness, but their efforts focused on the bushes and forest floor. Mercifully, no one looked overhead.

To Maria, it seemed her captors searched the entire night, but when their leader finally called off the search, dawn was yet hours away.

"The Bastard must be returned to London, and we'll not get our sleep chasing his whore," Mortimer said as he rounded up his knights. "Sussex is my main concern. Lady Rendell I will deal with another time." He held high his torch. "If the ground were not plagued by a foot of snow, I would set fire to the underbrush and flush the bitch out."

"She's probably halfway to Hereford by now," Ranulf said. "If not, mayhaps we'll yet meet her on the road."

Mortimer stroked his beard thoughtfully. "Her husband has a manor near here. I wonder if we should lie in wait for her."

"Every moment we waste might give the Bastard opportunity to escape. Besides, I know Phillip Rendell. A proud man so openly and painfully cuckolded by his wife would never welcome her. I do not think she would be foolish enough to beg his help."

The earl nodded. "I can always deal with her at my leisure. Perhaps I'll even send her the head of her lover in a basket." He barked out a loud laugh. "A present from Roger Mortimer, baron of Wigmore, and someday mayhaps, king of England."

TWENTY-TWO

eerhurst's fields stretched in a ghostly blanket, deserted save for cows drifting toward a milking shed and occasional flocks of bleating sheep. Approaching the manor castle's crenellated towers, Maria was too exhausted to worry about her probable stormy reception. Since early morn she'd been walking, and her wet boots had rubbed painful blisters on her feet. Contractions increasingly plagued her, sharp and insistent.

"Do not betray me now, my wee one," she whispered. "Just a bit more and mayhaps we'll enjoy some hot spiced malmsey and a bed. If Phillip will just not turn us away."

Pray to God that her husband was at Deerhurst, for she knew not where else to go to seek help. The city of Hereford was miles farther and unfamiliar to her. Besides, it would be crawling with the queen's loyalists. Even if Maria reached the city, what kindness could she expect from townspeople who had so gleefully destroyed Hugh Despenser? They might string me up as well, she thought, as she limped along the road. She'd encountered few people during her journey, but she was careful at the first sight of riders to hide in the woods, ditches, or any available shelter. She feared Roger Mortimer, and England was filled with those who shared his sentiments. She could not trust anyone. Her lone stroke of luck had been her proximity to Deerhurst. If she'd escaped in alien territory she'd surely have perished.

When Maria reached Deerhurst's drawbridge the sergeant-at-arms, who was beginning to lower the portcullis, challenged her entrance.

"I beg a bit of bread and a place out of the wind for this night, nothing more." Maria did not recognize the man and prayed he hadn't been there during her residence, now nearly a decade past.

As the sergeant looked her over, Maria grew increasingly nervous, but he finally waved her past. "Be off with you then."

As she walked across the outer bailey she remembered arriving at Deerhurst as a bride. She had awaited Phillip's return from the castle's battlements, given birth to her son in its solar, and received the news of her mother's death by the stables. Her eyes filled. She had been so young and innocent, so untouched by the world. That Maria Rendell is long dead, she thought, as she approached the cookhouse from which servants were scurrying. The dinner smells made her stomach growl. Her knees suddenly went weak. She leaned against the castle curtain and closed her eyes until the wave of exhaustion passed. Then she approached a page, dawdling at the cookhouse entrance.

"Sir, might I talk with you a moment?" The young man possessed a round, pleasant face and looked more accessible, as well as less busy, than the others.

The page's brown eyes widened in surprise as he noted her manly attire, as well as her belly. "Aye . . . madam."

"Could you tell me whether Sir Rendell is in residence?"

"That he is." The lad had cocked his head to the side and was openly studying her. "In truth, I saw Sir Rendell in the hall not an hour past."

After pausing to consider, Maria slipped her marriage ring from her finger and placed it in his hand. "Would you take this to Sir Rendell and ask him to meet me in Deerhurst's chapel?"

"M'lady, 'tis nearing suppertime and I have duties . . ."

Removing a silver-and-amethyst locket from around her neck Maria pressed it into the lad's palm beside the ring. "The

[253]

necklace has some value. If you'll but relay my message, 'tis yours."

The page pocketed the locket. "Aye, I will."

In the chill gloom of the chapel Maria awaited Phillip. She slumped against a wall in the nave, near the font where Tom had been baptized. He'd been such a sweet babe, and now she might never see him again, as she might never see Richard. Slowly she sank to the ground.

The door opened. Maria raised her head from her knees, then struggled to her feet. Humphrey, not Phillip, had entered the chapel.

Humphrey's face flushed a deep red. "You!" he hissed. "When Brian showed me the ring I could not believe you would be so bold as to show up here. But I should have known. You are brazen enough to attempt anything."

Maria was too tired to argue. "I would talk with my husband, Sir Humphrey. I did not know you were master of Deerhurst as well as Winchcomb."

"Who do you think looked after his property when Phillip was traipsing about the world? Think you I would entrust prime land to a lackadaisical steward? And now my brother mopes about so much he cannot give proper thought to anything, save his troubles, troubles caused by you—you meddlesome whore."

Maria looked past Humphrey's bulk, which blocked much of the doorway. "He is not here, for which I thank God, bitch. Now be gone before I call my men to extricate both you and that unborn brat you are carrying."

"I need not you to fight my battles, Humphrey." Phillip, who had entered unnoticed, moved between his brother and Maria. "I will take care of this myself."

Humphrey looked as if he were suffering the first throes of an apopleptic fit. "I've seen how well you take care of your personal life. In the same way you administer your land—half-assed."

"Deerhurst is still mine, no matter how you covet it, and if you do not immediately leave my chapel, I will have you removed."

After Humphrey left, cursing and muttering, Phillip addressed Maria. "Now, tell me what you are doing here and why you are dressed so strangely." His eyes carefully remained away from her stomach. "Where is Richard?"

"Mortimer has him. We were bound for sanctuary, to Wales, when he captured us, not far from here. I escaped, but Mortimer is taking Richard to London where he intends to have him die a traitor's death."

Phillip thought of Hugh Despenser's body, twisting from the gallows, its thud as it plummeted to the earth, the thump of his head as the executioner cleaved it from his body . . . "So." He turned away, struggling with the images and the past he could never escape. Richard and Maria lying together, betraying him. He saw them as clearly in his mind's eye as if he'd personally witnessed their perfidy—as he'd witnessed the favorite's death.

"What care I for the Bastard's fate?" he asked softly. "I hate him with a lasting hatred. You were a fool to come here seeking help."

"I had nowhere else to go." Looking into his carefully controlled face Maria longed to reach out and touch him, to somehow bridge the gap separating them. Three years had passed since Phillip had left England. She'd lain in another man's arms and loved him. She still loved him. But she knew now her feelings for Phillip were not dead. "Who would have thought we would come to this?" she whispered. "I loved you so much. I am beginning to realize I still do."

Phillip turned around. A disbelieving laugh emerged from his lips. "Aye. Your body shows ample proof of how faithful and loving a wife you were."

"If you had not left me I would not have turned to Richard."

In the light from a stained-glass window his profile was outlined to perfection. His profile had been the first thing about him that she'd found unforgettable. She still found it so.

"You and Richard were as inevitable as rain in spring,"

Phillip said. "I know that now, but I cannot live with it. You belonged to me, Maria. You were my property, and nothing in heaven or hell had the right to take what was mine. I did not ask or want much—a loyal wife and one man I could call friend as well as lord."

A sudden sharp contraction caused her to press her hand over her stomach. "Richard is your friend, Phillip. He loves you well."

"I do not call it friendship to steal another man's wife. I call it treachery." A spasm of emotion flickered across his face and was gone. "I am so poor with words. I cannot sort things out in my mind, or in my heart, it seems. I only know that I am not capable of forgiving him—or you." He looked above and beyond her to the shadowed altar. "Did you know, Maria, I had to force myself to stay away? A fortnight after I left England, I wanted nothing so much as to return, but I kept telling myself I was weak and that if I just went to Paris, then Milan, and then Rome I could recover the excitement I'd previously felt. There was not one day I did not think of you and the children."

"Then why did you not return? Everything could have been so different."

The pain showed so naked on his face she looked away. "I think not, Maria, and that is why I cannot help Richard, even if I would. He chose to side with Edward. He knew what might happen to those who remained loyal to the king, the risk he took. We cannot cheat our destiny. Not even Richard would say different."

"But we do not know our destiny until our lives are over, and it might be that Richard is not meant to die. Mayhaps he is meant to be rescued, to return and wrest England from the tyranny of Roger Mortimer. We must try, Phillip. Mayhaps to do less is cheating destiny, not fulfilling it."

Drained beyond further argument, she slumped against the chapel stones. Perhaps her husband was right. Why struggle and scheme and have your heart torn out by hurt and love and unhappiness when life was but a shadow passing upon a wall?

The lightest contraction tightened; something warm trailed down her leg. Jesu! Has my water broken? What is happening? The chapel receded. Darkness seemed to swallow her up. Raising her arm, Maria clutched at empty air.

"Hold on to me." Phillip's voice emanated from a long narrow tunnel. "I will take you inside."

Maria leaned against him. "Get me a midwife, someone, please. I think I'm losing my babe."

A damp washing cloth rested cool upon her forehead. Maria tried to open her eyes but it required too great an effort. How long had she been lying here? She had lost all track of time and had only a vague recollection of what was occurring around her. Her mind had withdrawn into a primeval past where only pain registered, and all else she could not grasp.

Far in the distance Maria heard church bells. Deerhurst's bells had rung to aid her through Tom's birthing, but this birthing would not result in a healthy babe, that much she knew.

"Here, Maria," said a gentle voice. "Drink this." Hands eased her up. She looked into Lady Jean's face. Aye, now she remembered. Phillip had sent to Winchcomb for his sister-in-law as well as a midwife, and then disappeared. Through the haze of faces, the cacophony of voices, she'd searched for him and prayed for him, but her prayers remained unanswered. If only I did not have to suffer through this alone, she thought, in one of her more lucid moments. But 'tis not Phillip's babe, and I am reaping the whirlwind, just as I knew I must.

"Jesu!" Maria clutched her stomach and arched her back, as yet another contraction knifed through her. Only this contraction would not wane. It rose and melded into subsequent contractions until she felt as if she were splitting in two. She writhed on the bed and held on to Jean's hands until her bones cracked. Still the pain would not leave go.

"Dear God, help!" she screamed, as her agony reached its

crescendo. She saw Jean's face and the face of the midwife
bending over her, and then her world went black.

She awoke to see Lady Jean sitting on a padded bench beside
her bed, watching her. The room was dark save for the light
from the fireplace. It was quiet. She could hear the sound of
logs cracking from the flames, even her sister-in-law's
breathing. From the chamber windows she saw a sprinkling of
stars against an inky sky.

Maria wet her lips. "Jean." Her voice sounded so weak she
could scarce believe it was her own.

Jean came to her. Her eyes were bright with unshed tears,
but she smiled. "You've been asleep for hours."

"Thank you. I did not want to be alone."

Jean's tears overflowed. One dropped upon Maria's forehead.

She did not want to ask the question, but she knew she must.
To complete her loss. "My babe did not live, of course?"

Jean's face crumpled. She shook her head and turned away.

Wearily Maria closed her eyes. A part of her wanted to ask
after her child, whether it had been boy or girl, large or small.
But it was none of these things. It was simply dead.

Maria awakened from a dreamless sleep, momentarily
disoriented. The room was familiar but it was not Fordwich.
She'd lain in this bed with her son, with Tom. But Tom was
serving his knightly apprenticeship, and she'd just lost her
babe.

The door opened and Lady Jean entered, bearing a tray of
gruel and oatcakes. "You look much improved this morning."

"I do not feel improved. I feel empty."

Jean reached out and patted her hand. "Every woman loses
at least one babe. It is the natural order of things."

Tears slipped from the corner of Maria's eyes. "'Tis my
retribution. And there will be more. I've lost Phillip, and

Mortimer said he would send me Richard's head."

Jean groped for the proper words. Her quiet, conventional life seemed so far removed from her sister-in-law's she was not certain what might soothe Maria. "Your son is here, you know. Would you like to see him?"

"Tom?" The first joyous leap of emotion was quickly extinguished. "He must hate me also, does he not? Has Phillip told him everything?"

Jean's cheeks darkened to a mottled pink. "Your husband is not a monster. He would not turn a son against his mother."

Maria swiveled her head against the pillow. "I would not blame him if he did."

At that moment the door opened, and Phillip strode into the solar. He was wearing his hauberk, and a black jupon without identification of any sort. When he pushed back his coif, Maria saw that his face was drawn and streaked with dirt.

Jean leapt to her feet. "I was just leaving." After throwing Phillip an anxious smile, she hurried from the room.

Phillip crossed to Maria's bed and looked down at her. For long moments he did not speak. "Richard had escaped."

"What?" Maria struggled to sit up.

"I have made inquiries. It seems a pack of knights descended on Mortimer when his troops left Brackley Castle at dawn this morning. His men were careless. They did not take proper precautions. Rebel knights attacked, and in the press Richard escaped."

"I do not understand. Men still loyal to Edward? But I thought all of England was against him."

Phillip turned toward the chamber window. His profile appeared worked in stone. "I am just relaying what I was told."

Maria tried to assimilate this stunning news. Phillip would not again risk his life for Richard, would he? Had he left her, not because he scorned her, but because he had ridden to save Richard? Why would he? Why should he?

"Richard's free then, and safe?" At least Maria would have one thing to be thankful for. At least God was not extracting his full measure of vengeance at one time.

"I did not say he was safe. I heard he was wounded, though I know not how badly. Mortimer is scouring the hills for him. But 'tis treacherous terrain there, where a man is better served on foot than horseback."

Maria sank back against the pillows. "But not a wounded man," she said tonelessly. "He will be all alone with no one to care for him." She plucked at the end of the woolen coverlet. "He'll die alone."

"We all must die sometime. And I would prefer dying peacefully with the sun upon me and a blue sky hovering overhead rather than an executioner's ax." He paused. "Michael Hallam was killed in the escape."

"Not Michael!" Maria could sooner imagine Richard's death than that of Michael, who seemed to her indestructible. She felt new tears well up inside, forced them back. If she was going to cry over every tragedy, she would weep the rest of her days. "How did he die?"

"When the knights attacked, Mortimer meant to kill Richard right then. Michael took the sword instead. Or so I was told."

"Poor Eleanora." Maria raised her eyes to Phillip. "Death is all around me now. You know I lost the babe."

Phillip looked away. "I know."

"It is what I deserved. But it will be . . . hard."

"Much of life is hard," Phillip whispered. "Much of life is not what we expected."

Maria remembered their first meeting, near ten years past. She had thought him so wonderful, a figure from a romance. She could still find him so, but perhaps her perception had accounted for their problem. She'd fallen in love with her idea of what a man should be, not what Phillip truly was. She'd cheated Phillip, but more, she'd cheated herself.

"Thank you for Richard."

Philip shook his head and turned away so that she could not see his face.

TWENTY-THREE

s the spring of 1327 nudged away winter, the isolated valley, tucked in Gloucester's Chiltern Hills, turned green and sweet. Following Richard's delirious arrival months ago at the secluded monastery, his slow recovery from a stomach wound, his life had settled into a certain comfortable routine. Remnants of the legendary Knights Templar lived behind the stone walls. Templars were holy men whose order had been outlawed fifteen years before, following peculiar rumors and the political machinations of greedy monarchs. With healing herbs, salves, and gentle care the aging knights had coaxed Richard back to health.

When his wound was fully healed, Richard participated in the daily tasks, helping in the kitchen, sharing housework, even shoveling manure from the stables. He found such menial duties surprisingly enjoyable. It was comforting to know that the fate of an entire country did not rest on his expertise at baking bread or cleaning the brothers' dormitory. He thought often of his dead squire, but though he missed Michael greatly he sometimes wondered whether Michael did not have the better end of it—no more worrying over political events and disasters, no more scheming or heartache. Surely now Michael at least had found peace.

Alone in his cell Richard sometimes studied from the available religious works until vespers and the even meal.

Though previously such a bland routine would have left him yearning for a stag hunt or hawking expedition, he no longer found it so. Increasingly he relished those quiet hours far away from the cares and troubles of a world swiftly receding into a dreamy, little-missed past. The past was dangerous and painful, though Richard could not completely free himself from its siren song. The Templars maintained perfunctory contact with the outside world by means of Fulk the Hermit, who sometimes begged along a main road to Gloucester and heard all manner of news. At Richard's urging his confessor, Father Raoul, had reluctantly sought out Fulk for information about Maria and King Edward. In January His Grace had been officially deposed by a Parliament rendered illegal by his absence. The stated reasons were that Edward was an insufficient ruler, a destroyer of the Church and the peers of the realm, a violator of his Coronation Oath, and a follower of evil counsel. Prince Edward, now Edward III, officially occupied England's throne.

Concerning Maria, the hermit had heard only that she'd returned to Fordwich. 'Tis enough to know she's safe, Richard told himself. I need nothing more. But with the first blossoming sweet violets, the soft scents from the orchard's budding apple, pear, and plum trees, passions that had lain winter dormant now sprang forth with disturbing vigor. The golden sun spread its warmth; bees droned in the apiaries while gentle breezes caressed his skin as lovingly as Maria once had. Are you yet at Fordwich, he wondered, or with Phillip at Deerhurst? Have you reconciled? He told himself 'twas safer not to know too much, and when past demons hovered he sought to keep them at bay by the hard physical labor of planting and hoeing in the monastery's large garden located just beyond the walls. I won't think of the past; I won't think of her, he vowed, as he cleared two rows to the other knights' one. His heart, however, remained unconvinced. This placid valley, disturbed only by the occasional call of a cuckoo or a monk's singing, should be an oasis from the world's cares. If here I cannot find peace, he despaired, what will I do?

Daily confessions to Father Raoul provided only temporary solace. Maria followed him everywhere. At night she came warm and willing in his dreams. Such times Richard would fling open the shutters of his window and, resting his elbows on the narrow ledge, gaze at the powdered heaven, the elusive moon, and torment himself with unanswerable questions.

When he discussed his unhappiness with Father Raoul, the priest nodded sympathetically. "We all have ghosts we must someday confront. You must pray, however, for the right time to face those ghosts. And believe it or no, sire, you are not the only one who has fallen short of God's grace or been tempted by weaknesses of the flesh."

Looking into the priest's furrowed face, Richard was certain he'd never succumbed to any such weakness. "You are Knights Templar, father, and closer to God than ordinary men."

"We are flesh and blood like any other."

"Nay, you are something more. You have always been, since the first crusades. When I was a page in my father's house I used to sneak from Westminster to Fleet Street to watch you there. I thought then there was nothing so fine as your long beards and crosses of red and white, and I told myself this is what I want to be—a knight devoted to God and the protection of man. The Templars are the most worthy of all."

"Your brother felt otherwise," Father Raoul said. "He packed many of us off to the tower."

Richard dropped his gaze. "He never believed those absurd stories of demon worship and human sacrifice."

"Nor does it matter—for it was all God's will."

"God's will," Richard repeated. "If only I knew what that was. Certain enough I've followed no will but my own. No wonder I cannot find the peace I read on all of your faces."

Father Raoul laced together his fingers. When his gaze met Richard's, his expression was oddly guarded. "We are old men, sire. With old men's dimming passions. 'Tis easy not to hear the world's siren song."

* * *

The Feast of the Holy Face occurred on July 1. For much of the preceding week a palpable though unspoken excitement had charged the monastery's usual placid atmosphere. Richard surmised that the change had something to do with the feast and certain Templar rites. The Holy Face was considered their most important holy day, though he didn't know why. While it wasn't a usual fast day, none of the knights came to table, but rather all went to confession and spent the day in prayerful contemplation. Even Father Raoul appeared distracted, offering Richard little more than perfunctory advice in the confessional, and later, when he returned to the chapel, the door was barred. Feeling vaguely apprehensive, Richard spent the rest of the day in the garden and roaming about the woods. What was happening?

The night was hot and humid. Hungry from fasting, haunted by visions of Maria, Richard could not sleep. Naked, he lay on his cot watching the moonlight stream through a crack in the shutters and thinking about other such nights . . .

Trying to subdue troublesome memories, Richard sought to bury them in sleep—but sleep, as well as peace, eluded him. Finally giving up, he stood and opened the room's shutters. From the position of the moon he judged it past midnight. Not a breath of air stirred; not a sound came from the adjoining room where the brothers slept. The humidity weighed oppressively. He felt sticky and unclean, as well as a bit unnerved by the silence. Surveying the shadowed courtyard Richard noticed light filtering from the chapel's windows. Odd. The chapel should be dark at this hour. The large stained-glass scene above the altar was positioned away from the yard, but its colored patterns pierced the darkness.

At that moment he heard a faint chanting, and the hair on the back of his neck prickled. It was no ordinary thing to celebrate a feast day in the dead of night. Its secretiveness, the lights dancing like fairies in the darkness, disturbed him. Tucked away in his cell, he was certain he was the only man in the monastery absent from the ceremony. Recalling the peculiar activities of the day, the taut, expectant faces, listening to the eerie voices, Richard's mind suddenly ran to childhood stories he'd heard about the Templars. What had people said? Some swore that during their time in the Holy Land they had turned away from Christian worship to Satanism. They were said to kneel before an idol in the form of a black cat, Baphomet—and human sacrifice supposedly numbered among their practices.

Quickly he crossed himself and inhaled air into his lungs, consciously trying to slow his racing heart. "Such a thing cannot be," he whispered. "These saintly men couldn't be capable of such abominations!"

The sound of chanting intensified and from its body a distinct word emerged—one that caused his stomach to constrict in fear.

"Yallah!" cried the Templars.

"The heathen Saracen's war cry!" Richard breathed. Were those long-ago tales then true? Before his brother had purged them, Westminster had buzzed with strange rumors. The Templars were accused of conducting secret midnight ceremonies during which they prostrated themselves before a fearsome bearded head. They were also believed to toss the bodies of newborn children about in a circle and then, after murdering them, burn the bodies and smear the resulting fat on their idols.

"Absurd." Though the possibility seemed considerably less so this eerie night.

Slipping on his breeches, Richard left the small cell. Moonlight streamed through the adjoining dormitory windows onto the deserted beds. The stones, daily scrubbed, felt cool and smooth to his feet.

The cloister was not even lit by wall torches. Shadows hung from the overhead rafters and lurked in invisible corners. From the stables Richard heard the neighing of restless horses. A breeze sprang up to rustle the nearby arbor leaves, and overall, like a heartbeat, sounded the Templars' chant. "Yallah! Yallah!"

As he neared the chapel Richard saw a crack of light from beneath the door. Walking on tiptoe, he approached the door. Expecting it to be locked he eased against it. It opened.

The chapel was brightly lighted. Several rows of candelabra had been placed about the altar illuminating the window scene of Christ at the Resurrection. Vivid in their crosses of red and white, the knights grouped near the front, where Father Raoul was celebrating.mass. The consecration was nearing, but it was unlike any consecration Richard had ever witnessed. Neither was the host elevated, nor the usual responses of the mass used. Rather the Templars chanted a psalm he recognized from the Bible.

> . . . *Selah.*
> *God be merciful to us*
> *And bless us.*
> *And cause his face*
> *To shine upon us.*
> *Selah!*

"Selah!" he whispered. "'Tis not Yallah but Selah!" They weren't praying to a heathen deity at all, but to the Christian God. So the stories must be false, he thought, ashamed of his earlier fearfulness. Squinting, he peered beyond Father Raoul in his white vestments. The candles threw the scene into imperfect relief, but to the side of the rood Richard saw a long ivory cloth of some sort. It hung suspended from a rod attached to the ceiling by two chains. The cloth was about seven feet long and appeared to be either stained or dirty, but perhaps it was just the play of light.

Fascinated, Richard watched the unfolding scene. At communion time the brothers came forward, but not to receive the customary host. Instead, each approached the shimmering cloth, prostrated himself before it, and raised its hem to his lips. Watching the hesitant, even fearful movements, Richard felt a chill that had naught to do with the breeze crossing his bare torso. What is this mysterious cloth? he wondered. Why does it inspire such reverence?

Too quickly, the service ended. When the knights rose to depart, Richard slipped inside an alcove hidden by the shadowed grape arbor. With folded hands and downcast eyes, the brothers passed. After the last one had disappeared, he again approached the door. Inching it open Richard saw that all the candles, except for those on the altar, had been extinguished.

Cautiously he approached the altar, his eyes held by the cloth, dancing in the uncertain light. As he neared, the straw-colored stains assumed a blurred, indistinct shape. Once Richard thought he glimpsed the full-length figure of a long-haired, bearded man, hands crossed over naked loins in an attitude of death. When he blinked the image disappeared. Although Richard had worshiped at countless shrines there was something about this object, whatever its identity, that shook him to the depths of his soul. At the altar step, he stopped—and could not move. The cloth shimmered before him, sometimes surely showing the outline of a man, sometimes nothing more than a patternless stain.

"My lord Sussex!" From the vestiary Father Raoul appeared.

"What is it?" Richard whispered.

"I'm not sure you should have come." The priest's expression was troubled. "I am not sure 'tis the proper time."

Richard's eyes remained locked to the cloth. "Tell me, father, what it is."

As he looked at the cloth, Father Raoul's face was transformed by adoration. He turned back to the earl, studying, weighing. Reaching out, the priest touched his arm. "Come, sire. Let us sit on these steps. 'Tis time, I think, to tell you a story."

Inwardly composing his thoughts, Father Raoul looked down

at his gnarled hands. "During the last crusade," he began, "our knights conquered Constantinople, which was then called the Queen of Cities, because of her art and culture and fine palaces. However, after our crusaders took her she was reduced to a sad state. 'Twas such a pity . . ." He shook his head as if ridding it of unpleasant memories.

"What followed was a black mark on Christendom. Our knights ransacked Constantinople. They held nothing sacred; they hacked and plundered and destroyed without mercy.

"At Blachernae there was a certain church, the Church of the Virgin Mary, which was known to contain the most sacred relic in the world. When the crusaders went mad, several of my order entered the church and spirited the relic away to Castle Pilgrim near Acre. There it stayed for near a hundred years."

Father Raoul closed his eyes, as if pulling forth long unused memories. "Now Castle Pilgrim was a grand place," he continued. "Though I was a young man then, I'll not forget the gardens and orchards, the cool running stream, and fields of grain tucked behind its walls. Who would think such a fortress would ever fall . . ." His voice trailed off. The furrows around his mouth appeared even more pronounced.

"The rest of the story you well know. Soon afterward France's Phillip the *Unfair*, craving the Templars' riches for himself, rounded up our knights, tortured them, and burned many at the stake. To keep the relic from falling into his greedy hands, several of us smuggled it to England. Your brother, God be thanked, felt more kindly toward us than that French devil. While some of us were jailed, none of us were tortured or put to the stake—and after a time King Edward granted us our freedom. We were left again to do as we pleased.

"For a time we hid at Wetherby in Yorkshire. Fearing that that preceptory wasn't remote enough, our group searched until we found a more secluded spot to guard our relic. We settled here, and here we've stayed these past dozen years or so."

Standing, Father Raoul made a sweeping arc in the direction

of the cloth. "Before you is the secret of the Templars, the truth of all the rumors, the ultimate cause of many deaths—for what man would not gladly give his life for even one glimpse of this most sacred miracle?"

Richard felt suddenly faint. "But what exactly is it?"

"Do you not yet know, my lord?"

As he shook his head a sudden panic gripped his heart.

"You asked me once why we have such peace. Before you hangs the answer. Behold, Richard, the burial shroud of Jesus Christ!"

The words exploded in his brain. His mind, his very body went numb.

The priest approached the shroud. "Come here, sire. Come and touch it."

"I cannot." Richard's body trembled more violently than it ever had preceding battle. "I am a bastard and adulterer. I have killed men and betrayed friends. I am unworthy."

The priest's lined face softened with compassion. "You are no less worthy than any man. Our Savior would not have come had we already achieved perfection." Taking his hand, Father Raoul led him forward. At his touch Richard acquiesced and, as a criminal condemned to his inevitable fate, approached.

Around him, candles flickered. As Richard stood before the shroud, his breath rasped. Intending merely to touch the garment's hem, he raised shaking fingers to the cloth. The figure suddenly sprang to focus, the indistinct facial features leapt out at him. Clearly now Richard saw the staring eyes, strong nose, forked beard framing a sensitive mouth, the center-parted hair that appeared to be topped by an indistinct caplet. Unbidden, he reached up to touch the eyes, mouth, face of Jesus Christ—and in the next moment, fainted into Father Raoul's arms.

TWENTY-FOUR

oger Mortimer stalked into the Painted Chamber in the Palace of Westminster. Queen Isabella was seated in a window seat, around which had been painted large, boldly colored figures of the Virtues. On either side snuggled her two daughters, listening to her recital of the ballad of the Clerk and the Mermaid.

"Madam, I have unpleasant news," Mortimer bellowed. The chamber door slammed against the wall with the force of his entrance. The sound cracked like a whip along the cavernous ceiling, decorated by ornamental paterae. Immediately the queen's ladies scurried for any available exit. No longer did Mortimer maintain even the most perfunctory façade concerning his personal relationship with Isabella—whether in happy times or sour.

As Joan and Eleanor's nurses grabbed their hands and scooted them toward a door, Isabella turned to her lover. Mortimer's face matched the scarlet hues that provided partial background to the Painted Chamber's multifarious frescoes. "What is it, Roger? What has happened?"

"Your husband has escaped from Berkeley Castle!"

"What?" Isabella's hands automatically clutched across her heart. "'Tis impossible. We had him moved there because Henry Leicester feared just this sort of occurrence at Kenilworth. You told me Berkeley would be safer."

"Safer than what?" Mortimer paced the long, narrow room like a panther scenting new blood. "Fools everywhere scheme for the idiot's release. We could not take him north because even God would not dare trust the northern lords to properly watch him, and that damnable earl of Mar is seeking a Scottish rescue. You yourself said we could not risk the Tower of London. The mob would either tear the whoreson to pieces or recrown him king."

Isabella struggled to maintain her temper. She did not dare chastise Mortimer, especially when in such a brutal mood, but she misliked his ugliness concerning her husband. Though the queen loved Roger beyond the bounds of reason, she sometimes missed Edward's less volatile nature. At least she had never had cause to fear Edward's temper.

"I realize that since the deposition there has been a certain shift in public opinion, my darling, but is that not to be expected? Our people still love me and my son." She could not add her lover to the equation. Not that he cared.

"I care not a whit for whom the people love or their opinion, public or private. I only care that your milksop of a husband has escaped." He shook his fist at an imaginary foe. "When I find those responsible I will string them all up."

"Do you have any idea who masterminded the escape?"

Mortimer ceased his pacing. "Aye, madam." He fixed her with a feral grin. "He is an old friend of yours—the Dominican Thomas Dunhead."

Isabella's eyes narrowed. The very name of Edward's confessor aroused hatred. Dunhead had been an ambassador to the papal court and it was he, rumor said, who had once approached Pope John about the possibility of Edward obtaining an annulment. "What are you doing to find him?"

"My men are scouring Gloucestershire. They'll not get far." Mortimer planted his feet in a truculent stance. "Your husband is getting to be a tiresome waste of time, madam." When Roger was angry he always referred to Edward as her husband. "We are going to have to seek a more permanent manner of dealing with him." Spinning on his heel he left the room.

Rising from the seat Isabella moved absently about the chamber, finally coming to rest beside the bed, which dominated the room. Henry III had commissioned his artists to paint a panel, ten feet by six, behind the bed of the coronation of Edward the Confessor. Isabella had lain often in the Painted Chamber with her husband. As Edward slept she had silently bemoaned her lot and, despairing of sleep, counted the surrounding sea of faces that danced like demons in the flickering rush lights. 'Tis strange, she thought, sinking down upon the counterpane. I still count the faces.

Staring blindly into the distance, Isabella fiddled with the golden row of buttons fastened upon her tight sleeves. She knew, for the sake of her son's reign and her and Mortimer's power, Edward must be recaptured. Since the deposition, which had occurred six months past in January, enemy voices had become increasingly strident. Some even dared maintain that ther son's entire reign was illegal. Her husband had been deposed by a Parliament that, the troublemakers declared, was invalid because it had been held apart from the presence and authority of the king, who had refused to travel to London. Without Edward's presence, Parliament had no authority to meet, let alone depose a reigning monarch. Nor was there any known law by which a king could be tried and disposed. "God alone can punish a king," some of the braver clerics had said.

When she'd questioned Mortimer he'd merely waved the debate aside. "The voice of people is the voice of God, in this matter at least."

Isabella did not dare question him further. Roger hated her to nag or appear weak and uncertain so she often affected a coldness she did not feel. Only once, since their return to England, had he even seen her weep. When Parliament had met to officially depose Edward, terrible things had been said about him. Outside the mob had clamored for his deposition— even his death—and inside prelates and peers had cried "Let it be done!" She had openly wept when Prince Edward had refused to take the crown unless his father willingly abdicated. Mortimer had mistaken her tears for frustration over her son's intransigence, but she had cried because of the hatred ruling Parliament—and all of it directed toward her helpless husband, who must step aside, in unnatural fashion, and allow his son to sit on a throne that should rightfully remain his until death. Isabella's hatred had died with the death of Hugh Despenser the Younger. She had none left to nurture, and Parliament's antagonism unnerved her.

Tears slipped along the bridge of her nose, dropping onto her full pleated skirt. Bishop Orleton, one of Edward's chief antagonists, had been among those who had traveled to Kenilworth to inform the king of Parliament's wishes. When she could not sleep, Isabella replayed that scene in her mind as clearly as if she'd personally witnessed it. Bishop Orleton, he who had preached many seditious sermons and helped engineer the Despensers' downfall, had reported it all to her and Mortimer in loving detail. Her outward indifference had nearly cracked when Orleton had described how, after listening to a list of the crimes for which he faced abdication, Edward had fainted, only to be cruelly propped up by Henry of Leicester and the bishop of Winchester.

After Orleton had finished with his diatribe Edward had said, "I am in your hands. You must do what seems right."

Then William Trussell, who had condemned both the Despensers, had broken fealty with him for all his subjects. "I account you as a private person, without any manner of royal dignity." The white staff of office had been broken—as was customary upon the death or deposition of a royal master.

"I am aware that for my many sins I am thus punished. Have compassion on me." When Orleton had related this to Mortimer, both men had laughed. Roger had mimicked Edward's words and Isabella had longed to flee the room.

Edward had ended his humiliation by saying, "Much as I grieve at having incurred the ill will of the people, I am glad they have chosen my oldest son to be their king." In defeat her husband had shown himself surprisingly dignified and gracious. Defeat showed well a man's character—as did victory. She thought of Mortimer's actions since his ascendancy. Criticism of him was becoming increasingly vocal and commonplace. Some even dared say he was proving himself as greedy as the Despensers.

"'Tis not so," she whispered. But Mortimer had indeed showered himself with lands, honors, wardships, titles, and offices—yet his ambition remained unsated. On the day of Edward III's coronation, four of the baron's sons had also been knighted, and among other acts, Mortimer had received lands once belonging to the dead favorites. Isabella's son was not proving himself always so easily manipulated, however, and she sometimes sensed behind the polite façade his dislike of Mortimer. She also sensed that Edward III possessed more of his grandfather's strengths than his father's weaknesses.

The queen's thoughts had come full circle, back to her husband. "You are no match for Roger," she whispered. "Enjoy your freedom, my husband, for it will be brief."

In August Maria heard wondrous news. Richard had ridden to Berkeley Castle, where the deposed king was incarcerated, and turned himself over to the keeper there. Maria had never allowed herself to believe in the possibility of her lover's death and constantly supplicated a God who, she was certain, had turned away His face. The news was the one happy occurrence in nine difficult months. Driven by guilt, Maria had tried to make up to her children for the months of separation. Tom was continuing his apprenticeship at Deerhurst, but Phillip had sent him home at Eastertime, and Blanche she saw daily. It was never enough—not the stories she told her daughter, the walks they took in the cherry orchard, the hawking parties upon which she accompanied Tom, or the pair of staghounds she'd given him. She had abandoned Blanche and, at the very least,

humiliated Tom. Always she sensed their unspoken accusations, as well as the disapproval of everyone with whom
she came in contact. She had failed as a mother, as well as a
wife, and she knew not how to remedy her acts.

'Twould be so much easier, she thought, if I could make my
heart love neither Phillip nor Richard. Then I would not care
that Phillip will not see me, or that Richard might momentarily
suffer a traitor's death. But even though her insides sometimes
felt hollow as a dried-out gourd, she could not long detach her
emotions. When she was not tormented by worries about
Richard's safety, she yearned for Phillip, for some sort of stable
home life. Though Phillip had not started annulment
proceedings, neither had he contacted her, save concerning her
son or to send for Blanche, who often visited Deerhurst. She
longed to somehow refit the shattered pieces of her life, but had
no idea how even to begin nor how to reconcile her love of
Richard with her need for her husband and children. I will lose
them both, she thought, Phillip through divorce and Richard
through death. I will end up alone; and 'twill be what I deserve.

With Richard incarcerated at Berkeley Castle, Maria began
concentrating her energies on somehow visiting him. With
Roger Mortimer's star ever in the ascendancy, both Richard's
life and that of his brother might possibly be measured in days.
Rumors abounded—that both men were being slowly poisoned,
that Richard was going to be taken to London where he would
stand trial for treason, that he had undergone some sort of
religious experience that had transformed him. Sometimes
Maria wondered whether Richard might not have changed. His
recent actions seemed at odds with the Richard she knew. Her
Richard would not voluntarily allow himself to be imprisoned.
With the political climate and changing sympathies, he would
have raised an army and freed his brother.

Maria began writing letters to Berkeley Castle and to
Edward III at Westminster, pleading to be allowed to see
Richard. Though she would rather have approached the king
personally with her request, she dared not travel to London for

fear of Roger Mortimer. Edward answered politely, but noncommittally. Thomas Berkeley answered not at all.

I must see him, she thought. A sense of urgency permeated her actions, a sense that time was running out.

Then she thought of Queen Isabella. Isabella understood about forbidden love. Perhaps she would help. Maria wrote yet another letter.

Isabella responded immediately. "Be at Berkeley Castle on September 1. I will instruct Lord Sussex's guardian, Thomas Berkeley. Do not relate to anyone your visit."

Maria was surprised, as well as gratified, by the queen's response. She'd not really expected Isabella to circumvent her lover, or trouble herself with Maria's affairs.

"If you should also see my husband, please tell me how he is faring," Isabella continued. "I have not had true word since his recapture and I can no longer personally see to his health."

Maria stared at the paragraph, mulling over the implications of Isabella's request. So, my queen, she thought as her fingers traced the royal seal, you are also trapped in a web of your own making. If Isabella was not allowed knowledge of Edward's care, and was reduced to soliciting information from a third party, events were indeed at a dangerous pass.

Berkeley Castle, which had been owned by the Berkeley family since the eleventh century, nestled amidst a wood in the southern part of Gloucestershire. From its turrets Bristol Channel could be viewed and the hazy waters of the River Severn. The castle's proximity to the channel made rescue attempts by water a constant threat. As fall approached, rumors abounded that yet another plan was being hatched to free Edward and Richard. Roger Mortimer sent out spies to ascertain the truth behind the rumors. Increasingly he cursed his royal prisoners, who, even while in captivity and stripped of their power, continued to plague him.

The Templar monastery, where Christ's shroud was kept,

was also located in Gloucestershire. As Richard had again begun contemplating his return to the outside world he'd known his continued presence constituted a threat. The monastery was not so secluded that it could not be found. What if the shroud fell into Mortimer's hands? That possibility, plus Richard's desire to tie up the loose ends of his life, had caused him to surrender himself at Berkeley Castle.

Richard's quarters at Berkeley were small and none too clean, but he counted himself content. Meditation and prayer took up much of his time, and while his warden, Thomas Berkeley, was married to Mortimer's daughter and had been imprisoned by Edward until Isabella's invasion, he was nevertheless kind.

Though Richard sensed his death drawing near, he accepted, even embraced, that knowledge. With eternity beckoning, how could his present life hold any allure? Death only opened the door to Jesus. From the moment he'd touched the shroud the hatred, ambitions, guilt, self-loathing—all the emotions that had been so much a part of him—had been replaced by love, the Savior's love for him. Jesus' love had penetrated to the innermost reaches of his soul, leaving him forever transformed. Richard could not explain the mechanics of the act; he only knew that it had happened. Initially, he feared that the intensity of his experience would fade, that the old Richard who had died would be resurrected. That had not happened.

Only three people I would once again see, he told himself. Edward, Phillip, and Maria. Edward because he is my brother, Phillip to obtain his forgiveness, and Maria? Because I loved her more than life.

Thomas Berkeley entered Richard's room. "You have a visitor," he said. His eyes darted about the room; his fingers nervously worked the folds of his tunic.

Richard raised up from his rope-frame bed, which comprised the area's only furniture. "Edward?" Though he'd repeatedly requested to see his brother, Thomas had always maintained a meeting was impossible.

"You have not much time. 'Tis a dangerous matter for all concerned." He cast a furtive look over his shoulder, as if expecting Roger Mortimer to materialize. "And speak softly. No one else must know who is here." Quickly, Berkeley exited, leaving the wooden door slightly ajar.

Richard had barely stood before Maria was in his arms, burrowing against him. Her hood fell back and he buried his face in her hair, inhaling its fragrance, marveling at the feel of her, her vibrant presence, which lightened the room as surely as a torch.

"I cannot believe 'tis you," he breathed. "I prayed to see you, but who would have thought . . ." His arms tightened around her.

"I've missed you so," Maria managed, before her voice choked on unshed tears.

She leaned back in the cradle of his arms, the better to view him. "Sometimes I feared you dead, and despaired of ever seeing you."

"Have you reconciled with Phillip? Has he forgiven me? Tell me about our babe. I have not heard anything."

"Phillip will not see me. And the babe . . ." She shook her head. "I lost it soon after our escape." Before he could comment, she rushed on. "Let us not talk of me. I want to know how you are. Have you suffered here? Has Berkeley treated you ill?"

"Nay. And I think I suffered less than those who loved me and were forced to wait for true word these months. I thought of you so often, Maria. 'Tis a miracle that you are here with me. Mayhaps now I'll be able to right at least a measure of the wrongs I've caused."

"You've done me no wrong." Her eyes caressed the beloved planes of his face, the skin stretched taut across high cheekbones, the new lines touching his eyes and mouth. "You've changed, my love. 'Tis marked upon you."

Richard looked past her, to the silver crucifix upon the far wall. "Aye. I know now that earthly influence, the things of this world matter not."

Surprised by his words, Maria again drew back to study him. Something about Richard's face reminded her of mystics she'd seen, of holy hermits who lived along the roadways and experienced religious visions. She wondered suddenly whether the rumors, for once, had been correct. "What does matter then, my love?"

Richard's arms fell from her waist. "Have you dwelt upon Our Blessed Savior and His love for mankind?"

Richard's words made no sense. The conversation was taking a peculiar turn that she could not grasp. "I mislike thinking about God," she said finally. Though Maria obediently went to church and prayed, she had ceased thinking of God as anything but an angry being who would never forgive her her transgressions or cease meting out punishment.

"After I escaped from Mortimer," Richard continued, "some monks found me and cared for me. 'Tis hard to explain what happened at their monastery, but they had a miraculous relic there, a certain cloth . . ." Searching for the proper phrasing he paused to run a hand through already tousled locks. The combination of soft light and golden hair created a nimbus round his head.

Watching him, an eerie sensation shivered through Maria. "Please, my love, no more. I do not want to talk about this. We have but a few moments together and . . ."

"There are things in life that we cannot be certain of," Richard continued as if he had not heard. "But of one matter I have no doubt. Our Saviour died on the cross for our adultery, paid the cost of our sin with His blood long ago."

She stiffened. "I have committed grievous sins in my life, but loving you does not number among them."

"We knew love, Maria, but not like the love Jesus bears us." Richard's face glowed as luminously as Christchurch's windows when pierced by sunlight. His face frightened her.

[279]

"Our Savior loves us both more than we could ever love each other."

"Nay! Not more than I love you!"

Reaching out, Richard brushed her cheek with his fingertips. "Someday soon, you'll know, as I do. This world seems so permanent and yet we are here such a short span . . ."

Maria felt Richard's touch to the very wellspring of her being, not erotically, but as if it were an extension of herself. An overwhelming sense of loss pierced her heart. She had lost her love. "'Tis true, what the monks said," she whispered. "Life though pleasant is transitory." She raised shimmering eyes to his. "And our love, was that also transitory?"

"Nay. I loved you well and truly. I still do." Richard paused. "But 'tis different now."

"I cannot believe some magic cloth, some months closeted with monks could so change you."

A sharp rap interrupted them, signaling the end to their moment.

Flinging her arms around Richard's neck, she clung to him. In her secret heart she knew she'd never again feel his embrace or look into his beloved face. Closing her eyes she tried to imprint upon her memory their last physical contact. "I do not care what you say or how you feel. I will love you into eternity."

Thomas Berkeley opened the door. "'Tis time, my lady. Your escort is already mounted and waiting in the bailey."

Richard's grip tightened round Maria's waist. His lips brushed her ear as he whispered, "'Twas a grand cherry fair we had, was it not?"

TWENTY-FIVE

rom the narrow window of his room, Richard glimpsed the sight of distant oaks, beginning to flaunt the boldness of fall. Since Maria's visit he'd scratched a mark on his wall for each passing day. The marks numbered thirteen.

This morning he'd seen his brother walking in the courtyard of Berkeley's inner ward, which was shaped similar to a college quadrangle. Even a hundred feet away, Edward of Caernarvon appeared a broken man. The cut of his black serge was mean and cheap. The slump to his broad shoulders spoke more eloquently than a thousand words of his sorry pass.

Richard heard a rattle of keys, a scraping in the lock. After knocking, Thomas Berkeley poked his head inside. "I am here to tell you I am leaving for a few days. I've been called away on business to Chepstow."

Berkeley's eyes could not meet Richard's. Something in his voice warned of danger. "What manner of business, Tom?"

"I am unsure. 'Tis an emergency, or so I've been told." Berkeley ducked his head, pretending great interest in the hem of his tunic sleeve. "I heard Thomas Gurney say that they might soon allow you to see your brother."

"I thank you, Tom, for your past kindnesses. May God keep you on your journey."

Thomas hesitated, then, after looking over his shoulder,

approached Richard. "Mortimer has uncovered another plot," he whispered. "The Welshman, Rhys ap Gruffyd, was scheming with several magnates to rescue you and your brother and remove you by means of the channel. Everything was set when Mortimer's lieutenant in North Wales, William Shalford, sent word to his lord. I do not think Mortimer will risk another escape attempt."

"Nor do I." Richard turned his eyes to the silver crucifix.

With Thomas Berkeley's departure, Richard and Edward were left at the mercy of keepers hand-picked by Mortimer— Sirs Gurney, Ogle, and Berkeley's brother-in-law, John Maltrever. Secretive faces appeared at Richard's door with an occasional tray of tasteless food. Thomas Gurney sometimes enjoyed taunting Richard but he, too, appeared preoccupied. Among his infrequent jibes, however, he relayed one interesting bit of information.

"Your brother has been removed to another part of Berkeley. To a room more in keeping with his changing station." Gurney laughed.

The underlying insinuation of the words was disturbing.

"When will you let me see Edward?" Richard had asked the question a hundred times previously and always received the same negative response.

This day, however, Gurney grinned. "Soon, Bastard, soon!"

Richard turned away and knelt before the silver cross. Grant me strength, Lord, to endure, he silently prayed. Death he did not mind. But pain—Richard was still enough a part of this world to be frightened by the very possibility.

Evil stalked Berkeley's halls. Richard sensed its presence as surely as the chill breath of darkness seeping through the castle walls. He had no doubt he and Edward would be murdered, perhaps this very night. On his cot, Richard slid in and out of terrifying dreams. Awake, he tensed at the slightest sound—the baying of a hound below, the scampering of an invisible rat across the room.

Footsteps in the passageway. Jerking upright, Richard reached instinctively for a sword that was no longer at his side. Guttural voices stopped outside the door; he heard the click of a turning key. Thomas Gurney stepped into the room. Behind him huddled Ogle and Maltrever, carrying torches. Their mouths were set in ugly slashes; their determined eyes looked cold upon Richard.

"Come, Bastard," Gurney said. "'Tis time to see your brother."

Warily, Richard arose. He felt certain they were not taking him to Edward, but to his own death. Suddenly, every instinct cried to fight, to break for freedom. Better to die with a blade to the back than strapped to the rack, or the hand-crushing pilliwinks. He inhaled deeply and a calmness descended; a gentling hand soothed away his fears.

Richard followed his jailers up narrow vices, along ill-lit passages. He had no clear idea where he was, where they might be headed. Of one thing Richard was certain, though—the increasing stench. A rotten smell that had at first soured in his nostrils, and now revolted his stomach, all his senses.

When the fetor grew so overpowering Richard thought he would vomit, they reached a narrow door. Maltrever unlocked the door and motioned him inside. Richard swallowed back a gag as he stepped into the tiny airless room. He noticed first a rude table scattered with remnants of a meal, and beyond a crucifix attached to the rough stone wall. A fire blazed in a narrow fireplace; a poker rested, tip inward, among the glowing coals. In one corner was located a gaping pit.

The dungeon, as it was called, was Berkeley's charnel house. Here were thrown the rotting carcasses of cattle, bones, entrails, and moldering, maggot-ridden heaps of garbage. The odor emanating from the pit literally made Richard's eyes water. Fear knotted his stomach. Sometimes prisoners of low birth were thrown in charnel houses and left to die. If such was his jailers' intent, they would have to kill him now. He'd never allow them to throw him down that hellhole.

As Richard turned to Gurney, his eyes caught a figure slumped on a cot thrust against a shadowy wall. The man's head rested in his hands.

"Edward!"

Edward looked up. The deposed king's face was sunken, his unkempt beard looked as if it had been hacked with sheep shears. Cheap serge clung to shoulders that had once worn velvets and brocades, matted hair to a forehead that had worn the crown of England. It was Edward's eyes, though, that had most changed. Vacant, hopeless eyes, red-rimmed, staring. Eyes that did not immediately recognize Richard. And then, with a strangled cry, Edward rose. Immediately, Richard was at his side. The two men embraced.

"Oh, Ned!" he whispered, drawing back. "What have they done to you?"

Edward's eyes misted; he clung to his brother. "Since my escape they've been so cruel. Isabella used to write to me at Kenilworth, you know, and send me fine clothes. But now I never hear from anyone." He choked back a sob. "When they captured me they never let me sleep or stay in one place. They made me shave with dirty water brought from a ditch in an old rusted helm. They made me sit in an ant heap." Edward buried his face against Richard's neck. Richard patted his back, struggling to breathe in the fetid closeness and warmth of the room, to ignore his brother's rags and filthy hair, the lice-ridden bedcovers piled atop his sagging bed.

"I can see but a tiny patch of courtyard with slimy paving stones and crumbling wall," Edward continued. "They have not let me walk in days, and the stench, I swear, is killing me by inches." Pleading eyes met Richard's own. "Help me, Dickon," he whispered, reverting to a nickname unused for twenty years, dropped on Richard's fourteenth birthday.

"Come!" He eased Edward down on the rude bed, sitting

beside him. He stroked his brother's arm and murmured soothing nonsense that seemed to momentarily calm Edward. "Now I am here, brother, and naught will harm thee, that I promise." Empty words—if Edward knew how empty . . .

"Here, drink this." Standing over him, Thomas Gurney held out a cup of wine to Richard.

He shook his head. Edward shrank against him; his hands clawed Richard's forearm. The blackguards had physically abused Edward, of that he was certain. What had they done to so reduce the carefree, physically powerful man to little more than a sniveling boy?

Gurney shoved the cup in Richard's face. "Nay!" Richard slapped away his hand. "Leave us be!"

Red wine splashed across Gurney's hand, stained his light-colored sleeve. "Drink, Bastard!" he snarled. "Or I'll pour it down your treasonous throat."

Richard's head jerked up; his eyes probed Gurney's own. The wine contained something—a sleeping draught, poison, what? Would they drug him to unconsciousness before killing Edward, and then perform a second murder? One thing was certain. His jailers did not intend that either he or his brother live to view another dawn.

"Have some wine, Dickon. They gave me a nice meal tonight, and the wine tasted like what we used to drink at court . . ." Edward's voice trailed away. He wiped his nose on a tattered sleeve.

Angry words threatened to erupt on Richard's tongue. How could these men do this to their king, to his brother? Again the invisible restraining hand. Hadn't they done worse to Jesus?

The wine cup was now less than half filled. Richard gulped down the contents and threw the empty cup across the room in the direction of the dungeon. The goblet bounced off the rough stones, careened down the narrow shaft.

Gurney laughed low in his throat.

Poison, Richard thought. God grant that the end is quick. "Now leave me be with my brother." He slipped his arm around Edward's shoulder. Trusting as a child, Edward nestled against him.

"You know what they did to my Hugh, don't you, Dickon? They daily tell me, over and over, torment me with the memory of his execution."

"Do not think on him," Richard murmured. "He is long in the arms of the Savior."

"I did try to rule well, I did." Edward began sobbing. "Dickon, Dickon, how came we to this?"

Richard had no answers. He opened his mouth to make reply when the room suddenly pitched downward; the hearth fire seemed to burn in his stomach. The floor leapt upward. Righted.

"I would have been happy, Dickon, to have plowed the earth and designed ships, to have been a gentleman farmer or a yeoman. I did not ask to be king of England."

Richard stumbled to his feet, lurched forward. He must reach the cross on the opposite side of the room, must make ready for his journey to the Savior.

"Dickon!"

Richard staggered to the cross, knelt. The room pitched again; knives stabbed his stomach. He slumped over on his side, trying to see through vision suddenly blurred.

Noise, movement. The dinner table was suddenly in midair. Plates fell, food splattered, utensils bounced, goblets shattered. Ogle and Maltrever were holding the table atop a thrashing Edward, pinioning him to the bed.

Richard tried to rise. He could not move. The guardroom wavered, swam. He saw double. He blinked, and as his vision cleared he saw Edward's flailing legs and arms, Gurney hurrying from the fire, a long pipe made of horn in one hand, a glowing poker in the other.

"No! No!" Did the scream remain locked inside? Pain sliced Richard's stomach, a thousand times more fierce than before. He was retching; he could barely lift his head above his own vomit. Sweat chilled his forehead; he began to tremble. He tried to rise. He must stop Gurney. Gurney bent over Edward, threw back his gown. Edward, crying, struggling; Maltrever and Ogle throwing all their weight to the table to keep him trapped.

Gurney jammed the horn against Edward's twisting buttocks. Into the horn he thrust the fire-tipped poker. A brutal shove and Edward was screaming, screaming. The smell of burning flesh cut above the charnel stench. Richard sucked the smell of his brother's burning insides into his lungs as he retched again. Screams shattered Richard's eardrums but he could not discern whether they were Edward's or his own.

Since her return from Berkeley, Maria spent most of her time gazing out her chamber window. From her vantage point she watched the barley and wheat harvests, watched the workers swing their sickles, bind the awkward sheaves, and stand them upright. On the last day of harvest she saw teams of reapers race to finish the remaining ridges and, in ancient ritual, throw their sickles at the last sheaf until it fell. She watched the castle steward walk Fordwich's fields, tallying his accounts for the new fiscal year. Autumn's moon rose like a beacon above the treetops and Maria watched the high flight of the "Gabriel Hounds," as the wild geese streamed across its golden face.

She felt the air cool and chill at even time and greeted the arrival of autumn's rain with tears of her own. She wept for Richard, for the past, her dead babe, and for reasons she could not name. Increasingly, Maria sensed something dreadful was going to happen, sensed it as certainly as she had the death of her mother. If only Eleanora were here so that I might question her, she thought. But Eleanora had entered a Benedictine nunnery soon after Michael Hallam's death. Maria had no one with whom to share her fear.

One late September afternoon she left her chamber to walk in the cherry orchard. A recent rain had stirred the scents of the earth—the long grasses and fruit trees, the cloying sweetness of fallen cherries that were beginning to rot. As she walked among the bare branches the past whispered about her; ghostly figures hovered just beyond her view—her mother, Edmund Leybourne, herself, and Phillip—for their youth had died somewhere unnoticed along the years. "You were a better husband than I was a wife," she whispered. "I wish I could tell you."

"Maria."

At first Maria thought the voice was only a trick of her heart. She turned around.

"Your father told me I would find you here."

Phillip looked exhausted. His jupon was splattered with mud; dirt streaked his face. Even his movements seemed dulled by fatigue. "I rode straight through, two days straight. I wanted to be the one to tell you."

Deerhurst was a hard hour's ride from Berkeley Castle. Phillip would have been among the first to know. Maria closed her eyes. She swayed ever so slightly before righting herself. "Richard's dead."

Phillip nodded. He took a step toward her, but a great distance yet separated them. "There were so many rumors, no one could sort them all. We just knew something was going to happen." He looked away, beyond the bony branches of the cherry trees, searching for the proper words. "I cannot say how he died. Only that both he and Edward were together, and that two such convenient deaths must have the foul hand of Mortimer stirring the brew."

Richard murdered. Maria held her arms tight at her sides and balled her fists. Tears leaked from beneath the closed eyelids. She willed herself to remain rigid. She would not further humiliate her husband by openly mourning her lover.

"I have lost everything," she said. "Richard and you. I cannot seek refuge in the past for 'tis but chasing the wind. And I have no future." She began to shake and turned away so he would not see. She felt as if she must shatter into a thousand shards, like a dropped piece of pottery.

Phillip came up behind her and slipped his arms around her

waist. "I know you loved Richard more than me," he whispered. "It no longer matters."

Faintly, she heard the sounds of Christchurch bells, announcing to the world Edward's death. And Richard's.

"I loved you differently, that's all. But 'twas you I hurt; you who deserved better." The pain stirred, rose inside like a live thing, began devouring her. Swiveling in Phillip's embrace, she clung to him, pressing against his warmth. "I cannot imagine life without him, Phillip, I just cannot."

His arms tightened around her waist. "Neither can I."

TWENTY-SIX

sabella left Parliament with her head held high, her hand grasping her lover's arm. The questions put to them by the Privy Council had been brutal and persistent. The lords had been unnerved by Edward's death, but when word leaked out that both the deposed king and his brother had died, panic had gripped the Council, and riots had occurred throughout the city. Isabella knew the only way to stop the rioting and the gossip of detractors was to tell the truth.

"There was no foul play," Roger Mortimer had insisted, as he faced members of the Privy Council. "And did you not all read the letter sent by Abbot Thokey of St. Peter's in Gloucester, exonerating us? He stated that he rode immediately to Berkeley, and said prayers over Edward's body. He said there was not a mark of violence upon it."

Young King Edward shot Mortimer a look of naked hatred. He'd accepted the death of his father as natural, or so Isabella assured herself, but two deaths? Why did they both have to die so suddenly? One death could be interpreted as fortunate; two was a scandal.

"What about Sussex?" spoke up Edmund of Kent, Isabella's brother-in-law. "Why has not anyone been allowed to see his body?"

"My physician will send back a detailed report," Mortimer

replied haughtily. "The wind blows cold off Bristol Channel. It does not surprise me that he succumbed to a sickness in the lungs."

"In the fall, Lord Mortimer?" Kind Edward asked, his voice edged in contempt. "And a strong man thirty-four years of age?"

Isabella spoke up. "Both my husband and Richard of Sussex are to be embalmed, and their bodies will be displayed at Berkeley's chapel for all to see. That should silence the skeptics."

She and Mortimer had left then. Her body trembled with the effort of maintaining an unruffled exterior, though Mortimer seemed unconcerned. As they walked across New Palace Yard toward their apartments, she noticed everywhere the white lion of Mortimer. Roger's troops were out in force and armed. He was taking no chances with disgruntled Londoners.

Church bells began calling out vespers. Isabella started, then composed herself. Following Edward's death, every church from mighty St. Paul's to the smallest had joined in an endless wrangling of sound, rolling through the streets, accompanying her every waking moment, intruding even into her restless sleep. Always the funeral knell—as omnipresent as God, and as accusatory. But we did nothing wrong, she told herself. We have the proof. The abbots said that the physicians . . .

"There goes the she-wolf and her lover," someone shouted. "Murderers both."

Isabella's eyes swept the staring faces; her nails dug into Mortimer's arm. He did not even notice. His thoughts writhed like a serpent's. Events had not gone according to his design. He had planned to announce Edward's death, and months later, when his power was more solid, an indifferent public would hear of the Bastard's unfortunate demise. Now he and Isabella would just have to brazen out the scandal. And scandal there would be, he was certain of that. Englishmen were as fickle in their loyalties as the heart of a whore. Six months past Edward's very name was a curse, yet now people flocked to the churches, bent their knees, and called him and his brother "saints." Mortimer's mouth twisted. Upon news of Edward's death, priests had rent their garments, women had fainted, and those lords who had stood against him had openly wept. Mortimer felt nothing but contempt for such mawkishness. Edward had been a fool and a weakling and he'd deserved death. As had his meddlesome brother.

When they reached the privacy of their apartments, Isabella dismissed the servants. She intended to discuss with her lover the deaths, to obtain certain concrete assurances, but when she opened her mouth, Mortimer said, "I do not like you in mourning black. Take off that damnable widow's barb. It makes you look like a nun."

Isavella obediently complied. Mortimer turned his back to her as he fed bits of chicken to one of his falcons, lashed to a perch.

"They really did die of natural causes, didn't they, Roger?"

Mortimer laughed.

"It seems such a strange thing," Isabella continued. "God must truly be on our side." She began twisting her hands together. "We must not hide anything, for 'twill make us appear guilty. Our hold is yet tentative, and Edward grows daily more silent. I know not what he thinks, but sometimes I'm certain he despises you."

"I quake in my boots at the very thought of his wrath. Really, madam, how could I fear someone sprung from the loins of Edward Caernarvon?"

"He is my son, as well." Isabella began replacing her widow's barb. "I think you are shortsighted to treat him with such contempt. As you also treat me."

Mortimer threw back his head and laughed so loudly that the startled falcon thrashed its wings. "I can treat you any way I please, madam. We are wedded, you and I. Wedded by blood and ambition and tied as certainly to each other as this hawk to its perch."

Isabella moved away from him, to her dressing table filled

with pots of sheep fat, cochineal paste, and other beauty aids. Blindly, she worked the stopper on one of her creams. I hate you, she thought. You are callous, greedy, and incapable of kindness. I wish I had never become your lover. Isabella sighed heavily. But the past could not be changed, no more than the future could be seen. And Roger was right. They were inextricably linked and nothing, save death, could sever that link.

Phillip entered Berkeley Castle's small chapel. The mourning candles surrounding Edward's corpse flickered in the sudden draft and leapt toward the ceiling, swathed by darkness. The entrance of the chapel was guarded, but by Thomas Berkeley's men, not Mortimer's. Phillip had experienced little resistance in arranging this late-night visit. Richard and Edward had been available for public viewing a fortnight now, and the controversy surrounding their deaths was already beginning to fade.

Illuminated by dozens of candles, Edward appeared to float above his bier. The cream-colored velvet tunic he wore shimmered in the reflected light. As if he were still breathing. The bier and Edward dominated Berkeley's nave. Phillip paused at the king's side only long enough to cross himself before he continued on to a secluded corner where Berkeley's patron saint was venerated. Here Richard had been placed.

Phillip's boots whispered on the stone floor; his elongated shadow leapt after him, ending near the rood positioned above the altar. The chapel was filled with shadows, just beyond the light. He suppressed a sudden shiver. He'd seen a multitude of dead men in his time, but he'd never viewed a king. Or Richard.

A lone pair of candles had been positioned to illuminate Richard's hands, which clasped a silver crucifix. The rest of Richard's body was swallowed by darkness.

Phillip's step slowed. Momentarily he experienced the eerie sensation that a second whisper of footsteps mocked him. But he was alone with two dead men, no one else.

Richard's bier was plain to the point of meanness. Removing one of the wax candles from its holder, Phillip played the light over Richard's face. The hair was neatly combed, the beard clipped to accentuate the mouth. Phillip held the candle closer. Not even the ministrations of professionals could smooth the unnatural twist to the lips. It confirmed what Phillip already knew. Richard had died in agony. He moved the light along the earl's length. The inspection revealed no further clues. Poison, most likely, he thought.

Phillip raised the light so that it illuminated Richard's face. Richard's face and yet not his. The skin appeared translucent, the features sculpted like a marble effigy rather than flesh. The expressiveness, the uniqueness that had comprised the essence of Richard had vanished with his life's breath. His face was smooth and beautiful, near a mask of his brother's, of any man.

"Where have you gone, my lord?" Phillip whispered. He closed his eyes. The last time he'd truly looked into Richard's face had been at Dover. The time of betrayal. It seemed now centuries past, such an inconsequential thing.

Phillip placed a tentative hand over Richard's own. The fingers were long and blunt, a warrior's hands. His fingers stroked Richard's own. Cold and unyielding. Not Richard's hands at all. A shudder of emotion passed through Phillip, quickly suppressed. Their lives had been inextricably intertwined since Bannockburn, thirteen years past. Their friendship had threaded through political events and private, winding through wars and laughter and betrayal toward death.

"We had devised another plan to rescue you," he said. "If you could have but held Mortimer at bay another fortnight, you would now be free."

The candle sputtered and smoked. Phillip replaced it upon its holder. He stared down at Richard's hands. If only he had something more, if only he did not feel so alone here in this drafty chapel, with its very stones exhaling the unyielding coldness of death. If only he could feel Richard's presence. If only God would grant him that much. But even if He could not, Phillip knew he must still say the words. "I cannot blame you for Maria. If I had not left, you would not have betrayed me. I know that now."

A great emptiness welled inside Phillip. He had not thought their relationship would end so unsatisfactorily, with bitterness rather than reconciliation. He had not expected life to prove so fleeting. "I forgave you long ago. I just wanted you to know." He inhaled shakily. "I wish you were Richard and could answer me. I wish it were not all so unfinished."

Leaning over, Phillip kissed the icy forehead. "When we meet again, my lord, then I will tell you."

TWENTY-SEVEN

he interior of Canterbury's Christchurch Cathedral was a crowded and brilliant sight. The walls and soaring ceilings were brightly painted; colorful cloth hangings hung from rods running from pillar to pillar. Usually the quarreling or gossiping press of people, the lords and ladies ambling about with their favorite hawks on glove lent Christchurch the aura of a fishmarket rather than a house of worship. But not today. Today the assemblage flanking Trinity Chapel and spilling out past the Norman nave to the cathedral precincts was silent. Expectant faces were turned toward the chapel that contained the shrine of Thomas à Becket. The minster bells began tolling a funeral knell. From the south aisle of Trinity Chapel appeared six prelates, flanking a barefoot woman wearing a hair shirt. Afternoon sunlight from the towering stained-glass miracle windows danced across the woman's unbound hair.

Maria kept her eyes locked to the mitered head of the man in front of her, Henry of Eastry, prior of Christchurch. Behind her walked John Fyndunne of St. Augustine's Abbey, the man with whom Richard had once negotiated for the sale of the Leopard's Head. Since Richard's death Maria had felt as hollow inside as a drained keg of ale. Hollow and alienated. Today was her first step toward reconciliation. Christchurch Cathedral was famous because of the murder of Thomas à Becket, and

King Henry II's subsequent public penance. Since childhood she'd lived with the tale of Henry's barefoot trek through Canterbury's streets, his scourging. His sins had been great, but so had been her own.

The smooth paving stones chilled her bare feet. Between the tolling of the minster bells she could hear the stiff rustle of the surrounding Benedictines' robes. With each step Maria's hair lightly brushed against her buttocks. Minutes from now the luxurious tresses that Phillip had wound around his fingers, Richard around her breasts, would be gone. Adulteresses sometimes had their hair cut off, sometimes were publicly exposed, naked to the waist. Abbot Fyndunne had given her a choice. Her hair would grow back.

Maria inhaled; the roughness of her hair shirt scored her flesh. Perhaps God no longer turned his head from her as she often believed. The calm she'd felt from the first moment she'd decided to undergo public penance remained strong inside.

Keeping her chin raised, her eyes on Christchurch's triforium with clustered columns, on the soaring vaulted ceiling itself, she shut out the crowd and surrounding Benedictines. When they reached the end of the Norman nave, the cathedral's carved wooden doors creaked open, as if by an unseen hand. The October sunlight momentarily blinded her.

The cathedral precincts were filled with people, stretching past Christchurch Priory's domestic buildings to the ragged stone walls. Her penance had been public indeed, announced from here to London and beyond. Her legs began to tremble. Reaching out for support Maria found only emptiness. Her eyes darted over the vivid blur of people. At least her family did not number among them. Eleanora had received permission to leave her nunnery, but Maria had ordered her to stay. Tom was at Deerhurst, and she had requested that Hugh remain at Fordwich with Blanche. "You did not commit my sins," she'd told them. "And I'll not have you witness my pain."

As if bestowing benediction, Henry of Eastry slowly moved the slender iron cross he was holding in a half circle from one end of the crowd to the other, quieting them. Maria sensed their curiosity, pity—and hatred. She was dismayed at her heart's frantic pounding. The calm was deserting her. God—someone—you must help me, she silently pleaded. I must be strong.

Abbot Fyndunne's powerful hands settled on her shoulders. "Time for your public statement."

The massive throng of people terrified her. "Oh, I do not think I can." She turned as if to flee. Fyndunne's fingers dug into her flesh. Henry of Eastry faced her. The bottom of his iron cross scraped across the paving stones.

"Time, my daughter."

"Father, I cannot."

"You must!" Fyndunne pressed against her back, pushing her forward.

The prelates, all in white and lined on either side of her watched her expectantly.

She stepped forward. She had rehearsed the speech countless times. She looked beyond the precincts toward the anemic sun. "I, Maria Rendell, have committed great wrongs." Her voice quavered, gathered strength. "I deliberately severed the vows of marriage, repaying love with betrayal, neglected my children, and was driven only by my own pride and selfish desires. I confess before God and my church that I am heartily sorry for my many sins. I ask not only their forgiveness but the forgiveness of my husband and children." She had not mentioned Richard. No one would ever convince her that loving him had been wrong.

Stillness, then a low murmuring. Maria turned to the priests, who helped her kneel. Her head bent forward, the heavy hair cascading past her stomach in coppery waves. Maria's neck was exposed, and she thought suddenly of Thomas Lancaster and the Hugh Despensers, who had been beheaded for their sins. She sensed some of their terror, vulnerability. But I will rise and walk away, she reminded herself. I can endure it.

Lifting a handful of Maria's tresses Abbot Fyndunne hacked

at it with a pair of Toledo scissors. The scissors must have been dull, for he pulled and jerked. Finally her hair began to fall around her, coming to rest on the gray paving stones. Catching the light from the sun the threads seemed to writhe. Maria closed her eyes. It will grow back. But with each thrust of the scissors, each falling strand a part of her femininity, her womanhood, seemed also to drop away. Tears oozed from neath her closed lids. Richard is dead and Phillip is gone, she told herself, so what does it matter?

When Abbot Fyndunne finished, her hair was a ragged chin length. Without its covering she felt naked. Thank God she would not be bare-chested for the scourging, exposed for all the world to see. At least she had been allowed to retain a measure of her pride.

Reaching within the folds of his robes the Abbot withdrew a knife and inserted it inside the neck of her shirt. He jerked and hacked downward until Maria's back was exposed. Stunned, she half rose and twisted to face him.

"Nay! You assured me you'd leave me dressed . . ."

"Orders from Roger Mortimer, my lady. We are to show you no mercy." She shrank from the sudden malevolent light in the abbot's eyes. Not only Mortimer, she now knew. Abbot Fyndunne was repaying her for his loss of the Leopard's Head. He shoved her back down on the stones, bruising her knees. "Since you once willingly bared yourself before the Bastard, you should relish a wider audience."

"Nay!" Maria clutched the pieces of hair shirt protectively about herself.

Fyndunne's mouth twisted contemptuously. He flicked his wrist and by prearranged design two prelates stepped forward. Each wore carefully impersonal expressions; their eyes looked no higher than her neck.

"Do not struggle," said the younger priest, not unkindly. "Aim your thoughts and prayers heavenward, and the reality of this moment will soon fade to insignificance."

Maria shrank from his grasp. When he touched the material

above her shoulder she slapped his hand. "You promised me you'd leave me decently clothed. Just my hair, you said. All of you."

Seeing Abbot Fyndunne's gloating expression, Maria felt new strength spring from her deepest being. Her hands fell away from her breasts. She raised her chin and stiffened her spine. Whether or not she begged and pleaded the end result would remain the same. They would expose her to the world and she'd not allow that same world the pleasure of seeing her cower. She allowed the separate pieces of the hair shirt to drop to the ground. Even as the crowd pointed and gaped, she forced herself to erectness, forced her arms to remain at her sides instead of shielding her breasts. A light wind caressed Maria's bare flesh. Never had she felt so vulnerable. Her hair could not hide her; nothing could.

When the prelate bearing the flogging scourge stepped behind her, Maria squeezed shut her eyes. I'll not cry out, she silently vowed, but the declaration sounded like braggadocio.

She heard the whistle of the lash, stiffened, and gasped at the sting of leather on flesh, but the pain was much less than she'd imagined. Fifteen lashes. I can well endure it.

The lash repeatedly rose and fell, retracing the same trails upon her flesh. The pain increased a hundredfold. Maria gritted her teeth, clenched her fists, willed herself not to twist away from the relentless bit of leather. The crowd, the prelates receded and two things existed—herself and the scourge. She felt the sticky wetness of her blood. Sweat broke upon her forehead, trailed downward to her eyes, along her cheeks. Maria lost count of the strokes. Surely she'd been here hours. Had Mortimer and Fyndunne conspired to flog her to death? She bit at the inner flesh of her mouth to keep from crying out. Screaming could not help, but she could not quite swallow back a sob as the lash hissed against her flesh. She swayed. In her consciousness swam Fyndunne's contemptuous gaze, Richard's fingers tracing the smooth curve of her backbone,

Phillip exploring it with his lips. Flawless it had been and would never again be so.

The crowd began counting off, "thirteen—fourteen—fifteen." Maria scarcely noticed that the pain no longer descended. She could think of nothing save the all-encompassing agony, and though she willed her back to remain rigid, her body betrayed her. Slowly, she keeled over. The paving stones felt cold against her side. Far away she heard voices, which she could not identify.

Hands grasped her arms helping her up; fingers dug into lacerated flesh. Crying out, Maria swayed against the sleeve of a rough robe.

"You must make the walk, m'lady," someone said.

"Walk!" Fyndunne commanded. "Do not help her. She must perform the entire penance alone."

When the support was removed Maria's knees gave way and she crumpled to the ground. On her hands and knees she swayed like a dazed animal. She shook her head, trying to clear her vision. She must make the walk to Becket's shrine in Trinity Chapel, must chant the required psalms and orisons. Struggling to her feet, Maria regained a shaky balance. She stared down at her feet, willing them to move but was unable to execute the command. She opened her mouth intending to say "I cannot," but an unintelligible croak emerged.

She locked her eyes on Christchurch's interior, lit by hanging torch wheels that appeared to shimmer with an unearthly light. Inching one foot in front of the other, she shuffled forward. 'Tis your back that was flogged, not your legs, she silently chided. Make them work.

The shadows of Christchurch seemed to cool her back. When she reached the doorway, Maria paused. The nave swayed as did the crowd gathering on either side of the opening. She reached out, grabbed the doorway for support. The scene steadied. She saw the heads turned to her, remembered her nakedness, did not care. The important thing, the only thing was to reach Becket's shrine. The nave, with its chaotic plethora of altars, chapels, and chantries, appeared to stretch forever. Narrowed by distance and architectural design, Trinity Chapel appeared as impossible to reach as the Holy Grail.

One foot in front of the other, Maria willed herself to take just one more step. And another. She reached the first set of stairs. The twelve steps appeared as impossible to climb as the Chiltern Hills. Easing herself down she began crawling up the shallow stone steps, the centers of which had been worn down by the press of millions of pilgrims. As Maria struggled up the granite the dried blood on her back pulled at her lacerations, causing fresh bleeding. At the top of the stairs, she rested, gulping into her lungs great amounts of air. The painted wooden canopy above Becket's shrine wavered—still forty feet away. She shook her head, trying to disturb the sweat dripping from her forehead into her eyes. Tendrils of wet hair stung her cheeks.

I cannot continue, Maria thought, yet somehow she forced herself once again to erectness. Her knees now shook so badly she knew she'd not complete the walk. But perhaps she could complete just this one step. She did.

As the lengthening sun streamed through Christchurch's miracle windows she triumphed over a second set of stairs, but her legs no longer possessed the strength to propel her upward. Locking her arms Maria pushed herself up, then to her knees. Across ten feet of mosaic tile was the final flight leading to the shrine. A groan escaped her raw throat. More stairs! But her destination lay just beyond. Even now she glimpsed the stone arches holding up Becket's marble tomb—veined marble reputed to possess curative powers.

Dizziness assaulted her; she toppled over onto the tiles. So close, she thought, her eyes on the soaring roof overhead. I cannot fail now. She forced herself onto her stomach. Spreading her fingers across the tiny tile squares, across the refracted patterns of colored light from the stained-glass windows, she inched toward the first rise. The floor scraped her breasts, her stomach. Maria's heart pounded so loudly in her ears, her thoughts were so single-mindedly concentrated she did not at first hear the angry rush of voices behind her.

Abbot Fyndunne's voice pierced Maria's intentness. "Leave her be! Do not help her!"

"You'll kill her." The man's voice was distorted by distance and Christchurch's cavernous dimensions. The voice sounded familiar, but it could not be—Phillip was days away at Deerhurst. Besides, no one could help her. She must do it all herself.

Maria reached the steps leading to Trinity Chapel. Without pause she dragged herself up the steps, forcing her body onward, crossing the last barrier, and collapsed before Thomas Becket's shrine. I did it! And I did not plead or cry or shame myself! Euphoria momentarily replaced exhaustion.

Rolling onto her side Maria faced Becket's tomb. Heaven could not glow more brightly. Diamonds, rubies, emeralds, countless jewels set in gold filigree sparkled around the shrine proper. The stone figure of an angel pointed to the greatest of these—a diamond large as a hen's egg. On the ledge where the chapel's precious relics were kept she glimpsed the famous statue of the Blessed Virgin, covered with pearls and other precious stones. The statue was known to have spoken often with St. Thomas, providing counsel and advice. Maria stared into the Virgin's painted face. The expression remained blank, lifeless. She closed her eyes.

Rustling robes, the soft slap of sandaled feet. A heavy weight fell across her shoulder. She opened her eyes to the white hem of a priest's garment.

"Cover your nakedness," Abbot Fyndunne commanded.

She tried to raise her arm. The weight of the hair shirt was too heavy.

From behind hands eased her up, worked her arms and torso

into the hair shirt. The rough material clawed at her back. Maria tried to twist away. "Jesu!" Her voice was a sob. "Do not!" The fabric settled against her brutalized flesh, tormenting her at her slightest movement.

Henry of Eastry approached. Almost apologetically he held out a portion of Becket's skull encased in silver for her to kiss. When she could not reach the relic he bent and pressed it against her cracked lips.

"We will leave you to your prayers now, daughter. You have conducted yourself courageously. Our Blessed Savior, I know, is well pleased."

Two prelates leaned Maria against the stone arches of Becket's shrine, clasped her hands together before her in an attitude of prayer. Then they departed.

Distantly she heard the movement and murmur of the dispersing crowd. Soon I will be alone—just me and Thomas Becket and God. Readying to chant the required psalms and orisons, Maria forced a thickened tongue over her lips. Instead she collapsed against the arches, and as the cathedral wheeled, slumped to the paving stones. Lights danced before her eyes, lights more brilliant than all the stained glass in Christchurch. Then the lights exploded.

Someone called Maria's name. At first she thought it was Richard and she knew she had died. She felt his hand caress her brow. She lay quiet, wondering why her body hurt so, where God was, why she could not see anyone. Her eyelids fluttered open. Christchurch was crowded by shadows and emptiness, alleviated only by the flames from the candelabra located on the high altar. A face swam across her vision. Phillip's face.

Ignoring the pain, Maria struggled up.

"Nay, I will help you." Calloused hands slid beneath her armpits, infinitely careful hands that edged her upward. "I have sage ale to drink and an ointment to ease your wounds."

He rested the smooth rim of a wooden cup against her lips,

Maria allowed barely enough liquid to wet her tongue before she pushed it away. She wanted only to look at Phillip, to gaze into his beloved face. Once she would have believed he merely wanted to view her pain. Now she knew better. She wanted to tell him, but speaking seemed impossibly difficult.

"'Twas a brave thing you did, Maria. I do not think I would have possessed your courage."

"You did not possess my sins." She raised her bruised arm and cupped his cheek. She wanted to ask him, to beg him to please stay, but she could no longer properly maneuver her tongue.

Phillip brushed the ragged length of hair from her face. "We are going home now, to Fordwich. And this time I'll not leave you."

"Truly?"

"What years remain to us we'll live them together. Richard's death has taught me that much." He wanted to say more, but as always, words came uneasily to him.

For Maria, however, the words were more than enough. She pressed against him, delighting in the strong beating of his heart, the feel of his arms around her. This day God had indeed performed a miracle, and she would spend the rest of her life in thanksgiving. The miracle was that Phillip had returned to her; the miracle was that he would stay.